ARKANGEL

ALSO BY JAMES ROLLINS

Tides of Fire
Kingdom of Bones
Unrestricted Access
The Last Odyssey
Crucible
The Demon Crown
The Seventh Plague
The Bone Labyrinth
The 6th Extinction
The Eye of God
Bloodline
The Devil Colony
Altar of Eden
The Doomsday Key
The Last Oracle
The Judas Strain
Black Order
Map of Bones
Sandstorm
Ice Hunt
Amazonia
Deep Fathom
Excavation
Subterranean

BY JAMES ROLLINS AND REBECCA CANTRELL

Blood Gospel
Innocent Blood
Blood Infernal

BY JAMES ROLLINS AND GRANT BLACKWOOD

The Kill Switch
War Hawk

ARKANGEL

A Σ SIGMA FORCE NOVEL

JAMES ROLLINS

WILLIAM MORROW
An Imprint of HarperCollins*Publishers*

FIRST EDITION

Library of Congress Cataloging-in-Publication Data has been applied for.

ISBN 978-0-06-289316-1 (hardcover)
ISBN 978-0-06-289323-9 (international edition)

24 25 26 27 28 LBC 5 4 3 2 1

To Julie and Robbie Grant, whose friendship has
helped buoy me through some rough seas

Acknowledgments

It's always a long journey to the end of a novel, but thankfully I don't have to go on this trek alone. First, let me thank those fellow travelers who have offered wise counsel, great friendship, and a wonderfully discerning eye to each page of this story: Chris Crowe, Lee Garrett, Matt Bishop, Matt Orr, Judy Prey, Caroline Williams, Sadie Davenport, Denny Grayson, Vanessa Bedford, Lisa Goldkuhl, and Royale Dziak. And a special thanks to Steve Prey for both his critiques and for the production of the book's front maps. I also have to single out David Sylvian for all his hard work and dedication in the digital sphere to make me shine all the brighter. And Cherei McCarter, who has shared with me a bevy of intriguing concepts and curiosities, several of which are found in these pages. Of course, none of this would happen without an astounding team of industry professionals whom I defy anyone to surpass. To everyone at William Morrow, thank you for always having my back, especially Liate Stehlik, Kaitlin Harri, Josh Marwell, Richard Aquan, Lindsey Kennedy, Beatrice Jason, and Caitlin Garing. Last, of course, a special acknowledgment to the people instrumental to all levels of production: my distinguished editor, Jennifer Brehl, and her industrious colleague Nate Lanman; and for all their hard work, my agents, Russ Galen and Danny Baror (along with his daughter Heather Baror). And as always, I must stress that any and all errors of fact or detail in this book, of which hopefully there are not too many, fall squarely on my own shoulders.

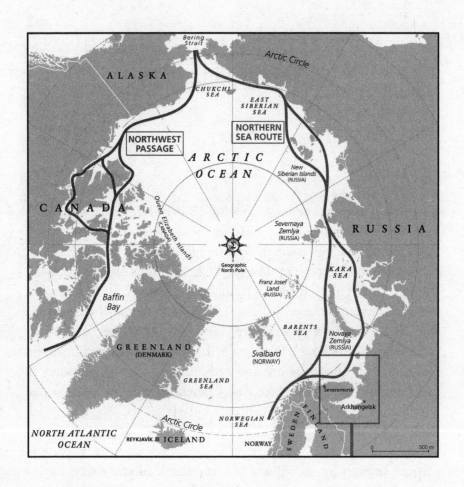

Cast of Characters

Sigma Force

GRAYSON PIERCE—current commander of field ops
SEICHAN—former terrorist/assassin, now working alongside Sigma
MONK KOKKALIS—specialist in medicine and bioengineering
KATHRYN BRYANT—expert in intelligence-gathering operations
JOSEPH KOWALSKI—specialist in munitions and explosives
PAINTER CROWE—director of Sigma Force
JASON CARTER—computer specialist at Sigma Command

From the Eighteenth Century

VASILY CHICHAGOV—commandant of Arkhangelsk Port
MIKHAIL LOMONOSOV—polymath and state councilor to Empress
    Catherine II
ORLOV—lieutenant under Chichagov
RAZIN—captain of the Spitzbergen whaling station

Russian Contingent

ALEX BORRELLI—monsignor with the Vatican
VADIM—student from Moscow State University
IGOR KOSKOV—archivist with Moscow's Museum of Archaeology
ANNA KOSKOV—novice from the Novodevichy Convent, sister to Igor
SERGEI TUROV—commander of White Sea Naval Base
OLEG ULYANIN—deputy chief of staff to Turov
LEONID SYCHKIN—archpriest of the Russian Orthodox Church
YERIK RAZ—monk and aide to Sychkin

Bogdan Fedoseev—Russian industrialist
Yuri Severin—Bogdan's head of security
Elle Stutt—research botanist
Arkady Radić—underworld courier
Nikil Yelagin—bishop of the Russian Orthodox Church
Uliana, Natalia, and Maria—nuns at the convent in Sergiyev Posad
Vinogradov, Sidorov, and Fadd—comrades of Yuri Severin
Osin—*spetsnaz* lieutenant
Bragin—*spetsnaz* lieutenant

Crew of the *Polar King*

Oliver Kelly—captain of the icebreaker
Byron Murphy—ship's navigator
Omryn Akkay—engineer and Chukchi local
Ryan Marr—security officer
Harper Marr—ship's doctor
Renny—dive team member
Mitchell—dive team member

Others

Finnigan Bailey—prefect of the Vatican Archives
Tucker Wayne—former Army Ranger
Kane—seven-year-old Belgian Malinois
Marco—eleven-month-old Belgian Malinois
Valya Mikhailov—leader of the Neo-Guild
Nadira Ali Saeed—second-in-command to Mikhailov

Notes from the Scientific Record

A new Cold War is brewing—in this case, literally.

Nearly everything north of the Arctic Circle has been a no-man's land for most of history. Eight nations border this region—Russia, Canada, Finland, Norway, Sweden, Iceland, Denmark (via Greenland), and the United States—but no country has any territorial claim to a vast majority of the Arctic. The United Nations Convention of the Law of the Sea (UNCLOS) set a country's economic boundaries to be 200 nautical miles off its coast—unless a country's continental shelf extends farther, then that boundary could be extended to 350 nm. Everything beyond those margins is out of bounds. This international treaty has protected most of the Arctic from full-on exploitation for decades.

But that's all about to change.

With the ice cap rapidly melting, access to the seabed has become far easier and more tantalizing. Already more than four hundred oil and gas fields have been discovered north of the Arctic Circle.[*] Additionally, new shipping routes—normally frozen over and impenetrable—have opened. For centuries, traveling the Northwest Passage across the top of Canada was nearly impossible. Now, you can book a cabin on a commercial cruise ship and travel this historical route with ease.

The change to the Arctic has been so rapid and sudden that the National Oceanic and Atmospheric Administration (NOAA) has declared "the Arctic as we've known it is now a thing of the past," even

---

[*] "Arctic Nations Are Squaring Up to Exploit the Region's Rich Natural Resources," Mark Rowe, *Geographical*, August 12, 2022.

coining the phrase the "New Arctic" to describe this fundamental shift.[*]

There are currently more than nine hundred infrastructure projects in development, totaling over a trillion dollars in investment. A majority of which is being undertaken by Russia. They've reopened abandoned Soviet-era military installations and established a slew of new seaports across their northern coast. Even China—which has no territorial claim to the Arctic—has expanded its global infrastructure initiative, known as Belt and Road, to include projects across the Arctic Circle. China envisions creating a northern sea route that could cut travel time between Asia and Europe by a third. To this end, China is building a fleet of hardened ice-capable cargo ships and fuel carriers to traverse this future "Polar Silk Road."[†]

With each passing year, the stakes in the Arctic continue to climb— as does the tension. It's estimated that a quarter of the planet's oil and gas remains hidden there.[‡] It is also a treasure chest of rare earth minerals (neodymium, praseodymium, terbium, and dysprosium) that are vital to the world's renewable energy projects, including the surging production of electric vehicles. In the Russian Arctic alone, the mineral value is estimated to be upwards of two trillion U.S. dollars.[§] Then there are the vast new seas open to fishing, where conflicts are already arising.

Unfortunately, matters are steadily worsening as nations vie for the resources of the melting Arctic Circle. Back in 2007, Russia went so far as to send two submersibles beneath the ice cap to plant a titanium flag under the North Pole, symbolically staking a claim.[¶] In 2022, the country also attempted to extend its territorial reach by seven hundred

---

[*] "Russia and China Vie to Beat the U.S. in the Trillion-Dollar Race to Control the Arctic," Clay Dillow, CNBC.com, February 6, 2018.

[†] Ibid.

[‡] "A Treasure Map of the Arctic," Frank Swain, *New Scientist*, February 2, 2018.

[§] "Arctic Nations," Rowe.

[¶] "Russia Plants Flag on North Pole Seabed," Tom Parfitt, *The Guardian*, August 2, 2007.

square kilometers, brushing up against Canada and Greenland.* And this is no idle thumbing of their nose at the Western world. Not only has the Far North been culturally and historically significant to the Russian people, it's also vital from a military and security standpoint.

To that end, Russia has already begun defending its space vigorously. It has conducted a series of unannounced military exercises across its northern borders, involving thousands of troops and scores of ships and submarines, including from its nuclear arsenal. In addition, the Russian fleet has more than *forty* icebreakers in service, including ten nuclear-powered ones. Whereas the U.S. Coast Guard has only *two*, although six more are in the works with completion dates sometime after 2025.†

This disparity in polar strength has sharpened tensions and increased military activity across the Arctic Circle. It would not take much—an accident, a misunderstanding, an error in judgment—to destabilize the entire region.

But there is one danger above all that threatens to set off this icy powder keg.

A new Arctic discovery.

Something unexpected and unforeseen.

Something that could set nation against nation in a race to secure it.

And that discovery . . .

It's about to happen.

---

* "U.S. Is Seen as Laggard as Russia Asserts Itself in Warming Arctic," Steven Lee Meyers, *Business Standard*, August 30, 2015.

† "U.S. Coast Guard Calls for Larger Icebreaker Fleet to Compete in the Arctic," Zamone Perez, *Defense News*, July 14, 2022.

Notes from the Historical Record

Interest in the Arctic has not been limited to the present day. Throughout the ages, it has been a source of mystery, adventure, and tragedy.

The ancient Greeks called the Far North *Arktikós*, the "Land of the Great Bear," named after the constellation of Ursa Major. According to their myths, the Arctic was the birthplace of the North Wind (Boreas), and even farther north was a mysterious land called Hyperborea (which translates as "Beyond the North Wind"). This land was said to be deeply forested, rich in wildlife, and a place of gentle breezes. It was also inhabited by the oldest of human races, a nearly immortal people who could live for centuries. More importantly, these Hyperboreans were the favorites of Apollo, the Greek god of sunlight and wisdom. He traveled to their lands so frequently that he is often referred to as the Hyperborean Apollo.

But this god was not the only one who sought them out.

This myth of a fecund and rich continent hidden in the Far North persisted for centuries. Over the passing millennia, adventurers and explorers have sought out this lost land, this *terra incognita*. Stories persisted in Roman legend, in medieval tales, and texts of the Enlightenment period and beyond.

But could there be any truth to this legend of Hyperborea?

In the fourteenth century, a Franciscan friar from Oxford traveled the North Atlantic, conducting business on behalf of King Edward III. He produced a volume titled *Inventio Fortunata* (or *Fortunate Discoveries*) that contained an astounding description of the North Pole and the surrounding seas, lands, and its peoples. This volume vanished into history, but later texts referred to it, including a Dutch account written by

Jacobus Cnoyen, called the *Itinerarium*, which summarized the friar's travelogue. Unfortunately, by the sixteenth century, Cnoyen's text also disappeared.[*]

Luckily, a Flemish cartographer, Gerardus Mercator, quoted extensively from it in a letter to his friend, the mathematician and royal adviser John Dee. This letter remains preserved in the British Museum. More importantly, Mercator used Cnoyen's description to craft a detailed map of the Arctic—the *Septentrionalium Terrarum*—the first such chart to be centered on the North Pole.[†] It is a wild map of magnetic mountains, fierce whirlpools, and lost continents—including the former home to the Hyperboreans. This map and its astounding claims persisted in various forms for more than a century until later Arctic explorers gained further knowledge and dismissed the reality of a lost northern continent.

Still, the myth persisted. Even today, there are those who espouse a firm belief that Hyperborea once existed.

One current advocate is Russian philosopher Aleksandr Dugin, who wrote *The Hyperborean Theory* in 1992. He firmly believes this lost land lay north of Siberia and that the Russian people are the modern descendants of these ancient Hyperboreans. This ultranationalist viewpoint led to the man's work being required reading by the Russian military and continues to be taught at the country's political science academies. It is said this theological view of Russia's destiny was used to justify the invasion of Crimea and Ukraine. Dugin and his beliefs continue to remain so influential that he is sometimes referred to as "Putin's Brain" or "Putin's Rasputin." In 2022, there was even a car bombing attempt on the man, which killed his daughter.[‡]

So be warned. Myths still hold power, especially as there remains *one*

---

[*] "The North Pole, Land of Pygmies and Giant Magnets," Frank Jacobs, *Strange Maps*, July 23, 1010.

[†] "The Mysteries of the First-Ever Map of the North Pole," Cara Giaimo, *Atlas Obscura*, February 27, 2017.

[‡] "Alexander Dugin: Who Is Putin Ally and Apparent Car Bombing Target?," Pjotr Sauer, *The Guardian*, August 21, 2022.

historical Russian account—involving a secret decree—that I've not mentioned. It offers further insight into a lost Hyperborea, a legend that continues to fuel sentiment today.

Turn the page and read closely to discover how a myth could destroy the world.

Worst of all . . . we may already be too late to stop it.

Not here! the white North has thy bones; and thou,
Heroic sailor-soul,
Art passing on thine happier voyage now
Toward no earthly pole.

—Alfred Lord Tennyson, poem etched on the Westminster
Abbey memorial to Sir John Franklin (1786–1847), who
vanished during the search for the Arctic's Northwest Passage

The North is not just a compass point but a state of mind.

—Christopher McIntosh, *Beyond the North Wind:*
The Fall and Rise of the Mystic North

There are two kinds of Arctic problems, the imaginary and the real. Of the
two, the imaginary are the most real.

—Vilhjalmur Stefansson, an Arctic explorer

May 23, 1764
Spitzbergen Archipelago

The bow of the ship's tender grated across broken shale and frozen sand, making landfall on the rocky island of Spitzbergen. Those aboard had come to seek the counsel of the damned, for even dead men had tales still to tell.

"We shouldn't be here," *Poruchik* Orlov warned, clutching a Russian Orthodox crucifix to his chest.

Commandant Vasily Chichagov couldn't argue with his lieutenant, but that didn't change matters. "We have our orders," he reminded him with a bitterness as icy as the morning breeze.

Behind them, three large frigates—the *Chichagov*, the *Panov*, and the *Babayev*—rocked amidst shattered ice floes that covered the seas. Though it was spring, the Arctic remained trapped in winter. Most of these waters would not melt until midsummer—if even then.

Vasily clenched his fists as much against the numbing cold as in frustration. He pulled deeper into his fur-lined coat, his lower face wrapped in a wool scarf. He waited for the oars to be stored and the tender to be secured before heading ashore.

While waiting, he glanced back to the trio of ships. The lead one bore his name, which was both an honor and at times an embarrassment. Vasily had joined the Imperial Navy when he was sixteen, quickly gaining fame and rank, and now served as deputy commandant of Arkhangelsk Port on the coast of the White Sea. The three frigates had left the port a fortnight ago. Their assignment was to survey and inspect the whaling camps that were established across this frozen archipelago each spring.

As soon as the seas began to melt, the competition here grew fierce for the best spots—not just by Russians, but also by Norwegian and Swedish whalers. During this volatile period, Vasily's naval forces would

maintain order and protect the Russian stations. Within a month's
time, after each camp had dug in and established itself, his ships could
head home. Skirmishes would continue throughout the summer, but
nothing that would require the intervention of Russian imperial forces.
After this crucial period of settlement, the whalers would begrudgingly
respect one another's stakes and claims. So it had always been, going
back two centuries, to the time when Willem Barentsz, a Dutch mariner,
discovered these islands while searching for the elusive Northeast Passage
to China.

Vasily sighed and stared across the ice-choked seas to the east. Last
summer, he himself had tried to find that route, but to no avail.

Gruff voices drew him around to the island. Across the beachhead,
men gathered around a bonfire set before a scatter of stone shacks.
Arms pointed toward them, surely wondering at the tender's arrival.

According to reports, this station had been set up a month ago.
Already, a carcass of a bowhead whale floated in the shallows. Even
with its flukes sawed off, its body stretched fifty feet. The tons of blubber flensed from its body lay stacked in dark hillocks. Elsewhere, crews
manned copper pots, boiling oil from the fat. Closer at hand, racks
dotted the shoreline, hung with drying U-shaped drapes of baleen. Off
the beach, the remains of the stripped whale had become a floating
feast for hundreds of seabirds, which wildly assailed the carcass with
raucous cries.

The presence of the whale continued to serve another purpose. It was
the anchor to which this camp was set. With this success, no other crew
would dare accost or contest this beachhead. Among this superstitious
breed of hard men, it boded ill luck to trespass upon another camp after
they'd had a successful hunt.

Even Lieutenant Orlov knew this. "Why have we landed here,
Commandant? These whalers seem adequately settled, are they not?"

"*Da*, but it is not these men we seek."

With the tender secure, Vasily waved Orlov ashore, ignoring the
man's curious glance back. Vasily had not shared the true reason they'd
come ashore.

As Vasily climbed free of the boat, he absently patted his jacket pocket. It held a letter from Empress Catherine II, written by her own hand. It contained a secret directive that had only been handed to him after his trio of ships had set sail across the White Sea.

The man who had delivered that missive sat at the tender's stern.

As if sensing Vasily's thoughts, Mikhail Lomonosov stood and crossed the boat. He was a sepulchral figure dressed all in black, from heavy frock to a wide brimmed hat. He had kept to his cabin during the journey here, ensconced with books and maps. Only a handful of people knew he had traveled from Saint Petersburg to Arkhangelsk, bearing the empress's decree.

Though only in his fifties, Lomonosov had already earned the civilian status of state councilor—equivalent to that of brigadier general in the army or captain-commander in the navy—outranking even Vasily. The man had achieved this lofty position by proving himself a genius in a wide spectrum of pursuits. He had a long list of accomplishments across esoteric fields: physics, chemistry, astronomy, geography, minerology, even history and poetry.

Lomonosov joined him on the beach. "I've forgotten how frigid it is this far north."

This was not stated as a complaint but spoken with a wistfulness. It reminded Vasily of a detail in the man's biography. Lomonosov hailed from these icy lands. He had been born in the village of Mishaninskaya in the Arkhangelsk Oblast. As a boy, he had traveled with his father, a prosperous fisherman, across these very seas on trade missions. So, this journey here was as much a homecoming for the man as it was in service to the empress.

"Now that we've made landfall," Vasily groused through his scarf to Lomonosov as the councilor joined him, "perhaps you could share what was left unwritten in the empress's letter."

"Once we're alone," Lomonosov stated with a taciturn expression. He pointed to a tall figure approaching them. "That must be Captain Razin, head of the whaling crew."

Vasily agreed. The heavily bearded Cossack appeared oblivious to the cold, wearing only pants and an open-collar shirt. What little skin showed was salt-scarred and burnished to the color of dark copper.

There was nothing welcoming in his manner, a sentiment reinforced by a sheathed saber at his side and a holstered pistol over his shoulder.

He spit into the sand before speaking, a heavy gobbet that splattered near Vasily's boot. Orlov took a threatening step forward, but Vasily motioned him back.

"Finally," Razin said, "I sent word of the bodies a month ago. Before much longer, they'll be thawing and stinking. My men won't go near that cursed stretch of beach until they're all hauled off, and I need that space if we hope for a successful hunting season."

"We will secure the dead in short order," Vasily assured the captain. "But first we wish you to show us what you found among them."

Razin sneered, glanced around the five-man party, then mumbled under his breath as he turned away. "Should've burned them all when I had the chance."

Lomonosov heard him. "You were right to send word back to Saint Petersburg. The bodies mark a team from the Imperial Academy, explorers who vanished two years ago while trying to discover the Northeast Passage. You and your crew will be rewarded for your service to Russia."

Razin looked back. "Rewarded how?"

"The recompense will be commensurate with what we find here today and where it might lead."

Razin frowned, clearly struggling with the councilor's verbiage.

Vasily translated. "You'll share in any bounty gained from the recovery of these men."

"As I should," Razin concluded and grunted for them to follow.

Lomonosov turned to Vasily. "Best we limit this first survey to just you and your lieutenant."

Vasily nodded and waved for the other seamen to remain with the tender, then set off with Orlov.

Vasily quickly drew alongside Lomonosov. "Now that there are fewer ears, maybe you could explain the reason behind all this subterfuge. Why does the discovery of a lost crew from the Imperial Academy require a sealed order from Empress Catherine? Many have sought the Northeast Passage, me included."

"It's because this team was dispatched by Catherine herself—and not to search for a route between the Atlantic and Pacific."

Vasily drew Lomonosov farther aside from the other two men. "Then what were they searching for?"

"At the moment, the secrecy is less about what they were searching for and more about what they might have found—especially due to the record that Captain Razin made of their belongings. I was sent to confirm what the captain described and determine the best course of action from here."

Vasily sighed, resigned to the fact that he would have to let this play out.

In silence, they followed Razin across the camp and through oily clouds of boiling blubber. The stench choked the throat and lay thick on the tongue. Once upwind of the station, the air eventually cleared, growing cold and crisp. The sky remained an aching blue, but a dark line at the horizon warned of incoming weather.

They hiked another quarter mile, following high cliffs that bordered the rocky beach. Razin seemed to be leading them nowhere. There was no sign of any dwelling in sight.

Razin finally stopped, lifted an arm, and pointed. "You'll find them in there."

It took Vasily another full breath to spot a shadowy break in the cliff face. It marked the mouth of a cave. He searched the neighboring seas but failed to spot any evidence of a shipwreck. The doomed crew must have abandoned their ship, maybe after it had been trapped and crushed by winter ice. It was a sadly frequent tragedy this far north, one he came close to experiencing himself when he sought out the Northeast Passage. He grimaced as he imagined the crew trekking across the frozen sea to reach land and seeking shelter where they could.

Not that coming here had done them any good.

"I've work to see to," Razin said sourly. "I'll leave it to you crows to pick among the dead."

When no one objected, the captain turned and headed back to the smoke-shrouded camp.

Lomonosov did not wait and set off toward the cave. Vasily and

Orlov hurried after him. Once at the entrance, the lieutenant ignited a lantern and lit their way down a short tunnel.

The walls were heavily coated in ice that reflected the lamplight. Meltwater ran underfoot. The tunnel emptied into a small cavern—now an icy crypt. Four bodies were stacked at the threshold, tangled and frozen together, creating a macabre dam across the entrance. The dead men had either been washed there by the tides of melting and freezing waters or perhaps they'd been purposefully stacked there to act as windbreaks for the other five crewmembers who lay sprawled inside the cave.

To enter, Vasily and the others had to climb over the dead men. As they did, hollow eyes stared up at them. Jaws hung open in silent screams, showing blackened tongues and white teeth.

A misstep by Orlov shattered a frozen hand under a bootheel. The lieutenant hurried away, as if fearing retribution from the dead.

Once inside, Vasily fought down his revulsion and circled a ring of stones, dark with ash, marking an old firepit. The crew must have burned their sleds after using them to transport gear and food. Still, at the back of the cavern, one object had been spared the flames. Even as the crew froze to death, they hadn't torched this artifact. It spoke to the value placed upon it.

Lomonosov stepped briskly toward this prize.

Off to the side, Orlov lifted his lantern toward a neighboring wall. A long row of names had been chiseled into the rock, likely an accounting of the crew, an epitaph written by the dead.

A gasp by Lomonosov drew Vasily's attention back around. The councilor stood before the large artifact preserved at the back of the cave. It was a huge horn of ivory, curved, and longer than a man's outstretched arms.

"What is it?" Orlov asked.

"A *maimanto* tusk," Lomonosov answered. "Also dubbed *mammon's horns*. Many such finds have been discovered in washed-out riverbeds of the north, often by the Samoyed clans of Siberia. They're believed to be from a long-dead species of sea elephant."

Vasily shrugged. "But why did the crew go to such lengths to drag it here, to protect it?"

Lomonosov waved to Orlov. "The lamp . . . bring it closer."

Vasily nodded for his lieutenant to follow this instruction. Lomonosov pointed to a section of the tusk.

Across most of its curved length, the coarse exterior husk had been shaved down to the ivory beneath, creating a canvas for an ancient artist. Fine scrollwork had been engraved into the ivory. Unfortunately, age and weather had shattered the handiwork into fragmented pieces.

Still, there remained enough to reveal glimpses of some city, one marked by pyramidal structures.

Lomonosov choked on his words. "It's . . . it's just as Captain Razin described . . ."

"But who etched it?" Orlov asked. "Was it one of the crew?"

Lomonosov ignored the question. Even Vasily knew this couldn't be true. This was far older than any of the dead men.

Lomonosov confiscated Orlov's lamp and set about examining the length of the tusk. He illuminated every surface, occasionally revealing other glimpses: a broken tower, a decorated throne, a sliver of a moon.

"What's being depicted here?" Vasily asked.

Lomonosov stiffened and brought the light closer to the ivory. He stared at a section for several breaths—then passed the lamp to Vasily. "Hold this."

After Vasily took the lantern, Lomonosov stepped back and fumbled through the inner layers of his heavy frock. Vasily used the moment to study what had triggered such a reaction in the man.

The lamplight revealed another scrap of scrollwork, just a sliver, but enough to reveal a trace of writing, one that looked more crudely inscribed, perhaps a hasty addition.

Vasily squinted at the letters. "This writing . . . it almost looks—"

"Greek," Lomonosov confirmed as he withdrew a small book from an inner pocket. "I believe it's a name. One that has echoed across millennia."

"What name?" Orlov asked, looking warily back at the bodies.

Lomonosov leafed through the pages, then stopped and showed Vasily a passage. "This is written by Pindar, a Greek lyricist of the sixth century B.C., from the tenth section of his *Pythian Odes.*"

πλοον. ναυσι δ᾽ ούτε πεζος ιων κεν εύροις
ες περβόρεοι αγωνα θαυματαν οδον.
παρ᾽ οἷς ποτε Περσευς εδαισατο λαγετας,

Vasily frowned and shook his head, failing to understand the significance.

Lomonosov sighed and tapped a finger under a single word in that passage. "Does this not look familiar?"

Vasily stared between what was written on the page and what was engraved on the horn. "It looks like the same word—at least a fragment of it—has been carved into the ivory. But what does it mean?"

"Like I said, it marks a name, a mythic place." Lomonosov returned to study the depiction of the pyramids.

"What place?" Vasily pressed him.

"Hyperborea."

Vasily scoffed with disbelief. All who sailed these seas had heard of the legendary lost continent to the north, a land free of ice, richly forested and populated by a nearly immortal people. Many explorers had gone in search of—

Vasily straightened as understanding struck him. He gave Lomonosov a hard look. "Is that what these poor souls had gone looking for—not the Northeast Passage, but Hyperborea?"

"At the request of Empress Catherine," Lomonosov confirmed.

Vasily clenched a fist. "Then they were doomed from the start."

Lomonosov kept his gaze on the curve of tusk. "It was indeed a daunting task given to them. To quote Pindar, '*Neither by ship nor on foot could you find the marvelous road to the meeting-place of the Hyperboreans.*'"

"In other words, a fool's errand."

Lomonosov stared at Vasily with a raised brow. "Do you dare call our empress a fool?"

Vasily winced, reminding himself to be more cautious with his words, lest he be hung for treason.

"Catherine is no one's fool," Lomonosov insisted. "In fact, she has done that which no man or woman has ever accomplished." The man shook his head, and his lips thinned, as if reminding himself to be careful with his own words. "Suffice it to say, she did not send them off without any guidance."

Vasily wanted to press this last detail further, but he knew Lomonosov would not relent. So, he changed tack. "Regardless, why does the empress seek out this lost continent? I've heard stories about the inhabitants of Hyperborea, of an elixir that grants centuries of life. Securing such a treasure has been the ambition of many explorers. Is that what she hoped to discover?"

Lomonosov sighed heavily. "Again, you call her a fool without stating it outright. The only immortality she seeks is to lift the Russian Empire to greater prominence, to have us shine brighter than the Europeans who look down upon us as savages. The discovery of Hyperborea—even remnants thereof—would bring far greater glory to the empire than even the discovery of the Northeast Passage."

Vasily doubted this was true, but he returned his attention to the curve of tusk. "And you believe this might be proof that the first expedition had been successful?"

"I . . . I do not know, but it is a hope. A place to start."

Vasily sensed the weight of the other's words and what he left unspoken. "And you intend for us to finish it."

"That is why Empress Catherine sent me with her decree."

Vasily glanced back at the icy crypt, praying he and his men wouldn't suffer the same fate. He noted Orlov standing to the side, near the tip of the horn. The lieutenant's neck was craned back. He stared not at the tusk, but at the wall behind it.

With the lantern still in hand, Vasily stepped over to Orlov and raised the light. Like the names of the dead chiseled into the cavern wall, someone had chipped out a final warning into the rock.

Orlov read it aloud. " *Never go there, never trespass, never wake that which is sleeping.*'"

Vasily turned to Lomonosov. The councilor's gaze remained on the tusk, on the ancient metropolis etched into the ivory. The man's eyes glowed in the lamplight.

In that moment, Vasily knew the truth.

No dead man's warning would stop them.

FIRST

1

The silence of a tomb hung over the subterranean vault, but it was not sarcophagi that lined its floor. Instead, a dozen steel-strapped chests were arrayed in a semicircle under an arched brick roof. The only noise was the echoing drip of water from the labyrinth of tunnels that the group had traversed to reach this site.

Monsignor Alex Borrelli entered the space with a shiver that was part delight and part trepidation. His heart pounded in his chest. He felt like a trespasser, maybe a grave robber.

"*Porazitel'nyy!*" Vadim blurted out with youthful enthusiasm. "Just as I described, *da?*"

"It is indeed astounding," Alex confirmed.

Vadim was a student from Moscow State University. A week ago, he and a motley group of fellow subterranean adventurers had stumbled upon this locked vault far below the streets of Moscow. Luckily, the young man had recognized the importance of his discovery and alerted the city's archaeological museum.

At the time, Alex had taken the discovery to be a sign of heavenly providence, especially as he was already here in Moscow. As a member of the Vatican's Pontifical Commission of Sacred Archaeology, Alex worked closely with the Apostolic Archive back in Rome. Alex's professional interest was in the *history* of the holy library, on establishing the provenance of its collection. Over the decades, he had uncovered many astounding and sometimes sordid tales behind various volumes.

In fact, this was why Alex had come to Moscow, to meet with his counterpart at the Russian Orthodox Church. For the past several years, the patriarchate's Holy Synod had been demanding the return of hundreds of tomes held in the Vatican library, which truthfully had been stolen from the country during the era of the tsars. The pope had personally sent Alex to oversee these discussions. The task would take some judicious diplomacy to discern who had rightful claim to the books in question. Some were of extreme historical value, and most were priceless.

Then a few days ago, word had leaked to Alex of the discovery deep beneath Moscow, of a cache of ancient books sealed up in a vault. His counterpart within the Russian Orthodox Church—Bishop Nikil Yelagin—had invited him to accompany the archaeological team, to help ascertain if the books were of any import. There were only a handful of others who had the knowledge and expertise to judge the significance of what might lay below.

Still, Alex knew this invitation was as much a part of diplomatic wrangling as it was a matter of his personal expertise. His inclusion served as a demonstration of cooperation by the orthodox church.

"How should we proceed?" Igor Koskov asked, joining him in the doorway.

"With care."

Alex turned to Igor. The lanky, dark-haired Russian was an archivist from Moscow's Museum of Archaeology. The young man was barely out of his twenties, four decades younger than Alex's seventy-two years.

"We should photograph everything before any books are moved," Alex warned. "Then go about meticulously cataloging each volume."

Igor nodded, letting Alex take the lead. "I'll spread the word to the others."

Igor crossed to his colleagues, a group of archaeologists, five men and a woman. No one was older than forty. After much gesticulating and some stern looks Alex's way, the team set off into the chamber, hauling in their gear. Like Alex, the team was dressed in dark blue coveralls and wore safety helmets topped by battery-powered lamps. The group started setting up tripods, measuring the room, and taking photographs, not only of the chests, but also the vault's walls and doors.

Alex respected their thoroughness.

Another did not. Clearly impatient with such meticulous work, Vadim waved to Alex. The student waited beside a trunk, one that had been left open by his friends. It stood to the left of the door, out of the way of the bustle.

"Come see," Vadim urged him.

"Don't touch anything," Alex warned. "The books will be very fragile."

Vadim scowled, but in a good-natured way, as if the young man was tolerating a scolding grandfather. "Не переживай. I would not let anyone touch anything. We only peek in trunks, *da*? No more."

"Very good."

Alex crossed to the open chest, trailed by Igor, whose eyes glinted with curiosity.

Inside the trunk, rows of leather spines were cradled within oak racks. It appeared more trays lay below the topmost one, stacked one atop the other.

Alex waved the beam of his helmet's lamp over the upper collection. He read a few of the titles. "Plato's *Timaeus and Critias* . . . Aristotle's *De Partibus Animalium* . . . Ptolemy's *Almagest.*" He leaned closer. "That looks like a Byzantine copy of *Corpus Hippocraticum.*"

The books were centuries, if not millennia, old. And all well preserved.

Alex rubbed an ache in his chest as his breathing tightened with excitement.

"*Neveroyatnyy* . . ." Igor mumbled with awe, plainly equally amazed.

The archivist reached and hovered a finger over the leather-bound volume of *Corpus Hippocraticum.* The book was a collection of sixty ancient Greek medicinal works, attributed to the physician Hippocrates. But it was not the subject matter that most interested the man.

Igor turned to Alex. "A *Byzantine* copy, you said."

"*Maybe* Byzantine," he cautioned, knowing what the archivist hoped this meant.

"If so, it could be evidence that these trunks, these books, came from the Golden Library."

Alex glanced over to the archaeologists as they labored across the room, whispering in Russian to one another. He knew the hope that they *all* held.

For centuries, hundreds of men and women—historians, explorers, adventurers, thieves—had been searching for the Golden Library, a treasure trove of volumes hidden away by Ivan the Terrible and lost after his death. But it wasn't even Ivan's collection. It was his grandfather—Ivan the Great—who had gathered together that vast library during the fifteenth century. A majority of it came as a dowry when the emperor married his second wife, Sophia Palaiologina, a Byzantine princess, who carried the collection with her after the fall of the Byzantine Empire. It was said to hold the most treasured volumes of the Library of Constantinople, including manuscripts from the ancient Library of Alexandria.

Alex looked enviously across the arc of chests. According to records, the Golden Library contained documents written in Greek, Latin, Hebrew, and Egyptian, even Chinese texts from the second century.

"If we could ever find it," Igor extolled, "just think what we might uncover? I read how a nineteenth-century historian—Christopher von Dabelov—claimed to have seen a list of the library's titles. That list included all hundred-and-forty-two books of Titus Livius's *History of Rome*. Only thirty-five of those volumes still exist today. Dabelov also noted an unknown poem written by Virgil. And a full version of Cicero's *De Republica*. Can you just imagine what such a discovery would mean?"

Alex tried to temper Igor's enthusiasm. "I know of Dabelov's account. It's highly suspect, likely a fraud. In fact, the Golden Library may no longer exist. It could've been burned or destroyed long ago."

Igor shook his head, refusing to accept this. "Ivan the Terrible valued that collection, hiring hordes of Russian translators to work through the library. It is well documented that he purposefully hid the collection somewhere underground—either in Moscow or elsewhere. There are stories that he discovered mystical texts that would grant Russia great power. So firm was this belief that many of the scholars working on the translations quit and fled, fearing Ivan would use black magic found in those books to wreak great harm."

Alex cast him a skeptical gaze.

Igor shrugged. "No matter the truth of such legends, it is well known that Ivan believed the future of Russia was tied to that library. If he truly put such stock in its collection, he would have hidden it well and not let it be destroyed."

Vadim interrupted their discussion, likely indifferent to the esoterica of lost libraries. He pointed into the trunk. "Look. Something shine in there. Down deeper."

Alex leaned closer, following his finger. "What do you mean?"

"Under the top books." Vadim stepped in front of them. "I show you."

The student reached to the handles of the oak rack, preparing to lift it off and expose what he had spotted.

"Don't!" Alex called out.

"*Ne!*" Igor reinforced.

Vadim ignored them and lifted the top tray of books out of the trunk.

With the damage done, Alex waved the young man off. "Be careful. Carry the rack off to the side and gently place it down. Somewhere dry. We'll want photos of that tray and books."

Vadim sighed heavily and lumbered off with his burden.

Alex shook his head and watched after him.

"He was right," Igor said, drawing back Alex's attention.

Alex stepped closer and shone his light into the trunk's depths. The next layer held similar books, but the middle row was taken up by a nine-volume set of tomes. Alex noted the titles on their spines.

"My God, it's a complete series of *Histories* by Herodotus." Alex gaped at the Greek books from the fifth century B.C.E. "No intact collection has ever been found. I wager this set is older than the Codex A at the Biblioteca Medicea Laurenziana in Florence. That copy has served as the model for most modern translations."

"But why is that fourth book in the series the only one covered in gold leaf?"

Alex frowned. It was puzzling. All nine volumes were leatherbound, but the fourth in the series was adorned with gold. Its reflective shine must have caught Vadim's attention.

Unable to stop himself, Alex reached a finger and carefully slipped the book free. Equally curious, Igor stepped closer, raising no objection. As Alex pulled the volume out, something snapped inside the trunk, loud enough to make the men jolt back.

A breath later, a thunderous boom shook the space.

Alex lost his footing. "What's happenin—"

Igor grabbed him around the waist and shouldered him out the vault door, all but carrying him. Once across the threshold, Igor leaped headlong with Alex as the entire room collapsed behind them.

Behind Igor's shoulder, Alex caught a glimpse of Vadim, half-turned in their direction. Then he and the others were gone, crushed under a thunderous rockfall of bricks and stone.

Outside, a wall of dust swept the two sprawled men, blinding and choking them.

Alex gasped, struggling to understand.

Igor explained, waving away the dust and helping Alex up. "The chamber . . . it must've been booby-trapped."

"But why?" Alex moaned.

The two staggered closer to the ruins of the doorway. For several minutes, they called and shouted, but Alex knew it was futile. Even hope could not withstand the weight of that collapse. It was plain that there could be no survivors under the tonnage of rock.

More rumblings—likely aftershocks—continued, threatening further rockfalls.

Igor pulled Alex away and pointed up. "We can't stay here."

2:07 P.M.

Fleeing the death behind him, Alex clambered up the stone steps carved out of the city's bedrock. He clutched what he could save to his chest. His heart pounded against the flaking gold-leaf cover of the book that he had rescued, the fourth volume of Herodotus's *Histories*.

He had dropped the Greek text after being thrown free of the collapse, but he had recovered it from the floor. He had briefly inspected it, shaking dust from its pages, wiping silt from its gilded cover. It was only then that he had spotted something that he still struggled to understand.

Despite that, one thing was certain.

"I can't let this be lost . . ." he gasped out to the darkness, casting the beam of his helmet's lamp up the spiraling staircase.

"Let me carry the book for you, Monsignor," Igor offered, raising an arm. "We still have a long way to climb."

Alex glanced back at the archivist. Igor's eyes squinted with the pain of their loss. Terror and grief had drained his features to a deathly pallor.

Alex pulled the ancient text harder to his chest. "This is my burden to carry. It was my foolishness that killed them all."

Igor lowered his arm.

With a heavy heart, Alex continued his climb. His cardiologist back in Rome had warned him against this journey, but it was not his recent angioplasty that made each breath an agony. Guilt tightened his chest. Each thud of his heart felt like a hammer blow against his ribs.

"I shouldn't have rushed matters," Alex said.

"No one objected to your timetable," Igor argued. "We couldn't risk word spreading. We had to secure it before anyone else ransacked the site."

Alex swallowed hard. He had used that same reasoning yesterday, urging the group to proceed quickly. But that wasn't his only motivation. With his failing health, he couldn't let this chance pass him by. At his age, he had come to learn a hard truth.

Patience was a luxury of the young.

Guilt-ridden and heart-sore, he rounded another turn in the stairs. He swiped sweat from his brow with his free hand. The air was stiflingly humid; the walls were slick and damp. As his lips moved in a silent prayer for the dead, his heel slipped on a patch of black mold. With a cry, his arms windmilling, he crashed to his knees. He felt the impact all the way up into his molars. The precious text flew from his hand, struck the wall, and bounced down the steps.

Alex winced, less from the pain than from the harm he might have wrought. Down on one hand, he craned back. "Is the book damaged?"

Igor hurried over, recovered the volume, then climbed back up to him. Alex tried to stand, but Igor waved him down.

"We should rest a moment. Are you injured?"

Alex settled to a seat with a sigh. "Just my pride."

The young man dropped to the stair next to him and handed him the book. "Looks only scuffed. Its binding, while old, has proven stubborn."

Relieved, Alex rested the ancient text on his lap. He pictured all that had been lost under the tons of rock. Any recovery, if even possible, would take weeks. Beyond the loss of lives, he remembered the books he had briefly spotted, a treasure trove of Greek and Roman texts.

Plato, Aristotle, Ptolemy, Hippocrates . . .

Alex sat straighter, startled by a sudden realization, a recognition of a theme to this hidden collection—or at least what had been stored in the open trunk.

"The books," he mumbled. "They were all scientific treatises."

Igor glanced over to him. "Monsignor?"

"They all pertained to Greek and Roman efforts to understand the natural world." Alex rested a palm on the book in his lap. "Even Herodotus's *Histories* is less a historical text than it is an analytical travelogue. It deals more with geography and the peoples of various lands. The massive work is said to be based on Herodotus's travels across the known world of his time."

Igor frowned. "If you're right, why would such books be locked away? To what end?" He searched down the dark stairs. "And why booby trap the collection? What were they trying to hide?"

Alex shook his head. "I think it was more about *protection*. To keep a secret."

"What secret?"

"The location of the Golden Library."

Igor gasped next to him—half shocked, half scoffing.

Alex ignored him and stared down at the bright leaf that adorned the leather cover. He knew it was that sheen that had made him pull the volume from the others. But it was not a lust for gold that had drawn his hand.

It was a longing for lost knowledge.

"If we could find it . . ." Alex started, but he left the rest unspoken.

Maybe such a discovery would help atone for the deaths below.

Igor's shoulders slumped. "If it truly exists, maybe the library is cursed, as many have claimed over the centuries."

Alex shook his head, refusing to give in to defeat. "Even the trap . . . someone set it centuries ago. It suggests that the collection of scientific texts was left purposefully. Maybe it was meant to be a test, a bread-crumb left behind that would lead to the greater collection. That is, if someone was wise enough to understand its clues and not be killed."

"But how can we be sure?" Igor pushed to his feet, clearly ready and anxious to continue climbing out of the maze.

Alex took hold of his wrist and drew him back down. "I must show you something. It's important."

Until now, he had not shared what he had truly discovered below. There had been no time. He had barely caught a glimpse of it while dust filled the air.

"What is it?" Igor asked.

Alex carefully opened the flaking leather cover of Herodotus's text. On the inside, someone had inscribed an intricate design. The most prominent being the drawing of an open book, one gilded in gold like the outside cover. It was clearly a more recent adornment—as in two or three centuries ago versus the age of the Greek text itself.

Igor stiffened as Alex focused his lamp's beam on the gilded drawing of a book.

The gold reflected the light, making the image of the sketched tome shine all the brighter. It was a single volume, splayed open in the middle. It glowed above a detailed drawing of a building, likely a church. The rest of the page was marked up, but most of it had faded into obscurity, though some faint writing was still discernible.

Екатерина II Великая

Igor squinted at the page. "Are those Norse runes off to the side?"

"I believe so. Also some Greek writing. And maybe scientific notations."

"But what are we looking at? What's being depicted here?"

"I believe it's a map. One encrypted in pictures, letters, and numbers." Alex hovered a fingertip over the top of the gilded book. "A map to the Golden Library."

Igor's eyes grew huge.

"Whoever drew this—or commissioned it," Alex continued, "they likely set that trap tied to this book."

Igor nodded. "She must have found the library and wanted to protect her secret from anyone unworthy of its discovery."

Alex tore his gaze from the book. "*She?*"

Igor pointed to a line of Cyrillic at the bottom, plainly meant to be a signature. He read it aloud. "*Yekaterina Velikaya.*"

Alex frowned, struggling to understand.

Igor clarified. "Or as she was better known . . . Catherine the Great."

3:33 P.M.

After taking a few precautions to help preserve their discovery, Alex set off with Igor. They climbed for another hour before reaching the top of the stairs. Yet, they were still deep in the maze, a long way from sunlight and open air. They would've gotten lost, except Vadim had left chalk marks along their path. Igor followed those guideposts across a warren of passages, crawlways, and shattered breaks in old walls.

Alex touched each scrawl in silent thanks to the intrepid young man.

Before setting off here, Alex had read up on this subterranean world. It stretched for hundreds of square miles, even burrowing beneath the Kremlin, though access to those regions had been sealed off long ago. The first tunnels had been excavated in the fourteenth century by Prince Dmitry Donskoy, as a secret exit from the Kremlin. Later, the patriarchs of the Russian Orthodox Church had also dug passageways beneath their cathedrals and basilicas, connecting them to Donskoy's tunnels, so the clergy could flee to the Kremlin in times of distress.

Over the passing centuries, the warren slowly spread wider and deeper. It was used by spies, by assassins, by illicit lovers. Bodies were dumped down here. During the sixteenth century, Ivan the Terrible had used the maze to hide a cache of weapons, guns that were discovered in 1978 by Soviet workers who were expanding the city's subway.

But that's not all that Ivan had hid underground.

Alex firmed his grip on the ancient Greek text.

Igor noted this. "Do you truly believe Catherine the Great discovered the Golden Library?"

"I don't know, but if she did, the larger question is *why* she kept it secret. Such an astounding discovery—a library to rival the greatest in the world—would've brought great fame to the Russian empire and her rule."

Igor bobbed his head in agreement. "Catherine was dedicated to her adopted country. She was well-read, interested in literature, philosophy, and science. Her greatest desire was for Russia to rise in prominence and notoriety, to become an empire to rival any European country."

"If so, then why keep the discovery of the Golden Library secret?"

Igor shrugged his thin shoulders. "She must've had her reasons. Maybe if we can decrypt her code, we could solve that mystery, too."

"But first, we have to escape this confounding maze."

By now, stabbing pains shot through Alex's chest. Three months ago, he had four stents placed in various cardiac vessels. He swore he could feel each one as his heart pounded heavily, both from the exertion and from the weight of the responsibility he carried.

Seven souls died for this . . .

He refused to let their sacrifice be for nothing.

"There!" Igor pointed ahead. "I recognize those stairs. They should lead to the door out of here."

"Thank the Lord," Alex muttered with relief.

They hurried together toward the steps. Igor led the way up, which ended at a rusted metal door. He shoved the heavy gate open. Bright sunlight filled the passageway, blinding them both. The two men shielded their eyes against the glare and pushed into the open air.

They exited into a basement level of a building under construction. Scaffolding and ladders climbed all around them, along with piles of bricks.

Steps away, the shining edifice of the Cathedral of Christ the Savior loomed high, topped by its gold cupolas. Stalin blew up the original cathedral in 1931 in his war against religion. He eventually built a public pool in its place. But after the fall of the Soviet Union and a resurgence of religious belief, the Russian Orthodox Church had been funded to restore the cathedral.

The construction site here was destined to be a future domicile for the cathedral's clergy and church officials. It was being built on the site of the old Soviet-era pool, marking it as a visible example of the expanding role of the Russian Orthodox Church.

Last week, Vadim and his band of urban explorers had cleared a pile of rubble on one side of the old pool and exposed the door. But the unearthing of it hadn't been pure chance. The young student had studied an account by a laborer—Apollos Ivanov—who described his own discovery of the door back in 1933, after Stalin's bombing of the cathedral. Ivanov ended up exploring these same tunnels, stumbling upon skeletons and the sealed passageways beneath the Kremlin. Vadim had used this old account to estimate where the old entrance might be and spent weeks doggedly searching for it—until he found it.

Only to be killed for his ingenuity.

Alex squinted against the glare of the low sun.

"We must alert Bishop Yelagin about the tragedy below," Igor said. "Get the authorities to start a recovery effort."

Alex fumbled his cell phone free of his pocket. "I can try to reach him. If I can get a signal."

He lifted the device to his face, and the screen bloomed to life. He swung the cell through the air, testing for a connection. In the process, he almost dropped the book.

"The call can wait another moment," Igor said. "We're only a few blocks from my museum. We can alert the bishop from there. I can also get my colleagues to secure the book and to start the restoration process. If there's any hope of deciphering that illuminated drawing, we must make it more legible."

Alex agreed. "At the Vatican Archives, I used UV fluorescent imaging to bring out the faded writing in a thousand-year-old Archimedes Palimpsest. With care, we should be able to do the same with this text."

"*Da.* There are other methods I'd love to try, too. I read about Dutch scientists at Leiden University who employed x-ray spectrometry to reveal hidden pages in the bindings of old medieval texts. Who knows what other clues Catherine the Great built into this tome? You already noted the handwritten annotations in the margins of several pages within the book itself, along with other drawings and underlined passages."

"We don't know if any of those were done by Catherine or by prior scholars who had been studying the text."

"Still, we must pick this book apart if we hope to discover the location of the Golden Library."

"Assuming it's not a wild goose chase."

Determined to find out, Igor and Alex worked free of the construction site and reached the open street. In the distance, over the top of the neighboring buildings, the towers of the Kremlin glowed in the last rays of the evening sun, setting the domes and spires on fire. The Moscow Archaeological Museum lay within a stone's throw of Red Square.

The pair set off down the street, which was lined by the detritus and refuse of last night's Victory Day celebration, a raucous party and military parade that commemorated the Soviet defeat of the Nazis in 1945. Being the day after, the street was mostly deserted as people slept off the drunken revelry.

Alex gingerly picked his way across a debris field of vodka bottles, beer cans, and crumpled fast food bags. He could only imagine the sight of them hiking through the streets in caked coveralls and caving helmets.

As they reached the end of the street, the full breadth of Red Square opened up. On the far side rose the walled fortress of the Kremlin. At one corner, a star shone brightly atop a hulking brick clock tower, glowing like a small sun in the twilit gloaming. Elsewhere, a dense cluster of domed cathedrals framed the darkening sky. The most prominent of all was the gilded cupola of the Ivan the Great Bell Tower, which glowed like a golden torch.

Igor drew his gaze away and pointed in the opposite direction. "We should get to the museum."

As Alex turned, a sharp crack made him jump. Igor looked at him with a confused expression. The young man sank to his knees. A dark bloom spread across the chest of his blue coveralls. Igor opened his mouth as if to voice a question, but blood flowed over his lips. He toppled to his side.

Alex backed away—into the grip of men in dark clothes. He lost his footing, but he was held up by iron fingers. More figures closed in out of the shadows, all masked by swaths of cloths over their faces.

The group parted, and another figure pushed forward, clearly their leader.

The figure marched up to him, drawing nose to nose with him. "Where is the library?"

Alex quailed back—not from the threat, but from the raw venom in that voice. He stared at the ice blue eyes above the drape of cloth. He was shocked to realize his interrogator was a woman.

He pushed down his shock and stammered, "I don't know what—"

The woman silenced him with a flick of her wrist. A steel blade appeared in her fingertips as if out of thin air. "I've been paid well to find the truth."

The point of her dagger lifted his chin and freed his tongue.

"We . . . we found a chamber," he admitted, aghast at how quickly word must have spread about Vadim's discovery. "A vault. With trunks of books. But it was booby trapped. The whole place collapsed. We barely got out alive."

Her gaze shifted to what he clutched to his chest. "But not empty-handed, it seems."

He pulled the book tighter. He couldn't help from doing so, though it likely hinted at its value. "It's an old Greek text. All I could grab. But it's only of academic value."

She reached and ripped the book from his hands. "We shall see about that."

He tried to snatch it back, but it was to no avail. It only made her eyes narrow suspiciously.

She pressed him, "And there was no evidence the collection below was connected to the Golden Library."

"None at all," he lied.

She huffed heavily and swung away. Her arm waved back as if dismissing him—but a sharp line of fire ignited across his throat. "Then you're of no use to me."

A hot dampness poured down his chest. It was only then that he realized her dagger had sliced deep under his chin. Shocked, he coughed more blood. As he was released, he fell to his hands and knees. His heart pounded hard. Agony flared in his chest. Pain narrowed his sight.

"No . . ." he choked out.

His captors ignored him, stepping past him.

He reached into his pocket, clawed out his phone, and cradled his body low over it. He tried to hide his efforts as he tapped and swiped rapidly. Blood pooled on the red bricks under him.

Before darkness could overwhelm him, he struck the last button, an address. He heard the whoosh of the text as it sent off a cache of photos. They were pictures he had taken on the stairs with Igor's help.

Alex's efforts were finally noted—whether from the noise or the shine of the screen.

The woman lunged back toward him, knocked him over, and grabbed the phone. She cursed thickly in Russian. The vehemence made her underlings lurch back.

Alex let his head fall to the cold bricks. His gaze drifted to the shining golden cupola of the Ivan the Great Bell Tower, which still glowed brightly against the purple sky. The tower was a monument to Ivan III, whose grandson—Ivan the Terrible—hid the treasure that led to so many deaths this day.

The library must be indeed cursed . . .

Darkness finally snuffed out the golden torch, taking the world with it. Still, Alex took solace in his final act. The new prefect of the Vatican Archives had given him an address to text in case of emergency. It came with no name, not even a number, just a symbol.

A single Greek letter, which Alex took to be providential.

He pictured it as he took his last breath, praying it was significant.

Σ

2

Commander Gray Pierce raced his motorcycle through the afternoon rush hour of D.C. traffic. His bike, a Yamaha V-Max, was two decades old, but its well-maintained engine rumbled like a pissed-off puma between his thighs.

Its ferocious timbre matched his mood.

He sped along Jefferson Drive through the heart of the city. To his left, the greensward of the National Mall shone a bright emerald, bisected by sandy paths. But ahead, the street was shut down, cordoned off with cement barricades and patrolled by police on horseback and on foot. A pair of army Humvees were also parked beyond the barrier, guarding the ruins of the Smithsonian Castle.

Seven weeks ago—on the first day of spring—a series of bombs had ripped through the red-stone structure. The Castle, a national treasure built in 1855, was the Smithsonian's oldest building. It had survived fires and political storms over the past century and a half. Now it was a pile of rubble, though its east wing and two of its Gothic towers still stood. The remainder of the building was a blasted mix of crumbling walls, caved-in roofs, and blown-out windows.

Thankfully, there had been only three deaths, workers who had been inside the building at the time. Since the start of the year, the Castle had been undergoing a major renovation and was closed to the public, so the building had been nearly deserted.

The radio inside Gray's helmet squawked with static, then a stern voice warned him. "Move your ass. We're going to be late."

A sleek Ducati Scrambler—a dark Nightshift edition—sped past him through the traffic with a roar of its engine. The rider, decked in black leather, boots, and helmet, looked back at him. Though Gray couldn't see through the polarized face shield, he pictured the narrow-eyed glare cast his way.

Gray throttled up and closed the distance with the other bike. "We're fine," he radioed back. "The meeting isn't scheduled for another—" He checked the holographic heads-up display glowing inside a corner of his helmet and grimaced. "Two minutes."

An irritated growl answered him—coming from both rider and cycle. The Ducati shot away, taking a sharp turn onto Twelfth Street, leaving the National Mall behind. Gray leaned hard, nearly scraping his knee on the pavement, to follow.

As he did, he caught a last glimpse of the bombed-out Castle.

He knew what the damage represented.

A declaration of war.

Over the past weeks, no one had claimed responsibility. Actually, some had, but their assertions were quickly refuted and dismissed. The true culprits remained unknown. Surveillance footage, both from cameras and satellites, had failed to reveal who had planted the bombs or how such a heinous act could have happened.

The Joint Terrorism Task Force continued orchestrating daily bomb sweeps of the area. Cable news channels debated, pointed fingers, and stoked conspiracy theories. Still, for those who knew the Castle's greatest secret, the target of the attack was obvious.

Gray hunched lower in his seat.

It was us.

Of that he was certain.

Gray was a member of Sigma Force, a covert team of field operatives working under the auspices of DARPA, the defense department's research-and-development agency. They were all former Special Forces soldiers, recruited in secret and trained in various scientific disciplines to protect the globe against all manner of threats. Their name arose from the Greek letter Σ, which represented the "sum of the best," the merging of brain and brawn, of soldier and scientist. Their motto was a simple one: *Be there first.*

In this case, as the other rider attested, Gray was failing in that mission.

He trailed close behind the Ducati and merged onto Independence Avenue. The pair circled behind the Castle, where gardens spread to the rear of the building. Fifteen years ago, Sigma had constructed its headquarters in a series of abandoned WWII-era bomb shelters beneath the Castle. The long-forgotten bunker served the agency well, both for its level of secrecy and for its proximity to the Smithsonian Institution's many labs and resources. Additionally, the Castle was within an easy walk to the major touchstones of governmental power—which of late was more of a problem than a boon.

Sigma's director—Painter Crowe—was dealing with a political firestorm after the bombing. While only those with the highest security clearance knew Sigma even existed, all of them had been bearing down upon the agency, especially the group's overseer, General Metcalf, the current head of DARPA.

Everyone needed answers—and if not that, then a fall guy to blame. Gray hoped this priority summons from the director was about the bomber's identity and not about dissolving Sigma, which was a grim possibility.

His helmet phone chirped with an incoming call. He took it, wincing slightly, expecting it to be Director Crowe. "Go ahead," he answered.

"Where are you two?" It was Monk Kokkalis, a fellow Sigma operative and his best friend. "Painter is pacing a hole through his office rug."

"We'll be there in a few minutes. We're about to head underground."

"Get here. Something major is up. Kat won't even look at me, but her face is drawn as tight as a drum. She clearly knows why we were summoned."

"Understood."

Captain Kathryn Bryant was Sigma's chief intelligence analyst and Monk's wife. She was also the agency's second-in-command.

"We'll be right there." Gray ended the call.

Gray swung into the entrance of a nondescript parking garage on the opposite side of the street from the Castle. A metal security gate ratcheted up, responding to a transponder in his helmet. Both bikes dove down a ramp and into a subterranean space. From there, they circled into a tunnel that ran beneath Independence Avenue. As they sped down the passageway, a series of electronic checkpoints registered their progress. The route led deep under the four-acre garden behind the Castle.

Finally, they reached a subterranean motor pool directly beneath the Castle. The space was full of Land Rovers, German sedans, and a handful of motorcycles. Gray joined his bike with the others and cut the engine. He quickly dismounted and removed his helmet.

The entrance into Sigma Command was sealed off by vault-like steel doors. He headed to a biometric reader and registered a retinal scan and palm print, but the door remained locked. The electronic surveillance in the garage had recognized another was present who had not yet identified themselves.

Gray turned to the Ducati as its rider swept off the bike. "Seichan, you'll need to scan in, too. They've upped security since the last time you were down here."

With the snap of a chin strap, Seichan yanked off her helmet. A drape of ebony hair fell to her shoulders. She gave Gray a scathing look and tugged down the zipper of her leather jacket, exposing a maroon blouse.

"Heightened security?" she scoffed. "Better late than never, I suppose."

She crossed to him, moving with a leonine grace, all sinew, muscles, and long curves. The almond complexion of her skin—marking her Eurasian heritage—shone through a sheen of perspiration. Her emerald eyes smoldered with barely restrained fury.

"Crowe better have answers," she warned. "If this is just some organizational pissing contest . . ."

Gray understood the source of her frustration and anger. The two had left their two-year-old son at the safehouse. She did not like being away from Jack's side—especially now.

Following the attack, the entire agency had gone into lockdown.

Painter was taking no chances, especially when a hit-and-run maimed a pair of operatives shortly after the bombing. Another agent was killed by a sniper while out jogging.

Someone was clearly targeting Sigma teams.

Since the lockdown, there had been no more incidents, but no one was fooled into believing that the threat was over. The enemy had only momentarily retreated, likely to regroup and reassess before striking again. Everyone remained guarded, knowing they were in the calm before the storm.

Gray hooked an arm around Seichan's waist as she joined him. "We'll get back to Jack as soon as possible."

She scowled at him, but she still leaned into his side, allowing herself this rare moment of reassurance. Despite her stoic front, cracks showed from the tension. Her lips were bloodless and thin; the curve of her jaw was hard from clenched muscles.

It was the *unknown* that wore on her, on all of them, but she was taking it especially hard. And it wasn't just the lack of knowledge about the bomber that kept her on edge. It was the unsettled fate of the organization.

If Sigma were shut down, Gray had plenty of options open to him. He had joined the armed forces when he was eighteen, become a ranger at twenty-one. Painter had personally recruited him into Sigma. He had been picked less for his military background and more for what Seichan described as his *strange mind*, his ability to perceive patterns where no one else could.

He didn't know where that talent came from. While growing up, Gray had always been pulled in different directions. Maybe his upbringing had made him look at things differently, to try to balance extremes. Or maybe it was something genetic, ingrained in his DNA, that allowed him to see those patterns.

No matter the source, he knew it was a skill set that other agencies would value.

The same was not true for Seichan.

She had been an assassin for an international criminal organization.

Brutalized and molded from a young age, she had developed her own bloody skill set, but it was not something easily included on an application or résumé. While she had eventually turned against her bosses and come to work with Sigma, she remained estranged from the surrounding world. Few knew her true background. Several countries' intelligence agencies, including the Mossad, still maintained a kill-order on her.

Sigma had become her home—first out of necessity, later out of hope for a different life, and now it offered a new beginning with Gray and Jack. No one, not even Painter, could say what her fate would be if Sigma folded. The agency was her cover, her protection. Without it, she would become unmoored—and as much as she tried to hide her feelings, it clearly terrified her.

"We'll be okay," Gray said lamely, drawing her closer. He lifted his left hand to show the gold band encircling a finger. "And we still have a wedding to plan."

Her attempt at a smile came off as a grimace. "I don't know which is worse: dealing with a bomber or figuring out the seating chart for the reception."

Seichan slipped out of his embrace and stepped to the biometric scanners. After her identity was confirmed, the reinforced steel doors parted. Gray felt his ears pop as the positive pressure ventilation wafted over them, maintaining the clean-room nature of the facility.

They headed together into the lowermost level of the command center. Gray stared up, picturing the director's office three flights above.

For better or worse, let's discover our fate.

4:34 P.M.

Director Painter Crowe remained seated behind his desk as he waited for the latecomers to settle in. A tension headache had taken root behind his eyes.

But, at least, I still have a head.

He had been in his office when the Castle had been bombed. He had heard the explosions, felt the quake of those blasts. The lights had failed for several dark seconds before the emergency generators had kicked in. He had ordered an immediate evacuation of the facility, fearing it might collapse—but in the end, the old WWII shelters had proved to be as bomb-proof as their name attested. The deep bunkers had sustained minimal damage.

As Commander Pierce entered, Monk gave Gray a brief hug and clap on his back. The other returned it with the same affection. They shared a bond deeper than mere brotherhood. It was forged of blood-shed, tragedy, and sacrifice.

Outwardly, though, the two could not be more different.

Monk was a former Green Beret and still looked it, from his stocky bulk to his shaven scalp. The crown of his head barely reached Gray's chin. He wore a loose windbreaker over a tight-fitted T-shirt with a growling bulldog, a countenance not all that dissimilar to the man's own face. But that tough exterior hid a mind as sharp and quick as any chess champion.

Gray, on the other hand, stood six-foot-two, with a lean musculature that masked the lethality of his quick reflexes. His ruddy complexion marked his former Texas roots, as if the Lone Star sun had permanently branded him. But his Welsh blood showed in his strong jaw, intense blue eyes, and dark hair, which he kept lanky on top and shaved close on the sides.

Painter waved to the chairs. "We should get started."

Gray took his seat, but he kept his leather jacket on, as if he did not intend to stay long. Seichan dropped next to him, looking equally impatient.

Painter recognized the tension they were under and their worry for Jack. The pair's son shared the same safehouse at the edge of Rock Creek Park with Monk's daughters. The two families had been sheltering this storm together.

The last member of the meeting strode into the room. Kathryn Bryant had been shuffling throughout the day between Painter's office and Sigma's intelligence nest, which was her fiefdom and domain.

She touched Seichan on the shoulder as she crossed to Painter's desk. This gesture—from one worried mother to another—was a warm one.

Still, Kat's manner was otherwise stiff, angry. She carried herself as if she were about to go to war—which might very well be the case.

Like all Sigma members, Kat had a military background. In her case, it was in naval intelligence, but no one would mistake her for a pencil pusher. Like her husband, she had not shed the taut mannerisms drilled into her by the armed forces. Her shoulder-length auburn hair was combed and braided in the back, as conservative as her attire: navy blue suit, crisp white blouse, black leather pumps.

"Now that we're all here," Painter started.

"This is everyone?" Gray sat straighter, glancing around. "I thought this was an all-hands-on-deck briefing. In fact, why aren't we heading off to the conference room?"

"This is a *need-to-know* sort of meeting," Painter corrected. "I've not even shared this intel with General Metcalf, or anyone at DARPA. In fact, there's much I haven't shared with any of you."

Seichan frowned. "What do you mean by—"

Painter held up a hand. "First, let me say we may have caught a break on the bomber. Unfortunately, what we've learned in the last eight hours does not necessarily equate to certain guilt. As you know, every military and government office tied to national security, counterterrorism, and intelligence operations has been hunting for the bomber—or for any organization, domestic or foreign, who might want to target the Mall. But most of those hunters have one hand tied behind their backs."

"Because they don't know about us," Gray answered.

Painter shrugged. "Some do, some don't, some suspect. Still, failing to know the intended target is a huge handicap. Metcalf has advocated for pulling us out of the shadows, to expose our organization."

Monk groaned. "Which would cripple our effectiveness."

"If not destroy us," Gray added.

"I've managed to hold him off for now, mostly because there haven't been any further attacks. But if that should change . . . ?"

Painter let that question hang in the room for a breath.

Gray finally shrugged out of his jacket and settled deeper in his chair. "What have you learned?"

Painter turned to his second-in-command. "Kat, can you bring up the video from ADX Florence?"

"Give me a moment to transfer the footage." Kat slid around the desk to access Painter's terminal.

He moved aside to allow her room, which wasn't hard. His office could be considered spartan at best. Beyond his mahogany desk, the only nod to luxury was a Remington bronze seated on a pedestal in the corner. It featured an exhausted Native American warrior slumped atop a horse. It had been a gift from his former mentor, Sean McKnight, who had founded Sigma and died to protect this bunker years ago.

And now I may lose it all.

Guilt tightened his jaw as he found himself staring at the bronze.

Sean's gift was meant to honor Painter's heritage. When Painter was younger, few people recognized his mixed Native American status, but as he approached fifty, his skin had grown ruddier, his cheekbones more prominent. And while his hair remained dark, a single lock of white now crested over one ear, looking like an eagle feather.

For Painter, though, the statue no longer represented his heritage. It had come to embody his burden as Sigma's director. The mounted warrior's face hung low, etched with exhaustion and grief. To Painter, it reminded him of the cost of battle for any soldier.

And maybe that was Sean's intent in this gift, too.

Kat finally cleared her throat and straightened. "I have the video from ADX Florence keyed up. I'll bring it up on the left monitor."

Painter swung around. Three large 8K monitors covered the walls behind and to either side of his mahogany desk. He sometimes scrolled different landscapes to create the illusion of windows in his confined office, but they only reminded him of how trapped he was underground.

"Here we go," Kat said.

The monitor's screen filled with a picture of a series of low-brick buildings, cement towers, all surrounded by tall fences encased by curls of razor wire. It was all backdropped by a wall of mountains.

"This is ADX Florence," Kat said.

Seichan uncrossed her legs and leaned forward. "Which is what?"

Gray's brows pinched with confusion. "The Alcatraz of the Rockies."

Painter nodded. "It's a supermax federal penitentiary in Colorado. It houses prisoners deemed to be the most dangerous, especially to national security. One cell block has been dubbed Bomber's Row, due to the various domestic terrorists who have been housed there over the years. Timothy McVeigh, Terry Nichols, Ramzi Yousef, Ted Kaczynski."

"I don't understand," Monk said. "What does a supermax facility in Colorado have to do with the bombing here?"

"Good question," Painter said. "It's why it took us so long to make a connection."

Kat tapped on the terminal keyboard. "This is footage from inside, from a visitor's center."

A grainy video from a closed-circuit security system started rolling on the screen. The image was split, showing both sides of a glass partition that separated prisoners from visitors. The room was deserted, except for a single posted guard and two figures seated at one booth. The pair leaned in close, phones at their ears.

"Is there any audio?" Monk asked as the video ran silently.

"Restricted," Kat answered. "This was a privileged conversation between a lawyer and his client."

"Who's the prisoner—" Gray's words choked off as the man leaned out far enough to reveal his face. "That bastard."

"Senator Kent Cargill," Kat confirmed. "Or rather *former* senator. He's better known as Inmate 4593."

Painter waited for the shock and anger to wane. The man had betrayed his country. His actions had led to hundreds of deaths. Sigma had exposed him a couple of years ago, but prior to that, the senator had also sat in one of these office chairs after his daughter had been kidnapped.

"Kat and her team have been canvassing, reviewing, and interviewing anyone who had knowledge of Sigma Command's location."

"And who might hold a grudge against us," Gray added.

Kat nodded. "It took us this long to come across this video. It was taped a month prior to the bombing."

Monk sighed. "But what's the significance of this one meeting between Cargill and his lawyer?"

"His lawyer's colleague," Kat corrected. "A junior partner in the firm, according to a background check prior to the visit. It was Jason who noted how this particular visitor was very coy with the cameras, as if they had foreknowledge of their locations in the room."

Jason Carter was a twenty-six-year-old former hacker who had been recruited by Sigma a few years back. His black-hat skills, raw ingenuity, and sharp eye had earned him a position at Kat's right side.

"But the lawyer made one slip-up," Kat said.

She sped the video forward. The visitor leaned down to remove something from a satchel. Kat froze the footage. The camera had captured a three-quarter profile.

"Kat was able to nab a few other photos during the intake process," Painter added.

She nodded and brought up a row of pictures, some blurry, others full body, of the visitor.

"It's a woman," Monk said.

"Not just any woman," Kat said. "And certainly not the junior associate of Cargill's law firm. Though, the make-up and prosthetics made her look very much like that junior partner."

Gray swore harshly.

Monk stiffened.

Kat continued, "The NSA has developed some sophisticated facial-recognition software. Jason improved on it. We ran these images through the program, inputting photos of the most likely suspect."

"And you got confirmation," Gray said.

Kat tapped a button. On the screen, the three-quarter profile shed its artifice to reveal a pale, phantom face beneath. Someone they all knew well.

Painter studied those gathered in his office.

Only one of them remained stoic and unsurprised by this revelation.

5:02 P.M.

Seichan shook her head, accepting the inevitable. Sigma had made many enemies over the years, so had she. But there was only *one* foe whom both she and Sigma shared.

"Valya Mikhailov," she muttered.

Seichan studied the spectral visage hidden behind the mask on the screen. The features appeared pale, but not as ashen as the woman's true complexion. Valya suffered from albinism. Her skin was the color of Carrera marble, her hair chalk-white. Yet, defying the assumption that all those afflicted had red eyes, her irises were an ice blue.

The only other blemish—visible even on the ghostly image—was the shadowy remains of a black tattoo. It depicted half of a black sun, casting out kinked rays across her left cheek and brow. It was a *Kolovrat*, a pagan solar symbol from Slavic countries. It had once been tied to witchcraft but later was co-opted by nationalistic parties, including Neo-Nazis.

But Valya was far from a *nationalist* of any country.

She and Seichan had both been assassins with the Guild, sisters in the same deadly profession. After Seichan had helped Sigma destroy the organization, Valya had survived, bitter and vengeful. In the power vacuum left behind, Valya had gathered new forces, slowly rebuilding the organization under her own merciless leadership.

Sigma had crossed paths with them several times, embittering both sides.

Gray shifted in his seat, drawing Seichan's attention from the screen. "Cargill must have told her where our command center was located. Did anyone question him? Confirm that he told her our location?"

"We tried," Kat answered. "He lawyered up. We'll get nothing out of him. He certainly doesn't want any culpability for the bombing placed on his shoulders."

"So even with this information," Painter said, "Valya's guilt is not certain. Her culpability in the bombing has yet to be firmly established. Still, we all know she certainly has *motive* to attack us."

"What about *opportunity*?" Monk said. "Is there any evidence she was in D.C. at the time of the bombing?"

"None," Kat answered. "If she was here, she covered her tracks well. The problem is that whoever planted those devices knew well enough to stay out of sight."

"Plus," Painter added, "there were glitches in eight of the Mall's surveillance cameras, which happens periodically, but those cameras were likely taken out. We know Valya has plenty of resources at her disposal, while being unbound by the restrictions and restraints put on us."

"So, she had the *means* to attack us," Monk huffed out.

Kat nodded. "With the Castle undergoing renovations—with its spaces gutted and emptied—many of its interior cameras were non-operable. It was the perfect window for Valya to attack. That is, if it was her."

"Screw *if*." Seichan burst up, bumping her chair back. "It *was* her."

Gray tried to draw her back down, but she shook free and stalked the edges of the room.

"We all know it's her," she said. "We've suspected it from the beginning."

Painter held up a palm. "True, and I have acted accordingly. Like I said, there are some details that I've not shared with anyone, not even you all."

"Like what?" Gray asked.

Kat answered, "Early on, I had compiled a list of the most likely suspects, with Mikhailov at the top. Since the attack, I've been in constant contact with various intelligence services, both here and abroad. While Valya herself is a ghost, a handful of her associates—low-level operatives and contacts—are known well enough for us to trace her organization's movements, not in any granular detail, but enough to glean a general trend of direction."

"And?" Seichan pressed. "Spit it out. What are you dancing around?"

"After the attack, we suspected she retreated to Eastern Europe, maybe Russia, perhaps to lay low for a spell. It's also where we believe she's set up her headquarters. In her home country."

"Her and her brother's," Seichan reminded them.

The room quieted, reminded that Valya's grudge ran deeper than simply thwarted global ambitions. There had once been *another* who carried the other half of that black sun, only across his right cheek and brow—Valya's twin brother. Four years ago, Anton Mikhailov had been killed during a Sigma operation. He had died helping them.

Still, Seichan knew *who* Valya truly blamed for the loss of her sibling.

Gray cleared his throat. "If Valya's holed up in Russia, it will be hard for us to reach her, especially with the current political climate."

"Perhaps," Painter said, "but having already suspected who we might be dealing with, I took some preemptive countermeasures."

"What do you mean?" Seichan asked.

Before the director could answer, a commotion erupted at the doorway. Jason Carter burst into the room. "We've got trouble."

3

Captain First Class Sergei Turov waited for the summons. As the commander of the White Sea Naval Base, he had an expansive view from his office of the three shipyards, which glowed through the ice fog of the cold night.

As he stood vigil, frustration warred within him. It was written across the reflection of his face. His ice-gray eyes remained pinched. Deep lines furrowed his brow, under hair that had gone an ashy white. He was dressed in a starched uniform of navy blue. A matching cap sat on the desk behind him.

For the past seven years, the base had been under his charge. He had started his career as a submariner with the Northern Fleet, as a navigational engineer. Forgoing family and a home life, he had risen steadily in rank over the past decades—even as the Soviet Union fell and the Russian Federation formed.

And look where I stand today.

Since taking command, he had seen the base at the edge of the White Sea expand under his leadership. When he had first arrived, the station had housed dozens of submarines and scores of surface ships, all spread across two shipyards. During his tenure, he had built a third yard. He also oversaw the testing of ice-hardened watercraft, amphibious vehicles, and radar systems. Yet, it wasn't just hardware. A large section of the base was now devoted to training the Arctic Brigade—

seamen, marines, and infantry who had to be just as battle-hardened to the ice and cold.

I did all of this.

While he should be satisfied, he rankled at the lack of recognition. The prior leader of the White Sea Naval Base had advanced to vice admiral after only four years and now commanded the entire Northern Fleet.

Yet, here I languish.

And he knew why.

Four summers ago, he had participated in a massive war exercise called Ocean Shield. It had involved bases across the northern coast, encompassing hundreds of ships and three hundred thousand troops. But during the exercise, an engineering mishap aboard an Akula-class submarine had sunk the boat. All aboard had been lost. While the incident had been covered up, the blame fell on his shoulders—undeservedly so. Two months prior, the same sub had undergone repairs in his new shipyard. He had urged for the boat to be held back from the exercise, but Vice Admiral Glazkov had demanded it be included. Afterward, like the sinking of the sub, his reluctance to dispatch the sub vanished from all records.

The incident became a black mark on his record. All because of that bastard Glazkov.

Exasperated, he struck the window with a fist. A ring on his finger banged sharply against the glass. He lowered his arm and rubbed the band of white gold.

He took a deep breath and let it out slowly as he stared down at the heraldic image stamped on the ring, of a sword raised across a pair of wings. He also pictured the inscription engraved on the band's inner surface.

Архангел Общество

Those two words—*Arkangel Society*—held the promise of a brighter future.

Both for him and for all of Russia.

And maybe a way to right an injustice.

A knock on his door drew his attention. His deputy chief of staff, Oleg Ulyanin, entered and gave a slight bow of his head.

"I heard from Archpriest Sychkin," Oleg stated. "He says he has finished with the interrogation."

Turov grimaced. "Then let us be finished with this matter, too."

Oleg, ten years his junior, was a dour-faced mountain man from the Urals. His blond hair was shorn tight under a black beret, a hat that represented his past with the naval infantry brigade. While serving in Syria, the man had lost a leg, just below his left knee. Afterward, while recuperating, he had studied at the Arctic Marine Institute, gaining a degree in geology.

Oleg also shared more than just a professional role. The two had forged a deeper bond. It gleamed in white gold on the man's left hand. It was Oleg who had introduced him to the Arkangel Society, a group that had already opened powerful doors and held the promise of far more.

Turov clapped his friend on the arm, squeezing firmly, then collected an overcoat from a rack, along with a furred ushanka hat. Oleg already had donned a heavy woolen jacket over his uniform.

The two headed out of his office and into an elevator.

"Did Sychkin say if he was successful?" Turov asked as the doors closed.

"No. Only that there was something important he wanted to share with you."

Turov frowned.

What could that be?

11:55 P.M.

As Turov exited the administration building, the breeze off the sea cut through his fur-lined coat. Ice and salt filled his lungs. Though it was well into spring, the temperature remained frigid, dropping precipitously after sunset.

He and Oleg hurried through the dark streets, hunched against the cold. They strode quickly toward a building lit by flickers of gas lamps.

Unlike the base's utilitarian cement block and corrugated steel archi-
tecture, this structure was mortared stone, with leaded glass windows
and sills of hewn pine. Above it, a wooden steeple rose high, topped by
an orthodox cross.

It was the Church of the Holy Sacrament. It had stood on this spot
for more than a century. During the Soviet era, the structure had been
transformed into a jail. Now it had been returned to a place of worship,
though steel bars still covered its windows.

They headed up the stone steps and pushed through the heavy
wooden doors and into the church's dark narthex. Ahead of them, on
the far side of the nave, a few fat candles glowed warmly, reflecting off
the rich gold iconography of its altar screen. Closer at hand, the plaster
walls bore new frescoes, which still looked wet in the candlelight.

Turov frowned, resenting the expense it took to renovate the church.
Then again, the current regime in Moscow considered the restoration
of the Russian Orthodox Church to be a top priority, a means to a
spiritual renewal for the country, a way of instilling national pride—or
as cynics would believe, returning Russia to the theocratic values of the
tsarist era.

"The archpriest should still be below," Oleg said as he led Turov to a
set of stairs on the left.

They headed down steps into the church's basement. While everything aboveground had been returned to its former glory, this level
still clung stubbornly to its Soviet roots. The stone walls remained un-
plastered. Stark sodium lights lit the passageway. Cells lined either side,
closed by thick steel doors. Likewise, the purpose down here remained
the same.

This was still a prison, one that the Church had found little reason
to change. To Turov, it was the dark truth of the newly restored ortho-
doxy, what it hid from the world. The Church's word had become
absolute. Dissent was not tolerated. Only the Church was allowed to
do the questioning.

Like today.

When Turov had been down here earlier, screams had echoed in a
painful chorus. The place was now as silent as a grave.

Oleg led the way to a door halfway down the passageway. It had been left ajar, allowing firelight to flicker into the hall. Oleg pushed the way open and motioned for Turov to enter first.

With a hard swallow, Turov stiffened his back and stepped into the room.

Like the rest of the subterranean jail, this interrogation chamber had not changed from its role during the Soviet era. The room's walls were hung with all manner of torture devices, some sharp, others serrated. They gleamed with threat under the harsh lighting. A steel-doored firepit lay open along the back wall, heating the room to a blistering temperature.

The reek of scorched flesh struck his nose. Blood pooled and ran in tepid flows down a floor drain. The source of all of it came from two figures strapped to chairs. They had the shapes of the young man and woman who had been hauled into the church, but there was little recognition beyond that. Skin had been stripped, joints broken, fingers severed. Their heads hung to their chests.

Turov had believed them to be dead, but a low moan rose from the man. The woman's naked chest still moved.

The pair were students, part of a team of urban explorers who had discovered a vault deep beneath Moscow. The Kremlin kept close watch on such trespassers and had heard what they claimed to have found: an ancient trove of books, possibly part of the lost Golden Library.

Archpriest Leonid Sychkin turned at Turov's arrival and lifted an arm. The clergyman was only thirty-three, young for such a rank. He wore humble dark pants and a matching black shirt. His only adornment was the heavy silver crucifix that hung to mid-chest, just below the end of his thick, black beard.

"We were about to leave," Sychkin said, motioning to his assistant, a hulking monk who had taken a vow of silence.

Turov frowned. "Did these two have any further information about their discovery?"

"Nothing that we hadn't already discerned. It was unfortunate they had to be treated so harshly, but we had to be certain."

The word *unfortunate* seemed far too meager a description for what had transpired in this room. Still, Turov knew better than to object. Sychkin had the ear of the patriarch, the leader of the Orthodox Church. Likewise, the archpriest carried the same white-gold ring as Turov and Oleg, only it did not decorate a finger, but hung from a chain under his clothes.

The Arkangel Society had members across a spectrum of high-profile professions: politicians, military leaders, scientists, and religious figures. Their ambition was to seek paths to return Russia to its former glory, with a focus on its northernmost lands, an area that the society believed held the true origins of the Russian people.

In fact, the group's name came from the mythic history of the neighboring port city of Arkhangelsk, where it was said the Archangel Michael fought the devil and that the angel still guarded over the northern coast of Russia. The society's heraldic symbol of a sword-over-wings was a nod to that battle and represented their group's commitment to help Michael's cause.

But more than just guarding the northern coasts, the society's primary goal was to seek the true roots of the Russian people, to prove they had descended from a nearly divine race, one that Archangel Michael had wanted to protect and cherish. The society adhered to the philosophy of Aleksandr Dugin, a man who was held in high esteem by both the military and the current regime in Moscow. Dugin believed the roots of the Russian race came from a lost continent, what the Greeks called Hyperborea, the land beyond the North Wind.

The Arkangel Society's primary goal was to find *proof* of this truth. To that end, Dugin gave them his personal blessing, which helped the group quickly gain powerful allies.

Still, in his heart, Turov remained skeptical of all of it, but that had not stopped him from joining up, especially as the group's cause served his own ends.

For decades, Russia had been seeking ways to expand its territorial reach, to claim more, if not all, of the Arctic. Back in 2007, two Russian Navy submersibles traveled beneath the ice cap and planted a titanium flag under the North Pole, symbolically staking a claim.

Since then, Turov's mission was to turn symbolism into reality. Turov and Oleg—working in tandem with the Arctic Marine Institute—had used submarines to collect rock samples along the Lomonosov Ridge, a subsea mountain range that crossed the North Pole. Their effort was to prove geologically that the ridge was an extension of Russia's continental shelf, which would allow the federation to have territorial claim over most of the Arctic.

Unfortunately, ownership of the Lomonosov Ridge continued to remain in dispute. Canada claimed the mountain range was an extension of their Ellesmere Island. Denmark said it was a submerged section of Greenland.

In the end, Turov's efforts failed.

Still, he held out hope that he could find *another* similar site, one with both a *geological* connection to the Russian mainland and a *cultural* tie to its people. If he could find that, especially a location far to the north, then Russia could claim the Arctic for itself.

And I would get the honor.

Holding to that hope, Turov tolerated many of the wilder and arcane assertions of the society's members. He tempered what he heard and tried to cast it all in practical terms, but even he had his limits.

He stared at the ruins of the two young people.

This zealotry and cruelty strained his forbearance.

He scowled at Sychkin. "You truly believe that what these two found, a cache of old books, could lead to the Golden Library of the Tsars?"

"I do. It's why I wished to talk to you before I returned to Moscow and reported to the patriarch."

"About what?"

"From those trunks of books, a single Greek text was recovered. We've come to believe it holds the key to the location of the Golden Library."

Turov shook his head. "Even so, why is this library so important to the Arkangel Society?"

Sychkin took a deep breath, clearly weighing if this was a question that he should answer. He finally drew Turov off to the side, away from Oleg.

The archpriest's voice dropped to a whisper. "Because of the centuries-old accounts from two sons of Russia."

The stench of the room stoked Turov's impatience. "What accounts? What sons?"

"The first came from Pavel Chichagov. He was the son of the Russian admiral and Arctic explorer Vasily Chichagov."

Turov's interest sharpened. All who served in the Far North knew the name of the eighteenth-century admiral, a man who had once been the commander of Arkhangelsk.

Sychkin continued, "Pavel wrote a memoir about his father after his death. In that book, he stated something intriguing. It was already well known that his father repeatedly sought out the Northern Sea Route across the top of Russia, but Pavel makes mention of one particular excursion in 1764. Vasily left Arkhangelsk with three ships, but once he was underway, Pavel claims his father received a letter. A secret decree from Empress Catherine the Great. She ordered Vasily to travel north, toward the pole, to search for a lost continent."

"You think she was referring to Hyperborea?"

Sychkin lifted his bushy brows. "What else could it be?"

Turov waved for the archpriest to continue. "What happened during that voyage?"

"Pavel never says. All we know is that Chichagov returned with only one ship. Afterward, he quickly advanced to the rank of admiral." Sychkin shrugged. "Maybe as a reward?"

Turov scowled. "Even if this is true, it sounds like Pavel's father came back empty-handed."

"Maybe not. Especially when you consider the *second* account that I had mentioned." Sychkin stared hard at Turov. "That story came from Catherine the Great's own son—Paul. The young man was also friends with Pavel. In a set of Tsarist papers returned to us from the Vatican, we uncovered a single letter from Paul to Pavel, where the emperor hints that Chichagov had found *something* during that voyage. Paul's words are cryptic. He hints at the discovery of '*wonders and horrors*' far to the north. And '*a threat that could end all life.*'"

Turov scoffed. "That could mean anything."

"Except for one additional oddity in that letter. Paul tells Pavel that his mother, Catherine, hadn't sent Chichagov north without any guidance. He claims she had come across *ancient texts thought lost forever* and it was those books that guided her hand."

Turov understood where this was leading. "You're thinking she found the Golden Library and something in that archive revealed a path to Hyperborea?"

"I see the doubt in your eyes. Sometimes you must give yourself over to faith."

Turov heard the growing irritation in the other's voice, but he ignored it. "And if I don't have such faith? What if I want proof?"

The shadow of a smile shone through the archpriest's thick beard. "Within that recovered Greek text, we found an illuminated sketch of a gold book, an image we believe is meant to represent the Golden Library. More importantly, the illustration was signed in Catherine's name."

"Truly?" Turov could not help but be intrigued.

Sychkin nodded. "I believe—I have *faith*—that Catherine is guiding our hand to that library."

"A library that could lead us to a lost continent?"

"And maybe to a weapon hidden there. Catherine's son, Paul, warns of a great danger, one *that could end all life*. Still, either way, her explorers must have found something important. Why else keep her discovery of the Golden Library secret? Such a revelation would've brought great acclaim to her reign and to Russia. So why hide it?"

Turov could guess. He remembered what Paul had described was found to the Far North.

Wonders and horrors.

A stab of trepidation struck him. He pictured the collapse of the vault under Moscow. If the archpriest was right, Catherine must have been determined to preserve her secret, while also keeping it well guarded.

"We are close to the truth," Sychkin insisted with a note of exaltation. "As such, there will come a time when we will need your help, Captain

Turov—along with your Arctic Brigade. I ask you to gather a force, those you most trust, and wait for our word."

Turov gave a slight bow of his head in acknowledgment, recognizing this was the reason Sychkin had been so forthright about these details.

He needs my help.

Turov shared a look with Oleg, whose eyes shone with the same hope that stoked in his own chest. If all of this was even partially true, it could change Russia forever.

Turov turned back to Sychkin. "How long do you believe it will take you to find the Golden Library?"

Sychkin's smile widened. "From the drawing inside that Greek text, we suspect we already know *where* to look . . . or at least a general area. The search will begin in earnest tomorrow."

Turov could not hide his surprise, yet he could also not shake his earlier trepidation. He had more questions, but Sychkin turned away, clearly dismissing him.

The archpriest called over to his assistant. "Yerik, we're done here. Let us put these pour souls to rest."

The robed monk, who had been cleaning knives off to the side, nodded. He was a formidable figure. Even crouched over a table, the man towered taller than Turov.

He knew of the monk's past, how he had come to be Sychkin's aide. When Yerik was twelve, his mother had been part of a doomsday cult. She followed the self-declared prophet, Pyoty Kuznetsov, who founded what he called the True Russian Orthodox Church. The cult holed up in a cave with canisters of gasoline. It was only after some of them died during a fire, including Yerik's mother, that the group abandoned the cave. It had been black-cassocked members of the orthodox church who had guided them out. Sychkin had been part of that party and took Yerik under his care, who had been badly burned and still carried a gnarled scar across his neck and the side of his face.

After that experience, the monk would clearly do anything the archpriest asked.

Including picking up an electric drill, one fitted with a long stainless-steel bit.

Yerik carried the tool toward the two figures strapped in the chairs. The woman stirred, as if suspecting her doom.

Turov swung away as the drill's motor ignited with a feverish scream. More than ready to depart, he headed to the door with Oleg. A concern continued to plague him.

Maybe we should take heed of Catherine's caution in such matters.

Archpriest Sychkin had his own worry, announcing it over the grind of metal through skull. "Let us hope, Captain Turov, that no one else discovers what we've found!"

4

Following Jason Carter's warning of trouble, Gray and the others gathered inside Sigma's intelligence nest. It was down the hall from Director Crowe's office. Jason had insisted they all accompany him here, as there were details that he wanted everyone to see in person.

At the moment, the young analyst was hunched over a curved bank of monitors. Kat kept to his side. Jason had wanted to consult with her before addressing the group. The two whispered conspiratorially, using arcane jargon and cryptic acronyms.

All that Gray understood was the last question posed by Kat: "Have you been in contact with Vatican City and Italian intelligence?"

"Yes, also the *Sluzhba Vneshney Razvedki*," Jason answered.

Gray recognized the name for Russia's Foreign Intelligence Service, their equivalent of the CIA. Considering the discussion in Painter's office, the mention of Russia's involvement in this new matter rankled his suspicions.

And what the hell does the Vatican have to do with all of this?

The director was also losing patience. "What's got you both stirred up?"

Jason looked to Kat, who nodded for the young man to take the lead. In fact, she left his side and headed to her office, likely to pursue the matter further while Jason briefed them.

"Sorry," Jason said. "I should've caught this earlier, but with all that's been going on . . ."

"Caught what?" Monk asked.

Jason opened a window folder that had been hovering on his screen. "This file hit our systems a few hours ago, but it got shuffled to a low priority. Sigma's data-gathering algorithm didn't recognize the sender as a priority contact."

"Where did it come from?" Painter pressed him. "Who sent it?"

"A man named Alex Borrelli, a monsignor with the Pontifical Commission of Sacred Archaeology."

Gray shared a glance with Seichan, beginning to understand the Vatican connection. In the past, Sigma had dealings with the Holy See in Rome.

Painter stepped closer to the monitor. "What did he dispatch to us?"

"Nothing that makes sense. It's just a series of photos of an old Greek text. I was able to translate the name off its leather cover. *Histories* by Herodotus."

Jason opened the list of attached jpegs. They showed various pages, often photographed askew. It looked like the pictures had been hastily taken on a set of dark stairs.

Most of the pics were of yellowed pages filled with Greek writing. Several passages were boxed off or underlined. There were annotations in the margins, even a drawing on the bottom of a half-page. But there were also several snapshots of what appeared to be the inside cover. It showed a gold book hovering over the sketch of a building and faded writing.

Painter studied the array of pics. "Was there any explanation about *why* this was sent to us? What it might mean?"

"No, nothing. It's a puzzle, maybe one the monsignor hoped we could solve."

"Why us?" Monk asked.

Seichan sighed. "Has anyone called the priest back?"

Jason nodded. "It was the first thing I did. But my inquiry revealed that Monsignor Borrelli had been killed. Along with an archivist from Moscow's Museum of Archaeology. According to Russian intelligence, the pair were accosted and murdered by muggers at the edge of Red Square. From the timeline, it appears the monsignor sent us this packet of photos during the attack."

"While it was happening?" Gray frowned. "If so, then whatever he sent must be important."

Kat returned to the group, her brow heavily furrowed. "I contacted an associate, someone I've known for years at Russia's Foreign Intelligence Service. With some wrangling and a promise of future cooperation, he forwarded me footage of the attack." She took Jason's place and tapped at the keyboard and swiped a mouse. "This is from a street camera at the edge of Red Square."

As she stepped aside, the monitor's screen filled with a black-and-white view of a street corner. The image was grainy, and the light was poor. Two figures in jumpsuits and helmets entered the frame and hurried along the edge of the square.

"The attack occurred near sunset," Kat said. "This is the only camera that caught the assault."

One of the men pointed an arm, then lurched forward, raising a palm to his chest, then collapsed to the pavement.

"Shot from behind," Gray noted.

"Igor Koskov," Kat reported. "The museum archivist."

On the screen, a clutch of hooded men in black commando gear swarmed the priest. The leader of the group accosted the man and ripped a book from his arms, likely the Greek text that had been photographed. Then the monsignor's throat was savagely cut. He fell to his hands and knees.

Gray noted him struggling, not to save himself, but to paw free a cell phone. "That must be when he dispatched the file."

"But why send it to us?" Monk asked. "How did he even have our system's encrypted number?"

Gray remembered Kat's question about contacting Vatican City. "Father Bailey must have given it to him."

"*Prefetto* Bailey," Kat corrected. "He was promoted to the prefect of the Vatican Apostolic Library a few months ago. I just reached out to his office and asked him to call us back."

Gray frowned.

Finnigan Bailey was an Irish Roman Catholic priest, one who had a dual PhD in ancient history and classical studies. He also served the

Church in a more clandestine manner, as an operative of the Vatican's *intelligenza*. Few were aware that the Vatican had its own intelligence agency, its own spy network. For decades—if not centuries—it had dispatched operatives to infiltrate hate groups, secret societies, hostile countries, wherever the concerns of the Vatican were threatened.

Gray's history with this organization went back twelve years, when he'd first met Monsignor Vigor Verona, a former member of the *intelligenza*, an honorable man who would go on to save Gray's life and whose niece had once captured his heart. Both were now gone, sacrificing themselves to save the world. Before his death, Monsignor Verona has been the prefect of the Vatican library.

"So, Bailey continues to follow in Vigor's footsteps," Gray commented. "Even into those dusty archives."

"He's been of great help to us in the past," Kat reminded Gray. "And he may be able to give us some insight into all of this."

Monk turned to her. "Does your contact in Russian intelligence know anything about the attackers?"

"Not yet. Moscow has dozens of organized crime groups running black markets and trafficking enterprises. At this point, it could be anyone."

"No," Seichan said, drawing everyone's attention. "Run the footage again."

Kat nodded and rewound the clip. Seichan elbowed closer and leaned her nose to the screen. Again, the murders unfolded in black-and-white.

"Stop it there," Seichan said, getting Kat to pause as the monsignor's throat was sliced with a sweep of the assailant's arm. "I recognize that move."

Seichan stepped back and pantomimed pivoting on her left toe and sweeping her right arm out. She twisted her wrist at the last moment to deal a deadly and unexpected blow.

Once done, she stared down the group. "I was taught that same maneuver. But another was far more skilled."

Gray's stomach gave a sickening lurch.

Seichan pointed to the screen. "That's Valya Mikhailov."

7:28 P.M.

Seichan resented the doubt in all their faces. "It's her."

"Why would Valya's group be involved in a mugging?" Monk asked, clearly ready to dismiss this possibility.

Only Kat seemed willing to consider it. "If Seichan's right, this would confirm my earlier supposition about Valya's location. No doubt, the attack upon us would have been costly to her organization. The planning, the preparation, the execution."

Monk scoffed. "So she's refilling her coffers by committing petty larceny, by stealing an old book? That doesn't sound like her."

"Unless the book was important," Gray argued, coming around to Seichan's side. "The monsignor went to great effort to send that file. Something significant must be tied to it. And Kat's right. Valya is a mercenary. I wager some group with deep pockets—someone who could afford her services—hired her to interrogate Monsignor Borrelli and secure the book."

Monk looked unconvinced. "But to commit this murder out in the open, on the street, in view of a camera. That also doesn't sound like her. She's far more calculating."

"Unless she was feeling overconfident," Kat said. "Emboldened by being on her home turf."

Seichan frowned. "Or it's a trap."

Everyone turned her way.

"Maybe she wants to lure us out there." Seichan nodded to Kat. "To her own home turf, as you stated."

"Where we'd be at a significant disadvantage." Monk finally looked swayed to Seichan's side. "But do we fall for this bait?"

Kat sighed. "There's much we don't—"

A chime interrupted her, coming from a neighboring console as an encrypted call hit their systems.

Kat turned to Painter. "It's a video conference request from Father Bailey."

Painter nodded. "We might all as well listen in."

Kat completed the connection and tapped to accept the call.

A moment later, the familiar countenance of Finn Bailey filled the monitor. The priest sat behind a desk. Dark shelves climbed behind him, full of dusty volumes, suggesting he was calling from the depths of the Vatican Archives. He looked grim, a departure from his usual amused manner. He swiped aside a fall of black hair, a match to his priestly frock, to show a serious cast to his bright green eyes.

"Looks like you've got the band back together," he said with a thick Irish brogue, eyeing the group gathered at Kat's shoulder. His attempt at joviality was belied by a sorrowful expression.

He took a deep breath and continued. "First of all, thank you, Captain Bryant, for sharing what Monsignor Borrelli dispatched to you. While the Holy See has been informed of the murders, no one knew the monsignor had sent off this message, that collection of photographs."

"We were hoping you might offer some clarity," Kat said.

"I'll do my best. Monsignor Borrelli was one of my professors. In fact, Alex was my academic adviser for my classical studies dissertation." Bailey cast his eyes down. "He was also a dear friend. His loss will be mourned by many."

Painter shifted forward. "Can you tell us what Monsignor Borrelli was doing in Moscow?"

"He was there at my request," Bailey explained with a pained expression. "The Russian Orthodox Church is seeking the return of hundreds of books from our archives, volumes with questionable provenance. Alex had been dispatched to diplomatically sort the matter."

Seichan looked to the other screen, which still showed the paused image of the priest's throat being slashed. "He died wearing coveralls and a work helmet," she said. "That doesn't look like someone returning from a diplomatic dinner."

Bailey nodded. "True. Alex had been invited to accompany a team of archaeologists to explore the tunnels beneath Moscow. A week ago, some students discovered a cache of ancient books held in old steel chests and hidden away in a vault."

"Were they valuable?" Gray asked. "Worth killing over?"

"That's what Alex had hoped to determine." Bailey's eyes winced. "But that's not what had most excited my friend about this chance discovery."

"What do you mean?" Kat pressed him.

"I had a conversation with Alex yesterday. He had hoped that those chests might be part of a long-lost archive, one of inestimable value, a collection known as the Golden Library."

Noting their confused expressions, Bailey filled in the history of a Byzantine collection of ancient volumes that had been lost during the reign of Ivan the Terrible. "Treasure hunters and academics have been searching for that library ever since," he finished.

"And what of the vault?" Gray asked. "Was Monsignor Borrelli able to confirm his hopes?"

"We don't know. Russian authorities tracked down one of the students who had discovered the site and went down to look. They found the place collapsed by a huge rockfall. They're just beginning to organize a recovery effort. But it's believed the rest of the exploratory team died down there."

"Then maybe it was a simple heist," Monk said. "Someone heard about what had been discovered and sought to secure it for themselves."

Seichan frowned, still staring at the dead man on the other screen. "The monsignor went through considerable pain and effort to dispatch those photos. It was a desperate last act. He must have believed they were important."

"I reviewed the photos," Bailey said. "Whether true or not, I suspect Alex believed they offered a clue to the Golden Library's location. He needed the information to get to someone who could help find the treasure before those thieves reached it first."

"But Monsignor Borrelli sent those photos to *us*," Kat said. "Not the Vatican. Why?"

"I can't say for certain. Before he left, I had given him your encrypted address. In case he ran into an emergency."

Seichan scowled at the frozen footage. "I would say being murdered classifies as an emergency."

Gray shook his head. "I'm not buying that explanation. In that moment of desperation, the monsignor acted reflexively. The fact that he sent this file to *us*, an unknown group, suggests he must have distrusted sending it to Vatican City."

"But why?" Monk asked.

"Maybe he feared that someone in the Vatican had tipped off his attackers. Or at least, in that dying moment, he didn't know who he could trust." Gray stared at Bailey. "Except for a former student who had given him a failsafe number."

"A student who sent him to his death," Bailey reminded them with a somber sigh.

Seichan straightened. "Then what do we do? If all of this is true, we can't let Valya get hold of that treasure."

Bailey stiffened at her words. "Valya? As in, Valya Mikhailov?"

Seichan shrugged, remembering it wasn't only Sigma who had crossed swords with the former assassin. Bailey—in his past dealing with Sigma—had also run afoul of the woman and her cohorts.

Painter lifted a hand. "We *suspect* she may be involved. Not only with the attack on Red Square but the bombing here."

Painter sketchily briefed Bailey about their earlier discussion.

"Then I may be of help," Bailey said. "I'm scheduled to head to Moscow to retrieve Alex's body. I'm sure I can arrange for a few extra hands to accompany me. The Holy See has already informed Russia that it intends to do its own investigation. And, as prefect, I have the authority to nominate individuals to be temporary *nuncios*, emergency Vatican ambassadors. Such cover should help insulate those individuals from overzealous inquiries by Russian authorities."

"In other words," Monk said, "you want us to be spies for the Vatican."

Bailey shrugged, a slight twinkle returning to his eye. "I'm willing to vouch for your skills."

Gray turned to Painter. "Such a cover could help us get into Russia without raising as many red flags."

"Let's hope that's true," the director noted.

After some further discussion, details were settled between the two groups, and the call ended.

Painter faced the others. "We'll need to move swiftly. Ambassadorship or not, we can't count on the protection of the Vatican lasting long. But luckily, I've already established some groundwork out there."

Gray frowned. "In Russia?"

"Like I warned earlier, I've not been entirely forthright about every aspect of this investigation. With Valya at the top of our suspect list and Kat's belief she was holed up in Russia, I put boots on the ground out there."

"You sent someone?" Gray looked offended that he'd not been included. "Who?"

Seichan stared around the group, noting one conspicuous absence. In fact, she hadn't heard anything from the man in days. He had gone quiet—which was *not* like the guy at all.

Monk realized the same. "Where's Kowalski?"

Painter simply folded his arms.

Gray looked even more perturbed. "You sent Kowalski?"

"As muscle and firepower."

Seichan had to concede those two points. It perfectly described the man's skill set.

"But there's another who went with him," Painter added. "Someone who has helped us in the past with a Russian matter. He still has a meaningful contact there, an oligarch who owes him his life. I thought it was time to call in that debt."

Gray frowned. "Who are you talking about? Who did you send?"

Painter grinned. "I guess I should clarify. I not only put *boots* on the ground—but also *paws*."

5

Tucker Wayne pursued his target through a maze of dark alleys. It was still hours before dawn, but the city remained in a perpetual twilight. At this northern latitude, the sun barely sank below the horizon during the warmer months. Though, *warm* was not a term he would use for this spring night.

His breath frosted with each exhalation. His cheeks and nose were numb from the cold. He wished he had dressed more appropriately, but he had wanted his clothing to be nondescript: worn jeans, a battered olive-green coat, a wool cap tugged low. He hoped to pass as a laborer, returning home from a nightshift. With his sandy blond hair, he certainly looked Russian enough.

Still, he kept his six-foot frame hunched as he headed down the alley. He caught glimpses of the Neva River between buildings. Its waters were shrouded in heavy mist.

An hour ago, he had followed his target over a bridge and onto Aptekarsky Island. The night's hunt had begun in the industrial Vyborgskaya District, a corner of which was run by Russia's *mafiya*.

He didn't know why the man had come to this island. Tucker had familiarized himself with the area after arriving in Saint Petersburg a week ago. Back in the eighteenth century, Aptekarsky Island—or Apothecary Island—had been transformed by Peter the Great into the site of the country's Medical Clerical Office and laboratories. It continued in that respect today, with many research institutions dotting the large island, but a majority of the land was now filled with apartment complexes that formed a labyrinth of pedestrian walkways, pine-lined avenues, and narrow alleys.

As Tucker headed deeper into the maze, he periodically checked a digital tablet that he kept close to his chest. Its display glowed with a street map. A tiny blip moved down a neighboring thoroughfare. The street ran alongside the Neva River and paralleled the alleyway.

Tucker kept pace with his target along this backstreet.

Where the hell are you going?

His target—Arkady Radić—was a thirty-two-year-old Serbian with ties to extremist groups across the Balkans. He served mostly as a courier. According to Sigma, the man had periodically worked for the Neo-Guild—what Sigma had unimaginatively come to call Valya Mikhailov's new organization. The Serb's location in Saint Petersburg, versus his usual haunt in the Balkans, had made him a person of interest.

Still, even with this intel, it had taken Tucker until two nights ago to track the man down. Tucker had been forced to work carefully. He couldn't risk being caught—not by Radić, and certainly not by Russian authorities. Last night, the Serb had drunk himself into a stupor at a bar and ended up snoring in the bed of a mistress or girlfriend.

But that's not where he's headed now.

This stoked Tucker's suspicions.

A few hours ago, Director Crowe had informed him about what had transpired yesterday in Moscow—and about the possible involvement of Mikhailov. Painter had wanted Tucker to immediately head south to the capital city, but he had refused.

He trusted his gut.

Radić must be in Saint Petersburg for a reason. If it had anything to do with Mikhailov, then whatever was transpiring in Moscow would likely get the man to stir, to possibly lead Tucker to other operatives of the Neo-Guild in the city.

And from there, hopefully to Valya herself.

Tucker touched his throat mike and radioed his partner. "Kowalski, you receiving the tracking information?"

A gruff voice filled his ears. "I'm circling ahead of his position now."

"Keep your distance. Don't want to spook him."

"It's not *me* you should be worrying about."

Tucker scowled. "Kane knows what he's doing."

Tucker studied the video feed flowing across the top half of his tablet. It showed a low-angle view of the misty river. His other partner ran through the parkland bordering the Neva's banks. White-barked birches, leafless and skeletal, flashed past. Manicured bushes were skirted, benches ducked under.

Kane needed little guidance from Tucker.

He definitely knows what he's doing.

The Belgian Malinois—a former military working dog—had been Tucker's partner throughout multiple deployments in Afghanistan. After leaving the service, he had taken Kane with him, but it seemed the duo's unique skills were still needed. Back in the Army Rangers, the pair had served as trackers: for search-and-rescue operations, for extractions, for hunting down targets of acquisition.

Like now.

He pictured Kane's seventy pounds of lean muscle, flowing swiftly, ears stiff, tail low. A K9 Storm vest—waterproofed and Kevlar reinforced—covered the dog's body, camouflaged to match his black-and-tan coat. Hidden in its collar were a thumbnail-size wireless transmitter and a night-vision camera, allowing the two to be in constant visual and audio contact with each other.

Not that any further communication was needed.

Earlier, in the shadow of the bridge behind him, Tucker had identified the target. He had pointed two forked fingers at Radić and gave a simple command: TRACK. Tucker then qualified this order by bringing those fingers to his lips: COVERTLY.

Afterward, Kane had burst away, vanishing into the misty darkness. Tucker trusted the dog to follow this instruction and improvise as needed. A microchip embedded between Kane's shoulders allowed Tucker to track his partner, and in turn, keep tabs on Radić's position.

As Tucker continued down the alley, the radio in his ear chirped with a query from Kowalski. "Where do you think that bastard's going?"

"Not a clue. Could be a wild goose chase. If this doesn't lead anywhere, we'll head to Moscow in the morning."

"To join Gray and the others?"

"To drop you off. I've done all I can."

"But—"

"I'm not part of Sigma," Tucker reminded him. "At least not formally. I only agreed to come here because of my local connections—and we've pretty much exhausted those to find Radić. If Sigma is moving in other players, I'm removing myself from the board."

"What about Valya Mikhailov?"

"Screw that. I don't know the woman. She's your problem." Tucker fingered the puckered scar on his cheek. "And I've got enough problems of my own. Kane, too."

A year ago, his four-legged partner had nearly lost one of those limbs. Kane still walked with a slight limp in the morning, though the tough dog warmed out of it most days.

Still, he pictured Kane's shining eyes when the dog had headed off in pursuit of Radić. This was what the shepherd had been trained for, took pride in. Tucker knew this. It was why he had agreed to come to Russia. After the long rehabilitation, Kane needed to be out in the field.

And as much as I hate to admit it, I need it, too.

It wasn't a matter of Tucker being an adrenaline junkie, of longing for the whiz of bullets past an ear or missing the cordite smell of a firefight. His last sojourn afield had left him broken and shaken. Like Kane, he had busted up a leg, wore a boot splint for months. He had reason enough to lay low, to find a quieter life—and he might have made that choice.

But back in South Africa, he remembered standing at the porch rail of the lodge where he had been recuperating. Below him, Kane had sat on his haunches at the edge of the grassy savannah, his ears pricked. The dog would occasionally glance back, his eyes shining brightly.

Tucker had understood.

Handlers had a phrase to describe their relationship with their dogs: *it runs down the lead*. Over time, the two learned to read the other, requiring no communication. Their bond ran up and down the leash that tied them together. And that was certainly true of him and Kane. The pair were bound tighter than any leash, each capable of reading the other, a connection that went beyond any spoken word or hand signal.

In that moment back in Africa, Tucker knew what Kane was telling him.

Let's go already.

The two were not meant to be rooted down. A wanderlust had been growing over their long recuperation. Tucker had always felt the most alive with open roads ahead of him, paths stretching toward unknown horizons.

Kane, too.

So, when Crowe had called and asked for his help, he had agreed. Plus, there was another reason why—

"Something's happening," Kowalski radioed with a note of urgency.

"Heard," Tucker responded.

He focused back on the glowing street map and the blip of his target. Radić had been approaching the edge of a sprawling park that bordered the river. The landmark was the fifty-acre Botanical Garden of Peter the Great, where medicinal herbs and plants had been grown and cultivated during the eighteenth century. It was the crown jewel of Apothecary Island and Russia's oldest botanical institution.

Radić left the main thoroughfare, abandoning the river behind him. He took a side street that edged the gardens.

Tucker slowed.

Where are you going now?

Across the top of Tucker's screen, he watched Kane close in on that same corner. The view swept from the riverside park and across the blacktop of the street. At this early hour, there was no traffic. Kane reached the corner and stopped. The view lowered as Kane assessed the situation.

On the screen, the dark figure of Radić sidled along an iron fencerow that enclosed the gardens. There were no streetlights, but Tucker toggled Kane's camera to night-vision mode.

The image on the screen scintillated into brighter shades of green, revealing more of the street, exposing a parked SUV—a Russian UAZ

Hunter. Two men climbed out. Radić hurried forward and met them. The trio huddled together.

"What are you all up to?" Tucker mumbled.

Only one way to find out.

He radioed a dual set of commands to Kane. "CLOSE IN. LAY LOW."

Tucker knew his partner would understand. The breed had been picked by the military due to their fierce loyalty and intelligence. Kane exemplified both, with a working vocabulary of a thousand words and an understanding of a hundred hand gestures. Even more impressive was Kane's ability to follow a chained link of commands. Only a few military working dogs could do this.

Pride warmed through Tucker.

Still, as Kane edged around the corner, Tucker held his breath.

Be careful, buddy.

With the commands branded into him, Kane rushes to a raised planter bed on the far side of the street from his prey. He stops and inhales the scents that wash through the narrow street.

He smells the sharp ammonia marker of other dogs that fills the air around the shelter. They are old . . . layered over the course of many days. Still, instinct stirs his desire to lift a leg, to claim this spot.

He drives that down and pushes the scent away. He draws in others, letting the smells build what his eyes can't see.

—the earthy notes of mold from a gutter.

—the acrid ripple of street tar.

—the burnt smoke of oil and engine.

—the musky ripeness of sweat and dank skin.

He concentrates on the last and dashes low, sticking to the shadows on this side. He reaches another planter and halts into a crouch.

His ears prick to the pattering timpani of cat paws on a steel balcony overhead. A strained hiss of threat follows, which he quickly dismisses. Instead, he turns the bells of his ears to the voices. They rumble in bass tones of urgency and furtiveness.

He can hear each utterance. But he knows from experience that this is not enough. The command still rings inside his chest.

CLOSE IN.

He leans out and spots the cluster by the truck. He waits until no eyes glint toward him—then sprints low. His ears continue to track for any sign of alarm. He reaches the next planter and keeps high. His muscles tense, claws hard against stone.

The truck now stands between him and the targets.

Voices carry, but not loud enough.

He ducks clear of the planter and stalks across the street to the truck. He drops behind a tire. It reeks of hot rubber and the singed hair smell of its brakes. He slips lower, satisfied with the intensity of others' rumblings.

This is confirmed in his ear. It is not a command, only acknowledgment of the truth.

"Good boy, Kane."

Tucker trotted through a crisscrossing of alleyways, maneuvering farther from the river. He made a final turn and increased his speed. He aimed for where the maze dumped into the narrow street bordering the botanical gardens. According to his map, he should exit thirty yards behind the truck.

He had already coordinated with Kowalski. The big man was rushing down the riverside thoroughfare to close off the other end of the street. Together, they would have the truck and the three men pinned down between them.

He continued to eavesdrop on the trio's conversation. They were speaking in Russian. A real-time translation program converted their talk to English, but with the three men arguing all at once, the program stuttered and lapsed.

Still, Tucker understood enough.

It seemed Radić had been hired for his usual services—to be a courier—but he was not being asked to be a drug mule or a money man. Instead, his *package* was trussed up in the back of the truck.

"*I don't move people,*" Radić emphatically argued. "*At least not without first being told. Preparations have to be—*"

"*You say no then,*" one man said. "*You refuse.*"

"*I didn't say that.*" A note of fear laced Radić's words.

Tucker reached the end of the alley and peeked around the corner. Thirty yards away, the bulk of the truck was just a larger shadow. One of the men from the vehicle puffed on a cigarette, a single red ember in the dark. The man paced near a gate into the gardens. A chain lay on the ground, likely cut through to gain access.

The two in the SUV must have ambushed and grabbed someone working at the gardens.

But why?

Tucker subvocalized to Kowalski. "What's your position?"

The answer came in gasps. "Two minutes out. Maybe three."

"*You take the truck,*" one of the men instructed Radić. "*Go now. You're expected at the rendezvous by noon.*"

Radić swore, but he didn't object. There was a jangle of keys, and a dark figure—Radić—circled the front of the truck, rounding toward the driver's door.

Tucker cringed, knowing Kane was hiding beside the rear tire. But his partner needed no warning to act. A small shadow ducked under the back of the truck and vanished beneath it.

Still, that protection would not last long.

Radić popped the driver's door, climbed inside, and slammed it shut. A moment later, the engine roared. The truck headed away from the curb, aiming in the river's direction.

Tucker had no time to strategize.

He yanked a Makarov PMM pistol from under the fall of his jacket. He radioed two commands, one to each of his partners.

"Kowalski, stop the truck heading your way." Tucker rolled out of hiding and ordered Kane. "TAKEDOWN BRAVO ONE."

The truck cleared the shepherd's position. It took the two men on the sidewalk a moment to react—to both the dog lunging out of hiding and to the figure racing down the street at them. Still, they moved swiftly, suggestive that they had combat training. Both reached for holstered weapons.

Tucker ran with his Makarov leveled, arms out, cradling the butt of his pistol in both hands. He centered on the cigarette's red ember and squeezed off two rounds. The first went wide; the second 9-mm hollow-point struck the man in the right eye. The Russian flew back and crumpled to the ground.

Kane made no sound as he struck the other. The only noise was a sharp scream and audible snap of bones. The shepherd's bulk took the target down. As they crashed together, Kane kept hold of an arm and rag-dolled the man with ferocious strength.

The Russian lost his pistol, but he yanked out a long knife from a sheath at his waist. He stabbed it into Kane's side—only to strike the camouflaged Kevlar vest.

Fuck that.

Tucker reached the pair, skidding to a stop. He leveled the Makarov at the man's head. He shouted an order, half-panicked. "RELEASE. TO ME."

Kane let go and spun away, evading another desperate swipe of the blade. The shepherd panted over to Tucker's side and paced away his adrenaline, tail whipping low.

Tucker closed on the man, intending to question him on the night's events. "Don't—"

The Russian sneered and stabbed his knife into his own throat, driving it deep.

Tucker lunged forward, but then stopped, recognizing the futility of any intervention. The man choked and frothed blood, then sprawled onto his back.

A loud boom forced Tucker into a crouch.

He twisted around and watched the departing truck swerve wildly. A front tire smoked and chattered off tread. The vehicle leaped the sidewalk and struck the garden's fence, crashing through a section of it.

Beyond the truck, a large figure ran toward the site.

It was Kowalski. He held a Desert Eagle at low ready. The weapon's .50-cal round must have taken out the front tire.

The truck's passenger door popped open, and Radić tumbled out. He staggered a few steps, looked in both directions, then dove through the broken fence and into the dark garden.

Goddamn it . . .

Tucker turned and ran to the gate with the broken chain. From the corner of his eye, he spotted Kowalski sliding over the SUV's hood on his hip, clearly intending to follow Radić through the broken fence.

Tucker radioed him. "There's a captive. In the truck. Check on them. Kane and I'll deal with Radić."

Tucker dashed into the botanical gardens. Kane kept pace alongside him. Tucker turned to his furry partner. Still gripping the Makarov, he touched two fingers to his own nose, then pointed in the direction that Radić had rabbited away.

"SCENT TRACK," he ordered.

Kane leaps off the sandy path and into the dark bower of tall trees. He rushes past bushes. He breathes deeply, drawing smells into the very back of his throat and sinuses. After an hour of tracking, the reek of his prey burns brightly behind his eyes. The breeze from the dank river carries that same scent.

He catches it and races along it.

He hears the crash of footfalls behind him as his partner gives chase, too.

Pride fuels him, as does a dark lust. The iron of blood is still on his tongue. His heart hammers with fiery rage. He has not had time to shed that fire. The hunt is still on. He races onward, drawn by the scent as he closes in on his prey.

As he does, a growing pain lances up his right forelimb. He ignores the old injury. It is familiar, known. He refuses to slow.

Especially as branches break ahead of him, drawing him onward.

He hears a panted breath, wheezing with panic.

The bitter salt of fear traces to him.

He aims toward it.

Then comes a faint tinkle of breaking glass—and all sounds muffle away.

Still, he remains confident. He has the trail locked in his nose—then in another three bounds, it all washes away in a single breath.

A sweet, cloying odor fills his senses, wiping out all else.

Kane is forced to slow, knowing he is defeated.

His partner reaches his side.
Kane whines his frustration and shame.
But a hand pats his side.

"It's okay, Kane."

Tucker had chased after his partner, following in the shepherd's wake through a spread of tall trees, flowerbeds, and manicured shrubbery. The path had led into a corner of the park that had been transformed into a Japanese garden, with ponds and arched bridges. A dense grove of cherry trees covered the grounds, all in early bloom. Pink and white petals drifted everywhere, carried on the night breeze. The sweet scent of those blossoms hung heavy in the air.

The smell must've overwhelmed and erased Radić's scent.

Tucker cursed the Serb's luck.

"Stay with me," Tucker said and took the lead through the Japanese garden.

After several meters, they finally cleared the cherry grove, but Kane's nose remained bunged by the heavy saccharine smell. From past experience, Tucker knew it would take the shepherd a few minutes to regain his finer senses.

Still, an obstacle rose ahead of them. It was a towering six-story glass arboretum, one of the garden's many elaborate greenhouses. It sprawled the length of a football field, enclosing an acre of grounds.

But which direction did Radić go? Right or left?

As Tucker slowed, Kane dashed forward.

Believing his partner had recaptured the trail, Tucker followed. The shepherd raced to the side of the main entrance and sniffed at a few shards of glass on the ground. Above, a low window had been shattered, its sill brushed clear of glass.

Bastard didn't go around—he went through.

Tucker crouched and peered inside the window. Humid air wafted out. The arboretum was filled with palms and orchids. It looked as impenetrable as the thickest jungle. Radić could be holed up anywhere inside, or maybe he was planning on breaking out the far side.

With no other choice, Tucker climbed through the broken window. Kane leaped after him, landing silently. Still, he noted the dog's right forelimb—the one nearly blown off—buckling before straightening again.

Kane was reaching his limit.

Tucker dropped to a knee. "Stay," he ordered firmly, then tempered with softer words. "Guard this exit. Can't have that bastard sneaking out behind me."

Kane rumbled, nearly inaudible, just a vibrato in his chest. The dog was not happy with this command.

Still, Tucker reinforced it, pointing at the broken window. "Guard."

Kane huffed, circled once, and stood stiffly.

Satisfied, Tucker set off into the depths of the arboretum.

This time I hunt alone.

6

Joe Kowalski crouched inside the rear compartment of the crashed SUV. He swept a penlight over the unconscious body draped across the back. It was a woman, late twenties or early thirties, with snowy blonde hair tied in a ponytail. A bruise was beginning to purple under one eye, but the blow wasn't what had knocked her out.

He checked her pulse and found it strong. A pass of his penlight over her eyes revealed glazed, dilated pupils.

Drugged . . .

He eyed that welt on her cheek.

"You put up a fight," he mumbled. "Good for you."

But who are you, lady?

The woman was wearing grayish-green coveralls. Even through the baggy clothing, she appeared fit. He shifted his light to a nametag clipped to a chest pocket.

"Dr. Elle Stutt," he read and squinted at the Russian Cyrillic below it.

ботаник-исследователь

Kowalski shrugged, not understanding, but he dismissed this mystery for now.

He slid out of the back of the truck. He had already hauled the two dead bodies into the bushes beyond the gate, but there was nothing to do about the pools of blood. He frowned at the spare tire mounted on the SUV's lift-gate.

Probably should change the blown tire.

Radić had abandoned the vehicle with the keys still in the ignition. If they were going to haul this woman with them, the vehicle would be useful.

Still, he took a moment to check his tablet. He had been monitoring Tucker's progress across the botanical garden. The glowing blip that tracked Kane's microchip had stopped.

Did they finally run the bastard down?

If so, it was all the more reason to get this SUV road-ready. With a sigh, he crossed and climbed into the driver's seat. He started the engine and reversed into the street. He then searched the SUV, found a set of tools, and set about freeing the spare tire. Bolts fell to the ground, then he tugged off the spare and dropped it to the pavement.

He took a breather to check the tablet again.

Kane's blip still hadn't moved.

Kowalski grimaced, suspecting something was wrong. "Two should've been headed back by now," he mumbled.

He looked at the broken section of fencing, then back to the woman sprawled inside. She should be out for hours. Or so he guessed. He was no medical doctor.

"Screw this."

He yanked his Desert Eagle from its holster. He hated being sidelined. If the mission was going south, he couldn't risk simply babysitting this unconscious woman.

Besides, I've been playing babysitter long enough.

He scowled at his small partner, who stood silently nearby.

"C'mon," he grumbled. "Let's get going."

4:33 A.M.

Tucker headed slowly through the heart of the arboretum. He had donned a pair of night-vision goggles from his pack, but the sun had risen a few minutes ago. The glare through the glass walls had grown excruciating. It threatened to blind his normal sight.

To save his vision, he toggled the lenses into infrared mode, which would allow him to detect heat signatures. But the view remained murky, wavering with the steamy warmth of this tropical greenhouse. All around him, palm leaves slowly dripped from the humidity. His face ran with rivulets of sweat.

With a grimace, Tucker finally pushed the goggles to his forehead, recognizing their uselessness. He continued forward, his ears straining for any telltale sign of Radić. He feared the bastard had already crossed the arboretum and smashed out a window on the far side. If so, then the target was likely lost to them.

Tucker pushed aside the frond of a huge fern. The view opened ahead of him, revealing a vast pond filling the center of the greenhouse. Huge lily pads, some a full meter across, covered the dark surface. Several stands of smaller pads were in bloom, lifting stalks of white and yellow flowers. The air was redolent with their musky, sweet scent.

Tucker paused and searched the pond's far side.

He spotted the reflection of windows in the breaks between the palms and bushes, marking the other flank of the arboretum. Tucker edged around the water, sticking to the cover of the foliage. On the far bank, a section of bushes suddenly shook. Tucker froze—but then jets from a sprinkler burst forth and doused the area, pebbling the pond with droplets.

He cursed under his breath and continued onward.

He reached the opposite bank and dropped lower. He crept through the last of the tropical garden. Once near enough, he stayed within a thicket of ferns and searched the spread of windows.

For as far as he could see, nothing appeared to be broken.

Tucker glanced behind him.

Is Radić still holed up in here somewhere?

The answer came with a crack of a pistol. A round clipped his shoulder just as he had turned. More shots shredded through the leaves, but Tucker had dropped flat. He rolled behind a palm trunk. He winced against the blaze in his shoulder and tried to figure out where Radić was hiding. Tucker fired into the foliage, warning Radić that he was also armed.

Then bushes exploded to his left.

Tucker ducked aside as a dark shape raced past his position.

Kane.

The dog must have heard the gunshots. His partner would never have broken the last command to GUARD—not unless absolutely necessary.

Caught by surprise, Radić panicked. His first round blasted near Kane's flank. The dog pivoted away, but his weakening front leg betrayed him. Kane slipped on the wet ground cover and toppled sideways into a tumble.

Tucker leaned out with his Makarov, ready to defend his partner, regardless of how exposed it left him.

He was too slow.

A gunshot blasted from Radić's position.

No . . .

Tucker cringed, but Kane remained uninjured. Glass shattered behind Radić's position.

Is the bastard using this moment to escape?

Tucker stood higher. Outside, a towering shadow loomed beyond the glass wall and cradled a raised pistol.

Kowalski.

The large man hollered a single command from out there: "TAKE-DOWN!"

Radić burst out of hiding and ran toward Kane—not to threaten the dog, but to escape another. A dark shape raced after him, low to the ground, having just leaped through the window that Kowalski had blasted open.

Radić reached the edge of the pond when he was struck from behind. The shepherd's bulk slammed into him and toppled the man headlong into the shallow water. The dog kept hold of an upper arm. As they surfaced, the beast thrashed Radić back and forth, like a shark with a seal.

The Serb screamed in terror.

Tucker hurried over, aimed his pistol, and shouted to the dog. "RELEASE."

The large shepherd stopped his rag-dolling—but he kept hold of Radić's arm. Fangs dug deeper; a growl flowed in a continuous threat.

"RELEASE," Tucker repeated.

The dog finally let go, gave a shake of his wet fur, and bounded out of the pond.

Kowalski joined them, picking a piece of broken glass from his jacket. He aimed his pistol at Radić, but the bastard would not be offering any further resistance.

The Serb knelt in the shallow water, holding his torn arm to his chest. Blood flowed thickly, showing white bone and shredded muscle.

With the man guarded, Tucker turned to the bloody-muzzled dog. The young shepherd—another Belgian Malinois—panted and paced, fighting the battle-rage inside him.

Tucker dropped to a knee and held out a hand. The young dog trembled all over. "I've got you," he whispered. "You did good, Marco."

His calm voice soothed the dog's shaking and smoothed the raised hackles.

The shepherd came over, looking for further reassurance.

Kane joined them, limping slightly.

Tucker cradled the young shepherd's muzzle and drew it close. He touched noses with the dog to let him know all was fine. "Good boy, Marco."

A tail wagged tentatively.

Kane came forward and butted a hip against his young brother.

Marco's tail swept wider.

Still guarding Radić, Kowalski explained, "I radioed Kane after I circled behind the greenhouse. Got here just as gunfire broke out. Told him to close quarters with the target, to keep him distracted until I could sic Marco on him."

Tucker eyed Kane.

So that's why you broke command.

Tucker reached over and scratched Kane behind an ear. He nodded to Marco. "He's not Abel—but we'll get him there."

During his tours in Afghanistan, Tucker had worked with *two* dogs, littermates, Kane and Abel. Abel had been killed, slaughtered during a fierce firefight, a loss that still debilitated Tucker at times.

Then eight months ago, while Tucker had been recuperating alongside Kane, an old friend—a former army veterinarian—had dropped off a pup, a Belgian Malinois who had flunked out of the military war dog training at Lackland AFB. The pup had been judged to be too feral, too irredeemable.

Tucker had intended to prove otherwise.

No dog is irredeemable.

He patted his newest brother and reassured him again. "Well done, Marco."

"We should get going." Kowalski waved his pistol for Radić to move. "Get this guy to talk. But first, I still have to finish changing a tire. And there's the matter of a drugged woman in the back of the SUV."

Tucker had forgotten about the captive and stood up. "I know who can help us—maybe with both mysteries."

11:45 A.M.

Seven hours later, Tucker paced before a panoramic window of a sprawling penthouse. The view overlooked a curve of the Neva River and the spread of the Hermitage Museum.

He barely noted the breathtaking sight. He had showered and had his bullet-grazed arm bandaged. The doctor who had been summoned to the penthouse had also given Tucker an injection that left his head fuzzy but had dulled the fire in his shoulder.

To the side, Kane and Marco were sprawled on the curve of a window seat. The younger dog rested his muzzle on his paws, snoring softly, adrenaline-weary. Kane matched that pose, except his eyes were only half-closed, feigning inattention. Tucker knew better. Kane missed nothing: *posture, hand-and-eye movements, respiration rate, perspiration.* The older dog had picked up on the anxiety in the air and continued to keep watch.

A gravelly voice rose behind Tucker. "How much more assistance must I provide before we consider our debt settled, *moy drug*?" Bogdan Fedoseev asked.

Tucker sighed and faced the Russian oligarch. The man, in his mid-sixties, sat on a velvet sofa, one leg up on it. He wore a thick robe, which barely constrained a prominent belly, but no one would mistake him as soft. He puffed on a Cuban cigar, casting redolent swirls of smoke around the room.

This was his penthouse. It occupied the top four floors of a high rise, one situated at the heart of the city's Golden Triangle, the richest section of Saint Petersburg.

"I guess it matters how much value you put on your life," Tucker answered.

Five years ago, Tucker had been hired by Bogdan, as both bodyguard and security adviser. There had been an assassination attempt on the man's life by Vladikavkaz Separatists, political terrorists whose main victims were the prominent Russian capitalists. And Bogdan certainly fit that description. The industrialist controlled hundreds of holdings across Russia: oil fields, mining operations, a shipping conglomerate. Tucker had saved the man during a coordinated attack during a worker's strike. Tucker had been paid well afterward, but he knew Bogdan still appreciated what he had done, even sending him Christmas cards and Russian dog treats each year.

"Speaking of my life," Bogdan said. "I still value it very much. Enough that I do not wish to find myself accidentally falling out a window. To help you Americans, I risk much, *da*?"

Tucker frowned at him, knowing the man was all but untouchable.

This drew a grin from the stern man. "Okay, I only risk *some*," he admitted. "Still, you come a week ago. You want information about *mafiya* and other gangs. I help you, *da*? And now you land to my doorstep this morning, hauling in two others. And don't even bring coffee."

Tucker looked across the penthouse. The space was too gilded for his tastes, decorated with Old World oil paintings on the walls. On the far side, a large gold fireplace danced with flames. Next to it, a closed door marked Bodgan's bedroom.

Inside, a physician still attended to the rescued woman. From her name tag, they had deduced she was a research botanist. The doctor and a nurse had established an IV and run a bag of electrolytes to help clear the sedatives out of her system. Shortly after, she had woken from her drugged stupor, aided by smelling salts. Initially, she had been frantic and panicked. It had taken some convincing to assure her that she was safe.

Unfortunately, Tucker still had no clue as to *why* Radić and the others had snatched the botanist. Any explanation awaited the not-so-tender mercies of Yuri Severin—Bogdan's head of security. He was in the kitchen with Kowalski. The two were continuing to question Radić, trying to discern how much he knew.

The bastard had been uncooperative at first, stubborn and close-lipped, but Kane had loosened his tongue. A hand signal from Tucker had sent the shepherd into a savage snarl, bearing fangs and snapping at the man's nose. After being mauled by Marco, Radić needed no further convincing.

Afterward, Tucker had withdrawn to the great room with Kane to give the others space.

Bogdan sat straighter, stubbing out his cigar. "You Americans cause me much hardship of late. That I must consider, too, when it comes to weighing our old debt."

Tucker turned to him.

Bogdan counted off on his fingers. "Sanctions, then more sanctions. Then the sabotage of gas pipelines."

"That wasn't us," Tucker said.

The industrialist wagged a finger. "Maybe, maybe not."

Tucker rolled his eyes, unwilling to argue—not because he feared offending his Russian benefactor, but because he cared nothing about geopolitics. Not any longer, not after all he had seen. He knew only one certainty.

I trust a dog better than any person.

Voices drew their attention across the penthouse. Kowalski and Yuri exited the kitchen and crossed the room. The two massive men wore matching expressions of disgust. In fact, they looked like roided-out brothers. The pair bore pale scars across the dark stubble of their cheeks and over their shaved scalps. Both were also former navy men, which showed in their salt-roughened complexions.

"What did you learn?" Tucker asked Kowalski as the pair joined them.

"Not all that much."

Yuri rubbed a set of bruised knuckles. "But I made sure he wasn't holding back."

"What *did* he say then?"

Kowalski grunted his frustration. "Bastard doesn't know *who* hired him. Or even *why*. All he was given was an address to deliver the woman to."

"In Moscow," Yuri added.

Tucker shared a look with Kowalski.

Where Valya had last been spotted.

Kowalski shrugged, indicating that the two circumstances might not be related.

Still, Tucker continued to trust his gut.

She's involved with this, but how and why?

There was only one place to find answers.

"We need to get to Moscow," Tucker said. "Check out that address."

"I can arrange transport." Bogdan pointed across the room. "What about our guest in the kitchen?"

"For now, keep him under wraps," Tucker said. "We don't want to alert whoever hired him."

"Then better to simply dump him in the Neva," Yuri offered.

Tucker shook his head. He had no sympathy for the bastard—especially after he had shot at Kane—but Radić could prove useful later.

And another might, too.

The bedroom door burst open. The kidnapped woman strode out, her eyes flashing angrily, her cheeks flushed. The botanist still wore the same coveralls. The back of her hand bled, from where she must have ripped out her IV. She spoke rapidly in Russian, clearly having had enough and wanting to be set free.

The doctor and nurse followed, urging her back with soft words, but she shook them off. She cast a suspicious glare around the room.

For better or worse, Tucker stepped into her path and held up a palm. "Dr. Stutt, *mne zhal'*," he apologized.

She gave him a furious look.

He hoped she spoke English. "We're trying to make sense of all this, too. We were tailing the man who met your assailants."

She lifted a finger to a purpled welt under an eye.

"He was hired to take you to Moscow."

"Moscow?" She frowned, then took a deep breath. "Why?"

"I don't know. We believe there is far more at stake here. If you return home, I fear you'll remain a target."

The muscles of her jaw tightened as she considered his words. "Then what am I to do?"

"You can stay here," Bogdan offered. "You will be safe."

She glanced around and looked little consoled.

Tucker suggested another path. "There must be a reason you were grabbed. Whatever it is could be important. We have a team arriving in Moscow this afternoon. If you're willing, they might help us determine your role in all of this."

She frowned, clearly no happier with this plan. Then again, why should she trust any of them? They were all strangers to her.

Tucker stared at her. "If you come with us, I promise we will do our best to keep you safe, to get you back to your life as soon as possible."

Her eyes narrowed. "Who is *we*?"

Tucker waved an arm to Kowalski, who gave a slight bow of his head.

Bogdan motioned to his head of security. "Yuri, too. You may need his expertise."

Tucker accepted the wisdom of this.

Dr. Stutt remained tense, clearly still unsure.

Finally, the last two members of the team joined Tucker. Kane slid up on his right side, Marco on his left. Tucker absently brushed their napes with his fingertips. It was a reflexive gesture of affection and brotherhood.

The woman stared from the dogs to him. "They're coming, too?"

Tucker grinned. "Always."

She considered the matter for two more breaths, then nodded. "I will meet with these others. But if they have no answers, that will be the end of it."

Tucker nodded his agreement. "Thank you, Dr. Stutt."

"Call me Elle?" She then qualified this offer. "For now."

The botanist turned to the physician and spoke rapidly in Russian.

Bogdan used this moment to draw Tucker aside. "Now that's settled. We must reconcile the other matter. With me lending Yuri to you—"

"It will further unbalance the scales between us," Tucker said.

"*Da*, but there is an easy way to right that imbalance." Bogdan glanced down. "Last time you were here, you came with only one dog. Now you have *two*. Maybe leave one. It will make us even."

Kowalski overheard this. "Buddy, you'd have more luck asking for one of his balls."

Bogdan scoffed, "I have no need for any more of those."

Tucker scowled at the two men. "My balls and my dogs are staying where they are."

"Then know I'm willing to pay . . . very well."

Tucker suspected Bogdan was seldom refused his desires, but he'd have to live with disappointment this time. "No deal."

Bogdan's face darkened, and his lips thinned, but he simply waved Tucker off. "We will talk again."

Tucker shoved past, hoping that he had not soured their relationship, or worse, made an enemy. He leaned down and brushed the flanks of his two dogs. No matter the cost . . .

I'll never part with my brothers.

Tucker joined the botanist as she finished conversing with the doctor. "We should get moving."

She nodded, but her hands wrung nervously as she followed.

Tucker flashed a signal to Kane. The shepherd rounded to her side, his tail wagging, ears tall. He pranced a bit on his paws.

His antics drew a small smile from the woman. She freed a hand and reached to rub his neck. As she did, the tenseness in her shoulders relaxed.

Watching her, Tucker noted the nametag on the woman's coveralls. It reminded him of a question that had been nagging him, one he had failed to ask.

"Dr. Stutt—Elle—you're a research botanist at the city's gardens. But what were you studying there?"

She brightened as she faced him, clearly happy to talk about her work. "It's a special interest of mine."

"Which is what?"

She grinned. "Carnivorous plants."

SECOND

Hunting Party

7

Gray rattled his motorcycle through an abandoned construction site that bordered the Moskva River. Other dirt bikes and ATVs sped across piles of sand and rock, using the area as a makeshift motocross track.

He did his best to blend in, riding a Russian-made IMZ Ural. The heavy-duty cycle had been designed for rugged terrain. He had also picked it for another reason. The Urals typically came outfitted with sidecars.

"Ahead of us," Seichan warned from the neighboring seat. "On the left."

Gray had spotted it, too, and sped faster. He turned away from the river, sending up a roostertail of dirt behind him. Seichan hunched under the sidecar's windscreen.

A wooded slope bordered the far edge of the construction site. Above its tree line rose the crumbling red-brick remains of an old fortress wall. A massive round turret—topped by a tall spire—loomed above everything. It was one of the surviving towers of a sixteenth-century monastic fortress. The Simonov Monastery had fallen into disrepair centuries ago. All that was left were sections of deteriorating walls, a trio of towers, and a handful of outbuildings. Attempts at reconstruction and repairs had been sporadic. The site had eventually been given over to the Russian Orthodox Church, where they had refurbished a small corner of the sprawling grounds, turning one building into a shrine dedicated to Theotokos of Tikhvin.

That church was their destination.

It matched the address that Tucker had obtained from one of the attempted kidnappers—which made no sense. *Why a church?* But the spot still had to be checked out, and the timetable was tight, if they were not already too late.

Two hours ago, Gray's team had landed in Moscow. While in the air, Gray had arranged for him and Seichan to canvass this area. According to what Tucker had overheard, the botanist had been scheduled to be delivered here at noon today.

That was four hours ago.

So even if the address was accurate, whoever had ordered the kidnapping was likely long gone.

Still . . .

Gray guided his motorcycle along the edge of the wooded slope, then nosed into a break in the forest. He cut the engine, which clicked and tapped as it cooled. He removed his helmet and turned to Seichan.

"Ready?"

She climbed free of the sidecar and tossed her helmet onto her seat. "Let's get this over with."

He dismounted, shouldered a small pack, and checked the SIG Sauer secured in a holster under his jacket. The two set off up the slope.

Gray hoped he had something to report to the others.

Back at the airport, Monk and Jason Carter had headed off with Father Bailey to meet with a representative of the Russian church: Bishop Nikil Yelagin. He was the man who had dispatched the doomed researchers into the labyrinth under Moscow. Their goal was threefold: to retrieve the body of Monsignor Borrelli, to establish their bona fides as part of the Vatican's investigative team, and to circumspectly question Bishop Yelagin.

The other part of their contingent, Tucker and Kowalski, would be arriving in Moscow in another hour. They were traveling from Saint Petersburg aboard a high-speed train, secured in a private car, courtesy of Tucker's Russian benefactor. It was quicker than flying and less problematic, especially with a pair of large shepherds in tow. The group was escorting Dr. Elle Stutt here for safekeeping, accompanied by the security chief of the Russian oligarch.

Gray stared up the slope toward the crumbling fortress wall.

What does a botanist have to do with any of this?

Her kidnapping could be unrelated—except for one intriguing detail. Gray had been pondering it ever since Tucker had reported in. It was one of the reasons Gray had headed directly here.

"There's scaffolding to the right," Seichan reported.

He looked to where she pointed and nodded. The watchtower—the Bashnya Dulo—was in the midst of a restoration. According to legend, it had gained its name after an invading Dulo khan was slain by an arrow fired from an upper tower window.

Now, the structure was circled by planks, ladders, and metal scaffolds.

As they drew closer, the need for repairs grew obvious. The steeple had already been restored, but the red-brick façade had huge cracks running from foundation to roofline. In an attempt to protect it, steel rings had been secured around its circumference, corseting it all together.

Gray climbed the last of the distance, but he paused at the edge of the woods. The tower and its steeple rose fifteen stories. He removed a small pair of binocs from his pack and scanned those heights. By now, all the construction workers should have left for the day. Still, he wanted to be certain there was no watchman left behind.

Then again, what's there to guard?

He kept a vigil for five minutes, until an exasperated sigh rose from his side. Seichan passed him and headed toward the nearest ladder. She mounted it and quickly scaled upward. Gray hurried to keep up with her. Upon reaching the third landing—which rose to the height of the flanking walls—they clambered across its planks to the tower's far side.

A panoramic view opened up.

Behind them, the curving expanse of the Moskva River swept off into the distance, its waters turned a rosy silver by the glare of the low sun. Ahead, the breadth of the monastic fortress revealed itself.

The southern wall stretched ahead of their position, interrupted by two more watchtowers. A small park lay outside it to the right, but the grounds inside the walls lay steeped in shadows.

Directly ahead and nearly as tall as the tower stood a five-story out-building. Its red-brick exterior was lined by rows of windows—mostly toothed by broken glass. From his study of the layout, he knew the dilapidated structure was the monastery's old "malter," or dyehouse, one of the oldest industrial buildings in Moscow.

For Gray and Seichan, it would serve as the perfect observation post.

Fifty yards beyond the dyehouse, the Theotokos of Tikhvin Church rose in all its majesty, one of the prime examples of Moscow Naryshkin Baroque. Its series of red-brick wings and stories were decorated with white limestone pillars and fanciful pediments, all roofed in blue-gray slate.

Gray studied the structure.

Why bring a botanist here?

The two set off down the tower's scaffolding and into the thick shadows of the grounds. They hurried toward the rear of the dyehouse, keeping the building between them and the church. They reached a broken-out window in the lowest level and ducked inside, cautious of the sharp shards that rimmed the opening.

"Now what?" Seichan asked, her voice frustrated.

He understood why. The interior of the old malting house had fallen into ruin, far worse than the exterior had suggested. Inside, the floors had collapsed across several levels, creating a labyrinth of broken beams, ribbed joists, and gaping holes. The nearby staircase was a pile of stone rubble, though someone had left a rickety ladder that looked as if it could have been original to the building.

Gray nodded toward it. "We'll get as high as we can."

They continued upward through the building, chasing a scurry of rats ahead of them. A few pigeons took flight with a flutter of wings and a pebbling of droppings. The place stank of urine and rotting wood.

"You sure know how to spoil a lady," Seichan whispered as they finally reached the fourth floor.

"I pick only the best places for you, sweetheart." Gray wiped a drape of sticky webbing from his face, then pointed ahead. "That window should offer a good enough vantage."

He feared going any higher. While this level was mostly intact, the floor had buckled with age. Still, they reached the window safely. Its jamb was empty of glass, but rusty bars had been sealed over the opening.

Gray took a deep breath of fresh air.

Seichan simply scowled.

From this high vantage, the view allowed them to spy on three sides of the church, which was circled by a narrow road and a small parking lot. Any closer approach would leave them exposed and in the open. The plan was to assess the area for anything suspicious and proceed accordingly.

"We're clearly too late," Seichan said. "Assuming this is even the right place."

Gray sighed, unable to argue. The tiny parking lot was empty. The only person in sight was a lone elderly man who swept the front steps with a broom. While some exterior lamps glowed in the shadows, the church's windows remained dark.

Gray passed a pair of binoculars to Seichan. "We'll keep watch for a half hour. If there's no sign of any activity, we can move in, circle the church once to be sure—then head back to meet Tucker's group."

Gray prepped some gear from his pack, including a digital monocular spyglass, one that was capable of taking pictures. He then set up a tactical parabolic microphone for eavesdropping. It had a range of six hundred yards, more than enough to cross the distance to the church.

But will I need any of this equipment?

Minutes ticked past with no sign of anything suspicious.

Even the rats got bored and traipsed past the interlopers with brazen disregard.

And apparently it wasn't just the vermin who needed some distraction.

"Our wedding," Seichan said abruptly, her voice neutral.

Still, Gray heard the slight catch in those two words. "What about it?"

"Maybe we should postpone."

He lowered his spyglass. "Why? July twenty-fourth is perfect. It's when we first met."

She gave him a sidelong look. "If you recall, we shot each other back then."

He shrugged. "It's our meet-cute."

She cast him a withering glare. "With everything in flux, with Sigma on the edge of termination, maybe we should wait until matters settle. Who knows where we'll be when—"

The growl of an engine cut her off.

They both turned to the window, lifting their respective scopes.

A black limousine wended through the monastery gates. Rather than heading to the church's portico, the vehicle circled to the back of the building.

"Maybe someone is preparing for an evening wedding," Gray mumbled. "Someone who hasn't gotten cold feet."

The driver climbed out and opened the door for a figure dressed in an ankle-length black cassock, sashed in gold. Even in the shadows, a large orthodox cross glinted under the man's prominent, oiled beard.

"If it's a wedding," Seichan whispered, "there's the priest."

Using his spyglass, Gray snapped a few pictures of the man.

From the other side of the limo, another figure exited, unfolding his large frame. He had to stand seven feet tall. He was dressed in a dark robe. As he straightened, he adjusted a cylindrical flat-topped hat, a clerical chapeau called a *kamilavka*, typically worn by an orthodox monk. Gray only knew such details because he had studied up on the owners of this place—the Russian Orthodox Church.

The tall fellow crossed around to the other, his shoulders and head dropping in clear deference to the priest. The monk's arms and hands fluttered for a moment. It appeared to be sign language.

Gray continued taking pictures.

"Too bad Kowalski's not here," Seichan whispered.

Gray understood what she meant. Kowalski—who had a deaf younger sister—was fluent in American Sign Language, but the Russian version was distinctly different due to cultural and linguistic variances, though likely a few phrases were shared.

The priest clearly understood the monk and waved to the church's rear. The large man headed up the steps to an arched doorway, which was flanked by ornate iron wall sconces. The priest remained below.

Gray wondered if the monk had any ties to this church. From his research, he knew the building had been turned into a museum in the twenties, then a cinema in the thirties, before becoming a school for the deaf and hard of hearing in the nineties. Even the services held in the current church were accompanied by sign-language interpreters.

Still, there was only one way to know more about these new arrivals.

Gray raised the microphone's parabolic dish to the window. The device was wirelessly patched to the earpieces that both he and Seichan wore and had been equipped with real-time translation.

The monk tapped an iron knocker on the old door. The amplified sound was loud enough in Gray's ear to make him cringe. The monk stepped back, folding his arms. He glanced back to the priest as he waited for a response.

Finally, the door swung open.

A tall, slim woman stepped out onto the landing. She was dressed in clothing that matched the monk, only her flat-topped *kamilavka* had a veil at the back, demurely covering her hair, marking her as an orthodox nun.

But this was no nun.

Seichan tensed next to Gray.

"Valya," she hissed.

Though the Russian's features were heavily powdered, covering her facial tattoo, the stark white of her hair could be seen in wisps from under her *kamilavka*'s veil. But it was her manner more than anything that gave her away. She stepped dismissively past the tall monk to confront the priest, who remained at the foot of the steps, as if he had no desire to move any closer.

"Archpriest Sychkin," she said with a note of bitter disdain. "You should've been here hours ago."

"I had other tasks that required my attention." The priest's voice was deep and forceful, perfect for preaching from a pulpit, but the translation came out a robotic monotone. "Why was your summons so urgent, requiring my personal presence?"

"The man I hired in Saint Petersburg never showed. Acquisition of the botanist was confirmed last night, but then nothing. Repeated attempts to reach the others also failed."

"And Dr. Stutt?"

Valya shrugged. "She has not been seen all day—not at her research lab, not at her apartment."

"What does that mean?"

"We've been exposed."

The archpriest stiffened. "By who?"

"Another party must've intervened."

"How could that be?" Sychkin reached to the cross on his chest. "Only a handful of people know what we found in that old book."

"Regardless, I took precautions after failing to hear from the others this morning. In fact, the intrusion by these others was not wholly unexpected, especially as I all but invited them here."

"What are you talking about?"

Gray knew the answer. He pictured the black-and-white footage of the attack on Red Square. Seichan cursed next to him. She had warned that the brazen attack could be Valya's attempt to lure Sigma into Russia, to get them involved.

But it wasn't just that.

"I knew Radić would be easy to break," Valya said calmly. "It's why I picked him as a courier. Especially as I knew he was compromised and likely to be watched."

Gray dropped his spyglass and grabbed Seichan's arm, but she was already moving, retreating from the window. Even without the scope, Gray noted Valya turn and face the old dyehouse. Her words, now in English, reached his earpiece from the parabolic microphone.

"But they will be dealt with."

Gray took another two steps when a series of explosive detonations tore through the building. The floor jolted under him, throwing him headlong. Flames brightened the darkness. Billows of smoke tried to smother it.

More blasts erupted, timed and positioned to gut the inside, to collapse the crumbling infrastructure into the basement.

Gray reached for Seichan—only to watch her fall away from him, tumbling down into the jagged ruins.

8

Jason Carter recoiled from entering the morgue. He had seen dead bodies before, but the stench of wet flesh, bleach, and embalming fluid made him balk.

He and Monk, along with Father Bailey, had driven straight from the airport to a beige brick building that had a mouthful of a name: *Federal'nogo Mediko-Biologicheskogo Agentstva Rossii Byuro Glavnoy Sudebno-Meditsinskoy Ekspertizy*. It was Moscow's Office of the Chief Medical Examiner. The morgue was in the building's basement, where the ventilation system dated back to the Soviet era.

Monk and Bailey led the way, flanking the chief medical examiner, a skeletally framed man named Dr. Lev Grishin. The examiner's face was etched with a perpetual scowl, as if disappointed in the world and his place in it. As such, he showed little patience or interest in these ambassadorial investigators from the Vatican.

"The causes of death are obvious," Grishin said, in fluent English. "For both men."

Jason reluctantly followed the group into the morgue. It was lined with five stainless-steel tables, two of which were occupied by draped bodies: Monsignor Alex Borrelli and the Russian archivist, Dr. Igor Koskov.

Grishin turned to Bailey. "Father, your team is welcome to examine your colleague's body, but you'll need permission from the family to do the same with the other."

Monk stepped forward. "That won't be necessary. Confirmation of the cause of death is a mere formality in this investigation."

Grishin's stiff demeanor softened. He was likely worried that his judgment would be contested.

According to Monk's forged credentials, he was a pathologist, which was not far from his true field of study. The man had been a medic with the Green Berets, but he had undertaken a doctoral program in forensic medicine after being recruited by Sigma. He eventually expanded his studies into biomedical engineering—though the latter was more of a personal interest. Monk had lost his left hand during a Sigma op and now wore a DARPA-designed prosthetic that was nearly indistinguishable from the real thing.

Bailey lifted an arm toward the doorway. "Dr. Grishin, if we could indulge your patience to allow us some privacy to perform our exam and to pay respects to the deceased."

"Of course." He appeared more than happy to oblige. He pointed to an intercom on the wall as he headed out. "You can call me when you're finished. In the meantime, I'll ready the paperwork to have the monsignor's body prepared for transport back to Italy."

Jason watched him hurriedly exit the room.

Clearly, he wants us out of here as soon as possible.

Once the examiner was gone, Bailey turned to Monk and Jason. "I asked Bishop Yelagin to join us here." He checked a wristwatch. "He should be arriving momentarily."

"At the morgue?" Jason asked. "I thought we were meeting the bishop at your embassy, to help solidify our ambassadorial role with the Holy See."

Jason was uncomfortable with this sudden change in plans. After working for five years under Kat Bryant, he had grown inflexible, preferring every detail of an operation to be prescribed and followed.

He had not always been that way. When he was nineteen, he had been trained as a systems analyst for the navy, but he had chafed at the military's endless rules and regulations. Especially considering the incompetence of those dictating those orders. His defiant attitude eventually got him discharged—that and the fact that, upon a dare, he had hacked into DoD servers with nothing more than a Black-Berry and a jury-rigged iPad.

Afterward, he had been offered a deal: join Sigma or serve time.

It was an easy choice, but one he had rankled against for months. It was Kat who eventually instilled in him a regimented work ethic—mostly because he had learned to respect her ethos and intelligence. Still, he couldn't fully shake his rebellious streak. He blamed his parents. Throughout his youth, Jason had been raised at the adrenaline edge of life. His mother was a paleoanthropologist, who often took Jason out into the field. His father—an Australian caver and diver—was known for his high-value rescue operations.

So, when this opportunity arose to head out with a Sigma team, he took it. With all that was happening—with the possibility of Sigma being disbanded—he didn't know if he'd get another crack at a field op.

Now, standing in a morgue, he began to question his life choices. He caught a reflection of himself in the polished bank of refrigerated storage cabinets. With his rail-thin physique and light blond hair, many mistook him for a teenager. Still, from the very beginning, Kat had never questioned his value or worth, respecting his analytic mind and his oily way of thinking through problems. She had also never doubted his physical prowess. They often worked out together in the gym or sweated through a marathon.

Before departing D.C., she had laid an extra assignment upon his shoulders. "*Keep Monk out of trouble,*" she had warned. "*That'll be the hardest part of this mission.*"

Her husband certainly looked perturbed now. Monk's brow crinkled as he pressed Father Bailey further. "Why *did* you change the venue of our meeting with Bishop Yelagin?"

Bailey winced. "Of late, friction between the Russian Orthodox Church and the Holy See has escalated. Especially considering the patriarchate's growing ambitions toward building a new—"

Monk cut him off. "In other words, you don't trust Bishop Yelagin."

"Let's say I'm being *judicious*. At least, until I get a better handle on him. By having Yelagin come here—to be face-to-face with the deceased, men he sent to their doom—perhaps he'll be more forthright with us."

Jason noted how Bailey's gaze lingered on Monsignor Borrelli's pale face. The priest clearly struggled with his own guilt.

"Plus," Bailey mumbled, "I do have a way to judge how willing Yelagin is to cooperate with us."

"What do you mean?" Monk asked.

Bailey shook his head. "All in due time."

Jason scowled, discomfited by the priest's obtuseness.

Monk simply shrugged and crossed to the table. He folded back the drape covering each body. Without touching either of them, he eyed their wounds. The monsignor's throat had been cut deep, exposing the white of his larynx. The Russian archivist had an exit wound mid-chest. The round had likely pierced the man's heart, killing him almost instantly.

Monk returned their shrouds to their respective chins. "The examiner is right. The causes of death are plain enough. Not that there was ever any doubt."

Bailey used this time to cross to a table and examine the monsignor's personal effects. Blood-stained coveralls had been neatly piled next to a pair of boots. Someone had piously wound a chain around a silver cross, forming a spiral atop the clothing.

As Bailey touched the crucifix, his shoulder sagged.

Jason hated to intrude upon the other's grief, but he had a pressing question. "Did they ever recover Monsignor Borrelli's phone?"

Bailey shook his head. "I reviewed the list of my friend's belongings. There was no phone."

Jason had hoped the attackers had abandoned the device. If he could've retrieved fingerprints or DNA evidence from the phone, then maybe he could've definitively confirmed that Valya Mikhailov was involved with all of this.

He stared over at the body of Monsignor Borrelli, picturing the deep slice across his neck. He did not doubt Seichan's assessment about who wielded that blade. He found his hands wringing together as time passed and his anxiety grew—not due to where he stood, but from one nagging certainty.

We're running out of time.

6:35 P.M.

Muffled voices rose from the hall outside the morgue.

Finally . . .

Jason let out the breath he had been holding. They all turned toward the door as it swung open.

Grishin led in two others. The medical examiner showed far more deference to these newcomers. The weary disdain had drained from his voice, replaced with a reverence.

"*Vot ty, Yepiskop Yelagin,*" Grishin said, with a slight bow of his head.

"*Spasibo, Doktor,*" the tall man acknowledged.

They shared a few more exchanges, then Yelagin raised a hand in a clear blessing. Afterward, Grishin backed out of the room and quietly closed the door.

Alone with the newcomers, Bailey crossed over with his arm out. "Thank you for agreeing to meet us here, Bishop Yelagin."

The man shook Bailey's hand. "Anything to help bring the murderers to justice."

Jason heard the slight catch in the bishop's voice as his gaze fell upon the two bodies behind Bailey. His face was pale above his long gray beard, his dark eyes haunted. A hand clutched the cross hanging from a chain over his black cassock.

Jason flicked a look at Bailey. It seemed the good father might have made the right choice when it came to leveraging the other's guilt.

Bailey introduced Monk. "This is Dr. Kokkalis, a forensic pathologist with Europol." He shifted his hand toward Jason. "And Dr. Carter, a lawyer and criminologist from the Hague, who specializes in cyber- and organized crime."

Yelagin nodded to them both. "The Moscow Patriarchate appreciates your help in this matter."

Jason turned his attention to the bishop's companion. A slender woman stood a step behind Yelagin's shoulder. She looked to be in her mid-twenties, maybe a year or two younger than Jason. She was dressed in a somber black dress that reached her ankles. Her hair was entirely covered by a discreet head scarf.

"This is Sister Anna," Yelagin introduced the woman. "A novice with the Novodevichy Convent in Moscow."

The woman trembled, but not due to the number of gazes turned upon her. In fact, she ignored them all. Her focus was on the bodies atop the steel tables. A small hand lifted to cover her mouth.

The reason for her distress became clear.

"Igor Koskov was her older brother," Yelagin explained.

Jason read the ache in the pained squint of her eyes, the tremor in her raised hand, the shortness of her breaths. He suddenly wished Bailey had stuck to their original meeting place at the embassy.

Yelagin continued, "Before heading here, I was informed by Dr. Grishin that you would need a family member's permission to examine Igor's body. Sister Anna is his only living relative. While she could've transmitted that consent, she asked to see him. I could not refuse her."

Guilt spiked through Jason. Their bit of subterfuge in luring Yelagin to the morgue had inadvertently trapped another, someone already grieving who didn't deserve to have her suffering stepped upon.

"I'm so sorry for your loss," Bailey intoned, looking equally regretful about this circumstance. "If you'd like some time alone with your brother . . ."

She shook her head, lowering her hand. She opened her mouth to speak, but she had to swallow hard to get her words out. "Thank you, Father," she said softly. "But I will find a time to grieve more fully. For now, I wish nothing more than to uncover the bastards who killed my brother."

Bailey's brows rose at her harsh tone.

Yelagin touched the young woman's arm. "Such language—"

She stepped away, her back straightening, refusing to apologize for her words. She circled the group and crossed stiffly to her brother's side. Unlike Jason, she did not balk. Fingers rose to touch her brother's cheek.

She then gently shifted the drape more securely, as if tucking her brother into bed.

A prayer whispered from her lips.

Bailey drew them to the far side of the room. "We've already completed our examination of the bodies," he told Yelagin. "We don't have to stay long. But there is another matter I wanted to discuss with you before we retired to the Apostolic Nunciature."

"Of course, anything. You've all had a long day of travel, and I know how dear Monsignor Borrelli was to you personally."

"Thank you."

"What do you need from me?"

"It concerns a photograph that Monsignor Borrelli dispatched to the Vatican archives prior to his death. We had hoped you might be able to help us about one aspect of it."

Jason kept his expression stoic. Bailey had not warned them about his intent to share this level of intel with Bishop Yelagin.

"Let me show you," Bailey said and drew out a tablet from a satchel.

The priest tapped open a file to reveal the photo of the ancient Greek book's gilded frontispiece. The image glowed brightly on the screen, only the good father had cropped out the top section that showed the golden book. All that was visible was the sketch of a building and part of the annotations surrounding it.

"We were hoping you might help us identify this place," Bailey said.

Yelagin held out a hand. "If I may?"

The father passed him the tablet. As Yelagin studied it, Bailey cast a quick glance over to Monk and Jason, his look heavy with import.

Jason understood.

This is the test that Bailey had mentioned earlier, to judge Yelagin's level of cooperation.

"I don't understand," the bishop said. "What does this have to do with the men's deaths?"

"We believe Monsignor Borrelli photographed a page from one of the books found in the vault under Moscow. For him to have dispatched it with such haste, I feared it might be important."

Yelagin's eyes narrowed as he mumbled, "Perhaps he believed it was some clue that would lead to the Golden Library of the Tsars."

Jason inwardly flinched.

How had the bishop made that leap? Especially without seeing the gilded book at the top of the page?

"Why do you say that?" Bailey asked, feigning confusion.

Yelagin sighed. "It was Monsignor Borrelli's hope—all of ours, actually—that the books hidden in that vault might be part of the lost library of Ivan the Terrible." He lifted the tablet. "This certainly makes me wonder if that might not be true."

"Why's that?" Monk asked.

"This sketch. If I'm not mistaken, it's an early rendition of the Holy Trinity Lavra in Sergiyev Posad, a town seventy kilometers outside of Moscow."

"Truly?" Bailey retrieved the tablet and tapped through to a search browser. He finally brought up a photo of a cluster of onion-shaped bell towers, fortified walls, and clusters of buildings. He positioned it next to the sketch. "You may be right."

He shared the photo with Monk and Jason to confirm.

Jason compared the two. The photo's main architectural landmarks certainly appeared to match the sketch—though the passing centuries had changed the religious site somewhat.

Bailey lifted one brow toward Jason and Monk. Plainly, the father had already deciphered this bit of the mystery. By getting confirmation from Yelagin, it suggested the bishop was willing to cooperate and not stonewall them.

Still, Jason had a question. "I'm familiar enough with the legends of the lost Golden Library. But, Bishop Yelagin, why did you ask about it when you saw this sketch just now?"

"Mostly because I know Monsignor Borrelli had been intent to look for clues that could tie the cache of books to the lost library. If he had sent this photo with such haste to the Vatican, it would suggest he had discovered something." The bishop frowned with clear disappointment. "Yet, I don't understand why he wouldn't have shared it with me. We had been on good terms, especially as I allowed him to accompany the archaeology team down into the vault."

"You said this was *mostly* the reason that you made a connection to the Golden Library," Jason pressed him. "What else made you think so?"

Yelagin pointed to the sketch glowing on the tablet. "The Holy Trinity Lavra was one of the locations outside of Moscow that many believe could be where Ivan the Terrible hid his library."

Bailey studied the tablet closer. "I thought everyone was convinced it was lost somewhere under the city."

"That was the consensus for a long time," Yelagin agreed. "The most ardent advocate for this location was a Russian archaeologist—Ignatius Stelletskii—who spent all his life looking for the Golden Library under Moscow. He searched until his death in 1949. Perhaps based on his lack of success, the search eventually extended outward. Since the 1990s, others have been looking farther afield. Mostly scouring any sites with historical ties to Ivan the Terrible."

"Like where?" Bailey asked.

The bishop ticked them off on his fingers. "Alexandrov, which was the capital of Ivan's fiefdom. The village of Dyakovo, where a secret door was discovered that led underground beneath the Church of St. John the Baptist."

Jason nodded to the tablet. "And the Trinity Lavra? It's connected to Ivan the Terrible?"

"Certainly," Yelagin acknowledged. "Ivan moved his court to Sergiyev Posad during the latter years of his reign. He was even the one who ordered the construction of the Lavra's Dormition Cathedral—what's now called the Cathedral of the Assumption. Ivan modeled it after the cathedral of the same name on the Kremlin grounds."

"And you say people have already searched the town, looking for the Golden Library?" Bailey asked.

"With no more success than anyone else."

Jason glanced over to Monk and Father Bailey. He read the hope in their eyes. Those other searchers didn't have what they had: the annotations and drawings from an old Greek text.

Could it be an encrypted map, one pointing to a hidden location within the Trinity Lavra?

With that prospect in mind, Jason was anxious to leave and settle into their rooms at the Vatican's embassy. He had some ideas that might help them analyze those series of photos in greater depth.

A new voice joined their discussion. "All of this? Is it somehow tied to my brother's murder?"

Jason turned to find Sister Anna approaching them. Her expression had hardened out of sorrow into a red-cheeked anger.

"Possibly," Bailey admitted. "If someone caught wind of such a discovery—a clue to the possible location of the Golden Library, a treasure house of inestimable value—they might have sought to steal it."

"You mentioned the Trinity Lavra and the town of Sergiyev Posad," she said as she reached them. "Just this morning, I heard of a new excavation that just started there. It has the whole town stirred up."

Yelagin's brow furrowed. "I was not informed of such a project. How did you—?"

"The sisters in the convent at Sergiyev Posad are well aware of all that happens within their town. And gossip travels quickly. They were abuzz with news of this excavation—and rightly so."

"Why?" Jason asked, drawing her eyes, which were an arresting azure blue. "Were the excavators looking for the Golden Library?"

She frowned. "No. The rumor is that they were searching for an early copy of the Tikhvin Icon. Maybe the very earliest—if not the original."

She said the last with a note of trepidation.

Jason narrowed his eyes. He recognized that name, but before he could ponder it further, Monk interjected.

"What is this icon?" he asked.

Yelagin explained, "It's Russia's most venerated relic, a holy icon said to have been painted by the Apostle Luke. It shows the Virgin Mary holding the Christ child in her lap. Many miracles and healings have been attributed to it."

"I don't understand," Monk said. "Has it gone missing?"

Yelagin sighed. "The history of the icon is rather clouded. Its path started in Jerusalem. But then, in the fifth century, it was moved to Constantinople. From there, it vanished for a time until it miraculously appeared to fishermen near the Tikhvin River in northern Russia in 1381. A church was built at the site to enshrine the icon. Centuries later, Ivan the Terrible added a fortified monastery around it, though the true protection of the church came from the icon itself, which was said to have repelled hostile enemies many times."

"Where is it now?" Jason asked.

"That remains controversial. During World War Two, the Nazis stole the icon from the Tikhvin Monastery. Eventually it ended up in the United States and was returned to Russia in 2004, where it is enshrined at the Tikhvin Mother of God Assumption Monastery."

Monk shrugged. "Then what's the controversy?"

"The bishop who transferred the icon to the U.S. had originally said it was only a reproduction of the original. He later claimed he had lied to protect it. In fact, hundreds of copies *were* made of the icon, many of which were also tied to miracles. Those reproductions are spread across dozens of churches, cathedrals, and monastic sketes, all dedicated to the icon. Because of that, scholars and historians have wondered if what is hanging at the Assumption Monastery is a copy, too."

Sister Anna interjected. "If so, it would mean the original remains lost, perhaps hidden away for safekeeping."

"Possibly at the Trinity Lavra," Jason said.

"Or any number of other churches dedicated to the Tikhvin Icon," she added.

Jason stiffened as he suddenly remembered where he had heard that name. *Tikhvin.* A hot flush of trepidation rushed through him.

Gray and Seichan had left to investigate the address that Tucker had given them, where the kidnapped botanist was supposed to have been taken. It was a church dedicated to Theotokos of Tikhvin. *Theotokos* was the orthodox title for the Virgin Mary. He realized the place must be one of the many churches dedicated to this venerated icon.

But is this just a coincidence or is it significant?

The answer came as his phone—an encrypted Sigma device—thrummed in his breast pocket. He reached for it, noting Monk doing the same with his own phone.

Uh-oh.

They shared a worried look and stepped aside to answer the call.

As soon as Jason put the phone to his ear, Kat's voice came through urgently, transmitting to them both via a conference connection. "We've got a problem. I've been monitoring local chatter and NRO sat feeds. There are reports of multiple explosions near the ruins of the Simonov Monastery. Sat footage shows a cloud of smoke rising from one of its outbuildings."

Jason swallowed hard, trying not to show any outward reaction, but all this intel boiled down to one conclusion: Gray and Seichan were in trouble.

"Local authorities are already responding," Kat added.

Monk grimaced at this news.

Jason understood.

Even if Gray and Seichan survived whatever was happening, if they were caught and exposed by the Russian authorities, the two would likely vanish into some icy gulag. Worse, such a black eye on U.S. intelligence operations would likely be the final nail in Sigma's coffin. It would destroy the agency.

At any cost, the pair could not be captured.

But first, they had to survive.

9

Enveloped in smoke, Seichan plummeted through a gristmill of fiery debris. A shattered chunk of floorboard struck her shoulder. She snatched it and twisted it around, bracing it like a shield before her.

As she plunged, splintered chunks and broken rocks pelted her. Something struck her head, hard enough to squeeze her vision into a tight knot. Exposed skin got ripped and lacerated. Her body jolted as she crashed through obstacles. She fought to keep hold of her shield, but a jarring impact cracked it in half.

She toppled headlong with a scream trapped in her throat.

Through slitted eyes, she watched a smoldering pile of wreckage rushing toward her. She had two heartbeats to react. She spotted a thick rafter laying crookedly atop the mountain of debris filling the basement level.

She curled her legs under her, aiming for the beam. Her boots struck it, but her legs went out from under her. Her chest slammed hard. Momentum slid her down the rafter's length. Splinters tore through the leather of her jacket and pants. From above, rocks and fiery shards battered at her.

She finally swung off the rafter and ducked into a small covey beneath it. She gasped and coughed, covering her mouth with the crook of her arm. Smoke grew thicker with every strained breath. The rain of debris quickly diminished into occasional crashes as the last of the dyehouse's interior collapsed in on itself, hollowing out the brick building.

She stared upward.

Luckily, she and Gray had been perched on the fourth floor, with only the attic above them. If they had been any lower, they would have been buried under the debris.

Still, she was far from safe.

She unzipped her torn jacket and yanked the SIG Sauer from its shoulder holster. She tried to assess her situation, but her ears still rang from the blasts. Her vision remained watery at the edges. Lines of fire traced her body, with blood dripping everywhere.

She ignored it all.

One pain remained paramount.

Where the hell is Gray?

She dared not call out. She didn't know if Valya and her team were closing in already. Though, knowing the woman, Seichan imagined Valya had fled with the black-robed men in the limo. The blasts and smoke would quickly draw the police and the military. Valya would not want to risk being trapped and questioned.

Still, Seichan had to be cautious. Even if Valya fled, Seichan could not trust that the assassin hadn't left a handful of gunmen to ensure the blasts had killed or immobilized her targets.

Wary of this threat, Seichan crept out from under the rafter and climbed across the treacherous debris field. Her ears strained for any voices or crashes that indicated the approach of an assault team. She kept to the thickest smoke and slowly found her footing across the broken landscape.

She retaped the radio mike under her chin and pushed the earpiece deeper into place after it had been knocked loose. She tried subvocalizing to Gray, her words inaudible to her own ears.

"What's your status?" she radioed out.

She waited, still searching, still straining.

There was no answer.

To her left, she heard a tumble of disturbed rock. She halted and focused that direction. Smoke obscured the view, but a fire glowed farther back. A shadow crossed in front of that smolder—then another.

Two men.

She tucked her pistol into her waistband and drew a throwing knife from a wrist sheath.

She set off in the direction of those shadows, using the various patches of flames to track her targets. She moved slowly, cautious of other hunters. She kept tight to the piles of wreckage, ducking under and through the deadfall of debris, careful not to disturb the teetering stacks.

In the distance, sirens warbled brightly, growing steadily louder.

Her heart pounded out the seconds she had left before they arrived.

She finally closed upon two figures who skulked with rifles fixed to their shoulders. One man freed a hand and chopped it to the left of a stack of rubble. The pair split off, preparing to circle the mound.

Seichan stalked behind the first. She was within a meter when her toe kicked a broken brick, sending it skittering to the side. The gunman whipped around—just as she had expected he would when she had bumped that rock.

She lunged beneath the reach of his rifle and stabbed her blade under his jaw. She pierced his larynx and twisted hard, silencing his scream to a gurgle—then slashed across his carotid.

As he slumped, she caught his weight on her shoulder and grabbed his rifle. She rolled him quietly to the ground, then checked his weapon, a Russian AK-308 battle rifle. A suppressor tipped its barrel. She wagered the weapon was chambered with subsonic ammo to further reduce noise.

She lifted the rifle to her shoulder and continued along the path the gunman had headed. She reached the far side of the rubble pile and heard the scuffle of the other assailant. She drifted back into a billow of smoke and waited until the other man circled into view.

Once in sight, he cast her a quick glance, as if confirming his partner's presence. Seichan lifted the rifle higher, hoping he would recognize the weapon's familiar silhouette in the shroud of smoke.

The man nodded and turned away.

She swiveled her weapon toward him, aimed her sights at the back of his head, and squeezed off a single shot. It sounded no louder than a soft sneeze. The crash of his body into a wood pile made far more noise.

Hearing that, Seichan retreated under an overhang formed by a broken section of wall. Furtive footfalls approached her position, drawn by the clatter of wood—but hopefully not the silenced rifle shot.

Another gunman appeared out of the gloom, circling wide, focused on that stack of wood. The hunter froze momentarily when he spotted the sprawled body of his teammate.

The pause was long enough.

Seichan fired from her shelter and dropped the man next to his mate.

She waited another three breaths for anyone else to appear. The sirens now screeched, maybe a block or two away. She heard the *thump-thump* of a helicopter's approach. Like her, any remaining hunters would need to evacuate before the authorities closed in.

With time running short, she slipped out of her shelter. A sharp intake of breath on her left was the only warning. She ducked and rolled. Rounds strafed overhead. She swung her rifle to return fire, but another gunman crashed toward her from the opposite direction.

The pair must have lain in wait, letting their teammate draw her out.

No way to get them both.

Still, she had to try.

She fired low at the first man, peppering him center mass in his chest. As he crumpled to the ground, she rolled to the other side—but the second man had his weapon leveled at her.

Too late . . .

Then a pistol cracked and the man's head snapped back, carrying his body with it. She turned and spotted a familiar figure hobbling her way, limping hard on an ankle, his face a mask of blood.

"Think that's all of them," Gray said.

She gained her feet and rushed over to him. She didn't know whether to punch him or hug him. "Why didn't you radio back?" she scolded harshly. "I thought . . . I don't know what I thought."

But she did.

I thought you were dead.

"I heard your message." He ran his fingers down his neck. "But lost my throat mike. So I kept hidden, then heard the firefight and closed in."

She hooked an arm around his waist to help him stay upright. "We need to get out of here."

He nodded as sirens roared up to the outskirts of the monastery's ruins. "Out of the frying pan . . ."

"Into the line of fire," she finished for him.

7:10 P.M.

Gray reached the window they had climbed through earlier. He had to shoulder aside a heavy beam that had fallen across it to make room. The effort left him trembling. He wiped blood from an eye. His body was lacerated, bruised, and battered.

Behind them, coming from the direction of the church, a bullhorn bellowed with Russian commands as the local authorities started a sweep of the monastery's ruins. The burning dyehouse would undoubtedly be their first priority.

We must be gone by then.

But the police weren't the only threat. Flames spread behind him, building into a bonfire at his back.

He peered out the window. The sun was nearly down. The open grounds between the dyehouse and the fortress wall were heavily shadowed. He had hoped to use the cover of smoke to aid their escape, but the wind blowing off the river had swept the area free, leaving only a slight pall across the weedy yard. Still, the steady breeze was driving a thick wall of smoke toward the church, where a majority of the police gathered.

"Stay low," he whispered. "We'll break for the tower."

The plan was to exit the way they came in.

"We'll be exposed once we're on the scaffolding," Seichan warned. "If anyone looks that way . . ."

He understood, but they had no choice. They were pinned down in this corner of the monastery.

Seichan lifted her stolen assault rifle. "I can try to lure the authorities away, draw them off, allowing you the time to scale over and reach the motorcycle. I'll rendezvous back at the embassy."

"And if you're caught?"

"I'm a known terrorist," she reminded him. "Not even a U.S. citizen, despite the forged papers that Sigma drafted up. So they aren't likely to tie me to Sigma."

"Seichan—"

She tapped him on the chest. "You can't be captured."

"Screw that," he countered firmly. "We stick together."

Brooking no further argument, he climbed out of the window and reached an arm back to help her. She ignored his hand and deftly rolled out next to him.

He pointed to the tower. "If we move quickly, we should make it. The others should be momentarily blinded by the smoke blowing their way."

Knowing such protection would not last long, Gray set off across the shadowy yard. Every step shot fire up his left leg. By now, his ankle had swollen tight inside his boot. Sweat ran thickly over his body, burning his wounds. Within ten yards, his run became a stumbling hobble.

Still, no alarm was raised behind them.

A glance back revealed a thick wall of churning smoke, filling the depths of the monastery ruins. Past the pall, the flashing lights of cruisers and fire engines glowed.

So far, so good . . .

As he faced back around, a gray-black helicopter—a military aircraft—swept over the southern wall to his left, coming from the direction of the children's park on the far side. It crested over the dyehouse with a throaty roar.

Seichan cursed—and not just because they were exposed in the open yard. The rotorwash of the aircraft's blades was quickly blowing away the obscuring smoke. The cluster of parked vehicles and trucks came into clear view—along with a row of uniformed men stalking toward the dyehouse.

While Gray and Seichan hadn't been spotted yet, it would not take long. They'd never make it to the tower's scaffolding, let alone scale over the wall.

Seichan shoved him forward, nearly toppling him over. "Run! Get to the motorcycle!"

She pivoted away from his side and headed toward the southern wall, drawing her stolen rifle to her shoulder. She clearly intended to circle behind the dyehouse and come out the far side, to draw attention away from him.

Gray hesitated, but only for a breath. With his bum ankle, he could never keep up with her. And she had been right before.

I can't be caught.

With a grimace, he set off for the tower.

7:14 P.M.
Seichan reached the alleyway between the dyehouse and the expanse of the southern wall. As she ran down its length, she clutched her rifle hard, wishing it was Valya's neck.

A moment ago, when the smoke had washed away, she had noted the black limo was no longer parked behind the church.

Valya must've taken off with the others.

Seichan understood. There was little reason for the woman to stay. If the blast didn't kill her targets, her gunmen still had a chance to capture them while they were stunned or injured. Seichan also knew Valya would want to prolong their suffering and, if possible, kill them herself. It was likely why she hadn't imploded the entire building on top of them. Plus, if all else failed, Valya had another way of damaging Sigma: by delivering her enemy into the hands of Russian authorities.

Despite her fury, Seichan had to appreciate such shrewdness. Knowing the woman, Valya must have planted charges across *all* the surrounding outbuildings, then hid inside the church, like a spider in a web, waiting for them to stumble into one of her snares.

Such measures spoke to Valya's growing paranoia, especially as the woman couldn't have been certain that Sigma would come to Russia or stalk one of her operatives in Saint Petersburg.

Yet, that hadn't stopped Valya from taking such a precaution—a safeguard that was about to prove costly to Seichan. Cornered now, she had little choice but to sacrifice herself.

As she ran along the far side of the dyehouse, she pictured her son Jack: his babbling attempts at his first words, his purpled face when he was frustrated, his bottomless joy at the simplest things in life.

She wasn't just making this sacrifice for Gray, but also for Jack, to make sure he still had a father.

Seichan had never truly known her own, and her mother had been ripped from her when she was a child. She remembered the hollow agony of that loss, of being orphaned, and would do anything to keep that pain from Jack.

She reached the end of the alley and paused. Once she stepped out, she would be in plain view of the men crossing the grounds.

And not just them.

Overhead, the helicopter circled into view as it passed over the grounds again. She couldn't let it swing toward the riverside wall, where Gray must have reached the tower by now.

She tightened her jaw and sprinted out into the open. She aimed her rifle high and fired at the aircraft. She focused on the tail assembly, the helicopter's most vulnerable spot. Its tail rotor was critical for stability.

Unfortunately, it was a small target, especially for a shooter on the run. However, her main objective wasn't to down the aircraft, but to distract it. She had already removed her rifle's suppressor. The weapon chattered loudly as she fired. Rounds pinged off the helo's undercarriage.

Then a sharper gunshot echoed behind her. A round sparked off the tail. The rotor remained undamaged, but the aircraft spun wildly.

She looked over her shoulder, knowing where the shot had come from, who had fired it.

Gray . . .

He must've reached the tower. She remembered him telling her the story behind the fortification, how an arrow shot from an upper window had killed a marauding khan centuries ago.

Gray must be trying to beat that sharpshooter's record.

Another round fired from his position, shattering into the chopper's windscreen. The aircraft bobbled, coming dangerously close to the rampart of the southern wall before veering off.

Praying the gunfire was mistaken as her own, Seichan ducked her head and sprinted away.

By now, the teams on the ground had also spotted her.

Bullhorns roared with orders.

Men shouted.

Rounds pattered around her, but the shadows, her speed, and the angry hornet in the sky all confounded their aim. The teams were fifty meters off and closing in fast.

She swung her rifle and strafed back at them. Earlier, she had stripped a spare magazine from one of the dead gunmen, but the additional ammunition offered her little comfort. She would soon run out.

A loud crash beyond the running men drew her attention. An armored van with a red shield emblazoned on it crashed through the church gate and headed straight across the grounds, bouncing over berms and curbs. She recognized the emblem. It was a unit of the Russian OMON—the *Otryad Mobilný Osobogo Naznacheniya*—the Federation's equivalent of a SWAT team.

Screw this.

She faced forward and concentrated on reaching shelter. The nearest outbuilding was the monastery's old refectory. She raced toward it. The red-brick structure was encased in scaffolding, but it was rusted and missing planks, as if a restoration attempt had been long abandoned.

Still, any port in a storm.

The refectory spread outward in two wings, each three stories high. Inside, there should be plenty of places to hide, to prolong this cat-and-mouse hunt, and possibly offer her a way to escape.

With that goal in mind, she sped toward the refuge.

As she neared it, a series of explosions erupted. Glass blew from the refectory's windows, accompanied by black smoke and flickers of flames. The blasts deafened her, but not enough to keep her from hearing the other detonations, erupting in all directions.

Stunned, she spun in a circle.

All the outbuildings had become dull torches, lit by fires inside, casting up thickening columns of smoke.

Seichan understood.

Valya . . .

Just as Seichan had suspected, the woman had planted charges across all the structures. *But were the bombs timed to explode after Valya left? Or is she spying from afar and spotted me trying to reach a hiding spot?*

With no way of knowing, Seichan turned and headed toward the southern wall. She had already studied the monastery's layout and noted there was a small archway that led through the wall and out into the neighboring park. Unfortunately, it was gated shut. She didn't know if the barricade was locked or not—but she had no other exit strategy.

She ran through beachheads of smoke. The helicopter had retreated higher, driven skyward by the blasts. The pilot must be assessing the situation, wary of the rapidly changing conditions below.

Likewise, the men on the ground milled in confusion.

Only one hunter remained on target.

The OMON van never slowed, bouncing and rattling straight toward her.

She sprinted faster, praying the gate was unbarred. She had no time to pick a lock or blast her way out.

Behind her, the van roared, sounding like a battering ram on wheels.

She flung her arm back and fired blindly toward the vehicle. She didn't bother conserving ammo and strafed on full auto. Rounds ricocheted off glass and pinged metal, but the van continued to hurl toward her.

Ahead, a gust of wind cleared the smoke, enough for her to spot the narrow archway and its barred gate. A heavy padlocked chain secured it.

No . . .

She swung her rifle toward it, but she had already emptied the weapon at the van. Gasping, she expelled the spent magazine and fought in another.

Frustration growled out of her.

Never make it in time.

Then a trio of sharp bangs cut through her complaint.

Ahead of her, the chain slithered to the ground. The old gate swung partly open.

She sped the last of the distance.

The van, only two meters back, roared at her.

She hit the gate with her shoulder and spun through it without slowing.

Behind her, the van crashed into the archway, as its wheelbase proved too wide for the narrow opening.

Seichan continued running—toward the IMZ Ural motorcycle. It idled on a brick pathway of the child's playground. Gray fired his SIG past her shoulder, discouraging anyone in the van from trying to exit.

But the vehicle wasn't the only threat.

Seichan leaped headlong into the sidecar, twisting at the last moment to land on her back in the seat. She lifted her rifle high.

The helicopter sped over the wall in pursuit.

Seichan took her time, aimed the rifle's sights to the rear of the aircraft, and fired a barrage of rounds into the tail assembly. The rotors exploded. The chopper spun wildly, tilting sideways. Its rotors chewed through the treetops. Then the helicopter rolled and slammed into the wall, bursting into a fireball.

Seichan lowered her rifle and turned to Gray. "Somebody had to finish what you started."

He shrugged. "I was short on time. Figured you'd try to make it to this side gate if you could."

"You shouldn't have stayed."

He gave her a stern look. "Don't think you're getting out of our wedding that easily."

Gray turned his attention forward. He already had the cycle moving, racing through the park. He stuck to the shelter of the park's trees. But with the sun setting and smoke rolling like a wave into the park, such cover wasn't necessary.

They burst out of the park's gate and headed away from the confusion on the far side of the monastery. They quickly buried themselves into the evening's rush-hour traffic and continued across the city.

Seichan looked back at the distant column of smoke. "At least now we know Valya is definitely involved in all of this."

Gray hunched over his handlebars. "And maybe the Orthodox Church, too."

Seichan frowned. She remembered how Monsignor Borrelli had sent those photos to Sigma—and not to the Vatican.

"Let's hope it's just the Russian Church," she mumbled.

10

Tucker hurried across Vadkovsky Lane with Kane at his side. Kowalski followed with Marco, while Yuri kept close to Dr. Elle Stutt. They headed toward an ornate century-old building at the corner. It rose in three stories of pinkish-orange stucco, decorated in a frilly Art Nouveau styling, with wrought-iron balconies and butterfly ornamentation.

It was their destination, the Holy See's Apostolic Nunciature.

"Why are we going to the Vatican embassy?" Elle asked.

For the sake of security, she had only been told their destination once the train had reached the station. Earlier, she had changed out of her work clothes and was dressed casually in a light blue windbreaker and jeans. They were all outfitted with similar streetwear. Even Kane and Marco had shed their Kevlar vests and wore simple collars and leashes.

Tucker glanced back at her, at all of them.

Just a group out for a stroll, walking their dogs on this spring night.

"The friends I told you about," Tucker explained. "This is where we were told to meet them."

She opened her mouth as if to ask a question, then closed it again.

Tucker led his party around the side of the building and over to a pair of black iron gates. It led into a parking lot behind the embassy. On the other side, a seventeen-story apartment complex loomed over the space.

He lifted a hand to ring a buzzer, but the gates opened on their own.

"About time you got here," Monk said and waved them all through. "Everyone's gathered inside. There's much we need to discuss and a short time to do it in."

"Why the hurry?"

"We're leaving at midnight."

Kowalski looked none too pleased. "We just hauled our asses here."

Tucker backed a step. "Hey, I'm only dropping everyone off. I've done all that Director Crowe has asked me to do. Me and the boys are headed home."

Monk frowned. "Your choice. But there's something you might want to hear first."

Tucker sighed, then shrugged. "If you've got hot coffee and something to eat, I might listen."

"We got dog treats, too." Monk glanced back at him. "Just saying."

Tucker cursed under his breath and headed across the parking lot.

Dr. Stutt shifted closer to him, brushing his arm with her fingertips. Her eyes were glassy with worry. "I don't know these people," she whispered.

Though she didn't say it out loud, she clearly did not want Tucker to leave.

"Let's hear what they have to tell us," he said in a noncommittal tone.

Monk led them to the embassy's rear door and herded them into a lobby. He pointed to a stairwell on the left. "Everyone's downstairs."

As they headed below, Tucker noted that the building's upper floors were dark and appeared to be mostly deserted at this late hour. He caught sight of a wobbling beam of light on the main floor, likely from a night watchman on patrol.

Once downstairs, Monk took them over to a conference room off to one side. A long mahogany table ran down its center. The walls were paneled in the same rich wood. A small fireplace smoldered against the back wall. Above the hearth, the papal symbol—a crown and two crossed keys, one gold and one silver—hung on the wall. The tabletop bore the same insignia, depicted in inlays of precious metal.

Contrasting with the regality of the ambassadorial space, a row of flat-panel monitors hung along one wall. They displayed silent news-feeds from various stations, all broadcasting chaotic footage of burning brick buildings surrounded by high walls.

Tucker could guess the source of that mayhem.

Commander Gray Pierce sat in a leather chair with a leg up on a neighboring seat. Tucker winced at the state of his condition. A bag of ice rested on his ankle. His face was darkly bruised, with Steri-Strips sealing dozens of cuts and wounds. It looked like the man had fallen through a plate-glass window—several times.

On one of the monitors, the fiery wreckage of a downed military helicopter smoldered.

Kowalski noted it, too. "Looks like you all were busy."

Gray motioned to the table. "Take a seat. We have a tight agenda."

Tucker signaled for Kane and Marco to retire to spots by the fire-place. The two shepherds loped over and settled there, though both kept their ears tall, wary of all the strangers.

Can't blame them.

Tucker drew a chair for Elle, then took the next seat. He eyed the trio of religious figures sharing the table. The one with the Roman collar had to be Father Bailey. Tucker had never met the man, but Kowalski had filled him in on the priest's past ties with Sigma. The other pair—an older, gray-bearded man and a slim young woman—wore robes of the Russian Orthodox Church.

Tucker struggled to understand their presence here.

Gray made introductions and then nodded to Elle. "Thank you, Dr. Stutt, for agreeing to come here."

"I don't think I had much choice," she said. "And I have many questions."

"Understandably so. Hopefully, we'll be able to clear up a few details. But right now, the situation remains . . . fluid."

"More like jacked up," Kowalski commented. The big man stood to the side, eyeballing the monitors, looking more disappointed than fazed, clearly frustrated not to have been in the thick of that firefight.

Gray pointed at Kowalski and motioned to the door. "Seichan is upstairs, coordinating with embassy security. The more eyes we have up there, watching our sixes, all the better."

Kowalski shrugged, likely happy to avoid a long talk, and headed toward the door.

Gray's gaze turned to Yuri—Bogdan's head of security—who still stood to the side. "Mister Severin, would you be willing to assist upstairs?"

Yuri's jaw muscles tightened, hardening his darkly stubbled face. He was clearly reluctant to leave, and not just because he would be abandoning the botanist, a woman who Bogdan had sent him to protect. Tucker suspected Yuri's boss, ever an opportunist, had assigned his employee to gather whatever intel he could about this whole situation.

Gray kept a firm stare on Yuri, but it was Kowalski who broke the standoff.

The big man grabbed the security chief by the elbow and drew him away. "C'mon. There's got to be food around here somewhere—and if we're lucky, maybe a bottle of vodka."

After the two left, Monk closed the door behind them, ensuring their privacy. Tucker knew most embassies had sophisticated jamming equipment to protect their premises, and undoubtedly the same was true here. Plus, he noted the black boxes with red LED lights affixed to the walls. They looked recently placed, probably by Gray's team, meant to augment the building's security with DARPA's latest tradecraft.

But why take all these precautions? What is really going on?

Gray waited for Monk to take a seat. "First, let's catch you up on what has happened and what we've learned . . . at some cost." He shifted the ice bag on his ankle and set about relating all that had transpired at the ruins of an old monastery—including *who* had been involved.

"So this Valya Mikhailov is behind all of this." Tucker was unable to keep the bitterness from his words. "Both that ambush at the monastery and the attempted kidnapping."

Elle stared from him over to Gray. Her face had paled, even her lips, as she took in his injuries, likely getting a better appreciation of the danger she faced. "This woman? What does she want from me?"

"It's not just her," Gray said. "We believe she was hired by someone who works for the Russian Orthodox Church."

Tucker began to understand why two representatives of the Moscow Patriarchate might be in attendance. Still, throughout his account, Gray's eyes would slightly narrow whenever his gaze swept their way.

He needs these others but doesn't fully trust them.

Tucker had little patience for such subterfuge. "What's this all about?"

Father Bailey answered, his focus still on the spread of photos before him. "It concerns a lost continent called Hyperborea." He looked up from the table. "And I believe someone found it."

9:12 P.M.

Always get the crap end of the stick.

Kowalski patrolled the rear wing on the third floor. Seichan had assigned him this lonely, dark section. While he would've preferred to keep watch somewhere closer to a kitchen, he hadn't argued with her, not after noting her injuries and the hard glint to her eyes.

She had taken over command of the embassy's security office, with its bank of CCTV monitors that showed every angle outside the place. The Italian guardsman had balked at this intrusion, but Father Bailey had arrived with a papal-sealed order granting them full control of the building.

When Kowalski had arrived at the security office, Seichan had immediately sent him off on patrol, likely to get him out of her way. She had been in no mood for anyone to second guess her. Not that he blamed her. She had been right about Valya luring Sigma to Russia and laying a trap for them, one that had nearly gotten her and Gray killed. Even that bastard Radić had been a rabbit that Valya had let loose for him and Tucker to chase.

He shook his head.

That tricky little witch . . .

Valya clearly was done underestimating Sigma.

And we'd better do the same with her.

Kowalski continued across the wing to check its far side. A penlight illuminated his way, but it only made the walls and ceilings draw closer—and the halls were already plenty tight in this old building. He had been forced by Gray to read up on the embassy, to memorize its layout, to know its history. The building was built more than a hundred years ago, when people must've been much smaller.

Definitely tinier than me.

He heard echoes of other men, embassy security, all speaking Italian. Their whispers carried eerily through the old structure, like disembodied ghosts. The floorboards creaked under his weight. This section of the embassy appeared little used. The offices were empty. The hallways had drapes of cobwebs that made his flesh crawl whenever he passed through them.

As with all embassies, these grounds were considered the territory of its home country—in this case, Vatican City. It was why Gray had agreed to make this their local safehouse. It served as the perfect shelter against any Russian incursion.

Though, right now, this place seemed less a sanctuary and more like a haunted house.

And I hate haunted houses.

He always had, even as a kid. The dark hallways, the cramped passages, the jump scares. It might've been because he had sprouted to his full six-foot-seven frame when he was only thirteen. He had been a gangly kid who didn't know what to do with his limbs, so narrow spaces had always challenged him. Add in costumed assholes who always seemed to target the tall, goofy kid, and it was a true horror show.

He did not expect any such surprises here, but he found himself moving slower, trying not to creak the old floorboards. As he turned a corner, moonlight shone down the next hall. He had reached the windows on this side of the wing. The vantage would allow him to spy across the expanse of the parking lot to the neighboring buildings.

Relieved to abandon the dark, tight spaces, he headed toward the light.

Once near the end of the hallway, he heard someone speaking Russian, sounding furtive, but also perturbed.

Kowalski stopped at the corner and took a fast glance down the hall that paralleled the row of windows. At the far end, Yuri Severin stood near a stairwell, bathed in moonlight. The man clutched a cell phone to his ear.

Kowalski eavesdropped. Unfortunately, he knew only a few words of Russian, most of them curses. Still, Gray had been adamant about them all going dark, forbidding any unauthorized communication.

Clearly, Yuri had chosen to ignore this order.

What's this guy doing?

Kowalski waited. He heard Tucker's name mentioned—and from Yuri's tone, it sounded like a curse word. Then again, so did most of the Russian language. Still, Kowalski stiffened when he heard the names *Marco* and *Kane*.

He remembered *who* had shown such exceptional interest in that furry pair.

Yuri's gotta be talking to his boss.

Bogdan must have given his head of security an order to regularly check in.

Yuri finished his call, lowered the phone, and spat out a few words that Kowalski did know. "*Yob tvoyu mat . . .*"

Kowalski grimaced at the rudeness of the curse.

Yuri ducked away and headed downstairs.

Kowalski pushed out of hiding and stared toward the stairwell. This was going to be a problem—but one that could wait for now. He would alert Gray and leave it to the commander to address.

Not about to wade into that shitstorm.

Besides, he had his own assignment. He returned his attention to the windows and used a set of binoculars to scan the apartment building on the far side of the parking lot. Nothing seemed out of the ordinary. He spied on people preparing a late dinner, others lounging in front of televisions, and one naked gentleman who was staring intently at a laptop across his knees.

Nope . . . enough of that.

He shifted his binoculars down to the parking lot.

He caught sight of a shadowy shape rushing low, heading toward that same apartment building. The figure vanished over the high embassy wall, as if it were a waist-high hurdle.

Kowalski frowned, having recognized the woman.

What is Seichan doing out there?

11

Gray scowled in frustration at Father Bailey. He had little patience for the priest's obtuseness, especially as his ankle throbbed with every heartbeat.

"A lost continent?" Gray pressed him. "What are you talking about?"

"Give me a moment to explain," Bailey said.

The Vatican prefect shuffled through a stack of photos spread across the tabletop, then leaned over and consulted with the bishop and nun from the Russian Orthodox Church. Since arriving here, the trio had been poring over the snapshots taken of the ancient Greek text. They had whispered amongst themselves, sometimes arguing, sometimes nodding.

Like now.

Gray remained wary of these two strangers, especially after witnessing Valya meeting with other members of the Russian Orthodox Church. He had initially balked at including these two in the meeting, but Bailey had insisted, vouching for them. Even Monk had said they were worth hearing out.

Gray had finally acquiesced, but only because he needed answers quickly.

Still, a lost continent . . . ?

Bailey picked out several of the photos and held them up. "Monsignor Borrelli was very thorough in recording anything of note in the old

Greek text. Besides photographing the book's gilded frontispiece with its sketch of the Trinity Lavra, he also took pictures of several other pages."

"I'm well aware of that," Gray said. "I was able to briefly review them on the flight here."

"Yes, of course. Then you must have noted the pages with sections that had been underlined or boxed off."

Gray shrugged in agreement.

Bailey continued, "What you must understand is that the Greek book—Herodotus's *Histories*—is more of a travelogue than anything else. It describes the lands and peoples of the known world at that time. Some regions Herodotus had experienced personally. Others that he wrote about came from accounts that he had heard while traveling."

Gray could guess the direction of this conversation. "Like this continent you mentioned? Hyperborea?"

"Precisely, Commander." Bailey spread the pages that he had picked out. "All of the marked sections are places where Hyperborea is mentioned in the text. Here is one, which Sister Anna helped me translate from ancient Greek. She had studied alongside her brother Igor to be an archivist . . . until she had a greater calling."

"I've not entirely abandoned my studies," she added quietly. "Presently, I serve our convent as its librarian. We have a collection that rivals many museums. Igor came often to assist me in cataloging and preserving our books."

Her voice caught slightly at the mention of her brother.

Bailey interceded, "As I mentioned, the passages she helped me translate all speak about the lost continent of Hyperborea." He read a couple of the underlined sections. "'*Among the northernmost tribes are the Hyperboreans, whose territories reach to the sea . . . Concerning the Hyperborean people, neither the Scythians nor any other inhabitants of these lands tell us anything.*'"

Monk leaned closer. "Who are these Scythians?"

Bishop Yelagin answered with a furrowed brow. "A Bronze Age people. Nomads of our northern steppes. They were known for their militant nature."

Yelagin gave a small shake of his head, as if struggling to put these pieces together. But the man's lips drew into hard lines, suggestive that he wanted to say more, but was holding off.

Bailey drew forth another page. "Here is an account of two maidens of Hyperborea who traveled to Greece, to the city of Delos. They came bearing offerings of bundled straw, a hay impregnated with medicinals that were said to heal the incurable."

Sister Anna nodded. "According to legend, the Hyperborean were a peaceful people from a verdant land and were gifted with long lives, many times a normal lifespan."

"Perhaps such long lives were due to this strange medicine," Bailey suggested.

Monk frowned. "If so, what became of these maidens and their miraculous cure?"

Bailey sighed. "According to Herodotus, the maidens were killed in Delos, which angered the Hyperborean people and caused them to close their borders. Afterward, Herodotus writes, '*In honor of the maidens, Delian girls and boys still cut their hair and make sacrifices with bundles of straw.*'"

Bailey lowered the page. "And it's not just Herodotus who writes about Hyperborea. Plato mentions it in *Charmides*. Pseudo-Apollodorus in *Bibliotheca*. And so many others. Virgil, Ovid, Seneca, Pliny the Elder, on and on."

Gray huffed in exasperation. "Still, this all sounds like hearsay. Does Herodotus—or anyone else—offer concrete information about this place? Like where it might be located?"

"No," Bailey admitted. "And I can't say for sure if these marked passages are even related to the Golden Library. Whoever annotated them could've done so long before the illuminated sketch was added to the front of the book."

"Then why are we focusing on this angle?" Gray pressed him.

"Because of those *other* drawings in the book." Bailey slid over a page. "Like this one. I've consulted with Sister Anna and Bishop Yelagin. From the exacting detail, the strokes of the lines, and the fade in the ink, we all believe this was drawn at the same time, possibly by the same hand, as the sketch of the gilded book and the Trinity Lavra."

Gray reached over and drew the photo closer. During the flight to Moscow, he had studied all the pics transmitted by the monsignor. This one had caught his eye, not only because of its strangeness, but also because it had nagged at him, and more so now—but he could not pin down what troubled him.

The photo was of a page from the book, likely a chapter ending, where someone had filled the lower half with a detailed sketch of jagged peaks surrounding a valley, one that contained what appeared to be a circular labyrinth, or maybe a shimmering lake, encompassing a lone mountain at its center.

Gray understood why Bailey had pointed out this page. "You believe this is a sketch of Hyperborea?"

"At least some corner of it. But whether the artwork was based on an eyewitness account or on some fanciful speculation, I can't say.

But the presence of this sketch—one that was drawn at the same time as the gilded artwork at the front—suggests that the marked passages concerning Hyperborea are related to all of this."

Gray sighed, recognizing that it was worth considering. Still, he could not shake the persistent sense he was missing something.

He stared again at the drawing.

Something about that sketch . . .

His rumination was interrupted by Bishop Yelagin, who had found his voice again, loosening those tight lips. "Commander Pierce, the two men who you saw at the monastery, could you describe them?"

Up until now, Gray had avoided sharing too much information with the Russian pair, but he recognized that the two had been cooperative so far. Plus, he wanted any information he could gather on those who had hired Valya Mikhailov.

Not that he wasn't already pursuing the matter on his own.

Since arriving here, Jason had sequestered himself in a neighboring room, working on a solo project, while also consulting with Sigma Command. Gray had already briefed Director Crowe about all that had transpired, and Kat was doing her own research into Valya's employers.

Still, if possible, he wanted any firsthand knowledge.

Gray drew out a handheld tablet and brought up the photos of the two men that he had taken with his digital spyglass back at the monastery. The pictures were grainy, especially facial details, but the images were clear enough.

Yelagin studied them for a breath, then closed his eyes and gave a small shake of his head, not in refusal, but in sad resignation.

Sister Anna leaned over to examine them, too. Her reaction was far more incredulous. "It can't be . . ." She glanced to Yelagin and pointed to the image of the hulking figure in a cassock and hat. "From his size and facial scar, that must be Yerik Raz, *nyet*?"

The bishop nodded.

Anna turned to them. "He serves commonly as a retainer for—"

"Archpriest Sychkin," Yelagin finished.

Gray kept his features flat, but this confirmed what he had overheard from Valya, who had named the priest back at the church.

Monk had his own query. "You recognize these two men? How? Does everyone in your church know each other?"

"While the patriarchate is growing rapidly, we are still relatively small in number," Yelagin confirmed. "But Archpriest Sychkin is well known by all. He oversees all our Tikhvin churches."

Gray stared over at the monitors that still ran with footage of the burning monastery. "Including the Theotokos of Tikhvin Church?"

The bishop glanced to the same row of screens. "Yes. In fact, Sychkin was the one who had orchestrated the church's restoration at the Simonov Monastery."

Gray slowly nodded. *No wonder the bastard had picked that site to serve as Valya's local base of operations.*

Yelagin sighed. "The Tikhvin Icon has always been Sychkin's passion."

"Why?" Monk asked.

"If you remember, back at the morgue, I had described the icon's holy status, but what I didn't relate—as it didn't seem important at the time—is another reason it's venerated in Russia." He stared around the table. "Many believe its arrival in Russia, appearing before the fishermen of Tikhvin, was a celestial sign that Russia was destined to be the Third Rome."

Gray frowned. "A Third Rome?"

Yelagin ticked them off on his fingers. "First, of course, there was the original Rome in Italy, and home to Vatican City. Then when Rome fell, Constantinople became the Second Rome."

"And where the icon resided for centuries after it was moved from Jerusalem," Monk noted.

"Correct. And when the icon vanished during the fall of Constantinople and reappeared in Tikhvin, it was taken as a holy sign that Russia was destined to be the Third Rome, the new seat of religious power in the world. It's a philosophy that drives the *Russkii Mir*—or Russian World—theology. It's one of the main reasons that a vocal number of the Russian Orthodox Church, including our patriarch, sanctions Russia's military conquest of other countries."

"Because it's God's will," Monk said dourly. "Formalized by the reappearance of the Tikhvin Icon on Russian soil."

Yelagin sighed. "Not all of us adhere to his political theology."

"But as a whole, the orthodox church has benefited from it," Anna said. "Our country's largest budget expenditure—after the military— is devoted to expanding our patriarchate."

Gray understood this investment. *Such funding had clearly helped garner religious support for Russia's militant expansionism.*

"Even the Trinity Lavra has benefited," Yelagin continued. "Millions are being poured into the religious site, with the aim of transforming it into a new Vatican City, symbolically preparing the Trinity Lavra to be the holy seat for the Third Rome."

"And let me guess," Gray said. "Sychkin is at the center of it."

Yelagin nodded. "He has curried favor with our Holy Synod for years, gaining the ear of our patriarch. So, know this, he is a powerful man."

"One you don't want to make an enemy of," Anna warned, but there was no shrinking in her manner, only a deep-seated fury that stoked brighter in her cheeks with each breath.

Gray understood.

She now knew that the bastard was behind her brother's murder.

Yelagin continued, "More importantly, Sychkin is also the *predsedatel'*— the chairman—of the Arkangel Society." He motioned to Father Bailey. "Which further confirms your suspicions about the significance of what was highlighted in the passages of Herodotus's text."

"About Hyperborea?" Gray said. "Why is that connection significant?"

"The *Arkhangel Obshchestvo* is founded on the ideologies of a revered Russian philosopher, Aleksandr Dugin. He has written books and trea- tises pertaining to the historical existence of a lost northern continent, claiming Russians are the descendants of these god-like Hyperboreans."

"Why does that matter?"

"Dugin believes—as do many—that the theological destiny of Russia is to resurrect our glorious past as the descendants of the Hyperborean people. To return to the divine status of those lost ancestors."

"Also," Anna said, "his take is very militant. He believes the only way to achieve that end is via an apocalyptic war between the East and the West. After which, all of Eurasia would return to the fold of Mother Russia."

Gray grimaced. "Which dovetails into this whole *Russkii Mir* theology tied to the Tikhvin Icon. So, I can see why this lost continent philosophy would appeal to Sychkin."

Yelagin sighed. "But do not be dismissive. Dugin's books that expound upon this ideology—*Foundations of Geopolitics* and *Fourth Political Theory*—are studied and taught at our country's military and political science academies. The current regime in Moscow uses his philosophies to support its ambitions to expand our borders—into Crimea, into Ukraine."

Gray struggled to accept this. "All because Dugin believes your people came from this mythical continent?"

"Myths can move mountains," Anna whispered.

"As can faith when it comes to the Tikhvin Icon," Yelagin added. "And whether the continent is myth or not, the Arkangel Society—an eclectic gathering of scientists, philosophers, religious figures—seeks to find proof to support Dugin's assertions."

As Gray stared across the spread of pages, a cold dread crept into him. He knew how heated the Arctic had become of late, and not just in terms of warming temperatures and thawing ice. Russia was reopening dozens of old Soviet bases along its northern coast and building new ones. Additionally, they were constructing hundreds of ice-hardened warships and training brigades of soldiers for fighting in the frigid, ice-choked seas.

Other nations were only beginning to take note of this aggressive posturing, ratcheting up tensions. The entire Arctic was a cold powder keg waiting for a match. One misstep and the next global war could erupt.

Gray remembered Yelagin's words from a moment ago.

Whether the continent is myth or not . . .

Even if Hyperborea wasn't real, just the *search* for the place in an area that volatile could be the flaming match that triggers Dugin's apocalyptic war.

And if that continent were ever discovered . . .

The result could be much worse. It would destabilize the region's fragile geopolitical landscape, wiping out established borders between

Arctic nations, blurring others. And considering the area's vast un-
tapped wealth, war over those resources would be inevitable.

And Russia has already set up the groundwork to win that icy battle.

From Yelagin's pallid features, he also recognized the danger to the
world. His next words grew defeated. "I suspect Sychkin first employed
Valya Mikhailov to simply secure the book, hoping it might be a clue to
the Golden Library. There have long been rumors that Ivan the Terrible
hid the collection because it contained mystical black arts that could
help Russia rise as a supreme Earthly power. That alone would have
drawn the archpriest's interest."

Monk pointed to Bailey's pages. "After securing the book, he must've
read those same passages that you just did."

Yelagin stroked his fingers through his gray beard. "I think he
believes—and maybe rightly so—that the Golden Library holds the
key to unlocking this mystery, to revealing the location of Hyperborea.
That's why he has grown so brazen." The bishop looked across the table,
to the woman who had remained silent through all of this. "Brazen
enough to order the kidnapping of a Russian botanist."

All eyes turned her way.

Dr. Stutt looked aghast, as confused as all of them. "But why me?
What do I have to do with all of this? With a lost continent?"

Gray answered as he stared at the spread of photos, "I think I may
know."

12

Valya appreciated having friends in high places. It had been Sychkin who had alerted her to where Sigma was holed up in Moscow. Unfortunately, he had refused to say *how* he had come by such knowledge.

Still, it was an opportunity she would not waste.

From her lofty vantage on the fifteenth floor of a housing complex, she continued to surveil the Apostolic Nunciature. The Vatican embassy squatted on the far side of a parking lot.

As she kept vigil, waiting for her team to get into position, her fist tightened on the knife in her hand. Behind her, the apartment's original occupants—an elderly couple—lay dead in their bloody bed. Valya had meticulously cleaned her blade afterward. The polishing ritual normally calmed her, but her heartbeat still pounded in her throat.

Frustration kept her on edge. The trap she had laid at the Simonov Monastery had failed to capture or kill her targets.

I will not repeat that mistake again.

Through an earpiece, she monitored the chatter of her assault team. It would not be much longer. She had confirmed her targets were inside the building. An hour ago, she had spied upon a group that had arrived at the embassy's gate. She identified one of them as a Sigma operative. They were met by another who ushered them inside. The group was escorting the Russian botanist whose kidnapping had been thwarted.

Valya hoped to correct that failing, too.

Oddly, the arriving group had come with a stranger—and a pair of large dogs.

She didn't understand their inclusion, but they would be dealt with, too.

Her earpiece buzzed on an encrypted channel. It was her second-in-command, Nadira Ali Saeed, a Syrian mercenary she had recruited three years ago. The woman had been part of an all-female commando squad, known as the Lionesses for National Defence, but her savagery and brutality had gotten her drummed out. Afterward, she had found a home in Valya's group, where she swiftly rose to her current position.

"We're ready, commander," Nadira reported in. "We're all locked down."

"How long of a window do we have before the local authorities respond?"

"We've jammed communications for three city blocks around the embassy. Once we engage, we'll roll out spike strips across the surrounding streets to thwart any vehicles coming into or out of the area."

"And our window of time?" Valya pressed her.

"Fifteen minutes, maybe twenty. After the monastery's firebombing, everyone is on high alert."

That will have to do.

The timeline was tight but manageable.

Valya lifted the old dagger in her hand. It had belonged to her grandmother, who had carved its black handle from a living Siberian spruce under a full moon. It was an *athamé*, a dagger used in magical ceremonies. Her grandmother had been a well-respected *babka*, a village healer. Later, during World War II, she had been drafted to fight the Germans, part of an all-woman unit, the 588th Night Bombers Regiment. The female pilots took to the air after sunset, gliding quietly across Nazi antiaircraft batteries to drop bombs on the unsuspecting enemy encampments. Their deadly efficiency earned them the nickname *Nochnye Vedmy*, or the Night Witches—which seemed appropriate for a woman who was a former village *babka*.

Unfortunately, after her grandmother's death, Valya's mother had tried to take up the mantle as a village healer. The family had needed the money, especially for a widow who had given birth to twins, both afflicted with albinism. And in such a rural area, notoriously prone to superstitions, it took only a few bad seasons for people to look for someone to blame. Valya's mother, burdened by two strange children, quickly became a target. Forced to flee their home, they made their way to Moscow. Penniless, their mother had turned to prostitution. Mercifully, she had died within a year, murdered by one of her patrons. Valya had come upon this crime, and in a fit of rage, she stabbed the man with her grandmother's dagger, turning a tool of healing into one of death.

Afterward, she and her brother, Anton—both twelve at the time— had been forced to fend for themselves on the streets, becoming savage and wild, until the Guild had found them and turned that anger into skill.

Valya studied her reflection in the mirror. She had powdered over her tattoo to hide the distinguishing mark, but the dark sun still shone through. She and her brother had disfigured their faces in this manner, as a promise to forever be there for each other.

But nothing lasts forever, she thought bitterly.

After the death of Anton, she was left with little else.

She gripped her witch's blade with white knuckles.

Except revenge.

13

Dr. Elle Stutt refused to shrink under the weight of those staring at her. Instead, she stiffened her back and sat straighter. "All this talk of lost libraries and continents . . . What does any of this have to do with me? Why am I here?"

She wished she was back at her apartment on Aptekarsky Island in Saint Petersburg. She had a small flat overlooking the botanical park—though most of her place's square footage was as much a garden as those manicured acres. She had a lab at the park, but that hadn't stopped her from bringing her work home. Each plant under her care—rare hybrids that she had bred—required precise lighting, humidity, and temperatures.

How much will be ruined while I'm stuck here?

Plus, she fed a stray cat who visited her balcony on a nightly basis. She had named him Nikolai—after Nikolai Vavilov, an agronomist and geneticist who had been jailed by Stalin due to a conflict in scientific belief. Vavilov died in prison, as much a victim of ignorance as Galileo.

Elle pictured the growling fury of the orange tabby.

Who will feed Nikolai now?

"If you'll bear with me," Commander Pierce said, drawing a pair of photos toward him. "I'll try to explain why I believe you were attacked."

She narrowed her eyes and rubbed a tender spot on her neck, just under the angle of her jaw, where her abductors had jabbed her with a sedative. Though freed now, she still felt trapped. The only reason she tolerated much of this—besides the personal danger—was the man seated next to her.

Even without turning, she felt Tucker's presence. There was a solidity that had a gravitational pull. He hadn't said a word during the discussion, but she knew he had absorbed it all with his quiet intensity. She also sensed the lethality behind that calmness, and it reassured her.

She realized he was much like his companions, the two shepherds. The pair sat to the side, silently alert. During the train ride here, she had noted how the three moved as one, through touch, whisper, and gesture, a coordination that was unnerving—and thrilling to witness. But their truer bond could be appreciated in quieter moments, a tenderness that was shared. The brush of fingers over ruff, the nudge of a shoulder, the contented rumble.

Tucker must have sensed the depth of her stress, the claustrophobic strain of this room of strangers. He reached over and touched the back of her hand as she clutched the edge of the mahogany table.

"Hear him out," he whispered in a graveled voice. "But just say the word, and we'll take off."

She nodded, and her grip on the table relaxed.

"Dr. Stutt," Gray said, "among the pages that were photographed in that old Greek text was a series of botanical drawings. I was hoping you might identify the specimens."

Despite her frustration, this piqued her professional curiosity.

Is this why I was drugged and grabbed?

Gray slid the photo to her.

Elle squinted at the picture. It showed a spread of two yellowed, grainy pages. The two halves contained line drawings of a cluster of plants, all with spiked stems and topped by bell-shaped lobes fringed by cilia.

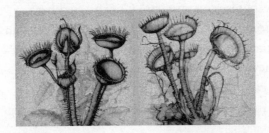

As she frowned at the pictures, her heart thudded harder. "I . . . I believe it's a rendition of *Dionaea muscipula*, the Venus flytrap, an insectivorous species. But the morphology is strange."

"How so?" Gray asked.

"*Dionaea muscipula* is not thorned. And its thigmonastic lobes—the leaves that respond to touch—are characteristically trapezoidal. Whereas these look more bulbous, more typical to species of pitcher plants."

"Which are also carnivorous," Tucker noted.

She turned to him. "What's drawn here could be a *hybrid*, or maybe even an ancient precursor to the modern species."

Gray leaned over with a pained expression as he strained his injuries. He shifted a second photo toward her. "How about this specimen?"

She pulled it closer, sitting straighter.

The next picture was of another set of open pages. Only the plants drawn here were odd, unlike anything she'd seen before. They rose on tall stalks, with fleshy structures at the top. There was also a long runner that extended outward from one plant.

"Do you recognize this species?" Gray pressed her.

"No, but from the level of detail, I believe it's a real plant. The leaves, the vining, the rootlike appendages. Even its pendulous calyx and corolla . . . they almost look primordial, as if it's nature's first attempt at a flower. I can't make sense of it."

"Maybe," Tucker said, "but it appears like someone got around to naming it."

Elle turned to him. "What do you—?"

Tucker tapped the picture's upper left corner, where someone had inscribed a snippet of Greek. She had barely noted it, as fascinated as she had been by the sketch itself. She drew the page closer.

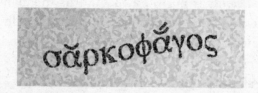

"I can't translate it," she admitted.

"I can." Father Bailey rose from his seat and crossed to her. He pointed at the page. "The word is *sarkophágos.*"

Monk frowned. "Sarcophagus? Like a tomb?"

Bailey shook his head. "I don't believe that's the intent of the artist. The derivation of sarcophagus comes from two Greek roots. *Sarkós,* which means 'flesh' and *phágos,* or 'eater of.'"

The priest lifted a brow toward Tucker. "So, the word's inclusion here is not the *name* of the species but a *description* of it."

Elle understood. "*Sarkophágos.* Eater of flesh. Whoever drew this was stating that this is another carnivorous plant. Like the other."

Gray stared at her. "Your knowledge of such species must be what drew Sychkin to coerce your cooperation."

"But to what end?" she asked.

"To help discover their origin," Bailey asserted firmly. "It's why I stated earlier that I think someone found Hyperborea—or perhaps another strange Arctic island. The mountainous sketch, those drawings of strange flora, it's as if someone were recording an account of such a place."

As Elle studied the sketches, she found herself no longer wanting to bolt from the room, to return to her apartment.

I'm sure Nikolai can fend for himself a little longer.

She stared across the table. "If these plants exist, if they're out there somewhere, I wish to be included in the search."

Gray gave her a small nod. "I believe that's what Sychkin wanted you to do, too—willingly or not."

Tucker raised the most important question. "Where do we even begin to look?"

Elle noted his use of the word *we*, as if he intended to accompany them. While a trickle of apprehension persisted, she found the tightness in her chest easing, making the room less claustrophobic.

Gray answered Tucker's question. "We start by finding the Golden Library. If Bailey's suspicions are correct, it must hold some clue to this continent's location."

Bailey looked none too happy to have his theories accepted—and for good reason. "While we suspect the library is hidden somewhere at the Trinity Lavra in Sergiyev Posad, the complex is vast. How do we even begin a search? Especially without being discovered."

"And keep in mind," Sister Anna reminded them, "we're not the only ones hunting in that spot. Someone is already excavating there, claiming to be searching for the earliest copy of the Tikhvin Icon."

"That's got to be Sychkin," Gray said.

No one argued with him.

"So where do we begin?" Monk asked. "What's our plan?"

The answer rose from behind them. "I may be able to help."

Elle turned to discover that one of the panels of the room opened into a side room. Past a young man's thin shoulders, she spotted a chamber full of computer monitors and other electronic equipment. Likely the embassy's communication hub.

Gray made an introduction. "For those who haven't met him yet, this is Jason Carter, our counterintelligence operative."

Elle frowned. It was a long title for such a small figure.

"I've been working on the photo of the illuminated frontispiece," he said. "We've all been under the assumption that the faded writing surrounding the drawings might be an encrypted code that would lead to the Golden Library's location."

Monk's eyes went wide. "You've broken that code."

Jason scowled and shook his head. "In less than an hour? I appreciate your confidence, but I'm not a miracle worker."

"If Kat were here . . ." Monk grumbled.

Gray waved to Jason. "Go on. What *have* you learned?"

Jason headed over to the row of monitors glowing on the wall. "There's been some astounding breakthroughs in bringing forth faded writing from old manuscripts. Using fluoroscopy and x-ray spectrometry."

Bailey nodded. "The iron gall in old ink glows a velvety black under UV light. I've used this technique to return ancient writings back to life."

"I tried that, but it didn't help much. Especially as it's a photo."

Bailey frowned, clearly disappointed.

Jason continued, "I then tried digitizing the page and employing an AI program, one that could detect micro-differences in ink. It only helped a little bit more. But what it *did* reveal was that there was something drawn *behind* the sketch of the church. It was faintly discernible through the church's outlines."

"A drawing behind a drawing," Bailey said.

Jason jabbed a finger at him with boyish exuberance. "Exactly. It reminded me of a recent discovery of a self-portrait of Van Gogh that was hidden beneath another of his paintings. It was discovered when an X-ray was taken of it, revealing Van Gogh's ghostly face buried behind paint and glue."

Sister Anna nodded. "Old masters often reused their canvases like that."

"Though, in this case," he said, "maybe someone was trying to hide the most significant clues to their code. To look deeper, I used the same AI program as before, only incorporating a digital technique that mirrors X-rays."

Jason cast Monk a glare. "And yes, Kat helped me."

"Of course she did."

Gray stepped forward. "Enough with *how* it happened. What did you discover?"

"Let me show you." He raised a clicker in his hand and pointed to one of the monitors. "Using this technique, I was able to digitally fade out both the gilded book and the sketch of the church."

On the screen, the footage from the burning monastery vanished and was replaced with a photo of a yellowed page.

Elle stood with the others and drew closer. If she squinted, she could just make out the phantom image of a splayed book and an outline of a cathedral. They looked like they were hovering over the page. Past them, in the center of the photo, the image of a large compass glowed. Scribbles of writing surrounded it, a combination of Nordic runes, old Latin, and even scientific nomenclature.

Monk whistled his appreciation and clapped Jason on the shoulder. "Kat did really good."

Jason frowned and shook out of his grip. "I don't know what any of this means, but on the way to Sergiyev Posad, we can try deciphering it."

"It's a start," Gray admitted. "Let's just hope our enemies haven't also figured this out."

Bishop Yelagin faced the table. "Once we're in Sergiyev Posad, I should be able to get a small group onto the grounds of the Trinity Lavra without raising attention."

Sister Anna added her support. "I know several of the nuns at the convent in Sergiyev Posad. Friends, who have no love for Archpriest Sychkin. They can offer additional cover for your group—as few people take heed of us."

"You'll need to be discreet with your friends," Gray warned her.

She gave a bow of her head.

Gray faced the group. "Then we should all get moving before anyone—"

It was too late.

An explosive blast shook the building.

Elle ducked, and Tucker shifted over to shadow her. Dust filtered from the ceiling. Gunfire erupted overhead—at first a few shots, then a furious barrage.

Tucker whistled to his dogs, who burst in his direction.

He then faced her. "Time to go."

14

Seichan crouched on a landing in the apartment building's stairwell. Moments ago, through a narrow window, she had spied the smoky passage of a rocket-propelled grenade. She hadn't seen it strike, but she had heard its blast.

She grimaced.

I'm too late . . .

The echo of gunfire reached her, too, muffled by the cement-block walls of the building.

She stared up the steps.

I had hoped for more time.

Earlier, while in the security nest at the Apostolic Nunciature, she had kept a continual watch on the CCTV cameras that surrounded the embassy. Nothing out in the streets had rankled her suspicions. All had seemed quiet.

Then the low static that had filled her left ear for hours suddenly went silent.

The noise had come from a radio transmitter that she had planted in the lobby of the neighboring apartment building. She had secured it shortly after arriving at the embassy. She had also hidden a camera there, but its signal had failed to penetrate the electronic buffer that protected the embassy. Still, the radio proved powerful enough to transmit to her earpiece.

She hadn't told anyone what she had done, not even Gray. When the two had reached the embassy, they had found Monk's group already inside—along with a bishop and a nun from the Russian Orthodox Church. Gray may have been willing to hear them out, but she couldn't stomach the sight of them.

Not after what happened at the monastery.

Furious, she had left the conference room and commandeered the embassy's security office. Before that, though, she had snuck off to the apartment building and planted her devices. She was certain, if there was an attack on the embassy, it would come from that site. The building towered over the squat Nunciature. Its windows offered hundreds of potential roosts for snipers.

To help monitor the building, Seichan had chosen the lobby to serve as her canary in a coalmine because if Valya attempted a siege, she would surely jam local communications to delay any response from the Russian authorities.

So, when Seichan's radio went silent, she knew something had gone wrong. She had immediately snuck off to investigate, to confirm the threat. With all the surrounding CCTV cameras still showing nothing, she couldn't be certain the sudden silence from the radio wasn't just a malfunction.

Even when she had reached the building's lobby, she had spotted nothing unusual. A few people had been watching a television in the corner, smoking cigarettes and cigars. A bored deskman worked on a sudoku puzzle.

She had discreetly recovered her radio and found that it was still operating, confirming that its signal was being jammed. She considered trying to contact Gray, but such efforts would also be blocked by the interference.

Even if it wasn't, she might not have alerted him.

If Valya had found their group, that meant *someone* in the embassy had alerted her to their presence. It was why Seichan had gone off on her own to investigate, not even alerting Kowalski. She feared the open radio would reach Yuri Severin, whom she didn't fully trust. Above all else, she couldn't risk forewarning Valya. Seichan's best chance of eliminating the threat was to act quickly and get a jump on the woman.

Plus, there was another reason she had come alone. This battle was a personal one. It always had been. Valya carried a grudge against her, for Seichan's betrayal of the Guild, for the death of her brother. Likewise, Seichan had her own reasons to hunt the woman down. Valya had kidnapped her in the past, tortured her, and threatened her unborn child. And then there was the woman's latest attack: bombing the Smithsonian Castle. Seichan took this personally, too. If Sigma were disbanded, it would strip her of her home, her future, all that she had painstakingly built.

But worst of all, just hours ago, Valya had come close to killing Gray, which would have left Jack fatherless.

Seichan slipped two knives into her hands, from the bracers of blades sheathed around her wrists and ankles.

And no one threatens my son.

Trusting Gray and the others to deal with the siege, she continued up the stairwell with one goal in mind.

Someone needs to cut the head off this snake.

By now, Seichan had reached the building's fifth floor. She had checked each level, still finding nothing out of the ordinary.

But now with the attack underway . . .

The door banged open above her. It was followed by a rush of boots down the steps. It could have been a panicked apartment dweller, fleeing the nearby firefight.

But she knew it was not.

She recognized the determined cadence in those steps. She stopped halfway up the next flight of stairs and flattened against its inner railing. The footfalls rapidly approached. She heard a grunt from the landing overhead, then a shadow swept along the wall across from her, cast by the someone descending the neighboring flight of steps.

When the figure reached a position directly above her, she burst up and stabbed her blade between the steel balusters of the railing. She aimed for the top of the man's boot. She severed his Achilles tendon with the razor edge of her knife.

A sharp cry of surprise burst from him. Pain and a flopping foot sent his body tumbling headlong. He crashed hard onto the next landing.

Seichan leaped to meet him.

Before he could get up, she landed on his back—where the tube of an RPG launcher was strapped. The man fought to free the arm pinned under him. His hand was in view, clutching a Russian MP-443 Grach, a standard military-issue sidearm. She plunged her second knife into the back of his hand, severing a finger. The weapon skittered off across the tile floor.

She held the other knife to his ear, while leaning tight to the same lobe.

"*Ne dvigaysya,*" she whispered coldly, intimately. She was fluent in Russian, a necessity in her former profession, where many mercenaries were from Slavic countries. "You don't want to feel this blade's kiss."

The man cursed and bucked under her.

So be it.

She kept her knife at his ear, but she flicked the other blade and sliced off his opposite ear. He hollered, but she pressed her forearm against the back of his neck, throttling the noise to a gurgle.

She needed him cowed, more fearful of her than even pain could achieve. She kept her voice cold. "You think your boss Mikhailov is a cruel *nadsmotrshchik*. Trust me, comrade, I am the one who gives that *kúrva* nightmares."

She had no need to pretend, to fake this threat.

I was a monster.

"You're going to tell me where she is," Seichan promised him.

He tried to deny her.

She shifted her knee to his neck and showed him she was not lying. Her vision narrowed as she let loose that monster. The Guild had taught her well, where pain and terror resided in a body. She used her knives until the man mewled under her. His blood spread wide across the tiles.

"*Stoy . . .*" he pleaded with her, his voice a croak of agony.

"Tell me."

"Fifteenth floor . . . 1509 . . ."

She retrieved his Grach and pointed the pistol at the back of his head. He did not even try to move. She breathed heavily, a slight tremble in her arm, as she fought the monster inside her.

Finally, she scowled, reversed the weapon, and struck him hard behind his remaining ear. Bone cracked, and he slumped limp into the pool of blood. She stripped him of his radio, then grabbed the RPG launcher and slung it over her shoulder.

She stared at the Grach in her hand.

Her breathing remained hard.

I won't be that monster.

Still, she leaned down and sliced his other Achilles tendon, hobbling him, making sure he was no longer a threat.

But I won't be a fool either.

15

How did Mikhailov find us?

The question burned brightly in Gray's mind, but the priority was to get everyone to safety. With the first rocket blast, Gray had burst to his feet—or tried to. Pain shot up his left leg from his ankle. He caught himself on the table's edge.

On the far side, Monk and Jason gathered Bailey and the two members of the Russian Church. A pained glance to Gray's left showed Tucker rushing out of the conference room, guarding over Dr. Stutt, flanked by his two dogs. The former Army Ranger had reacted with lightning reflexes, protecting the charge given to him, likely feeling responsible for hauling Elle here, for putting her in danger again.

Tucker's instincts—while well-intentioned—were going to get them both killed.

Monk spotted this, too. "I'll fetch them."

"No." Gray pointed to the others. "Get everyone to safety."

He headed toward the door, pulling free his SIG Sauer. He cursed himself for not warning Tucker of the team's contingency plan. Beyond the embassy's grounds being considered sacrosanct territory of the Holy See, the building's history had its own secrets—known only by a handful of the staff.

And certain members of the Vatican *intelligenza*.

Father Bailey strode quickly to the room's back wall. He pushed on a panel, and it popped open, revealing it to be a secret door, similar to the one that hid the embassy's communication hub. But this panel didn't open into a room. Behind it was a steel vault-like door.

Bailey reached for its electronic lock, which glowed an angry red, and swiped a black titanium card across it, a gift from the ambassador. The lock flashed green, and the large bolts that sealed the door slid away.

Bailey swung the door wide, exposing stone steps heading down. Lights flickered on. The staircase led into the labyrinthine tunnels beneath Moscow, the same maze where the cache of books had been discovered. The Vatican's century-old building, prior to being gifted to the Holy See, had been the Markin Mansion. As with many places of prominence built during that volatile period, it had incorporated a secret back door, taking advantage of those subterranean tunnels to use them for their original purpose—as a means of escape in times of emergency.

Like now.

"This way!" Bailey urged his two colleagues.

Gray reached the main door and called back to Monk and Jason. "If I'm not back in ten, lock that hatch. We'll regroup at our secondary safehouse."

Monk did not look happy with this plan, but they had civilians to safeguard. "What about Kowalski and Seichan? I can't reach either of them on the radio."

Gray headed out. "I'll check on them, too."

By now, the fierce firefight had died to sporadic bursts. The all-out assault had turned into a siege as assailants set about clearing the building, surely hunting for Gray and the others. From the sounds of battle, the Italian security guards continued to engage the intruders.

Hopefully, their efforts would buy Gray enough time to collect the others and retreat below.

He paused at the stairwell up to the main floor.

Tucker's trail was not hard to follow. Gray heard gunfire echoing above, accompanied by savage growling. In the past, Gray had witnessed Tucker's lethal efficiency—and that was when he only had Kane.

Now with two dogs . . .

No wonder the Ranger set off on his own with Elle.

Gray edged upward, climbing through a choking pall of smoke. Upon reaching the rear lobby, he saw four bodies sprawled across the floor. Beyond them, the door out to the parking lot had been hit by a rocket blast. The exit was blocked by a pile of rubble.

Gray turned and headed for the main floor.

A deafening barrage of gunfire burst ahead of him. He didn't know if it was Tucker or other defenders of this castle. Smoke grew thicker. Fires glowed in the distance.

Taking advantage of the momentary cover, he ducked into the next hall, intending to check on his other teammates. The hallway ended at the embassy's security nest. He sidestepped another two bodies— a guardsman and a combatant in black body armor. The floor was slick with blood, challenging his bad ankle.

Ahead, the door into the security room was ajar.

Had the others abandoned it?

He crept low and nudged it open with a palm, while keeping his SIG trained forward. A gunshot rang out. A round ricocheted off the doorframe and buzzed his ear. Gray ignored it and dove low, knocking the door wider. He slid on his shoulder across the floor and aimed his pistol where he expected the sniper to be from the bullet's trajectory.

But the shooter had already moved, anticipating this.

A large shadow loomed farther to the right, limned against the row of static-filled security monitors. A huge gun reflected the meager light.

Gray shifted his aim.

A harsh voice called to him, "Don't shoot."

It wasn't a command, only an urgent warning.

Gray forced his finger to relax on his gun's trigger. He recognized the accent and the scarred profile as the man leaned down.

"Yuri . . ."

The Russian security chief helped him up. "I retreated here when all hell broke loose."

Gray gained his feet and searched around. "The others?"

"No sign."

Needing some intel, Gray crossed to the bay of CCTV monitors. They all ran with static. Valya had knocked out all the exterior cameras.

What about those inside?

He flipped switches to the interior cameras. Many of them were also down, but a few screens showed views of the mansion. Smoke obscured several of the cameras, but he caught sight of a large form shambling down a staircase from the third level.

Kowalski . . .

The view also showed what awaited him below.

Oh, no . . .

10:28 P.M.

Kowalski leaned a large palm on the wall, struggling to stay upright. He clutched his Desert Eagle in his other hand, but it felt like an anchor. His vision remained watery. His hearing was muffled, as if he had been dropped down a well.

And I almost was.

While spying upon the neighboring apartment building, he had spotted the smoky blast from an RPG launcher. As the grenade rocketed his way, he dove for cover. Fire and glass exploded behind him, blowing out all the windows along this side of the embassy. The blast threw him hard against the wall. Between the concussion of the detonation and the blow to his head, he passed out for several breaths. The world had gone dark, then returned, all muted and wobbly.

He had gained his feet and stumbled away from the spreading fires, intent to join the others and, if possible, get a little payback.

As he descended, he rubbed blood from an eye, squinting through the stinging smoke. The arm holding up the Desert Eagle slowly sank.

Still, he noted the smoke stir near the bottom of the steps. He caught the glimpse of a figure in body armor. He fired before the assailant came fully into view. His Desert Eagle's fifty-cal rounds needed little precision. It was a weapon meant to inflict maximum damage.

The weapon blasted and bucked in his hand.

The body below got knocked back, wafting the smoke enough to reveal the ruins of a successful headshot.

Unfortunately, the fierce recoil of his handgun ripped the weapon from his weakened fingers. The Eagle fell and toppled down the steps—landing at the toes of a second man in black armor who appeared from the stairwell's opposite side.

An assault rifle pointed up the steps.

Kowalski had nowhere to go.

He raised his empty hands and flipped the guy two birds. "Screw you."

The bastard savored his kill. "*Nyet*, screw—"

A large shadow struck the man from the side, taking him down hard. A bloodcurdling cry erupted from him. The shadow thrashed atop him, ripping into his throat until that scream became a gurgle, then silence.

"RELEASE," came a familiar command.

Kowalski stumbled down the rest of the steps to meet Tucker. Kane leaped off the dead man, tossing his furry head, shaking blood from his muzzle. Behind him, Elle Stutt stayed close, her eyes huge. Marco kept tight to her side.

Kowalski struggled to clear his addled head. "What're you—"

"They've got the exits covered on the first floor," Tucker warned. "With heavy fighting. But there's a second-story balcony on the side of the building, over an alley, with a fire escape leading down. This way."

Tucker snatched up the dead man's rifle and headed off.

Kowalski hurried to follow, stopping to collect his pistol from the floor.

After crisscrossing several passageways, they reached a set of French doors leading out to an iron balcony. Kowalski watched the hall behind them, while Tucker searched below.

"Looks clear at the moment," he whispered.

"Let's hope we get more than a moment," Kowalski muttered.

Tucker flipped a deadbolt and edged the door open enough to slip out. He kept low and surveilled the dark, narrow alley. He then waved to Kowalski.

"You first."

"Why me?"

"You're barely on your feet," he keenly noted. "And someone has to secure that alleyway—someone who's also good at catching."

Kowalski bit back a groan, glancing over to Kane and Marco.

No way those two are climbing down a fire escape.

Out on the balcony, Tucker pulled the release and dropped the ladder to the alley floor. It clattered loudly, making them all wince.

Tucker waited to make sure the noise hadn't been noticed. When no alarm was raised, he stepped aside. Kowalski holstered his sidearm, squeezed past Tucker, and mounted the ladder. He clambered down and dropped heavily to the ground. He retreated to the side of a tall trash bin and did his best to watch both ends of the alley.

Elle followed next, half sliding down the ladder's length.

Once she was on the ground, he pushed her into the deeper shadows and stepped below the balcony. It was not a high drop from the second story, but Kowalski still wobbled on his feet. His arms felt leaden.

"Ready?" Tucker hissed down at him.

"As I'll ever be," he groused.

Never thought my new job at Sigma would be as a dogcatcher.

Above, a furry shadow appeared at the top of the ladder. Kowalski braced his legs and held out his arms.

"MARCO, JUMP," Tucker ordered his partner.

The dog hesitated, shifting nervously. The shepherd was only eleven months old, still a newbie in his training, with little to no field experience. Kowalski felt for the big lug, but they were running out of time.

"Just push him," Kowalski suggested.

Tucker ignored him. "You can do this, boy," he said with a calm assurance that spoke to a depth of patience that was beyond Kowalski. "JUMP, MARCO."

Likely drawing confidence from Tucker's tone more than his words, Marco made that leap of faith.

Kowalski grimaced, knowing Tucker would shoot him if he failed in this effort. Marco's body hit his arms. The dog's weight tossed him back. He hit his backside hard, but he kept hold of Marco in his lap.

"You okay?" Tucker called down quietly.

Marco panted, turned, and gave Kowalski's nose a fast lick. Kowalski shoved him off, but Marco appeared unoffended by his rejection and wagged his tail vigorously.

Kowalski took a page out of Tucker's book and patted the dog's side. "Good boy."

The tail wagged wider.

Kowalski held out his arms. "Next."

Behind him, Elle gasped out a warning, "On your left."

Responding to the panic in her voice, Kowalski ducked and hurried over to her with Marco. A cluster of seven men appeared at the end of the alley, all decked in body armor and helmets, moving fast.

Likely an enemy patrol.

Kowalski retreated out of view. He didn't believe they had been spotted, but the men would be upon their hiding spot in seconds.

Above, Tucker balanced his assault rifle on the balcony railing. Like Kowalski, he knew a firefight was inescapable. Their only advantage was surprise. Kowalski stared up, waiting for Tucker's signal. From his hiding spot, Kowalski had no sightline.

Tucker rested his cheek against the stock of his weapon.

Kowalski dropped to a knee, preparing to shoot low, while Tucker rained hellfire from above. He continued to stare upward.

C'mon . . .

Tucker finally gave a small nod.

Upon that signal, Kowalski leaned out with his weapon extended. He immediately got a bead on a target and fired. The man flew back. From on high, Tucker unleashed a merciless barrage. Another three men dropped under the assault.

But the element of surprise was over.

Return fire forced Tucker off the balcony. The remaining men took shelter: flattening behind low walls, ducking near trash barrels, retreating to the far corner of the alley.

Kowalski fired at one man who was too slow, felling him with a leg shot, then sending a second round through his throat. He had no time to target another combatant.

Bullets peppered into the trash bin, sparking off the rusted metal. He ducked back for a breath.

Tucker took over, strafing toward one of the assailants hidden behind a low wall. Kowalski had no view, but he heard the man's cry, followed by a death rattle.

Another down . . . two to go.

The odds had evened out.

Kowalski allowed himself a glimmer of hope.

Stupid mistake.

Elle clutched his elbow, while holding fast to Marco's collar. "Behind us."

Kowalski swung around. A large truck veered into view at the other end of the alley. It braked hard. From the open rear passenger window, the black tube of an RPG launcher shoved out.

Not again . . .

His head still pounded from the last rocket attack.

Kowalski gained his legs and fired at the truck. The rounds spidered the driver's side window and ricocheted off the metal. He knew he couldn't do any real damage—only buy time.

But would it be enough?

10:34 P.M.

Concentrating on the two targets still in the alley, Tucker had failed to identify the new threat—not until the gunmen burst out of hiding and fled away. He heard Kowalski's Eagle booming below. But it wasn't his gunfire that had driven the pair off.

A glance back revealed a Russian truck blocking the far end of the alley. He also spotted the RPG launcher. Below, Kowalski dragged Elle up. The big man fired blindly at the vehicle while rushing out of hiding.

Tucker twisted around and strafed at the truck, but he had a poor angle upon it. While the RPG launcher bobbled under his onslaught, it settled quickly again.

From the corner of his eye, he saw Kowalski clear the bin—but rather than running past it, he flipped its heavy lid, which banged open against the brick wall behind it. He picked up Elle and threw her inside, then grabbed Marco. The dog, not understanding, struggled in his arms.

Tucker continued his barrage at the truck, knowing that what was coming was inevitable.

Move it, Kowalski . . .

The big man leaped headlong into the bin, rolling sideways with Marco in his arms. They hit the cushioning trash that filled the space. A large arm reached up and yanked the lid closed with a resounding clank.

Just in time.

A loud huffing bang erupted below. Smoke burst out of the vehicle's open windows. The grenade struck several yards behind the trash bin— its aim thrown off by Tucker's onslaught.

Still, compressed by the narrow alley, the blast wave sent the bin cartwheeling and rolling down the alley. Tucker got tossed hard into the balcony doors.

As he scurried back, dark smoke smothered the alley, obscuring his view. Still, he saw men swarming the trash bin. It lay on its side, its lid fallen open. Kowalski was dragged out, limp and unmoving. They hauled him toward another truck that rushed into view at that end.

If they're moving him, he must still be alive.

But for how long?

Elle crawled out, then hands grabbed her, too. She gestured wildly, batting at the men. She momentarily broke free and rushed to the bin, not to seek shelter, but to pull Marco out. The dog stumbled a few steps, then shook off the worst of the tumbling. He kept close to Elle, still following the order to protect her.

His hackles rose, and he growled at the commotion.

Rifles leveled at the dog.

No . . .

Tucker flashed to when he had lost his other dog Abel—Kane's brother—during a firefight in Afghanistan. Panic narrowed his vision, choked his throat, leaving him momentarily paralyzed.

Not again . . .

But Elle dropped in front of Marco, sheltering the dog's body with her own. She yelled, getting the others to back off. Tucker couldn't make out what she said, but he knew the enemy wanted her, had been seeking to coerce her into cooperating.

Had she parlayed that into keeping Marco safe?

He couldn't know.

Still, she succeeded.

The pair were led at gunpoint toward the waiting truck.

Movement drew Tucker's attention below. Men had bailed out of the first vehicle. One shouldered the RPG launcher, already re-armed with another rocket. Free of the confines of the truck, the shooter swung his weapon toward the balcony.

Tucker twisted around.

"KANE, RUN! WITH ME!"

Tucker burst through the French doors and sprinted down the hallway.

Kane raced at his side.

The grenade struck the balcony in a brilliant flash. Smoke burst past them. Bricks and twisted iron clattered into the hallway. The concussion threw him far, sending him sliding over the tile floor.

He came to a stop near the mouth of a stairwell.

Kane rolled up next to him, then quickly clambered to his paws.

As Tucker pushed to his hands and knees, he heard boots pounding up the steps ahead of him. He reached for his rifle, knowing he only had a few rounds left.

He pointed to an open doorway on the left.

"HIDE," he ordered Kane.

Together, they retreated out of direct sight.

A moment later, a clutch of dark figures rushed into view on the steps.

Taking advantage of the smoke's cover, Tucker dropped to his belly and fired at those in front. Men tumbled back into the others, but the confusion lasted only moments. Curses in Russian spat his way. The enemy quickly regrouped on the stairs and shot back at him, using their dead as shields.

Tucker did his best to conserve his ammunition, but his magazine quickly emptied. He rolled to his hip and pulled out his Makarov PMM pistol. He had already reloaded its eight-round box magazine, but it would never be enough to hold off the remaining force on the stairs.

He had only one option left.

Take out as many as I can.

He extended his arm, cradling the pistol in his hands.

Then a new barrage erupted from the stairwell, sounding savage and fierce. Body-armored figures burst into view, fleeing from the threat behind them. Tucker aimed at those who fell into his sights and squeezed his trigger, dropping man after man.

He was down to his last round when no one else rose out of the stairwell.

He waited.

Eventually, two figures crept into view.

Tucker sighed with relief, then called from his position. "Gray . . . Yuri . . ."

The pair abandoned their caution and hurried forward.

Tucker rose to meet them, with Kane at his heels.

Gray cast his gaze around, quickly assessing the situation. "Where's Dr. Stutt?"

"Captured." Tucker clenched a fist. "Along with Kowalski . . . and Marco."

Gray absorbed this, showing no reaction. "Then we need to get clear of here."

This was reinforced by the rising scream of sirens in the distance.

Tucker stepped forward, then retreated. "I need to find where they're taking the others."

Gray turned on a heel, anger slipping into his voice. "You can't find them if you're dead."

Yuri grabbed Tucker's arm. "He's right, my friend."

Tucker allowed himself to be led back toward the basement. Fires raged everywhere, burning throughout the old building. They ran into two other combatants, who appeared to be fleeing, likely ordered to evacuate as the Russian authorities closed in. Those last two never made it out of the building.

Back in the conference room, Tucker noted the steel door at the far end. Bodies lay on the floor. All in combat gear. Monk stood shielded in the threshold, but relaxed when he saw who had arrived.

Monk checked his wristwatch. "I gave you an extra two minutes before locking up."

Gray clapped him on the shoulder, then turned to the others. "Everyone get below."

Yuri headed down, followed by Kane. When Tucker passed Gray, the commander grabbed his arm as the door was sealed behind them. Tucker expected to be berated, deserved to be.

I lost Elle, Kowalski, and Marco.

Tucker waved at the stairs. "I . . . I didn't know you had an exit strategy."

"There's merit to being a team player. If you'd stuck around long enough to find out . . ."

Tucker shook off his grip, as frustrated as Gray about the situation. He could not hold back his anger, stoked by loss and fear. "And you could've said something sooner, rather than waiting for a firefight to break out."

Gray stared him down, then sighed in acknowledgment. "That's not why I stopped you."

"Then what?"

Gray stared at the door, expressing aloud his own fear. "Have you seen any sign of Seichan?"

16

Seichan opened the stairwell door that led out onto the fifteenth floor. She crouched low and inspected the hallway. It was deserted.

As she expected it would be.

The explosions and gun battles had sent the apartment dwellers into hiding—which was no surprise. From the Soviet years until now, Russians had learned it was wise not to be overly curious. The phrase *zanimaytes' svoim delom*—mind your own business—was as common as *dasvidania*.

She straightened and exited the stairwell.

While climbing the ten flights, after ambushing one of Valya's teammates, she had eavesdropped on the enemy's chatter, using the radio she had stripped from the man she had hobbled. It had allowed her to roughly follow the battle at the embassy.

She had also discovered the channel where Valya communicated to her team leaders, including a woman named Nadira, who sounded like her second-in-command.

Seichan thumbed over to that channel as she continued down the hall. So far, there had been no indication over the radio that anyone was aware she was in the building. Even Valya's commands were ripe with a combination of gloating and growing frustration. The latter was understandable.

Her team had a limited time frame to carry out this attack.

The flurry of sirens racing here made that abundantly clear.

You're running out of time, Valya.

Then again, so was she.

As Seichan headed down the hallway, she kept to its center, carrying herself low, out of the sightline of the peepholes to either side. She feared Valya might have posted guards, hidden in a few of the rooms across this level.

But no alarms were raised.

No doors burst open.

She noted the odd-numbered apartments faced toward the Vatican embassy. It offered some assurance that the man she had interrogated had been telling the truth, but she had to be sure, especially as she carried her method of entry over her shoulder.

The RPG launcher hung heavy across her back. She intended to blast her way inside, then follow through the smoke and destruction to her target. But to avoid any collateral damage, she needed to make certain it was the *correct* apartment. Torture didn't always glean honest information, just desperate responses, anything to stop the pain.

A familiar voice burst into her radio earpiece. It was Nadira—Valya's lieutenant. "Good news. We have secured the botanist. And an unknown combatant with a large dog."

Seichan's pace slowed.

Were they talking about Tucker and one of his Malinois?

She struggled to understand how the pair had been captured. She expected Gray and the others to have been long gone by now, to have used the escape route into the subterranean tunnels. That had been the plan. It was why she had full confidence in abandoning the others and attempting to ambush Valya. Plus, this news further reinforced her suspicions that someone was leaking intel to Valya or her Russian employers.

It also supported Seichan's earlier decision.

To tell no one about this gambit.

Valya responded, "What about our other targets? Any sign of them?"

"Negative. But we have the building locked down."

Valya's voice grew more frustrated, biting off each word. "Then they must still be inside."

Seichan sneered, enjoying the woman's aggravation, and continued toward the door stenciled with the number 1509. She crept forward, dropping even lower below the line of peepholes.

Once at the apartment, she glanced back to make sure all remained quiet, then leaned her ear against the door.

In her other ear, she heard Nadira's warning. "The police and military are closing in. Two helicopters are inbound. And fires are rapidly spreading throughout the building."

"And the others still haven't shown themselves?" Valya noted. "Not even to flee that growing inferno."

Nadira didn't bother responding to this. Instead, she focused on the timeline. "Should I call a retreat?"

Valya stayed silent, then spoke with an icy certainty. "Yes. Clear out. The others must already be gone. Somehow."

As Seichan eavesdropped, she heard a muffled voice through the door. While she couldn't discern the words, the cadence and tone matched what was spoken through the radio.

Valya's definitely in there.

Getting this confirmation, Seichan pulled back and retreated down the hall. But Nadira's next question gave her pause.

"And our captives?"

Seichan listened more intently.

"Take them to Sergiyev Posad," Valya ordered. "Archbishop Sychkin will want his botanist. And I'll deal with the other. See what use we can make of the man."

As Nadira acknowledged these orders and signed off, Seichan backpedaled farther down the hall. Once at a safe distance, she dropped to a knee and lifted the RPG launcher to her shoulder. She squinted an eye and centered the weapon's sights on the 1509 stenciled on the door.

She waited for Valya to show herself.

Each second grew longer than the last.

C'mon . . .

Finally, the door opened. Voices carried to her. The first to appear was not Valya, but a hulking figure in body armor. The escort had a pistol in hand and an assault rifle slung behind him. He stiffened as he spotted Seichan down on a knee, with a weapon aimed his way.

Shock slowed him for a fraction of a heartbeat.

But even that was too long.

Seichan pulled the trigger. The explosion of the rocket's exhaust gasses deafened. Blue-gray smoke burst behind her. The grenade launched out the tube, traveling a hundred meters a second.

The gunman had no time to blink. The grenade hit the half-open door. The detonation blew his body into armored pieces. Black smoke blasted into the hallway.

Seichan threw the launch tube aside and burst forward, like a sprinter off a starting block. As she closed the distance, she slipped a dagger into a hand and pulled her SIG Sauer into her other grip. She ducked low through the smoke and spun past the shattered ruins of the doorway. Fires flickered all around her, casting up embers as she passed.

As she continued into the apartment, a breeze blew toward her, shredding the swirling mix of dust and smoke around her.

Damn it . . .

She knew what that must mean. She dove headlong to the left. A barrage of rounds tore where she had been. But that wasn't her main concern.

She hit the floor and shoulder-rolled into a low crouch. She spotted the source of the breeze. An open window fluttered with drapes. Past its sill, a dark figure hung from a rappelling line.

Valya.

It appeared Gray wasn't the only one with an emergency exit plan.

The woman slipped down the rope, vanishing from view.

Seichan rushed to the window and ducked her head out. She caught the barest glimpse of Valya sailing down, using her legs as brakes, one gloved hand on the line. The woman leaned back and fired up at her.

Forced away, Seichan lifted her SIG's sights to her eyeline and

waited for a breath. Valya was armed with an assault rifle, an un-
wieldy weapon when fired one-handed. The recoil from the barrage
would worsen that aim.

With rounds still bursting past the window, Seichan leaned out and
fired down at her target. By now, Valya had descended four floors,
making for a harder target. Even worse, the woman's body swung
wildly on the line, either purposefully or due to the gunplay.

Most of Seichan's rounds missed, but one bullet struck Valya's
shoulder, nearly tearing her off her rope. Valya lost her rifle, but she
snatched the line in a two-handed grip to secure her roost.

Recognizing a clean shot was unlikely, Seichan holstered her pistol,
reached out, and grabbed the rappelling line. She pulled the rope closer
and attacked it with her knife. She sawed with the blade's serrated edge.
One stroke cleared the outer sheath. The inner nylon weave proved
tougher. Still, her finely honed Japanese steel cut deep with every saw
stroke.

The line suddenly yanked in her grip, ripping free of her fingers.

She looked down.

Valya swung wide from the building, rappelling off the wall to gain
that distance.

Seichan cursed, suspecting the other's intent. She caught the rope
again as Valya's body rocked back toward the building. With two more
strokes, the line snapped and snaked away. But it was too late.

From the corner of her eye, she watched Valya dive feetfirst into an
apartment six stories below. Its window had clearly been left open, part
of Valya's emergency exit plan.

Seichan spun away, fearing the worst.

Knowing Valya, once she was safe and off the line, the assassin would
have an additional countermeasure in place if she ever had to use that
escape route.

Seichan raced through the smoke and growing fires from the grenade
blast. She hit the hallway at full sprint. She rebounded off the opposite
wall and sped away. Behind her, a deafening explosion tore through the
apartment, shaking the floor under her. Debris blasted into the hallway.

She kept running, praying that was it.

She hit the stairwell door and headed down. She knew she had no chance of closing in on Valya. Sirens echoed, coming from every direction. They all had to get clear of the area.

Still, Seichan took a circuitous path, crossing various floors and descending other stairs. Once halfway down, she called up an elevator, climbed atop its cage through a ceiling hatch, and rode it into the basement, where a three-level parking garage spread beneath the complex.

From there, she made her escape.

Amidst the chaos, she easily cleared the cordon of arriving police, ambulances, and fire trucks. She continued across the city, heading for the team's secondary safehouse, their fallback position. Behind her, helicopters buzzed the smoky column rising from the battlefield.

She scowled back, knowing this was only the opening volley of a greater war to come. She pictured Valya vanishing into the building and made a promise.

Next time, one of us won't be walking away.

Still, Seichan acknowledged another outcome, one that was just as possible—and maybe always fated to be.

She coldly accepted this, too.

Or neither of us will walk away.

THIRD

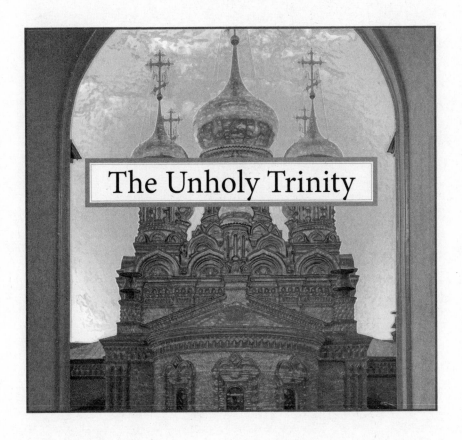

The Unholy Trinity

17

In the hotel bedroom, Gray whistled appreciatively as he eyed Seichan up and down. "I like this look on you. It's not a wedding dress, but it's definitely flattering."

She scowled and ran her palm down the black clerical robe that enveloped her body. She also wore an apostolnik, a cloth veil that covered her head, neck, and shoulders.

She tied the latter under her chin. "I've worn Muslim hijabs that were less constrictive."

"I'd be happier if we could cover your face, too."

"So you want me in a burqa?" She glanced over to the rumpled state of the bed. "You wanted me in far less clothing last night."

Gray reached an arm around her waist and pulled her close. "I'll take you however I can get you."

She drew against him, showing him exactly what was hidden under all that wool. The curves, the softness, the suppleness. She kissed him, at first gently, a brush of lips, then more passionately, bruising and rough.

Gray pulled back, still tasting her on his tongue. "Is that any way for a novice of the convent to behave?"

"After last night—and again this morning—you know I'm no *novice* at anything."

He glanced over to the bed. "I may need more convincing."

Gray's attempts at levity poorly masked the tension inside him. His fingers still held Seichan's arms. He didn't want to let her go. When she had appeared at the safehouse after the firefight at the embassy, his relief nearly felled him. Fear for Kowalski and the others had also tempered their reunion. Not that they'd had much time. Fearing any further exposure, the group had quickly vacated the site in Moscow and traveled the seventy kilometers to Sergiyev Posad.

Once here, they had checked into a two-century-old establishment: the Staraya Gostinitsa Lavry, or Old Lavra Hotel. It was ideally positioned, overlooking the front gate into the Holy Trinity Lavra. Due to the hotel's proximity, the sprawling, yellow-plastered building had served as a pilgrim's rest stop since its founding—and continued to do so today. According to Bishop Yelagin, many priests, monks, and nuns took up residence here, offering convenient access to the Lavra's many churches.

Yelagin and Sister Anna had secured the group's suite of adjoining rooms, then helped whisk the others inside—even Kane, who posed as a seeing-eye dog.

A knock at the door interrupted them. "Commander Pierce," Tucker called through, "Anna returned. Along with three of her sisters. We need to head out."

"We'll be there in a moment," Gray answered him.

He and Seichan shared a long look, and he kissed her again. "Keep your head down," he whispered afterward.

"I'll do my best to stay out of trouble."

"No, I mean *really* keep your head down." He pointed to the floor. "While you're all covered up, we don't want anyone spotting your face."

The plan was for Seichan to pose as a nun. With her head piously bowed, few should note her presence. The Russian Orthodox Church was staunchly patriarchal, even more so than its Catholic counterpart. Gray hoped Anna was right about people taking little notice of nuns. According to her, most people's gazes glossed over a nun's black garb, ignoring the woman under the habiliment.

"I should get going," Seichan sighed out, looking equally reluctant to leave.

After so short a time together, it was hard to separate again. She would be accompanying the trio of nuns, burying herself amongst them. The cloaked group would be trailed by Yuri and Tucker, along with Kane.

Their goal was to circle the Lavra's grounds. Archpriest Sychkin maintained a residence in an old family mansion on the far side. Seichan's group would circumspectly inspect the site, looking for any evidence that their captured members—Kowalski, Dr. Stutt, and Marco—had been taken there. According to what Seichan had overheard on her stolen radio, the botanist was to be hauled here, taken to Sychkin. The hope was that the other two would also be close at hand.

Gray had instructed Seichan's group not to engage, simply to surveil. Once confirmation was made that the others were at the mansion, then they'd put an extraction team together and attempt a rescue.

Until then . . .

He studied Seichan. In the dark of their room last night, he had sensed a desperation in their lovemaking, as if Seichan were trying to eke out every last moment with him. With the lights on now, he recognized the hard cast to her eyes, guarded and wary, and from the pinch at their corners, also anxious.

After reaching the safehouse in Moscow, she had explained why she had left on her own, describing both her tactic to try to ambush Valya and her suspicions about the others in their party. But Gray knew that her act of running off had been as desperate as their lovemaking.

She's fighting for her life—and not just to keep breathing, but to keep the life she made with me, the home and son they shared, for everything.

Valya threatened it all.

Seichan broke eye contact and turned toward the door that led to the suite's salon. "Do you trust that we're not still compromised?"

Gray studied the stiffness in her back, recognizing that she continued to lean on her paranoia, rather than addressing what truly troubled her. He tried his best to assure her. "Both Yelagin and Anna have given us information freely. Intel that we had no access to. From a strategic standpoint, such cooperation makes no sense if they were turncoats."

"What about the Russian?"

"Yuri?"

She looked back at him. "He has no loyalty to us."

"True, but during the embassy attack, he helped rescue Tucker versus simply running off or aiding Valya." Gray shrugged. "Still, I suspect he's keeping cards close to his chest. But I think that's just him being Russian."

Seichan frowned, clearly not satisfied with his assessment.

"The mole might not be any of us," he argued. "Father Bailey admitted that there were a select few in the Holy See who knew we were using their embassy as a safehouse. Not to mention the ambassador himself. And we already know that Monsignor Borrelli dispatched his photos only to us, possibly due to his own suspicions concerning the Vatican."

She stared pointedly at him. "And Bailey hasn't informed anyone in Rome about our location here in Sergiyev Posad or our intentions."

"No. I was adamant with him that we stay dark, and he didn't disagree—though, plainly our suspicions left him unnerved."

Seichan shook her head and concluded this discussion with a warning. "Still, watch your back."

"You do the same."

With the matter resolved for now, they headed toward the door. He wished he could go with her. After arriving at the hotel, Monk had administered a steroid injection and applied a soft splint to Gray's ankle. His mobility was much improved, but he was not at his best.

Still, that wasn't the only issue.

Those remaining behind had their own task to address: to solve a centuries-old puzzle. If the Golden Library was indeed hidden somewhere within the sixty acres of the Lavra, they needed to pin down its location.

But how?

As tired as they all were, no one had the verve to tackle that confounding riddle of ancient scrawls, small pictures, and strange scientific nomenclature. It remained a baffling mystery. But one member of their team had sought to clarify it as best he could, working throughout the night.

Then again, he's a decade younger than any of us.

Gray reached the door. "Let's see if Jason has made any headway."

18

May 12, 7:34 A.M. MSK
Sergiyev Posad, Russian Federation

This is going to give me an aneurysm . . .

Jason ignored the chatter from the main salon as he worked at a desk in a bedroom. He had a laptop open before him, flanked by two digital tablets. Three crushed cans of Yaguár—the Russian equivalent of Red Bull—lay toppled by his elbow.

He tapped a stylus on the desktop as he glared at the laptop's screen. The image that had confounded him all night glowed in the darkened room.

Earlier in the night, he had managed to strip away more of the frontispiece's overlaying sketch of the golden book and the Trinity Lavra, enhancing what lay underneath to a slighter degree.

It hadn't helped.

He took a sip from his fourth can of Yaguár, wishing it was the alcoholic version of the energy drink.

Maybe getting drunk would help make sense of this.

For the thousandth time, he studied the arcane writing, all surrounding a compass rose that might or might not be important. He shook his head, refusing to second-guess himself. He had come to a few conclusions overnight, just not enough to put the pieces together.

A voice cleared behind him. He stiffened in surprise and glanced over his shoulder. Gray stood there, leaning down, scrutinizing his handiwork.

Even with a bum ankle, the guy moved like a shadow.

"I see you've made some progress," Gray noted.

Jason stretched his arms, then let them drop in defeat. "But little else."

"You're likely too close to the problem by now. Can't see the forest through the trees."

"Maybe."

Gray pointed to the suite's salon. "Sometimes it helps to talk it out. To share what you might have discerned."

Jason groaned, not in refusal, but in exhaustion. He gathered his laptop and tablets and followed Gray into the neighboring room.

The salon had a cluster of sofas, a bar with a minifridge—well stocked with Yaguár—and a large television. But the room's main attraction was its tall bank of windows that offered a breathtaking view of the Trinity Lavra.

Only a hundred yards away, the monastery's towering white walls glowed in the morning light. A dozen watchtowers, roofed in green slate, dotted its mile-long circumference. Within the grounds itself, bell towers, domes, and onion-topped spires—shining in gold or painted in bright blue—protruded into the sky. It all looked like something out of a fairytale, ethereal and majestic.

Yet, somewhere in those sixty acres awaited a greater wonder still to be discovered.

Hopefully . . .

Jason turned his back on the view and crossed to the salon's dining table. He was surprised to find only Monk and Father Bailey, along with the two Russian clergy—Bishop Yelagin and Sister Anna—in attendance. Focused on his work, he hadn't even noticed that the others had left on their own assignment, to search for those taken by Valya.

Jason grimaced. Worry for Kowalski and Elle, even Marco, had plagued his concentration. He read the same anxiety in Monk's and Gray's faces. Guilt flared through him.

They're all stuck here, waiting on me to come up with a solution.

Gray waved to the table. "Show the others your work."

"It's not much," Jason admitted. "I was able to clean up that front page and bring out more of the faded writing."

He showed them the result.

The group gathered for a closer look.

"What do you make of it?" Monk asked, leaning on the table.

Jason sighed. "Either it's all gibberish, intentionally written to mislead, or it's too complicated for me to figure out."

Anna gave him a consoling look. "Or it might take someone from the eighteenth century to even understand its intent. We may be missing the context here."

Gray turned to Jason. "What's your assessment? Is what's written here nonsense? Could we be spinning our wheels?"

Jason swallowed, knowing the others were counting on him. "No. I don't believe so. All these scribbles must be clues to the location of the library. I'm sure of it. It's just an exceptionally *hard* puzzle. Plus, we may be missing clues that have faded into obscurity."

"If so, then we're never going to solve it," Monk groused.

Gray ignored him and focused on Jason. "Have you come to any other conclusions after working all night?"

"Maybe." Jason took a deep breath, hoping his assessment wasn't about to lead everyone down a rabbit hole. "During the night, I got to wondering *why* sections of this page were blocked out by the golden book and the sketch of the Lavra. Why would they do that? It took all my skills—and Kat's back in D.C.—to strip away those layers to reveal what was obviously hidden on purpose."

Gray's eyes narrowed. "Do you have any guesses? About why that compass and other pieces were overwritten?"

"I have a theory." Jason pointed to the compass rose. "I think that's the answer to the puzzle, to the location of the Golden Library. It's right there. Or at least a simplified version of it." With growing certainty, he straightened his back. "I believe someone drew that compass, one that points to the library's location—then got cold feet."

Father Bailey glanced at him. "What do you mean by cold feet?"

"I think someone—someone likely brilliant—concluded that this first encryption was too *easy* to solve, so they covered it up, and constructed a more convoluted puzzle around it, one that would challenge all but the greatest minds."

Jason stared around the table, daring anyone to discount his theory.

Gazes returned to the screen as everyone considered his words.

Gray simply picked up one of the tablets and tapped at its screen.

Monk shook his head. "This compass is the *easy* version of the puzzle?"

Jason shrugged and glanced at Anna. "Maybe for someone in the eighteenth century."

The nun leaned close to the screen, squinting at the page, as if struggling with something.

What is she doing?

Gray drew back Jason's attention. The commander pointed at a few icons drawn in various spots on the page. "Jason, can you bring up these small drawings onto my tablet?"

"Not a problem." He picked up a stylus and stepped to the laptop.

Sister Anna shifted out of his way. As she did, she retrieved the second tablet from the table. "May I?" she asked him.

"Of course."

While Jason set to work, the nun joined Bishop Yelagin and whispered in Russian, clearly consulting with him about something.

Jason used his stylus to circle the icons that Gray had pointed out. He had chosen tiny sketches of what appeared to be onion-shaped images in varied levels of detail. They were spread across the page, but Jason lined them up in a row and dispatched them to Gray's tablet.

Monk and Father Bailey stared over Gray's shoulder at the small icons.

"What are you thinking?" Monk asked.

Gray lowered the tablet and returned to the laptop. "That drawing in the center of the page. It's *not* a compass."

Jason stepped next to the commander, leaning shoulder to shoulder with him. "Then what is it?"

Gray pointed to a final sketch, just below the center one. "Here is another example of those orb-like drawings. Only this one is slightly more detailed in its functional design."

Monk stared over their shoulders. "That sketch looks like a crude version of the larger one in the center. Like a first attempt at drawing it."

Jason nodded. "But if it's not a compass, what is it?"

Gray turned to them both. "We've seen something like this before. Just a couple years ago." He nodded across to Father Bailey. "You did, too."

Jason shared a confused look with the other two men.

Gray straightened and brought up a new image onto his tablet, one he had already pre-loaded, as he had clearly come to this conclusion when he'd first picked up the tablet.

The picture he showed was of a tarnished brass globe, about the size of a baseball, engraved with symbols and Arabic numbers, all encircled by arched arms and etched bands.

"The hidden sketch on the page is not a compass," Gray impressed upon them. "It's a drawing of a spherical astrolabe, like the one shown here."

Jason understood, appreciating how much the photo matched the 2D sketch.

Anna and Yelagin came over to look, too.

The bishop frowned. "But what does it do?"

Gray explained. "This brass artifact dates to the fifteenth century, to the Middle Ages. It's part cosmic map and part analog computer, one capable of calculating nautical positions."

"But why draw an astrolabe," Yelagin asked, "then hide it?"

"I may know," Anna said, drawing all their eyes. She returned to the laptop and ran a finger around the circumference of the sketched astrolabe. "Mister Carter, there are symbols written along here. Can you make them more discernible?"

"I can try."

He took over her spot and boxed off each symbol, then tasked his AI program to bring those particular icons into better focus, to bring to life any hint of ink in the faded page.

Everyone gathered as the result slowly resolved into view.

Once done, Jason zoomed in on the astrolabe and its surrounding symbols, each one set off in its own assay box.

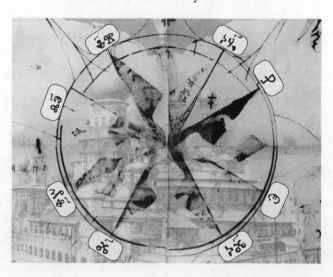

"I still don't get it," Jason admitted. "Those symbols . . . they look like arcane scribbles."

"They're not arcane," Anna explained. "They're just old."

"You recognize the writing?" Gray asked her.

"I do. So would my brother Igor." She lifted a hand and made the sign of the cross in the memory of Monsignor Borrelli. "As part of our studies to become archivists, we were exposed to all forms of Russian script."

"This is Russian?" Monk asked. "But it doesn't look anything like Cyrillic."

"It's not," Anna said. "It's Glagolitic, the oldest known Slavic alphabet, created sometime in the ninth century. It was eventually supplanted by Cyrillic. Though, many of Russia's oldest religious texts can still be found written in Glagolitic."

"Can you translate these glyphs, Sister Anna?" Bailey asked, half breathless. "Maybe they spell out the name of a church or structure."

"I should be able to, but from the little that I was able to discern earlier, I think they're mostly *numbers*, not letters."

Jason remembered her consulting with the bishop a moment ago.

Anna continued, "During the reign of Peter I—Peter the Great— Russia changed from Cyrillic numerals to the more common Arabic numbering system, to match the Europeans." She pointed to the screen. "Centuries prior to that, though, Glagolitic numerals were used."

Gray nodded. "Then whoever encoded this cipher, they had clearly wanted someone to know Russia's history, a history even further back than Peter the Great, to solve it."

Anna lifted her tablet toward Jason. "Mister Carter, if you can help me, I have a conversion chart. We should be able to quickly transpose these Glagolitic symbols into their modern equivalent."

"Gladly."

Working together, comparing the chart in hand to the symbols on the screen, Jason replaced each glyph with its corresponding equivalent. He stepped back and allowed everyone to see.

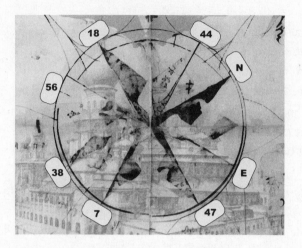

"No wonder the designers hid this work." Jason smiled. "It is rather simple."

"Perhaps for you, young man," Yelagin scolded.

Jason shifted back to his computer. In a corner of the screen, he lined up the Glagolitic symbols, splitting them into two halves, corresponding to the upper and lower hemispheres of the astrolabe—then matched them with their corresponding translation.

He showed his work to Yelagin.

$$\text{ᲠᲑ} \quad \text{ᲤᲶ} \quad \text{ᲜᲥ} \quad \text{Გ}$$
$$\quad 56 \qquad 18 \qquad 44 \qquad N$$

$$\text{ᲚᲤ} \quad \text{ᲝᲑ} \quad \text{ᲜᲥ} \quad \text{Ე}$$
$$\quad 38 \qquad 7 \qquad 47 \qquad E$$

"They're longitude and latitude designations," Jason explained. "Nautical positioning like you might work out with a spherical astrolabe."

Monk's brow furrowed. "But does it truly mean anything? Did our counterparts in the eighteenth century have accurate enough measurements to be of any use to us today?"

Gray answered, studying his tablet. He must have researched this very question before Jason had finished clarifying matters for the bishop. "Catherine the Great was a great advocate of science and innovation. By her time, latitudes were easily calculated and had been for millennia, all the way back to the ancient Phoenicians. Determining longitudes had been more problematic, requiring precise timepieces. It wasn't until John Harrison, a clockmaker from Yorkshire, developed the marine chronometer that longitudes could be accurately worked out. That was in the middle of the eighteenth century."

"So, a new invention of Catherine's time," Bailey said, "which, considering the empress's interest in the sciences, would have garnered her attention."

"But what about the prime meridian?" Monk asked. "Our longitudes are based on the one passing through Greenwich in London."

"True," Gray said. "It became the de facto standard a century later, but it was Harrison who recommended that the meridian be set at the longitude of the Royal Observatory in Greenwich—where it remains today."

"Why there?" Bailey inquired.

Gray smiled. "Harrison invented his chronometer to win a prize of twenty thousand pounds. It was offered by the English Parliament to anyone who could invent a practical method for determining longitudes. Britain's chief astronomer handed Harrison his prize money— during a ceremony held at the Royal Observatory."

"And that's why he picked the location for his meridian," Monk mumbled.

"It makes sense that Catherine would follow his example," Anna added. "Besides being an advocate for the advancement of science, she was also an Anglophile. She would've found this discovery astounding and would have likely adhered to the standards set by the British inventor."

Gray turned to the puzzle on the laptop's screen. "It's as if Catherine coded her cipher using a combination of science, history, language, and the arts."

Anna nodded. "A true test of all that she loved. She would want only the most brilliant minds to know the location of the Golden Library."

Monk sighed. "Then let's test how brilliant *we* are." He pointed to the tablet in Gray's hand. "Can you pull up the coordinates?"

Gray simply lifted a brow.

Jason knew the commander already had. "Where is it?"

Gray pointed toward the panoramic view. "The coordinates mark a spot along the walls that surround the Lavra."

"If so, that makes sense," Yelagin said. "It was Ivan the Terrible who, back in the sixteenth century, converted the Lavra's old wooden palisades into the stone fortifications that stand today."

"The same Ivan who hid the Golden Library," Jason added.

Monk pressed Gray. "But *where* along that wall do those coordinates point to?"

"At one of its twelve watchtowers. The *Zvonkovaya Bashnya*—or Ringing Tower." Gray lifted his tablet and tapped at it. "I'll pull up a picture."

Once he found one, he passed around his tablet, which showed a stretch of wall with a prominent tower, steepled with what looked like a belfry at the top.

Still playing the skeptic, Monk questioned Gray. "But how can we be certain that's the place?"

The answer came from Yelagin, who, after viewing the photo, had

returned to the laptop. "Because of a unique aspect of the Lavra's towers. All twelve are different—varying in size and shape—depending on
their specific use."

"Why's that significant?" Monk asked.

"Because it appears someone left us a clue. In case there was any
doubt."

The bishop pointed to a small sketch on the lower right of the page
on the screen. It showed a crude sketch of a tower that bore a strong
resemblance to the one in the photo. In the foreground, a robed figure—
maybe a monk—was drawn running toward it, as if late to ring that
steeple's bell.

"That must be the place," Gray said.

Monk nodded. "You'll hear no argument from me."

About time, Jason thought.

Still, this raised a concern of his own. "Where could someone hide a
vast library in that tower? One that's remained lost for centuries?"

Gray stared out toward the glorious spread of the Trinity Lavra.
"Only one way to find out."

19

Hiking along a trail through the wooded park, Tucker kept an eye on the clutch of black-robed women strolling along another path. Even knowing Seichan was one of the four, he could not pick her out.

The group moved with a silky brush of their robes, and though they kept a decorous stride, they spoke animatedly in Russian, often waving an arm back toward the Lavra's towering walls behind them or pointing at the spring flowers poking their buds out of the damp soil.

Just tourists appreciating the sights.

Their two routes paralleled each other, both aiming for the next street.

"That's the place, *da*?" Yuri whispered next to him. "Up ahead."

Tucker frowned at the hulking man, not because he was wrong, but because Yuri had been instructed to speak only Russian. They both wore green military fatigues, including matching berets. The plan was to blend in as two soldiers on leave. Yuri accentuated his disguise with a half-empty vodka bottle gripped by its stem.

Tucker had his own accessory to help maintain his cover. He held Kane's leash. The Russian army employed its own cadre of military working dogs, many of them Malinois. Kane was already wearing his vest, which to the casual eye looked like a stout harness. In addition to the visual look, the presence of Kane went a long way in discouraging any bystanders from approaching too closely or challenging Tucker's fluency in Russian. A stern nod from him had proved good enough so far.

Tucker responded to Yuri, subvocalizing to demonstrate the throat mike. "Yes, that's Sychkin's house directly ahead."

"*Da, o verno*," Yuri whispered, chagrined.

Ahead, at the corner of Ilyinskaya Street, a five-story brick mansion rose above the tree line. It was crowned by a steepled tower with mullioned windows facing the Trinity Lavra. The house sat on an acre of gardens. It had once been a *dacha*, a Russian country home—until eventually, the town grew around it.

The mansion was the residence of Leonid Sychkin, going back generations in his family. During the Soviet era, many of the rural *dachas* had been taken over and turned into communal living quarters, but not this place. Stalin had granted an exception to the Sychkin family. Mostly due to the largesse of Leonid's grandfather, who had gifted Stalin with one of the family's other *dachas*, one outside of Saint Petersburg.

Tucker had learned much of the family's history from the trio of nuns—sisters Uliana, Maria, and Natalia—who escorted Seichan. Having grown up here, they had no love for Stalinist partisans. Worst of all, none of them believed Leonid had come into his faith from a true calling, but more out of lust for greed and power, drawn by the new money flowing into the orthodox church's coffers and the resurgent patriarchate's growing status.

If so, Sychkin's interest in lost libraries and mythic continents made sense.

If Russia's star rises, so would his.

Reaching the edge of the park, Tucker stepped out onto the sidewalk, but he kept to the shadows of a maple tree. Closer now, he could discern the scaffolding and ladders around the mansion. The roof slates looked new. Several windows were temporarily boarded over, waiting to be replaced. The steeple had a shining layer of fresh gold-leaf, as if trying to rival the Lavra's gilded onion domes.

And clearly the work was ongoing.

Tucker frowned.

No way this costly renovation was done on an archpriest's salary.

He wagered Sychkin must be skimming off the generous flow of funds that were filling the coffers of the orthodox church. No wonder the nuns were so upset with the guy.

Tucker glanced down the street as those same women exited the park, stopping thirty yards to his right. He still couldn't tell which one was his teammate. Valya might be a master of disguises, using her pale face as a blank canvas, but Seichan was clearly equally skilled in such deceptions.

He radioed Seichan, rubbing his chin to further hide any movement of his lips. "We're all set here."

"The limo out front," she warned. "It's the same vehicle that Gray and I had spotted at the monastery ruins."

Tucker had also noted the stretch limousine. It was parked before the fence's ornate iron gate.

Then Sychkin must be inside.

The plan was for each group to set off in opposite directions and canvass the mansion as best they could. Cobblestoned alleyways, bordered by tall brick walls, ran behind and to the right of the building, separating the estate from its neighbors.

Seichan and her group headed toward the mouth of the alleyway to the right. She would inspect the house's front, too. Tucker and Yuri would surveil the mansion's left flank and the rear of the structure.

Their goal was to search for any evidence that the captured group had been brought here. The team had been ordered to do nothing more. If the others were here, Seichan's group would continue their surveillance—then, after nightfall, a rescue effort would be made to extract them.

Tucker's jaw tightened. While he recognized the need for caution, he chafed at the constraints, uncomfortable with having to follow orders. Then again, he had been taught a hard lesson last night. He pictured Kowalski being dragged off and Elle guarding over Marco. If there was any chance of rescuing them, he couldn't go it alone.

Not here, not in broad daylight, not with a military encampment nearby, stationed to protect the Lavra.

Tamping down his frustration, Tucker set off with Kane, trailed by Yuri. He reached the corner, noting Seichan's group had stopped by the entrance to the far alley. They chattered amongst themselves, unfolding a map. Though Tucker could not discern Seichan, he had no doubt she was studying the narrow cobblestone lane and her half of the mansion.

Tucker continued along the opposite side. The sidewalk was deeply shaded by the crowns of old rowan trees, a species revered by Russians, believed to have magical properties. The trunk of one of the nearest had grown past the garden's iron bars, swallowing the spars into its bark. It spoke to the age of the mansion and its grounds.

Unfortunately, the canopies occluded the view of the home's upper levels, but Tucker imagined that if his friends had been hauled here, they wouldn't be locked up high. While pretending to take a swig from Yuri's vodka bottle, he surreptitiously eyed the first floor and the half-sunken basement windows.

Most of the curtains were drawn, which further frustrated him.

He passed the bottle back and continued down the sidewalk. A bricked lot covered the rear of the building, with a six-car garage at the far end. A pair of large SUVs—Mercedes G-wagons—were parked near the steps at the back. One flight headed up to the door on the main level, another led down toward the basement.

Tucker could get no closer to inspect the vehicles or the mansion's rear. Tall electric gates closed off the parking lot.

But he didn't need to.

Kane whined next to him, lifting his nose high, pointing his muzzle toward the gate. That was enough.

"Good boy," Tucker whispered and added, "STAND DOWN."

This rescinded Kane's prior order: SCENT MARCO.

Tucker knew that if Marco had been hauled all the way here, the dog would need to relieve himself after the journey, going for the nearest post or bush.

Kane—who had lived for the past eight months with his new brother, eating, sleeping, playing, and training with the young Malinois—knew Marco's scent as well as he did Tucker's.

With this confirmation, Tucker continued past the gate. Kane followed with him, but the shepherd glanced over a shoulder with the faintest rumble of complaint.

Right there with you, brother. He patted Kane. *Don't worry, we're not leaving Marco behind.*

Tucker radioed Seichan. "They're here. Kane caught Marco's scent, like I told you he would. I'll meet you at—"

She cut him off. "Stay in position."

Tucker slowed as he reached the mouth of the back alley. "Why?"

"Sister Uliana suggested we make a house call."

"Why?"

"To go begging for funds for their convent. Apparently, they do that a lot. It seems little of that new orthodox money ends up with them. They've approached Sychkin in the past and been rebuffed. So, what's one more attempt?"

Tucker balked. "We were told to back off after we had confirmation."

He could almost hear Seichan shrug. "This will give me a chance to look inside. Assess the security and manpower. Until then, stay close."

He didn't have to ask *why* again.

He motioned to Yuri and drew him into the alley.

"*Chto sluchilos'?*" Yuri asked, remembering to speak Russian this time.

From the security chief's worried expression, the translation was easy.

What's wrong?

Tucker tried to stare through the brick wall and mansion to its front stoop.

"We're about to find out."

8:32 a.m.

Seichan climbed the steps toward a wide stone porch. She followed behind Uliana, Maria, and Natalia and kept her head bowed.

It was Sister Uliana—a scrappy seventy-two-year-old—who had suggested this course of action. Seichan had balked at involving them, but Uliana had waved away her concern with a mischievous glint in her dark eyes. The other two had nodded vigorously in agreement. While still paranoid, Seichan had sensed no deception in these women, only impish glee.

They must really detest Sychkin . . . or maybe they watched The Sound of Music *too many times.*

Regardless of the reason, Seichan wanted a peek inside—and not just with her eyes. She also palmed a matte-black spherical listening device. If given the opportunity, she would roll it across the threshold into a dark corner of the mansion's vestibule. While her team had secured the mansion's floorplans, the blueprints offered no intel on the level of security inside.

Time to find out.

Uliana led their brigade through the garden gate and up to the front doors, which were carved out of oak, patinaed darkly by age, and studded in iron. The nun pressed a buzzer. Chimes echoed out to them.

As they waited, Seichan noted a security camera and kept her face turned away. She shifted closer to the hinges and stayed behind Natalia's shoulders.

Loud footsteps reached them through the thick wood. A moment later, the door swung open. A huge figure filled the doorway, blocking the view. The giant was dressed in an ankle-length black cassock, the same as he had been wearing before, but he had shed his cap, showing black hair shorn in a pious tonsure. His exposed scalp formed the shape of a cross.

Even Uliana knew the commanding figure. "Brother Yerik," she greeted him in Russian, offering a slight bow. "I see from the limo that the Reverend Archpriest Sychkin has graced our town once again. We were hoping to beseech his generosity. Our need has grown most dire."

Seichan tried not to roll her eyes.

Yerik merely stared under heavy brows. The left side of his face and neck were scarred and pocked from an old burn. Seichan had heard about his past with an apocalyptic cult. His small black eyes took in the women, showing little regard for them. He lifted a palm, plainly telling them to remain on the stoop.

Seichan pictured his use of sign language back at the monastery. He was plainly continuing his vow of silence here, too.

He turned his back and stepped away, clearing the doorway.

Finally . . .

Past the foyer, which was darkly paneled and lit by gas wall sconces, a long hallway crossed the length of the building. Bulky men in black suits stood guard before a door at the far end. She also spotted the glowing eyes of security cameras high on the walls, both along the hall and in the parlors to either side.

She leaned down as if to scratch a knee.

With Yerik's back to her, she rolled her listening device across the threshold, aiming for a pedestal that supported a marble figure of the Virgin Mary. She quickly lost sight of it as it vanished into the shadows.

Unfortunately, something was far more eagle-eyed and noted the intrusion.

A siren burst across the mansion, winding into a screeching wail. Her bug's electronics must have tripped off a counterintelligence scanner inside.

Seichan swung around, pushed the shocked trio of nuns back, and pointed toward the steps. "Go!"

To buy the others time, Seichan did what she had wanted to do all along.

She rushed low across the threshold and ducked into a side parlor.

She radioed Tucker.

"Looks like we're done hiding."

20

Gray followed their tour guide across the expanse of the religious wonderland. Sister Anna led the way, walking backward with a clipboard in her hand. Bishop Yelagin came outfitted in the vestments of his office, including a silver-plated staff topped by a cross. He nodded piously as the nun extolled about the Lavra's history with much drama.

She spoke in Russian, but the team's earpieces translated her words. Monk and Jason flanked Gray. All of them were bundled into jackets, scarves, and hats against the crisp spring morning. The clothing also helped mask them.

Father Bailey was similarly attired, but with a white Roman collar showing above his scarf. He scanned the spread of baroque churches with wide eyes, looking astounded.

"A *lavra*," Anna instructed everyone, continuing her role as guide, "was originally a term used to describe a monastery formed by a cluster of caves where hermits or monks would seclude themselves, usually with a small church at its center. Later, such a designation was only given to monasteries of great importance, true cultural centers."

She waved an arm to encompass the breadth of the sixty acres. "Like the Trinity Lavra here. It was founded in 1337 by the monk Sergius of Radonesh, our most venerated Russian saint. Back then, the site was little more than what it was originally termed: a group of caves—with a few sacred springs—surrounding a small wooden church built by Saint Sergius."

She kissed her fingertips and lifted her hand high in thanks, then pointed to a white basilica topped by golden domes and onion-shaped towers. "In 1422, the wooden church was replaced by a stone one— The Holy Trinity Cathedral. Inside, you'll find the relics of Saint Sergius and icons painted by Russia's most esteemed medieval artists."

She stared meaningfully at Gray. "Unfortunately, you'll not be able to visit there today, as the cathedral is closed to the public for a special project."

Gray understood. Sychkin's team from the Arkangel Society must be excavating beneath such an important landmark.

And not just there.

Anna sighed with a mournful expression. "Alas, such work is also being done at the Church of the Holy Spirit, built by Ivan the Third in the fifteenth century." She nodded toward a smaller, squat church with an onion dome of bright blue and adorned with gold stars. "And sadly, the same is true of the Cathedral of the Assumption, which was constructed by Ivan the Fourth in the sixteenth century."

Gray could appreciate Sychkin's interest in those two buildings. *Ivan the Great* had secured the Golden Library, and his grandson *Ivan the Terrible* had hid it away.

So, of course, the archpriest would pick such places to search.

Anna drew them onward. They continued across the sprawling religious complex, aiming for a site far to the right of the Lavra's main gates. So far, Sychkin had shown no interest in the *Zvonkovaya Bashnya*—the Ringing Tower—a relatively nondescript structure among the baroque richness of the monastic complex.

Still, *another* belltower had drawn the archpriest's attention.

They circled past the Lavra's tallest structure. A blue-and-white tower speared three hundred feet into the sky. Its conch-shaped golden belfry shone brightly in the morning light. Under it lay one of those sacred cave springs, said to have been summoned forth by Saint Sergius himself.

But no one will be sipping from those holy waters today.

Currently, the belltower's entrance was cordoned off, guarded by a cadre of Russian soldiers with assault rifles. So, either an excavation was underway, or one was about to be started.

Anna led them past the tower and over to a tree-lined street, paved in bricks. The crowd of tourists dwindled around them. This corner of the Lavra was devoted to a theological academy. Three hundred monks still worked and lived here, maintaining the Lavra as a working monastery. Such academic pursuits drew little interest from the public.

Away from the crowds, Anna halted her act as a guide. There remained only a few people idling around this section's meditative gardens. She led their group toward the towering white walls that surrounded the Lavra.

The Ringing Tower rose directly ahead of them.

Gray searched, but he spotted no military presence. Clearly Sychkin had not solved the riddle drawn in the old Greek text.

But will we fare any better once we're inside?

Gray crossed with the others, passing by a small fire station to reach the tower's entrance. His left ankle throbbed in his boot. He had swallowed several tablets of ibuprofen, but the long walk challenged the meds' effectiveness.

To distract himself, Gray inspected the tower's four white tiers, all rising to a green-tiled belfry, some sixty feet above. Its elegant façade, decorated with arches and pilasters, was pierced by arrow slits, a reminder of the era when the Lavra needed such fortifications. Still, when this tower's bell would ring out during the eighteenth century, it was not to warn against intruders, but to mark the beginning and end of classes held at the Trinity Seminary, a theological school that continued to this day.

"We can enter through here," Anna said.

She drew everyone toward stone steps that led up to an archway. The tower's stout door stood open, but a small souvenir shop next to it was shuttered, a testament to the lack of interest in this remote corner of the Lavra.

They all crossed through the archway and into a cavernous entry hall. The white plaster walls and vault of the roof were decorated with a few faded frescoes of haloed figures. A single wall sconce cast a sad, bluish hue over the space.

"Looks like we have the tower to ourselves," Bailey noted, staring around the deserted space.

Jason frowned. "Just as well. We have no clue where to even begin looking for a lost library."

Bishop Yelagin inspected an alcove to the right, where a stone staircase spiraled upward. A rope closed off access to the heights.

"I don't hear any footsteps or see any lights up there." Yelagin brushed cobwebs from the velvet rope with his silver staff. "Definitely looks undisturbed."

Gray stepped to the opposite side, to another alcove, only this one's staircase led down. "If there's a library here, one that's remained undiscovered after so many centuries, it's likely under us."

He unhooked the rope barrier, careful not to disturb the dust, lest it give away that they had passed this way.

Monk headed down first, withdrawing a flashlight from his pack. "Nothing creepy about exploring a tower dungeon."

Jason followed next, trailed by Anna, Yelagin, and Bailey.

Gray took up the rear, resecuring the rope behind him as he set off down the winding staircase. He also deployed his own flashlight. Underfoot, the steps had been worn smooth, slightly depressed in the center, eroded by centuries of sandals traversing up and down. The walls were initially made of brick, part of the tower's foundations, but they eventually turned to raw limestone.

"How far down does this go?" Monk asked, his disembodied voice echoing up from the turns below.

"Each tower is different," Yelagin answered him. "This one had a wine cellar beneath it, where the monks stored hundreds of casks, enough to serve the whole compound."

"That may be why it's so deep." Anna ducked her head from the low roof. "Summers can be stifling, and winters bitter. But underground, an even temperature would protect the wine."

"And maybe *books*, too," Bailey astutely added.

Gray glanced up the steps. He pictured the religious school that was still operating as it had been during the time of Ivan the Terrible. *Had the tsar picked this site due to its proximity to that place of learning?* He remembered how Ivan had employed scores of scholars to translate the old books. If he ever wished to reopen his library, having it located here, steps from a school of higher learning, would make sense.

"Finally," Monk called back, clearly having reached the bottom.

They all wound down to him, spilling into a vaulted space carved out of the limestone. Someone had tiled the floor long ago, but it was cracked and aged, pocked with missing sections, showing raw rock. Niches had been carved into the walls, possibly to secure the most precious casks of wine.

Jason slowly circled in place. "I wonder if this could've been one of the caves that the monks had used during the Lavra's founding."

"It could be," Anna admitted.

Monk cast his flashlight's beam around. "If so, then they must have believed in communal living. It's a regular maze down here."

Other limestone caves—or wine grottos—extended in every direction, spreading past the reach of their lights.

"If we hope to search this place in a timely manner," Gray said, "we'll have to—"

"Don't say it," Monk pleaded with him.

Gray ignored him. "We'll have to split up."

Gray checked his watch and looked upward, remembering his team wasn't the only one on a mission. He imagined that Seichan and Tucker must have completed their canvass of Sychkin's mansion by now, but he had no way to confirm. Their radios had lost signal after descending into the wine cellars.

He stared toward the maze.

I hope they're having better luck than us.

21

May 12, 8:44 A.M. MSK
Sergiyev Posad, Russian Federation

Kowalski cringed as an alarm blared throughout the mansion. The sound ate into his skull—which still felt cracked after being battered inside the trash bin last night. It had left him bruised all over. His neck still had a throbbing kink to it.

He grimaced and rose from his cell's cot. He did his best to shrug off his aches and pains.

Eh, I've had worse hangovers.

Knowing something was wrong, he stepped over to the metal door. A tiny, barred window allowed him to peek out into the next room. When he had been hauled down here in the wee hours of the morning, along with Elle and Marco, he had done his best to get his bearings. He had noted a boiler room, running with copper pipes, then they had descended another level, to some subbasement dungeon, maybe part of a secret S&M club.

The latter was suggested by the handcuffs hanging from chains bolted to the wall.

At least, I hope it's a sex club.

Out in the hallway, a broad-shouldered man in a black suit guarded the steps that led up to the boiler level. The bulge under his jacket left no question that he was armed. The siren finally cut off, replaced by muffled gunfire echoing from above.

A trio of figures came rushing down. Two were cloaked and cassocked: a thin man with a prominent black beard and a hulking scar-faced giant.

The third was well known.

Valya Mikhailov scowled, her pale face darkening with anger. She carried her left arm in a sling, her shoulder heavily bandaged.

Someone must've tagged her.

Kowalski could guess who. Prior to the attack on the embassy, he remembered spotting Seichan slipping off and heading to the neighboring apartment building.

Once in the room, Valya grabbed the arm of the older robed figure. "Sychkin, I warned you. You should've let me bring in more of my team."

"No need." The man spoke with a calm assurance. "We're barricaded down here. My security team will deal with the intruders. Plus, we have a contingency plan already in place."

Another five men, all dressed in dark suits, rushed down the steps behind them. They were accompanied by a tall, muscular woman in motorcycle leathers. Her dark hair was drawn back in a ponytail. A thin scar ran across one cheek, from hairline to chin.

Sychkin turned to the cassocked giant, speaking in clipped Russian. Kowalski heard the name *Yerik*, and though he couldn't follow the rest, it was clear the man was being ordered to move the prisoners.

Yerik turned to the men and signed to them—which was weird, as the giant had clearly understood his boss, so he wasn't deaf. Maybe mute? No matter, the crew clearly understood, likely having worked with Yerik in the mansion. Pistols were pulled from holsters, and a pair of guards strode toward the next cell. The grating slide of a bar could be heard as the neighboring door was unlocked.

A threatening growl followed.

I feel the same, Marco.

The guards disappeared as they entered the cell. Angry voices were raised, both male and female. A moment later, Elle was led out at gunpoint. She had Marco leashed next to her. Someone had secured a locked muzzle around his snout. Still, the dog frothed and snarled.

Elle kept him close, glaring all around. She looked in rough shape after her ride in the rocket-blasted trash bin. A dark bruise shadowed her chin, and she had multiple bloody scabs marring her face.

Sychkin stepped closer, but not too close. He eyed Marco warily. He withdrew an old book from a satchel hanging over his shoulder. The leatherbound text was covered in flaking gold. Kowalski recognized it from the video of the assault on Red Square, the source of all this mayhem.

As Sychkin opened it and flipped through its pages, he challenged Valya Mikhailov. "What of the other prisoner?"

Valya's eyes swung toward Kowalski's cell. He didn't bother shying from her intent stare. "He was supposed to be bait."

Kowalski inwardly shrugged.

I've been called worse.

Valya stared upward. "But it seems he will no longer be necessary." She turned to the woman decked in leather. "Nadira, before we leave, we should get rid of our extra baggage."

Kowalski scowled.

Okay, that hurt.

Particularly knowing what it meant.

The two approached his door. Nadira pulled out a black pistol, a Russian MP-446 Viking. The weapon typically came with ten to eighteen rounds, not that they'd need that many. Especially as Valya drew forth a steel dagger with a carved black handle.

Kowalski backed up a step.

This ain't going to be pretty.

8:47 a.m.

Tucker crouched between the mansion's six-car garage and the brick wall of the alley. Yuri had taken up a post on the other side of the building. Tucker cradled his pistol between his hands. Two guards lay sprawled across the cobbles in a spreading pool of blood beside the two parked Mercedes SUVs.

He spotted no one else.

Moments ago, when the sirens had blared inside the house, Tucker had ducked down the alley, scaled the wall, and dropped into this sheltered position. Yuri had followed, but Tucker had to leave Kane in the alley with an order to keep hidden. With the mansion's grounds fenced and gated, there had been no time to haul his four-legged partner into this fray.

Without him, Tucker felt half-blind, stripped of his best weapon.

But he had no choice.

"All clear," he radioed Yuri.

Tucker ran into the open, using the bulky vehicles for cover, then ducked behind one of them. So far, no one had sniped at him. All attention must be inside, where a fierce firefight was underway, echoing out to them.

Seichan was offering him plenty of distraction.

But will it do us any good?

Yuri ran low and dropped behind the second Mercedes. "What now?" he called over, not bothering with the radio or speaking in Russian.

Tucker eyed the set of steps leading to a cellar or basement. If the others were being held prisoner, it would be down there. "Cover me. I'm going to strike for the basement door."

"*Da.* Go. I got you."

Tucker dashed for those steps. He was halfway across when automatic gunfire burst from above. Rounds sparked off the brick cobbles. Already committed to this course, he sped faster.

Behind him, Yuri returned fire from his hiding spot. Glass shattered overhead, showering shards across his path. Tucker raced through the sharp rain, hit the stairs, and slammed into the door. Momentarily out of range of the snipers, he looked back.

More gunfire erupted from other spots across the back of the mansion, pinning Yuri down.

"Keep them busy as best you can," Tucker radioed.

He tried the door. It was locked. No surprise there. Having anticipated this, he crawled out of the stairwell and skulked along the mansion's foundation. He reached a row of basement windows. Fearing those closest were likely to be watched, he continued until he spied a dark, enclosed space with bright copper piping.

Boiler room . . .

Good enough.

The basement window was only a couple feet tall. He smashed his elbow through its glass, then used the butt of his pistol to clear the frame of shards. He then belly-slid headfirst into the overheated room.

Once inside, he rolled into a crouch, keeping his pistol pointed toward the door. He waited a few breaths, long enough to reload and to make sure no one had heard his entry.

Satisfied, he headed to the door and pressed his ear. He heard no shouts, no furtive whispers. He reached for the handle—then stopped.

The gunfight continued above, accompanied by cries and barked orders. As he paused, footsteps ran past the door outside. It sounded like five or six men. Archpriest Sychkin must have a small army bivouacked inside the mansion.

Tucker lowered his hand.

One extra person wasn't going to be enough here—not to pull Seichan's butt out of this fire and certainly not to rescue the others.

Earlier, as the sirens blared, Seichan had successfully distracted most of the forces inside, allowing Tucker and Yuri to get into position.

But now the enemy had regrouped, redoubling their effort, putting Seichan in greater danger. Recognizing that, Tucker knew what he had to do.

Return the favor.

To aid Seichan—to help *all* of them—they were going to need a diversion.

A big one.

He swung around and faced the boiler.

That'll do.

8:50 A.M.

Seichan ran low along a hall on the third floor. It was heavily carpeted, the walls richly paneled, hung with paintings of Old World masters. Not that she had time to appreciate the opulence or art.

She carried an AK-15 that she had confiscated. By now, she had nearly emptied the weapon and run through her SIG's two magazines. A deep graze on her thigh bled through the habit she wore.

Ten minutes before, after ducking into the mansion, she had spotted the hulking form of Yerik Raz as he vanished behind a guarded door at the end of the long hallway. She had hoped to make short work of the two guards posted there and pursue him, but the archpriest's forces proved more stubborn and in far greater numbers than she had anticipated.

Overwhelmed, she had been forced into a game of cat-and-mouse across the sprawling wings of the mansion. At times it was a rolling firefight—others, a stealthy hunt.

During one of the lulls, she had heard a fierce gunfight break out across the rear of the mansion. Knowing it had to be aimed at Tucker, she headed there now, to assist him and hopefully combine their forces.

At the end of the hall, a door had been left ajar. She used the toe of her sandal to ease it wider—enough to spot a gunman poised by an open bedroom window, an assault rifle at his shoulder. She also spotted the spare magazines near his knee.

Definitely need those.

She headed over, moving silently. Gunfire erupted from other rooms along this side of the house. She dared not draw attention to this one. A single gunshot might be lost amid the flurry of blasts, but she couldn't take that chance.

She had her rifle slung over her shoulder and carried her new weapon in both hands. She reached the man and dropped the twisted length of her apostolnik—the clerical cloth that had draped her head—over his face and snagged his neck. She spun on a heel, drawing the rope tight, and yanked the man across her back, using his weight to choke him out. He gurgled and thrashed.

Once he went slack, she lowered his body to the floor. She gathered the additional magazines and glanced outside. She spotted Yuri sprinting toward the side of the house. The large man vanished out of sight.

Seichan searched the parking lot below, but there was no sign of Tucker.

Voices rose behind her, along with a pound of boots.

She swung around. A cadre of men rushed toward her. Whether they were reinforcements or she had been spotted on a camera, the end result was the same. Shouts rose. Men flattened against the walls or ducked into side rooms.

She leaped away, shoulder-rolling across the bed, as gunfire burst into the room.

She landed low, near a marble-topped nightstand, and tipped it over. She sheltered behind it and pointed her rifle at the door. She could hold them off for a time, but not forever.

This was made even clearer as a grenade bounced through the doorway.

22

May 12, 8:53 A.M. MSK
Sergiyev Posad, Russian Federation
Elle cringed and ducked as a large blast echoed from above, cutting through the gunplay and momentarily silencing it. She straightened and clutched harder to Marco's leash, keeping the beast between her and the archpriest. The young dog panted, clearly stressed and exhausted.

And he was not the only one under duress.

To the side, Kowalski was marched out of his cell at gunpoint. He held his hands atop his head.

"Down on your knees," Valya ordered him.

"If you're going to shoot me, I'd rather stand. Got bad joints."

The woman behind him—a mercenary named Nadira—looked ready to take him up on that offer. She lifted her pistol toward the back of his head.

"Stop!" Elle yelled.

Sychkin held up a hand. "A moment of patience, please." His eyes never left Elle. "I had hoped for a more leisurely conversation this morning, Dr. Stutt. To convince you to aid us in the days ahead."

"How? How do you think I can help you?" She did her best to look confused, but she knew damned well what he wanted of her.

He raised a leatherbound book. Its cover was leafed in gold. A finger held a page open. He parted it and displayed a spread of drawings that she had been shown before.

Her fingers tightened on Marco's leash.

"What do you make of this?" he pressed her, clearly testing her.

She knew this was an exam she must not fail. Especially as it wasn't only her life in the balance. Recognizing this, she saw no reason to lie.

She peered at the page. "It looks to be a rendition of a *Dionaea muscipula* variant, some carnivorous hybrid or ancestor of the Venus flytrap." She raised her gaze to Sychkin. "Possibly from the lost continent of Hyperborea."

She enjoyed the shocked look on his face.

He turned to Valya. "So, you were right about Monsignor Borrelli spreading the secrets of this book."

"I never doubted it," the pale woman said stiffly. She pointed her black-handled dagger at Kowalski. "As such, it's best we deal with these nuisances before matters sour further."

Sychkin agreed. "Definitely before we discover the Golden Library."

Nadira raised her pistol again.

"Wait," Elle called out.

Sychkin eyed her with irritation.

"If you harm any of them—" She looked down at Marco, then over to Kowalski. "I won't help you."

"I believe I can persuade you otherwise." Sychkin motioned to Yerik. "He can be quite convincing."

The monk remained deadpan and expressionless—which was far more terrifying than some leering threat.

"That . . . that will take time," Elle stuttered nervously. "And I'll serve you far better as a willing participant."

Sychkin lifted a hand and combed fingers through his beard. "I can appreciate that, so I will grant this largesse," he slowly stated. "On one condition."

"What's that?"

"You may pick *one*. To leverage your cooperation. I see no need to keep *both*." He stared hard at her. "You still have some distance to travel today, Dr. Stutt. So, tell me, which of these two will accompany you on this journey?"

She balked at making this decision. From the dark gleam in the arch-priest's eyes, he savored his cruelty.

To delay matters, she pressed the man. "Where are you taking me?"

Apparently, she wasn't the only one wondering this.

Yerik stepped forward with his brows pinched, as if he had the same question. Clearly, this *journey* was news to the monk. Their plans for the day must be rapidly changing due to the attack. Yerik signed to Sychkin with crisp movements of his arms, followed by hand gestures, as if he were spelling something out.

"*Da,*" Sychkin acknowledged him. "I'll have you escort Dr. Stutt, while I oversee the continuing search at the Lavra. Until we deal with these interlopers, I don't think it's wise keeping her so close. Captain Turov can secure her until she's needed." He turned to Elle. "We certainly don't want to lose you again."

Elle swallowed, gripping Marco's leash.

Sychkin's gaze swung between Kowalski and the dog. "Now, back to the matter of your decision, Dr. Stutt."

She backed a step. "I . . . I can't."

He feigned a sympathetic look. "I don't understand. I thought the choice would be an easy one. You'd truly balance a dog's life against this tall fellow?"

She knew the archpriest was right. Still, she stared down at Marco. As if sensing her attention, the shepherd glanced up at her with dark caramel eyes. All night long, Marco had kept beside her, even sharing her cot—but not to sleep. As she drowsed, the dog had never stirred, his head up, his ears tall, guarding over her.

Beyond her affection and appreciation for Marco, she also felt a responsibility for him, especially knowing Tucker's attachment to the dog. Marco was as much a brother to the man as any family member.

Kowalski coughed, drawing her eye, as if to plead his case to pick him. With his arms still above his head, he motioned at her in a strange, palsied manner.

Next to her, Marco whined, his neck stiffening. She stared down. His body trembled all over. She reached to him, but he collapsed under her—first to his chest, then to his side. His legs kicked in a hard convulsion, then went slack.

She dropped beside him. "Marco . . ."

8:57 A.M.

With everyone's attention on the dog, Kowalski lashed out. He swung his raised arm down and slammed his elbow into the woman behind him. He struck Nadira hard in the midriff, aiming for her solar plexus.

As she choked and fell backward, he spun and nabbed the MP-446 Viking from her hand. Kowalski squeezed off three rounds in fast succession, striking the security team gathered behind her before they could react.

Chaos broke out.

Kowalski ducked and whistled, swinging back around.

Marco leaped to his feet, guarding Elle with savage snarls.

The dog was quite the ham.

Tucker had once explained that the best tool of an extraction team— the duo's specialty—was a perfectly timed distraction. Still, when Kowalski had hand-signaled Marco to PLAY DEAD, he hadn't expected the dog to be so dramatic about it. Then again, the exaggerated display was likely purposeful, a tool of distraction when needed.

Kowalski grabbed for Elle's arm.

Unfortunately, such a distraction—even a perfectly timed one— only lasted for so long.

Especially when faced by a skilled opponent.

As Kowalski reached for Elle, Valya lunged forward and drove her dagger through his forearm. He reflexively yanked his limb back, ripping the blade's handle out of her grip.

Disarmed, with her other limb in a sling, Valya bowled into Elle, driving the botanist away from him and into the grip of Yerik.

The huge man snatched an arm around Elle's waist and carried her away, toward a passageway behind them. He used her as a shield, protecting Sychkin, who cowered behind the mute giant.

Valya and Nadira hurried with them.

Kowalski raised his pistol, but he hesitated, fearing he would hit Elle.

Any further choice was taken from him as gunshots ripped around him, coming from the remaining two guardsmen. The pair had collected themselves amidst the chaos.

Forced away from the tunnel, Kowalski backpedaled, returning fire. He retreated into his cell, where he was pinned down.

But his other teammate wasn't.

Marco had withdrawn toward the far passageway, likely still adhering to Tucker's original order to protect Elle—or maybe the dog's instinct to guard the woman was intuitive, born of a bond that had been clearly growing between them.

Either way, the dog was in the line of fire and had no Kevlar vest to protect him.

Kowalski bellowed to Marco, reinforcing Tucker's original command, trusting Elle to keep the dog safe. "GUARD PRIMARY! STAY CLOSE!"

Still, Marco hesitated, shifting on his legs.

"GO ON, DAMN IT!"

It wasn't one of the commands Tucker had taught Kowalski, but it did the job.

Marco spun and headed after Elle.

Kowalski returned his full attention to the two shooters. They had spread out, covering the cell door from two angles, which made one thing clear.

Not getting out of here any time soon.

Which was a problem.

He kept his pistol raised and tried to ignore the blood pouring over the fingertips of his other hand.

Valya's dagger was still impaled through his forearm.

8:59 A.M.

Seichan lay sprawled under the smoking ruins of the bed. She pointed her rifle toward the door. To one side, the nightstand that had sheltered her during the grenade blast was a pile of kindling. Its marble top— two inches thick—had cracked in half, but it had saved her life.

If not my hearing.

Her ears rang in a continual hum.

Following the detonation, she had used the smoke to roll into hiding, turning the ruins of the bed into a makeshift sniper's nest. She now had a direct line of fire through the door. Four bodies lay out in the hall, but there were more combatants, as evidenced by the occasional potshots into the room.

As of yet, between the smoke and her concealment in the bedding, no one had fixed her new position. She bided her time but knew she had to move. Someone would eventually lob another grenade in here.

And I have no other place to hide.

She did, though, have another possible *exit*, but to reach it would leave her exposed. She stared near the door, where a crater had been blasted through the floor to the level below. The opening was barely larger than her waist, all surrounded by jagged floorboards.

She'd prefer not to have to use that escape route.

But I may have no choice.

A buzzing vibration suddenly irritated her left ear, as if a gnat had flown in there.

But it was no annoying fly.

It was her radio earpiece.

Through the ringing from the blast, she made out a few words.

"*. . . where are you?*"

It was Tucker.

She palmed her throat mike, pressing it more firmly. "Third floor. South wing."

She waited for a response, but it either didn't come, or she was deaf to it.

What she did hear was the massive BOOM that shook the entire mansion. The ceiling cracked overhead, shaking down dust. A gout of flames burst up the main stairs at the end of the hall.

One of the combatants fled into view, attempting to escape.

She shot him in the back.

Smoke quickly flooded into the hallway, obscuring everything.

Knowing this would be her best chance, she crawled out of hiding and crossed to the crater in the floor. But the opening was narrower than she had thought.

She dropped to a knee—as a round burned across the crown of her head.

She ducked lower as two combatants ran toward her, shedding the smoke around them.

She swung her rifle up, but two sharp retorts blasted out in the hall.

Both men collapsed, shot from behind.

Through the smoke, Yuri appeared, running forward. His words were muffled, but she made them out. "Been radioing nonstop. Luckily, I was in this wing when you replied."

She pointed to her ears, but before she could explain, Yuri helped her up.

"Need to get going," he said. "Tucker blew the boiler. Flames are spreading fast."

She found her voice. "What about the others? Kowalski? The botanist?"

"Don't know. Let's hope they weren't in the basement. Tucker failed to account for the size of Russian gas pipes and a century-old boiler. A bad combination. In winter, we lose many houses that way."

Seichan stared below, a question foremost in her mind.

Where the hell are the others?

9:03 A.M.

Kowalski pushed himself off the floor of his cell.

Smoke choked him, filling the space.

What the hell?

He had been finishing a volley of return fire and ducking into cover when a thunderous blast had shaken the mansion to its foundations. Out of the corner of his eye, he had caught sight of a steel door, likely the one sealing off this subbasement, flying and rebounding wildly off the walls.

It struck a gunman stationed at the bottom, decapitating him.

A wall of flames followed, blasting across the main room.

Kowalski had rolled aside, dropped into a fetal position, and covered his head. Still, the heat had come close to parboiling him—and might still.

Have to get out of here.

He crawled to the door and searched outside the cell.

Through the smoke, he spotted a second body blown against the far wall. The man's clothing still burned. He turned toward the tunnel where Sychkin's group had fled. He hoped Elle and Marco had been far enough away when the world had exploded.

He squinted in that direction.

But where did that tunnel lead?

9:04 A.M.

With his pistol in hand, Tucker headed through the smoke-choked basement. Flames burned all around. The heat was blistering. He searched for any sign of the others, though if they were down here, he'd be identifying bodies.

He cursed himself, breathing hard—and not because of the foul air.

What have I done?

Yuri had already radioed in. He and Seichan were headed down to aid in the search. They would not have much time. Though it had only been twenty minutes since the start of the attack, there was little leeway left. With a military detachment stationed by the Trinity Lavra, the response to the blast would be swift. He had to hope that the prior firefight, which was mostly limited to the interior of the mansion, had not been reported.

As he continued across the ruins, he spotted an open doorway through the smoke.

Steps led downward.

Into a subbasement.

Such a level hadn't been on the floorplans for this place. Plainly, the Sychkin family was good at keeping secrets.

Hope flared inside him.

If the others had been kept down there—

A loud growl of a throaty engine drew his attention. The noise rose from outside, coming from the parking lot. Another engine joined it.

He could guess what that meant.

No . . .

He swung around and ran through the smoke toward the back steps. The exterior door had been blasted loose. It hung by one hinge. He climbed through the wreckage as a pair of black SUVs barreled out of the garage and sped toward the gate, which rolled open ahead of the vehicles.

Tucker leaped the steps as the vehicles swept past. He spotted Elle in a backseat. She hugged a dog in her lap.

Marco . . .

The vehicles didn't slow as they hit the street and careened away.

I can't lose them.

He raced to one of the bodies on the parking lot. He skidded through the blood and patted down the man's pockets. He prayed there were keys to one of the vehicles.

As Tucker pawed at a breast pocket, the nearest G-wagon chirped and blinked.

Thank god.

He yanked out the fob and rushed to the SUV. He flung open the door and threw himself into the front seat. As he did, he radioed Yuri.

"They're on the run," he gasped out. "I'm in pursuit."

With no time to summon Kane, he hit the ignition.

As he did, the other Mercedes next to him growled to life.

He froze for a second, confused.

Then he felt the pistol pressed against the side of his neck.

He stared into the rearview mirror as a pale face rose into view, framed by snowy hair. A dark tattoo stood out sharply.

Valya reached around and ripped off his throat mike. "Drive," she said. "If you hope to find where the others are going. Or die here."

Tucker had no trouble making this choice. He shifted the vehicle into gear and headed away.

The other Mercedes paced him across the lot. A scarred figure with a dark ponytail sat behind the wheel. He imagined the two women must have secured the second fobs to these Mercedes—and turned both vehicles into traps.

And I jumped right into one.

Valya leaned close as Tucker made the turn onto the street.

"You're not who I had hoped to catch," she said. "But you'll do for now."

23

Jason continued through his assigned section of the wine cellar's labyrinth. Sister Anna accompanied him. Twenty minutes ago, the team had broken off into pairs, all carrying flashlights.

Not that we're making any progress.

Crossing into the next chamber, he swept his beam around. He searched the walls, floor, and roof for any sign of a hidden library. Across the back of the space, splashes of graffiti glowed under his flashlight, shining in neon yellows, blues, and crimson.

Anna huffed her disapproval.

This wasn't the first sign of trespassers. There were piles of trash everywhere: broken bottles, crushed cans, crumpled bags. In one chamber, a stained mattress had been left behind, surely harboring an unknown number of STDs. More disturbing, in one cavern, someone had spread a set of matryoshka dolls—Russian nesting dolls—across a row of niches, with their faces all painted into leering, fanged demons.

Down in these shadowy caves, Jason had shuddered at the macabre sight.

While the grounds above might be sacred, there's nothing holy down here.

As the two continued, with each chamber failing to offer any clues, tension slowly built.

Jason tried to break it, asking a question that he had wondered about. "Sister Anna, your name . . . did you pick it when you became a nun?"

"I'm still a novice," she reminded him. "I'll take my formal vows next month. But, yes, I could change my name—and I did."

He glanced toward her, not sure if it was polite to ask his next question.

She smiled and answered anyway. "My given name was Iskra, which I was never fond of anyway."

"Iskra?"

Her smile widened. "I know. My parents wanted both their children's names to begin with the letter I."

"Like Igor."

She sighed, and her smile dimmed, darkening her face.

Jason kicked himself for bringing up her brother. He tried his best to recover. "Did you pick Anna . . . or was it selected for you?"

"I chose it. After Anna of Kashin."

He looked toward her.

She explained, "She was a Russian princess of Tver, who was twice canonized, after losing her family to Mongol hordes. She's considered the holy protectress of women who have lost their loved ones." She glanced down as they continued into the next chamber. "I picked her because Igor and I had lost our parents following an auto accident. We were only fourteen. Afterward, we were all we had, following in each other's footsteps, pursuing the same academic careers—until I was drawn to the church, pulled by my faith."

"Was there a moment when you knew about your calling?" Jason whispered, though the labyrinth's acoustic amplified his words.

"I had no heavenly visitation, if that's what you're asking." She looked at him, as if testing if he were mocking her.

"Not at all. I'm sorry for prying. I was truly curious."

She relaxed. "I've always found comfort in prayer. And later, during my studies to be an archivist, my interests slowly diverged from my brother's. He was drawn toward old scientific texts and treatises, where I was fascinated by ancient scriptures, lost gospels, even religious debates among Greek and Roman writers. It was in those yellowed, fragile pages that I felt myself called to a more meditative, worshipful life."

He nodded. "I think we can all use a little more introspection."

She smiled at him. "I'm sure there's a monastery that would love to have a resident computer expert. I heard many of them have websites now."

He held up a palm. "No thanks. Considering my work hours, I'm already living the life of a monk."

She lifted a brow. "That's too bad."

He glanced to see if there was any extra meaning there, but he reminded himself . . .

She's a nun—or, at least, a novice.

Flustered, he tripped on a loose tile and sent it skittering away. He caught himself, his cheeks warming with embarrassment. He followed the tumbling tile with his flashlight.

Anna gasped next to him.

He spotted it, too.

They both rushed over.

Jason picked up the tile. Like all the others, it was octagon in shape and had been kilned to an azure blue, though age had mottled it. Only this tile also had a sigil engraved in silver atop it, a single symbol. It was so tarnished that it was nearly indiscernible at first glance.

Still, he recognized the glyph. He had seen it before, scrawled along the edge of the astrolabe's sketch.

He turned to Anna.

"It's Glagolitic," she confirmed.

They shared an amazed look.

This must be significant.

With his heart pounding, Jason tried to radio his teammates, but the warren of rock defied his efforts. He gave up and cuffed his hands around his mouth.

"Over here!" he hollered, trusting the acoustics of the place to carry his message to the others. "We found something!"

Before his yell could echo away, Anna waved to him. "Look at this."

She had crossed deeper into the cavern chamber and swept her flashlight across the floor.

He joined her, standing at her shoulder. "It's everywhere," he whispered in awe.

Across the breadth of the room, hundreds of blue tiles were engraved with tarnished silver, shining with Glagolitic symbols in every shape and sigil.

He gaped at the sheer expanse, coming to one firm conclusion. "We need Commander Pierce."

9:31 A.M.

Gray shuffled across the tiled floor, shining his flashlight down. The others were spread across the chamber.

"What do you make of it?" Monk asked.

"Considering the symbols we found in the old Greek text, this must be important."

He examined another few tiles, rubbing a bit of tarnish off one, getting it to shine brighter. As he did, he felt something give under his thumb, accompanied by a barely perceptible *click*.

Huh . . .

He did it again, getting the same result.

He sat back on his heels and cast his beam across the expanse of tiles and letters. "I think there's some mechanism hidden under the lettered tiles."

The others gathered closer, and he demonstrated by pushing on the tile. It depressed a quarter inch, then popped back into position.

"Spring-loaded," he mumbled.

"It can't be *all* the tiles." Jason pointed to a gap in the floor. "I dislodged one. And there's only bare rock under it."

Gray joined him, dropped to a knee, and examined the spot. "You're right."

Bishop Yelagin stood to the side, leaning on his staff. "What does that mean?"

"We'll have to test each tile." Gray stood up. "Find out which of the engraved ones move and record each symbol."

Jason slipped out a digital tablet from a pack. "I'll build a database."

In short order, the team set about testing the hundreds of tiles. Even Yelagin used his metal staff to press lettered pieces. When anyone found one that moved, Jason snapped a picture of it and digitized the letter for clarity.

Anna, down on her hands and knees, offered a theory. "I wonder if this helps explain why Catherine's designers covered up the astrolabe and its Glagolitic symbols in the Greek book. Maybe it wasn't just that the puzzle was too easy to solve. Maybe she feared it was too direct of a connection to what lay down here."

"You could be right," Gray admitted, appreciating her insight.

After several more minutes, they had a complete recording of the mechanized tiles. Gray looked over Jason's shoulder to study the result. On the screen, a row of eleven sigils formed a neat row.

$$ℛ⅋⚜⚔✠⚕ℚ⚜ℙ⅃ℰᏚⱴ$$

Gray turned to Anna. "Can you translate these symbols?"

She nodded and took the tablet from Jason. "I still have the conversion chart saved. It should only take a moment." As she worked, her frown slowly deepened. "This makes no sense. It's just gibberish."

She shared the result with everyone. Each symbol now had a corresponding letter or number written below it.

$$ℛ⅋⚜⚔✠⚕ℚ⚜ℙ⅃ℰᏚⱴ$$
S L A Y V H I N E 4 C

"Maybe it's not gibberish," Monk offered. "Maybe it's an *anagram*. We just randomly recorded those symbols. They're not likely to be in the correct order."

Everyone tested aloud various options, coming up with answers just as nonsensical.

Gray took the tablet and studied it. "That's not the answer. In this list, there are no repeating letters. Most words and phrases, especially those with ten letters, would reuse at least *one* letter."

"What are you thinking?" Monk asked.

"Whatever the code is, it must require reusing some of the letters." He waved across the breadth of the room. "To spell it out, we may need to press some of the tiles two or three times."

"Or *four*," Anna added.

Gray heard a catch in her voice. "What?"

She took the tablet and tapped at the letters on the screen. As she continued, her frown lines faded. Her eyes grew wider.

"I'm right," she whispered.

Jason leaned by her shoulder.

"It's a signature." She faced the others. "The number four gave it away."

"Whose signature?" Jason pressed her.

"The egotistical tyrant who hid the library. The *fourth* of his name."

Gray understood and shifted closer. "Ivan the Terrible."

"Or his official name . . ." Anna typed onto the screen and showed everyone.

Ivan IV Vasilyevich

"But instead of using the roman numeral for four," Gray noted, "they used its Glagolitic equivalent."

Anna nodded as she continued to work. She converted the letters of his name using the limited number of Glagolitic symbols available to them.

ℙℰℹℸℙ℈ℰℹℛℙℬℤℑℰℙℙⅤℚ
I V A N 4 V A S I L Y E V I CH

"See. You can spell out his full name using only those ten letters and that one number," Anna explained. "This must be the code to unlock a hidden door."

Monk stared across the chamber. "Let's give it a try."

Clustered in a tight group, they searched the floor again for the mechanized symbols and set about pressing them in the proper order.

They finally reached the last one.

Gray waved to Yelagin. "Would you like to do the honors?"

"*Spasibo,*" he said with a grin.

The bishop reached with the butt of his staff and pressed the last tile, getting an audible *click*.

Gray braced himself, as did the others. Glances searched the room. But nothing happened.

"Did we spell it correctly?" Jason asked.

"I'm sure we did," Anna assured everyone. "Maybe it's just a coincidence that you can spell Ivan's name with those symbols."

Gray shook his head. "Not with that conspicuous number four. This must be the correct code."

Jason grimaced. "Then maybe the mechanism is broken, damaged by age and the conditions down here."

Monk huffed in exasperation. "Then what do we do?"

Gray closed his eyes, trying to picture the centuries-old mechanism under their feet: its metal wheels and gears, its pulleys and chains. For it all to work in synchrony, the locking mechanism would have to register each press of a tile and hold it until the entire sequence was completed. It would be a point of unbalance for the entire mechanism, one it couldn't hold for long.

In his ears, he again heard the small *clicks*, the tiles returning to their proper place afterward.

"I think we were too slow," he mumbled—at first tentatively, then with more assurance. "The mechanism must have a built-in timer. If you don't enter the code quickly enough, it resets mid-sequence."

"So, we have to enter it faster," Jason said.

"Let's hope so." Gray looked across the floor. "We should spread out and each cover a section of the tiles. That'll allow us to press the symbols in a timely manner."

Gray quickly assigned a specific area of two or three symbols to each person. Except for Anna. She kept hold of the tablet, ready to call out each sigil, using the symbols' proper Glagolitic names.

"All set?" she asked.

Once she got confirmation from everyone, she recited the code aloud.

Gray and the others pressed their respective tiles in the order she called. Gray had taken up a post by the last tile.

This had to work.

Otherwise, I'm out of ideas.

Anna called out the Glagolitic name for the final sigil: "*Spidery Ha.*"

With a hard swallow, he pressed the corresponding tile, and it clicked under his fingertips.

Before he could straighten, the floor shook with a metallic rumble. He stood up, balancing on his good leg. From a neighboring chamber, stone grated loudly against stone. He also felt a change of pressure, a slight popping of his ears.

Then all went silent and quiet.

They all stared at one another.

Gray finally moved and headed toward the next room. He drew the others with him, but he stopped everyone at the threshold. Flashlights lit the space, illuminating a fine dust swirling in the air.

On the room's far side, a section of the wall had lowered into the floor, leaving behind a foot-tall sill. Beyond it, a black tunnel opened. Something twangled loudly, and the door dropped the rest of the way down. It sounded as if a gear had broken, likely permanently damaging the mechanism, trapping the door open.

"Stay here," Gray warned and headed into the room.

He reached the mouth of a passageway and waved his light down it. The tunnel ran for five yards and ended at a set of stairs that spiraled down.

Looks like we're heading deeper.

Monk called to him. "What now?"

"We continue on."

"What about Seichan and Tucker?" Jason asked. "Should we try to reach them before we enter the lion's den?"

Gray nodded. "You're right. Someone should go topside where there's a radio signal and get an update. Let them know what we're doing."

He turned to Monk and Jason, looking for a volunteer.

Monk sighed. "I'll go. You've dragged me underground enough times as it is." He clapped Jason on the back. "Can't have our latest field agent missing out on all the fun."

Gray nodded. "Once you've contacted the others, come back down. We'll need someone to watch our backs and guard this exit."

"Understood." Monk set off into the cellar.

Gray faced the tunnel and stepped over the threshold. As he did, an uneasy twinge iced through him.

Something must be down there—but what?

The others crowded behind him, stoking his trepidation. He remembered the crushing fate of the other group of explorers who had trespassed into a lost subterranean library.

As he descended, a certainty firmed inside him.

We need to tread carefully from here.

FOURTH

Burying the Truth

24

Seichan paced the length of the suite's salon, staring out the windows toward the breadth of the Trinity Lavra. Kane had also taken up a post there, his gaze fixed outside, clearly worried about his missing partners.

She was, too.

Her team had returned to the hotel thirty minutes ago, fleeing the fires and the cordon of police and military vehicles. On the far side of the monastic compound, a column of smoke rose into the sky. A pair of helicopters circled around it.

She turned her back on the sight, leaving Kane to maintain his vigil.

Monk sat at the dining table. Kowalski scowled across from him with his wounded arm thrust out. A med kit lay open between them.

Shortly after Tucker had reported that he was in pursuit of Elle and Marco, Kowalski had stumbled out of the lower depths of the mansion. She and Yuri had hustled him off, collecting Kane from the alley. Minutes later, Monk had radioed them. He had reported that Gray and the others had opened a secret door, one possibly leading to the lost Golden Library.

In turn, Seichan had informed him of their own dilemma.

She stared over at the steel dagger with its carved black handle. It rested on the table. It was Valya's *athamé.* The blade had been impaled through Kowalski's forearm.

Needing Monk's skill as the team's medic, they had regrouped at the Old Lavra Hotel. Monk was supposed to return to the tower, but the priority was to attend to Kowalski. Even for such a big brute, he had lost a lot of blood.

"Quit squirming," Monk warned, pinning the big man's wrist down.

It looked as if it would take all of the engineered strength in Monk's prosthetic hand to keep Kowalski from yanking his arm back.

"Just put a Band-Aid on it already. I'll be fine."

"Do you want to lose your arm?"

"I can barely use it now."

"Enough whining. The nerve block will wear off in a couple hours."

Seichan ignored them as Monk continued suturing Kowalski's arm. She turned to Yuri. "Any response from Tucker?"

The Russian security chief shook his head. "*Nyet.* He still maintains radio silence."

Seichan frowned. There had been no further word from the man after he had taken off after the others. Kowalski had informed them about what had happened down below. It seemed the Sychkin family—with its generational history of illicit pursuits—had built an escape hatch out of their mansion, one leading through the garage.

Seichan clenched a fist. "Tucker wouldn't stay silent this long. Something's wrong."

Kane glanced up at her, as if he agreed with her. She knew Tucker barely tolerated teamwork, preferred being a lone wolf, just him and his dogs. It was a trait that Seichan often envied.

Just not now.

"Do you think he was captured?" Yuri asked. "By our enemy? By the authorities?"

"No way of telling. It could be a problem with his radio. But if I'm wrong or if he was captured by Sychkin's crew, then we need to know *where* the archpriest was taking the botanist. That's our only lead."

Kowalski lifted his good arm, raising a scowl from Monk. "I may know," he called over.

Seichan crossed to him. "How?"

"Elle raised that same question." Kowalski pointed toward the column of smoke in the distance. "Back in the subbasement. Before they took her. She was the only one courteous enough to speak English during the exchange. The others spoke in Russian."

"You don't speak Russian," Seichan reminded him.

"But I know sign language."

Seichan pictured Yerik Raz. "I thought Russian signing was different from the American standard?"

"It is. I have no idea what that big monk was saying, but he was clearly spelling something out with his hand during that exchange. Thinking it might be important, I memorized it." He demonstrated by signing with his fingers and wrist. "I'm pretty good at picking up gestures, but I can't promise I got it all."

Seichan turned to Yuri. "If we recorded it, do you know anyone who might be able to interpret it?"

"*Da*. Should be no problem. My boss Bogdan has many connections."

She nodded. "Then let's see if this leads anywhere."

They quickly videoed Kowalski's hand gestures as he repeated his demonstration. Yuri then stepped to the side with one of the team's encrypted phones and dispatched the file to his contacts, someone familiar with Russian sign language.

As they waited for a response, there was a knock on the door.

Seichan withdrew her SIG Sauer and stepped over. She squinted through the door's peephole. A woman, dressed in the hotel's crimson-and-black livery, stood in the hall. She held aloft a tray covered by a domed silver cloche.

About time.

She holstered her pistol and opened the door. She blocked the view inside with her body, then took the tray and passed over a thick roll of rubles. She thanked the woman, then closed the door.

With the tray in hand, Seichan crossed the salon and lowered it to the table. She removed the cloche, exposing two full blood bags, along with a transfusion kit.

Yuri had arranged this special delivery.

Kowalski sighed appreciatively. "Room service is good here. But they could've brought fries, too."

As Monk prepared to replace what Kowalski had lost, Yuri strode forward with the phone in hand. "I heard back," he reported. "But I don't know if this helps much. A couple signs were *absurdnyy*, my contact says. But others he got right."

Kowalski grunted. "Like I said, I wasn't sure I memorized everything perfectly."

Seichan focused on Yuri. "What was your contact able to make out?"

"I'll show you. But Russian sign language uses Cyrillic letters, not American." Yuri passed over the phone. "My friend sent this."

Seichan stared at the screen, which showed a line of Cyrillic letters with gaps at the beginning and the end.

<u>?</u> Е Л В М <u>?</u>

Seichan frowned. "So, the first and last letters are wrong?"

"*Absurdnyy*, like I said. All that is clear are the four middle ones. Translated they spell out E L V M."

Seichan showed the others the image.

"Looks like a game of Cyrillic hangman," Kowalski mumbled.

Monk nodded. "One we'd better not lose, if we hope to ever see Dr. Stutt and Marco again."

And possibly Tucker, too.

Seichan turned to Kowalski. "Show me those signs again."

At her insistence, Kowalski ran through the sequence a few more times. As he did, she recognized a pattern.

"It looks like your signs for the first and last letters are the *same*. Whatever error you made in remembering the first one, you repeated in the last."

"What does that mean?" Kowalski asked.

"It means those missing letters could be the same ones."

She and Yuri returned their attention to the screen. There were only thirty-three letters in the Cyrillic alphabet. It didn't take long to test her theory. The answer was found in the alphabet's second letter.

Seichan tapped at the screen and replaced the question marks with the Cyrillic letter *be*.

БЕЛВМБ

She glanced to Yuri, who nodded in agreement.

She showed the two at the table.

Kowalski shrugged. "Still looks *absurdnyy* to me."

"What is it?" Monk asked. "You and Yuri clearly know something."

"This spells out BELVMB," Seichan explained. "A military acronym for the *Belomorskaya Voyenno Morskaya Baza*."

"Which is what?" Kowalski asked, wincing as Monk inserted an IV catheter.

"The Red Banner White Sea Naval Base," Seichan answered.

"A huge place," Yuri added. "Up in Severodvinsk to the north."

Monk started the transfusion. "How can we be sure that's the right spot?"

It was a fair question.

On the phone, Seichan pulled up a map of the Arkhangelsk Oblast, where the base was located. She read aloud about the base's facilities: the dozens of submarines, the thousands of Arctic-trained troops, the hundreds of ice-hardened ships and equipment.

Seichan despaired. "The base's commander is a decorated naval officer named Captain Sergei Turov. If the others have been taken there—"

Kowalski jerked straighter, nearly pulling out his catheter. "Wait. *Turov*? I heard that name come up during the exchange. Thought it was just a Russian word." He stared over at her. "Then that's gotta be the place, right?"

Seichan nodded. She withdrew the veiled apostolnik from where she had tucked it away. It had been severely wrinkled after choking out the guardsman at the mansion. She had done her best to smooth it out to wear on the way back to the hotel, and no one had commented on it—

proof yet again that few people took notice of nuns, especially here, where they were as common as crows in a cornfield.

Let's hope that continues.

She pulled the cloth veil over her head.

"Where are you going?" Monk asked her.

She pointed to the window, toward the Trinity Lavra. "You need to finish patching Kowalski up. I'm going to take your place over at the tower."

Earlier, Monk had already bandaged her small bullet graze. The bloodstain hardly showed where it had soaked through the black wool of her clerical dress.

She turned and headed toward the door. "If we want to rescue the others, someone needs to light a fire under Gray's ass."

25

"It's getting warmer," Jason commented from the front of the group.

As they all filed down the never-ending staircase, Gray had noted the same. He wiped his damp brow. His ankle throbbed with every step.

Ivan the Terrible must have buried his library deep—if it's even down here.

Continuing the descent, Gray kept near the back of the group. He stuck close to Yelagin. The elderly bishop breathed hard, leaning heavily on his staff, picking his way down. Perspiration sheeted his face, both from the exertion and from the heat.

Below them, Anna offered a theory for the warming temperature. "This region is geothermally active, like much of northern Russia. The springs found here can be hot or cold."

Gray ran a finger along the limestone walls, noting it was rich in crystals that reflected their light like encrusted diamonds. The stone was dry to the touch, unlike the chilly dampness usually found in deep caves.

Was that the reason this site was picked? To help preserve the old books?

As they wound their way down, Yelagin cleared his throat and raised a question, most likely to keep himself distracted. "Do you truly think there could be a lost continent in the Arctic, one undiscovered after so long?"

Gray glanced over to him. "I don't see how. No such landmass has ever been detected by satellites. Though, in the past, eyewitnesses have claimed otherwise. Back in 1905, Robert Peary—the disputed first to reach the North Pole—said he spotted a distant land during one of his expeditions, a place he named 'Crocker Land.' But that was probably just a crock of sh—"

Gray coughed, covering his near slip in front of the pious man.

Still, Yelagin smiled.

Gray continued, "Another American explorer, Frederick Cook, confirmed that same sighting in 1908."

"Then maybe something is out there," Yelagin offered.

Gray shook his head. "Many others, including the Inuit, have made such claims. But such sightings were either fabricated or due to some atmospheric trick of the light. Modern satellite surveys have irrefutably shown that under all that Arctic ice is only an ocean and an even deeper mountainous seabed."

"But what if—in the ancient past—the sea levels had been much lower, exposing those submerged mountaintops? As I understand it, the climate was vastly different back then. In Greenland, fossils of palm and fruit trees have been dug up. Along with bones of camels and rhinoceroses."

"Ah, but that's from a time *long* before the ancient Greeks, the ones who named Hyperborea and wrote accounts of its inhabitants."

Yelagin sighed. "Still, *something* keeps this myth stirred up. The Arkangel Society is not the only group searching for evidence of Hyperborea. There are explorations ongoing right now. Across the Kola Peninsula and in the Karelia region. Even through the northern Ural Mountains."

"But have any of those explorers turned up anything?"

"Not definitively. What they have discovered are remote regions with vast fields of petroglyphs. Some are not far from us. Around Lake Onega. And over in the Murmansk region. In fact, Russian archaeologists are craning in a huge dome—ten meters high and twenty wide—to protect a huge collection of rock art, a grouping from two thousand years before the birth of Christ." He looked pointedly at Gray. "Well within the scope of our ancient Greeks."

"I have no doubt that a prehistoric people populated this region, as inhospitable as it must have been at the time."

The bishop gave him a pointed look. "Unless those people also had greener pastures to retire to during the harshest seasons or toughest years."

"Hyperborea?"

Yelagin shrugged. "It's just speculation. But some of the strangest discoveries of late were found on a handful of islands in the White Sea. Archaeologists uncovered remnants of pyramids, tombs, labyrinths, and, on one island, a giant stone throne—as if the former occupants had been quite tall."

Gray heard the change in the bishop's timbre at the last. "Why's that significant?"

"There was a Roman historian from the third century—Claudius Aelianus—who described a trio of Hyperborean brothers. To quote the ancient writer, *three in number, brothers by birth, and six cubits in height.* Which in modern measurements would make them three meters tall."

"If true, the king of those people would certainly need a large throne," Gray admitted, but he remained highly skeptical.

Yelagin looked hardly convinced himself. "Maybe the petroglyphs and other archaeological discoveries are evidence of some grander, more sophisticated prehistoric society, one that existed to the north before fading into obscurity. And the stories of Hyperborea are just overblown attempts to describe those lost people, casting them into mythic proportions."

"You could well be right."

"And those stories of the Hyperboreans' agelessness," Yelagin continued in melancholy tones, "maybe such acclaimed longevity came about because of a confusion involving the Arctic's cycle of day and night—where a polar *day* could last for many months. That would certainly make it harder to accurately measure a lifespan."

Gray had no answer to that, and any further discussion was interrupted by an excited shout from Jason, who had traveled some distance ahead.

"Everyone! Hurry up! Come look!"

9:58 A.M.

Jason stood at the bottom of the stairs, flanked by Anna and Bailey. He pointed his flashlight into a vast vault that opened ahead of him. Other shadowy chambers branched off from this one, forming a maze far larger than the wine cellar above.

Yet, similar to the grotto overhead, the floor here was tiled in blue. At the center of the chamber stood a massive oaken table, circular in shape and surrounded by chairs.

But Jason barely noted such details. What truly captured both his attention and his imagination were the hundreds—if not thousands— of niches carved into the limestone walls. They climbed a dozen rows high. The topmost would take a tall ladder to reach.

In each niche, there rested a sealed chest, banded in silver and plated in gold.

"We found it," Bailey said, nearly choking. "The Golden Library of the Tsars."

"Apparently that name was meant to be *literal*," Anna noted. "Not just figurative."

Jason shifted his flashlight higher, revealing heavy timbered beams that buttressed the roof. Even there, thick sheets of gold had been hammered over their lengths, adding to the richness of the space. Between them, bright frescoes had been painted, showing studious figures bent over huge tomes, while others used long quills to illuminate manuscripts.

The scuffle of boots and the thump of a staff announced the arrival of Gray and Yelagin.

As the bishop joined them, he looked as if he were about to fall to his knees—and not from exhaustion. His gaze swept the space. A hand covered his mouth in shock.

"I never imagined it would be so grand," Yelagin mumbled.

"Maybe we should have," Anna said with a huge grin. "Our dear Ivan was not only *terrible*, but notoriously *grandiose*."

Gray pushed forward. "I don't think that word quite captures the breadth of this space."

Drawn like moths to the golden shine, they all set off to explore the expanse, spreading out to either side.

Gray did not deter them, but he offered a warning. "Don't disturb anything."

Jason understood, remembering what had happened to the team under Moscow.

As they wandered and examined the collection, additional observations were made.

"It looks like these chests are sealed with wax," Bailey commented with his head cocked to the side, leaning close without touching.

"They're also marked in silver," Anna announced from another spot in the chamber.

Jason squinted at the tarnished sigil fixed under the lock of the nearest chest. "Glagolitic symbols."

"Numbers again," Anna explained. "Like the latitude and longitude markings around the sketched astrolabe."

Gray shifted down a row, looking closely. "I imagine it must be their equivalent of a Dewey Decimal system for this archive."

Bailey straightened and looked across their group. "If so, then there must be a catalog or index somewhere that lists what books are in each chest."

"And keys, too," Anna reminded them. "If we hope to discover where in this vast library are the hidden clues to the location of Hyperborea, we'll need both."

"True." Gray pointed his flashlight toward the labyrinth spreading out from here. "There must be a centralized office somewhere. We just have to find it."

Jason stared out at the branching expanse of chambers. "Should we split up again?"

"Considering the danger, not this time." He stared at the others. "We'd best stick close."

Determined to unlock the mysteries buried here, the group headed out. The beams of their flashlights speared in every direction, like wobbly spokes of a wheel. They peered into neighboring spaces, all of which looked roughly identical to the first: niches holding golden chests, a wide circular study table, and stout chairs, waiting to seat some future scholar. The only difference was each room's size and shape, which appeared organic versus designed.

"They must have used the natural contours of a cavern system to build this library," Gray noted.

The commander led them onward, stopping periodically to sweep his light to the left and right, then he would shift their path, using some arcane measurement known only to him.

As Jason followed, he tried to get his bearings. "It would be easy to get lost down here."

"A map would be nice," Bailey concurred.

"We might not need one," Gray said.

"Why?" Anna asked.

Gray stopped and glanced back at her. "If there's an organizational hub to this archive, it would either be at the bottom of those winding steps or positioned at the center of this sprawling archive. That makes the most sense. So, I've been leading us along a throughline across the library, trying to keep the same number of chambers to our right and left. Or at least, to the best of my abilities."

"Your *best* has served us well," Yelagin commented. The bishop had continued a few yards onward. He pointed his staff ahead. "That chamber looks very different from the rest of the library."

Jason hurried forward with the others. All their lights shone forward, aimed at the room where Yelagin pointed.

Ahead, an archway opened into an unusual space—one that was hard to fathom being buried this far underground.

26

Gray stood at the chamber's threshold. "What is this place?"

"It looks like a private study," Yelagin noted. "Maybe from the seventeenth or eighteenth century."

Both awed and dumbfounded, Gray peered at the baroque design inside.

The room's walls were paneled and shelved in mahogany, all full of dusty leatherbound books amidst a collection of artifacts. Overhead, its flat roof was raftered and plastered. To one side, a rich tapestry hung, running from ceiling to floor, and below it, a crimson rug covered the tiles. There was even a replica of a small fireplace in a back corner. Above its mantel hung the curve of a mammoth tusk.

But what drew Gray's eye stood in the room's center. It was a large satinwood desk, inlaid with silver and gold filigrees. A lone glass lantern sat atop it, surrounded by a spread of papers, inked maps, small brass tools, even a book that had been left splayed open.

It was as if some researcher had stepped away and had expected to return shortly.

"What do you make of this?" Bailey asked Gray.

"This room feels like an anomaly. From a different time period than the rest. I think this was always the central hub to the library, but it looks like someone installed this chamber later. Perhaps to conduct research in a more comfortable setting."

Anna shifted closer. "This may be Catherine the Great's handiwork after she discovered this library. She loved to put her stamp on old Russian sites."

"But who was working here?" Jason asked. "I can't imagine it was the empress herself."

Gray stepped into the room. "For now, it's *us*. If we hope to learn any clues about Hyperborea, it'll be found in this room. I'm sure of it." He turned to the group. "But take great care."

As the team dispersed to examine sections of the room, Gray crossed to the desk, drawing Anna with him. He stood over the spread of books and papers. Atop the tallest stack, a journal rested crookedly. Silver stenciling across its cover shone through a layer of dust.

Gray leaned down and blew across its surface, brightening the Cyrillic lettering.

Михаил Васильевич Ломоносов

He glanced over to Anna, whose eyes had grown wider.

"What does it say?" he asked her.

"It's a name. No doubt the owner of this desk, the one who was doing research in here."

"Who was it?"

She pointed to the Cyrillic stenciling. "Mikhail Vasilyevich Lomonosov."

Gray shook his head, not recognizing the name.

"He was the leading Russian scientist of his time. A genius and polymath. One who exceled across a breadth of subjects. Chemistry, physics, geology, astronomy." She turned to him. "He was also Catherine the Great's most valued scientific adviser, even given the title of state councillor."

Gray considered all of this as he gazed around the space. "If Catherine wanted someone to explore this library, to search for clues to Hyperborea, I can see why she handpicked him."

"Without a doubt. It's also been well documented that Lomonosov showed great interest in the Arctic, having grown up in the Arkhangelsk Oblast, not far from the White Sea. He was particularly interested in the enigma of the magnetic North Pole."

"And maybe in other mysteries of that frozen world," Gray added.

"Possibly."

"But considering the astounding discovery Catherine made here, recovering the Golden Library, why did she focus on this lost continent? What drew her so immediately on that course?"

"It was an obsession of hers—not Hyperborea—but to establish the roots of the Russian people. She first believed it was the Scythians who might be our forefathers."

"The militant nomads of the Eurasian steppes?" Gray remembered Bailey and Yelagin bringing up those Bronze Age people last night at the embassy.

"The same. Even today there is an offshoot of the philosophies of Aleksandr Dugin—a group who call themselves the New Scythians—who pursue this same ideology. In fact, there's been a lot of friction between the New Scythians and the Arkangel Society, both arguing about who is right."

"And where did Catherine land, during her time?"

"She turned away from the Scythians and became convinced our true origins were much farther north."

"In Hyperborea."

Anna nodded. "Her fascination is well documented. And there are rumors she dispatched ships on secret missions to the Far North, searching for this lost continent."

Jason called from the fireplace. "I'd say she found it—or at least, found *something*."

Gray and Anna turned to him.

Jason stood with his hands on his hips, his neck craned back, staring up at the length of the mammoth tusk. The room was decorated with other artifacts across its crowded shelves: large chunks of crystals, stuffed birds under glass domes, painted pottery, tiny bronze sculptures.

Gray couldn't understand why the tusk had captured Jason's attention. Still, he stepped closer. "What is it?"

Jason pointed up, using his other hand to wave dust from the artifact's surface. "Someone turned this huge horn of ivory into one massive piece of scrimshaw."

Gray squinted and saw he was right. The artwork engraved into the tusk was broken by age and incomplete, but he could easily identify a collection of pyramids, tiered buildings, and spires.

He looked across the room to where Bailey and Yelagin conversed in low tones, searching the shelves and walls on that side. He remembered the bishop mentioning an archaeological discovery on islands in the White Sea.

Pyramids, tombs, and thrones.

Gray studied the scrimshaw.

Is this a peek of what those crumbling sites once looked like? Or is it evidence of a more sophisticated civilization even farther north?

Anna pointed up, but not at the mammoth tusk. "There's a plaque on the wall. It's inscribed with a long list of names. Like a memorial to lost explorers."

Gray looked higher and saw she was right. "But what's written to the *left* of that list? Though it's Cyrillic, it doesn't look like a name."

"It's not. But I believe it proves that this is a testament to those who died exploring. Possibly those who sought out Hyperborea and never returned."

"What does it say?"

She read the phrase aloud, " '*Never go there, never trespass, never wake that which is sleeping.*'" She turned to Gray. "This may be part of the reason Catherine hid this library, kept her discoveries secret. She must have discovered something dangerous."

"Then why preserve all of this?" Gray asked. "Why plant seeds under Moscow—possibly other places, too—that lead here? She must have wanted the library to be rediscovered."

"Maybe *eventually*. She clearly believed the knowledge was worth safeguarding. Even if it was dangerous. Perhaps she feared those of her time weren't ready for it, couldn't handle it."

Gray slowly nodded. "She planted those seeds for a future generation to discover. Maybe as a test." He pictured the boobytrapped vault and the encrypted page in the Greek book. "To prove we're cautious enough and wise enough to receive such knowledge."

"But are we?" Anna challenged him. "My brother's team wasn't cautious enough and suffered for it. And while we might have proved clever enough in solving her encryption, it was only by *cheating*—by using our technology to peer through the Lavra's sketch to see her easier puzzle."

Gray couldn't argue with her.

Jason, though, raised a question that was far more important. "But how did Catherine and Lomonosov discover Hyperborea's location? And more importantly, how do we follow in their footsteps?"

Gray returned to the desk, where Lomonosov's labors were suspended in time.

There must be a clue to his methodology here.

He stared across the disheveled spread of papers, journals, and books. He noted two types of brass compasses—the magnetic kind to divine true north and instruments for drawing circles. There was also a tarnished silver sextant, along with a set of metal rulers and protractors.

All tools of cartography.

This realization drew him to a brightly colored map on the table, drawn in pinks, greens, and yellows. Its parchment was more cracked and yellowed than anything else on the desktop, suggesting it was far older.

He shifted toward it, wanting a better look, but a large book was splayed open atop it, obscuring most of the map.

Gray defied his own instructions and reached down and closed the book. He shifted it aside to reveal the full breadth of the chart beneath it.

It was a map he vaguely recognized, one of the foremost examples of early cartography. He had also come across it more recently, from his research on lost continents—for obvious reasons.

Leaning closer, he studied the finely drawn map, which was inscribed with notes and names in Latin. He hovered a finger over the bottom right corner, where a title was written: *Septentrionalium Terrarum.*

Anna peered over his shoulder, noting where he was pointing, and translated the Latin. "*Of the Northern Lands.*"

He glanced to her.

"It's a copy of the Mercator Map," she said, clearly recognizing it, too. "Considered the oldest chart of the Arctic. Drawn by a Flemish cartographer, Gerardus Mercator, in the sixteenth century."

Gray nodded. The map was a top-down view of the Arctic centered on the North Pole. He could even appreciate how much of the coastlines roughly matched existing lands. Except, in the center, surrounding the pole, was drawn a large landmass divided into four parts by rivers.

No wonder this map drew the attention of Lomonosov.

He glanced to Anna and pointed to the map's center. "Is that supposed to be Hyperborea?"

"Many have believed so. But Mercator never claimed as such. In fact, he was a meticulous cartographer, one famous, even today, for his accuracy."

"Looks like he went way off course with this one."

"You must understand that he constructed this map based on information gleaned from many sources, mostly charts and accounts from early Arctic explorers. And clearly *much* of what is recorded here is accurate. Most of the coastlines, some of the written notes—not only about the various lands, but also its peoples." She pointed to the lower right quadrant of the fanciful continent. "Like here."

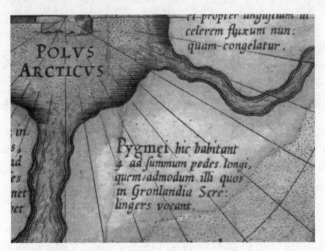

"As you can read," Anna continued, "this states that there are *pygmies* who live in this region. Most historians suspect Mercator is misidentifying the short-statured locals. Likely referring to the predecessors of the modern-day Inuit people."

"So, Mercator mixed truth with fiction. But what about the big landmass in the middle?" Gray circled a finger around the mysterious continent at the center of the map.

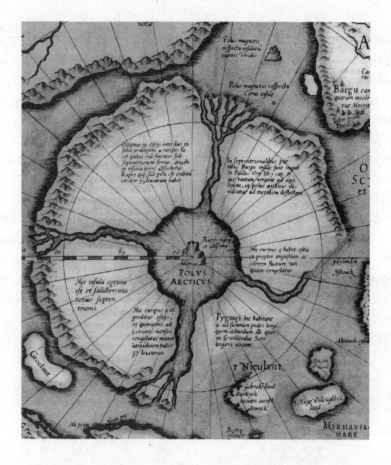

Anna studied it with a sigh. "According to Mercator's description, he states that rising at the North Pole is a huge mountain composed of pure lodestone, some thirty-three miles in diameter. It was where all compasses pointed, drawn by the pull of that magnetic peak. And not just compass needles, it also drew those four rivers toward it."

"Breaking the continent into its four sections," Gray noted.

"Correct. And where those rivers all met, at the base of the mountain, they formed a huge whirlpool that would empty into the world below."

"But there's nothing like that around the North Pole. For someone so accurate and meticulous as Mercator, how did he get it so wrong?"

"Again, he based his maps on eyewitness accounts from Arctic explorers."

"Like who?"

She shrugged. "There were many as I recall from my archival studies. For example, there was a pair of sixteenth-century adventurers, Frobisher and Davis, who traveled to northern Canada and reported vicious currents pulling icebergs toward the pole, towed—or so they believed—by those indrawing rivers."

Gray sighed and shook his head. "I guess this proves you should double-check your sources."

Anna scowled her disapproval. "Mercator *did*. The pair of Canadian adventurers weren't the only ones to tell this tale. Mercator's most influential source came from an English friar from Oxford, Nicolas of Lynn, who traveled to Norway in the fourteenth century and then continued farther to the north, sailing deep into the Arctic. He wrote a travelogue of his account, titled *Inventio Fortunata*, which he presented to King Edward III upon his return—along with an additional gift."

She glanced sidelong at him, as if this were significant.

"What was it?"

"The astrolabe that he used to navigate his journeys."

Gray stood straighter, picturing what was sketched inside the Greek book. He grew more interested in this tangent. "What was described in that travelogue?"

Anna stared down at the map. "According to Mercator, what you see here—a land of magnetic mountains and whirlpools—what you deem fantastical."

"But, of course, it *is*," he stressed. "Surely Nicolas, that English friar, had too many pints when writing his travelogue."

"We'll never know," Anna said sadly. "By the fifteenth century, all copies of the *Inventio Fortunata* went missing. We only know of it because of Mercator and a few others who had read and copied sections from it. Like Jacobus Cnoyen, a Brabantian explorer, who read Nicolas's travelogue and wrote about it in his own book—the *Itinerarium*."

She gave Gray another impactful glance. "Which subsequently also vanished."

Gray considered this. "It's as if someone was purposefully erasing all written records of this friar's book—and maybe of Hyperborea."

Anna shrugged. "All we have left are the shadows of it. Like Mercator's map. And a letter the cartographer wrote to a friend, a royal astronomer, where Mercator mentions the friar's travelogue."

Gray frowned. "If only we could get our hands on a copy of that book."

By now, Father Bailey and Bishop Yelagin had been drawn by the conversation, quietly following their discourse.

It was Bailey who broke the silence and pointed out the obvious, literally by reaching out a finger toward the desk.

"Isn't it right there?" he asked.

Both Gray and Anna turned from the map and looked at the book resting beside it. Gray had closed that same tome moments before and shifted it off Mercator's chart. So focused on the strange map, he had failed to note the importance of its paperweight.

Written in dark lettering and embossed into its leather cover were two words.

Inventio Fortunata

27

Tucker struggled to breathe through the cloth bag over his head. His wrists were cuffed behind him. His body jostled and rocked in the back of a van. He heard Valya on a cell phone in the front. Unfortunately, she was speaking in Russian, so he couldn't tell what she was talking about.

He could glean only one thing.

She's pissed.

Next to Tucker, the ponytailed woman with a thin scar—Nadira Ali Saeed—pressed a pistol into his side, aiming for his kidney.

Regardless of the threat, Tucker had no intention of struggling. He had heard Dr. Stutt's name come up as he eavesdropped on Valya.

If they're hauling me to Elle and Marco, I'll play the cooperative prisoner.

Still, the question remained:

Where are they taking me?

It had been roughly an hour and a half since he had been ambushed. By his estimate—after being forced at gunpoint from the Mercedes into a van—the vehicle had traveled some twenty or thirty miles. He heard increasing traffic noises: squealing brakes, honking horns, revving engines.

We must have returned to the outskirts of Moscow.

After another few minutes, the van swerved sharply, then jolted over a series of speed bumps. The latter threw him out of his seat. Still, the pistol never moved from his kidneys, which spoke to the deadly efficiency of the woman guarding him.

The van finally braked to a hard stop. Moments later, the door slid open. Even with his head bagged, the brighter light suggested they hadn't driven into a garage. He also heard the roar of heavier engines, both those rumbling in low timbres and others that screeched louder. He recognized the sounds of jets, landing and taking off.

An airport . . .

That was worrisome. He had hoped he'd be held somewhere closer at hand, to better his chances of a rescue.

Nadira nudged him with her pistol. He did his best to maneuver to the door. As he bent down to exit, a hand ripped the bag from his head. He blinked against the sudden brightness.

Valya stood there, holding the hood. "Sychkin wants to speak to you."

"I'm sure it'll be a pleasant conversation. But what about Dr. Stutt and my dog?"

"That beast is yours?" Valya said. "Didn't know Sigma had its own kennel. You've been a thorn in my side since Saint Petersburg."

"I'm not with Sigma," Tucker answered truthfully, enjoying the surprised pinch to Valya's brows. "I'm a hired gun. Like you."

"A mercenary?" Her voice rang with doubt.

"I prefer the term contracted employee. I was paid to track an operative of yours in Saint Petersburg. I was one of many tails placed on people in your organization." This last was a lie, but it sounded good to him. "My specialty is in hunting and extraction. After I secured Dr. Stutt, I was to keep her safe. So, if anything, you've been a thorn in *my* side."

Valya took this all in with a calculating expression, rubbing a finger along her jawline. He didn't know how much she believed, but he had no doubt she was assessing how best to put this to her advantage.

She finally swung to the side, clearing the way for him to hop out of the van, which was challenging with his arms secured behind him. He searched around and saw they were parked on the tarmac of a private airstrip, one next to a much larger and busier terminal. From the distance they had traveled, he guessed the main facility was Moscow's Sheremetyevo International Airport.

As he was led toward an open hangar, Tucker noted a small jet idling nearby. Its tire blocks were being dragged away by a sullen-faced employee, who showed no interest or surprise at the bound prisoner being marched at gunpoint into the hangar, as if this were a common occurrence.

Ah, Russia . . .

A voice rose from the depths of the building. "Tucker . . ."

It took him a few steps to pick out Elle's shape from the shadows. She stood before a closed office door. He also spotted a familiar four-legged figure. Marco had already recognized him as a breeze blew into the hangar, carrying Tucker's scent to the shepherd.

The dog whined and cried in a distressed greeting. Marco yanked on his leash, nearly toppling Elle over, who carried the other end of the lead.

"STAY," Tucker called over. "SIT."

Marco leaped once more toward him, then dropped to his haunches.

Tucker knew the familiarity of these simple commands would help calm the young Malinois. Dogs grew stressed in unknown situations, and with all that had happened, Marco was surely frazzled and drained. To hear Tucker's voice and to be able to fall back into the routine of his training was a warm hug of reassurance.

Tucker crossed toward the pair. They were watched over by the looming bulk of Yerik Raz. He carried no weapon, but his presence alone was intimidating enough.

Marching ahead of Tucker, Valya passed by the large monk and headed into the office without knocking. Tucker was left in the tender care of Nadira, who led him to Elle and Marco.

Once there, Tucker noted the muzzle locked around the dog's snout. Though he could appreciate the necessity on their captor's part, anger still fired through him.

Marco whined again in greeting, but the dog maintained his position, sticking to the last command. A tail swished behind the dog, but it was not the full swing of joyfulness. Only the tail's tip wagged, a sign of wary caution, as if Marco feared he had done something wrong.

Tucker wished he could reach out and console the dog. But with his wrists bound, he did all he could. He dropped to a knee and leaned his face close. "You're a good boy, Marco."

A tongue licked through the barred gate of the muzzle.

"I'm happy to see you, too," Tucker said.

Elle crouched next to him. "Are you okay?"

He turned to her and shrugged. "I've had better days."

The tension eased slightly in her shoulders. Her voice lowered to a whisper. "Do you know what happened to your friend, Mr. Kowalski?"

"He's not here?"

She shook her head. "He tried to help us escape, but we got separated."

Tucker frowned, hoping the big guy got out of the burning mansion. He focused on Elle. "What about you? How're you doing?"

"I've had better days, too." She glanced sidelong at Yerik. "They're planning on taking me north. To an Arctic base in Severodvinsk. I'm to be held there until I'm needed."

"Then just keep cooperating. We'll have to see what happens from here."

"And you?"

"That's still up in the air."

The door to the office opened, and Valya exited with Sychkin. Neither looked pleased—not about the situation, and for the archpriest, certainly not with Tucker.

"I've been informed that my *dacha* in Sergiyev Posad, an estate that's been in my family for five generations, has burnt to the ground." Each word was spoken with an icy bitterness. "And *you* were involved."

Tucker remained down on one knee, doing his best to look like less of a threat. "I was hired to search for Dr. Stutt. To use my dogs to sniff her out. Nothing more. This is not my war."

Sychkin eyed Marco. The dog noted the attention and curled his lips into a snarl, exposing fangs. A low growl rumbled from his throat.

"Quiet," Tucker ordered.

Marco's eyes narrowed, looking like he might refuse. The young shepherd had been stubborn from the get-go with his training. It was no wonder the pup had failed out of the MWD training center in Lackland. Still, Tucker recognized that stubbornness was born of intelligence. With time and the right training, he might outshine Kane.

Okay, maybe not Kane . . . no one else could be that good.

Marco's lips lowered, and his growl died away. Still, one long canine tooth remained bared.

Definitely stubborn.

Sychkin acknowledged Tucker's control of Marco with a small nod. "It seems Dr. Stutt has grown fond of your dog. If you can keep him under control, I see the worth of your presence. Still, if you are to continue with us, you'll need to *pay* for your passage north."

"How?"

"I want all the information you have on the group that hired you. Who they are? What do they know?"

Tucker swallowed, not sure how willing he was to comply.

His hesitation was noted.

Sychkin gave the smallest nod to Yerik, proving that the archpriest had as much control over the monk as Tucker had over Marco. Yerik drew a pistol and pointed it at Elle.

"Must I make my point clearer," Sychkin warned.

As Tucker stared at the archpriest, he imagined scalping that beard off his face. Instead, he said calmly, "You need her."

Sychkin smiled, but there was no warmth. "True." Another nod, and the pistol shifted to Marco. "But I don't need this dog. There are other ways to make Dr. Stutt cooperate."

Tucker's jaw tightened.

"Lie, and your partner's death will be prolonged. And you will watch every moment of it." Sychkin leaned closer. "So, I recommend that you tell me something worth the price of your safe passage north. Disappoint me, and we're done talking."

Tucker weighed his options. If he refused, he had no doubt that Marco would be slain, and Tucker would be next—but only after they tortured him for all the information they could get.

Later, Elle would likely suffer a similar fate.

So, it was either certain death at the hands of these monsters, or trust in Gray and the others' abilities. Tucker hated to put a target on their backs, but at least the others were still free and able to act.

Tucker felt the chafe of his cuffs, saw the muzzle on Marco, read the fear in Elle's eyes—and made his decision.

Sorry, Gray.

Tucker let out a long breath. He knew exactly what knowledge would gain him the most time.

"Well?" Sychkin pressed him.

"You're looking for the location of the Golden Library at the Trinity Lavra," Tucker said stiffly. "The others learned where it is. Or at least, the spot on those grounds where it's hidden."

Sychkin looked at Valya.

"I warned you that these adversaries are clever," Valya said, acknowledging that Tucker's claim was possible. "You best not underestimate them."

Sychkin turned back to Tucker. "Where?"

Knowing the cost of a lie, he answered truthfully.

"The Ringing Tower."

28

Deep under the Ringing Tower, Gray stood over Lomonosov's desk. Next to him, Sister Anna cradled the only extant copy of Nicolas of Lynn's *Inventio Fortunata* in her hands. Her arms trembled with the weight of all those centuries, of what had been thought lost forever.

He stared past the buried study's threshold and pictured the greater expanse of the Golden Library, spreading outward in dozens of chambers, all lined by golden chests that held the promise of many other treasures of antiquity.

"I wonder if there could be a copy of Cnoyen's *Itinerarium*, too?" Anna asked with clear wonder in her voice. "That other vanished book."

Gray focused on the task at hand. "I don't know if we need it. Lomonosov left the *Inventio Fortunata* atop Mercator's old map. Surely for a reason. It must be significant."

Bailey reached out for the precious volume. "May I?" he asked Anna. She passed it to him. "Of course."

Bailey treated the book with great care and reverence. He drew it open. "Maybe we must read it. It's written in Latin, but I should be able to translate it if given enough time."

Gray sensed they were running out of exactly that. "I don't think it was Lomonosov's intent that we read the entire book. He left the text open to a specific page. That must be important."

"Do you remember which one?" Anna asked.

"No," Gray admitted. He took the book from Bailey. "But it shouldn't be hard to figure out."

He carefully flipped through the yellowed pages, nagged by something he was forgetting. Still, it took all his concentration to find the set of pages that were coated in dust after being left open for so long. He finally located them and confirmed it was the right set of pages from the crease in the binding as he splayed the book open.

"This is the spot." He turned to Bailey. "Can you translate these two pages?"

"I better be able to, or they'll strip me of my degree in ancient studies."

Bailey set the book atop the desk and hunched over the pages. He read silently for a spell, hovering his finger over various lines. "Some sections are faded into obscurity, but the text seems to describe what you were discussing a moment ago. A great mountain—*Rupus Nigra et Altissima*, which translates to 'Very High Black Cliff'—and a huge whirlpool below it, fed by four great rivers."

Anna pointed to the map. "Mercator wrote those same words—*Rupus Nigra et Altissima*—next to the mountain on his map. Right in the center."

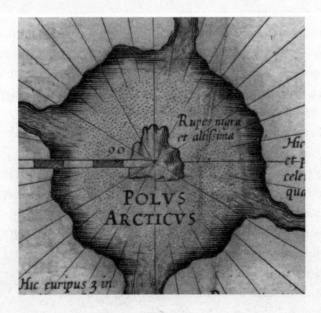

Gray nodded, still nagged by the sense he was forgetting something.

With his brows furrowed, Bailey continued reading. "This line elaborates in more detail. '*The land is most strange and should be shunned by all. Do not be deceived by its false pull, do not be lured by the wonders it hides, not even the long life it promises in stone and water. Instead, fear that which ended the people of Hyperborea. For if it ever breaks free, it will destroy all of us.*'"

Gray frowned. "That warning certainly supports what is inscribed on the wall plaque."

"And sounds even more dire," Anna added.

Bailey glanced up from the book. "There's also this. Someone—no doubt Lomonosov—underlined the phrase *falsum viverra*, or *false pull* in that line I just read. Could that be significant?"

Anna and Gray shared a look, but neither of them could make sense of it.

"And there's a section I can't read," Bailey admitted. "It's handwritten in the margin, a long passage, with an arrow pointing to another word in the text—*magneticus*—which means magnetic."

"The note in the margin?" Gray asked. "Is it too faded to make out?"

"No." He passed the book to Anna. "It's written in Glagolitic."

Ah . . .

Gray joined her, staring down at the crisp penmanship along the page's edge. "Can you translate it?"

"I'll try."

She turned to Jason, who hovered behind them. Jason pulled out his tablet, which still had Anna's Glagolitic conversion chart on it. They set about working on the mysterious message from Lomonosov.

Gray watched them, alone with his thoughts for the moment. As Anna tapped at the glowing screen, he suddenly recalled what had been nagging at him—both now and yesterday. The tablet in Anna's hand had reminded him.

He drew out his own device, turned it on, and flipped through the photos that Monsignor Borrelli had taken. He settled on one, realizing how much it looked like the description in the *Inventio Fortunata*—and what was drawn on Mercator's map.

It filled half a page of Herodotus's *Histories*, showing a mountainous valley that framed a lone peak at its center. Around it had been sketched a swirling pool.

Gray studied it.

Was this a glimpse of that same place, from someone who had been there?

Before he could ponder it further, Anna stepped back to them. "I think I have it all. Lomonosov's annotation was long, but not difficult to translate. Still, it makes little sense."

"What did he write?"

Anna stared down at the book in her hand and read the passage aloud. "'*Ah, dear Mercator, you hid well what you knew. Making large what is not. Building mountains where there are none. Burying the truth, like Catherine and I do now under a tower. Others should have looked more closely at what you drew, listened more intently when you claimed that this is not the truth—that it lies elsewhere.*'" She looked up. "Again, the last line points to the word *magnetic*—as if that's significant."

Gray closed his eyes, trying to unlock this riddle. Lomonosov must have written this for a reason, leaving this page open as centuries passed, sending a message into the future.

But what did he mean?

Gray talked aloud, trying to use his voice to tease out any answers. "Not only did that annotation point to the word *magnetic*, but he also underlined the words *false pull*, which possibly also suggests something magnetic."

"Or falsely magnetic," Jason reminded him, adding his voice to the puzzle.

Gray nodded.

There's something there . . . but what?

Gray squinted, trying to bring it into focus. "'*Building mountains where there are none.*' Could Lomonosov be referring to the fact that there is no magnetic mountain sitting at the north pole?"

"And '*making large what is not*,'" Bailey added. "Mercator drew a huge landmass, a veritable continent. But from what Nicolas wrote in his book, it almost sounds like he's describing somewhere far smaller."

"A place that Mercator blew up huge," Anna said. "Magnifying it, so he could delineate what Nicolas had described in a greater detail at the center of his map."

Gray returned his attention to the map. "'*Burying the truth.*' Maybe Mercator was trying to accomplish what Catherine and Lomonosov were doing here by keeping the Golden Library buried. To preserve knowledge—but keep it safeguarded and hidden."

"In Lomonosov's annotation," Bailey said, "he hints that Mercator drew the answer on this map. '*Others should have looked more closely at what you drew.*'"

Gray nodded. "And *listened*, too. According to Lomonosov, Mercator '*claimed that this is not the truth*'—pointing to the word magnetic—and '*that it lies elsewhere.*' Can anyone make sense of that?"

Anna stiffened, swearing in Russian, which earned a scowl from Yelagin, who leaned heavily on his staff, clearly exhausted.

"I think I know what he's talking about," Anna blurted out, sounding astounded with herself. "A well-documented part of the map's history is that Mercator *never* believed the central mountain he drew was the true magnetic pole. He told people many times that the magnetic *Rupus Nigra et Altissima*—Nicolas's Very High Black Cliff—lay *elsewhere*. But no one took heed of him."

"Where did he believe it was located?" Gray asked.

Anna pulled his attention back to Mercator's map. She pointed to a spot—an island from the look of it—positioned higher up the map.

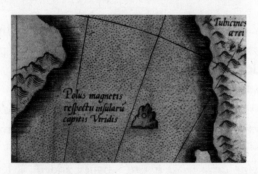

"Mercator even labels this spot *Polus magnetis*—the *magnetic pole*." She swung her finger to the center of the map. "While the mountain here he simply named *Polus Arcticus*—the Arctic Pole."

Jason frowned. "Could Mercator have been differentiating between the geographical North Pole and the magnetic pole of the Earth? They're in different locations. While the geographic pole is fixed, the magnetic one wanders all around."

Gray had to consider this, but it seemed unlikely, and for good reason. "No one from Mercator's time made that distinction. It wasn't recognized as two different locations until the middle of the eighteen hundreds. Three centuries after Mercator drew this map."

"Then what is that island on his map?" Jason asked.

Gray stared down at the tiny mountain in the ocean. "I think it's what Nicolas described—some island with a strong magnetic pull, one that *falsely* pulled his ship off course, drawing it away from *true* north."

Jason pointed to the large continent in the map's middle. "And what about the rest of what Mercator drew?"

"I think it was his attempt to expand what couldn't be drawn on that small spot on his map. Instead, he filled the Arctic's middle void with what Nicolas had described in his *Inventio Fortunata*."

ARKANGEL 271

"*Making large what is not*," Anna added, quoting Lomonosov.

Bailey leaned to peer at the small island. "But where is this place?"

It was a great question.

Gray stared across the charting and navigation tools spread atop the desk. "I think that's what Lomonosov was attempting to figure out here. He must have gleaned enough to send out an expedition to pin it down."

He remembered Anna telling him about the rumors that Catherine the Great dispatched ships on secret missions to the Far North, searching for this lost continent.

"But how do we continue from here?" Anna asked.

"I don't think we'll need all these sextants and compasses," Gray said.

He stared down at his tablet, which still glowed with the image of that strange valley, surrounded by cliffs, circling a swirling pool.

That's the location we need to find.

He closed the tablet's window and opened a map of the polar region, one that was not drawn from accounts of long-dead explorers and lost books. It was a modern atlas of the Arctic, produced in exacting detail.

Gray added in a set of crosshairs at the center, marking the geographic North Pole.

He then crossed over and took a few snapshots of Mercator's handi-work. Once satisfied with the image, he overlaid it atop the modern map. While the sixteenth-century version was not perfect in its rendition of every coastline, one detail was constant between the two, both past and present—the geographical North Pole.

He centered Mercator's mountainous pole atop the current map's spot, then played with the rotation until he could fix another point that was equally well mapped in the sixteenth century—the coastline of northern Europe.

With those two points overlapped and fixed, he boxed off the position of the mysterious island, the possible wellspring for all the mythology of Hyperborea.

He showed his handiwork to the others.

"It appears Mercator's magnetic island lies somewhere in the East Siberian Sea," Gray announced. "By tasking satellites with magnetometers, we should be able to detect any anomalous fluctuations in the magnetic field within that region and roughly pinpoint the island's location."

As the others studied the map, passing the tablet around, Jason waved Gray to the side. He did not look happy. His voice dropped to a whisper. "That's some fractious waters. The East Siberian Sea is one of the major shipping lanes for Russia's Northern Sea Route. If that island is far enough out into the remote waters of the Arctic, and Russia can claim it for themselves, it will vastly extend their territorial reach, consuming a large bulk of the polar sea. It risks destabilizing the entire region."

Gray understood. "We can't let that Arkangel Society get first crack at reaching the island. If we can expose this discovery—one with enormous historical implications—we may be able to keep a territorial war from starting. But to do so, we need to shine a big light on it."

Jason nodded grimly and stated the mantra of transparency. "Sunlight is the best disinfectant."

"Exactly. But there is a larger danger we must consider."

"What's that?"

Gray stared up at the warning on the wall, remembering Nicolas's admonition in his book: *Instead, fear that which ended the people of Hyperborea. For if it ever breaks free, it will destroy all of us.*

"Something dangerous must be out there. Something that frightened Catherine enough to hide her library." He turned back to Jason. "And I'm worried we're not the first to learn of this."

"You think Sychkin might know, too."

"He has possession of that stolen Greek text. He has access to the decades of research by the Arkangel Society. So, I would not be surprised if he came upon this knowledge already. Still, for the moment, we're one step ahead of him, but that lead will not likely last."

"Then what do we do?"

Gray shrugged. "We follow Sigma's motto."

Jason grinned. "*Be there first.*"

Gray nodded. "That still leaves one last concern."

"Which is what?"

"Is anything even out there?"

Yelagin cleared his throat, having clearly overheard this last exchange. "There must be."

He drew their attention.

The bishop leaned on his staff, standing by the fireplace. He stared up at the curve of the tusk. "No one noticed this, but there's a *word* inscribed in Greek along the bottom here. I believe it spells out *Hyperborea*, only some letters are missing or covered over."

The bishop reached up and rubbed his palm across the yellowed ivory, as if to polish the word clearer. As he did, the tusk shifted under his hand. It seemed the artifact was more delicately balanced than it first appeared.

Gray realized why and lunged for Yelagin. "Stop . . ."

But it was too late.

The trap had been opulently baited—not with gold, but with a wealth of ivory, poised to punish any potential thief.

In the neighboring room, a meter-wide door tore open from the roof. Water pounded down from some great cistern above. The force was strong enough to break the oaken table below.

And it wasn't only that one room.

It was *all* of them.

Crashing waters echoed from every direction, rapidly flooding the library.

"Make for the stairs!" Gray hollered.

He got everyone moving. As he did, he stared across at the row upon row of golden chests. Only now did he recognize the significance of an unusual feature to them.

All the boxes had been sealed with wax.

He now understood why.

The trap's designers needed them to be watertight.

Gray grabbed Yelagin by the arm. Bailey came to his aid, too, while Jason helped Anna, whose eyes were wide with terror.

"Go, go, go . . ." Gray urged.

Water swamped into the small study, going from ankle-deep to knee-height before they could wade clear of the room. As the level rose, a certainty grew.

We'll never make it to the exit.

Jason gasped, hauling through the deluge. "Where's all this water coming from?"

Gray knew the answer, remembering all the stories of Lavra's sacred springs, fonts of miraculous healing. With this realization came a hard truth.

We're all about to drown in holy water.

29

Seichan stood at the headwaters of a raging cataract and despaired.

No . . .

Steps away, a huge flume of water pounded out of a trapdoor in the staircase's roof and formed a heavy torrent tumbling down into the depths. A backwash of cold spray wet her face and soaked her clerical dress.

Several minutes ago, she had crossed through the maze of a wine cellar beneath the Ringing Tower, following a rough description that Monk had given her. As she reached the secret door that Gray had opened, she heard the birth of a waterfall deeper down. It had roared like a buried dragon. Fearing the worst, she had rushed headlong until she came face to face with the monstrous flood.

Poised before it now, she leaned forward on her toes, weighing whether to throw herself into the maelstrom and hope for the best. But she recognized that she would either drown or be battered to death before she ever reached the staircase's bottom.

She fell back onto her heels, knowing she could not risk it. But it was not only about protecting her own life.

Jack can't lose both of us.

Still, she stood there for several breaths, inwardly cursing, refusing to accept what roared in front of her, what it meant.

Unable to take it anymore, she flung herself around and fled up the steps.

She prayed that either Gray had already left or that he had some other plan.

She clung to that hope as she ascended the rest of the stairs and crossed the wine cellar. Still, her breathing choked into gasps. Her legs went leaden.

Hope had never been kind to her, proving false all too often.

Please, not this time . . .

She reached the stairs that rose out of the cellars and hauled herself up the steps to the tower's entry hall. As she did, she heard raised voices—sharp shouts and crisp orders—coming from outside.

She shifted to the tower's exit, careful to stay hidden in the shadows. Outside, a group of soldiers—a dozen or so—headed through the gardens surrounding the theological school. The men wore combat gear and carried assault weapons. Someone in the lead pointed toward the Ringing Tower.

Seichan rolled out of view, a question foremost in her mind.

Why are they coming here?

Had whatever triggered the flooding sounded an alert, drawing the armed men? Or had Sigma's group been exposed?

She expected it was the second explanation.

For the past half day, she had tamped down her paranoia about a mole in their midst. After the embassy attack, no one seemed aware that Sigma had traveled into Sergiyev Posad. Her suspicion of the two members of the Russian Orthodox Church—Yelagin and Anna—had dimmed. Likewise with Yuri, who had saved her life only hours ago.

As soldiers pounded across the cobbles toward the tower, she regretted such trust.

I should've known better.

While *hope* had failed her many times, *paranoia* seldom did.

She rushed across the entry hall. The tower had no back door—at least not on this level. She slipped under a velvet rope that closed off the stairs leading up. She was careful not to touch it, to leave it swinging, lest some soldier should notice it.

She escaped up the steps, climbing to the tower's third level.

Voices echoed up from below, along with the tramp of many boots.

She fled from them, over to one of the open windows that circled this tier. They were old arrow slits used to target attackers. She squeezed sideways through one, then got stuck. Struggling only wedged her tighter.

She closed her eyes, ignoring the voices drawing closer, coming up the steps.

Calm down.

A large part of her anxiety had nothing to do with the approaching soldiers. Fear for Gray and the others kept her tense, stiffening her honed flexibility.

She forced herself to stop struggling, to exhale slowly, to narrow her chest. As she did, her body slid through the opening. She let herself fall. Twisting in midair, she landed in a crouch atop the roof of the Lavra's towering wall. She balanced herself on the thin ridge in the middle, then took off.

The damp tiles underfoot were treacherous and slippery.

Fearing a fall, she kicked off the drab sandals that completed her disguise as a nun and ran barefooted. She gained speed. Still, she waited for a shout to rise behind her, for gunfire to pursue her. She could only imagine what a bystander below might make of her flight. She must look like a huge black crow sweeping atop the wall.

As she ran, she let the winds blow the apostolnik from her shoulders. It fluttered away, like a scrap of shadow. Her hair fanned wide. Despite the danger, she felt far freer, able to cast aside her fears for Gray.

She reached the next tower and easily scaled through another arrow slit, vanishing away from sight. Once inside, she sent a plea to Gray— willing to give hope one last chance.

Come back to me.

30

Gray forged through the rising flood. The water level was waist-high and climbing fast. Dozens of crashing torrents echoed from the chambers on all sides. A hazardous flotsam of broken chairs and slabs of tabletops confounded the group's passage, swirling and forming dams.

Jason called, yelling to be heard above the crashing waters. "Help!"

Gray turned at his frantic shout. The young man struggled with Anna. Her long dress—already clinging and weighing her body down—had snagged onto one of the logjams of debris.

Gray pushed Yelagin toward Bailey. "Take him. Keep going."

Gray and the priest had been hauling the bishop between them.

Bailey nodded. "I got him."

Gray set off, kicking and paddling over to Jason and Anna. Once he reached them, he drew a knife from his belt. The woman's eyes were wide with panic. The shifting blockage was dragging her under.

He felt along the fabric to where it was snagged. The cloth had twisted into a hard rope.

He let it go, knowing it would take too long to saw through it. He shifted behind Anna, lifted his blade, and slit her dress from neckline to waist. She understood and wiggled free with Jason's help, shedding her garment, swimming away in her bra and underwear.

"That's better," she gasped out.

Jason headed after Anna.

Even this brief stop had cost them valuable time.

Ahead, Bailey had an arm hooked around Yelagin's waist. The bishop used his staff like a rafting pole to help propel them along.

By now, the water had reached neck high. They'd all be swimming soon. And terror made it look as if the roof were closing in on them.

He had to accept the truth.

No one's escaping this trap.

Gray's heart pounded in his ears. He wished Lomonosov's study had been closer to the staircase. Still, even alone, Gray doubted he could've crossed that distance in time. The remote location of the study had made it a deathtrap.

Wait . . .

He halted in mid-stroke.

That makes no sense.

His mind spun—and he knew the answer.

"Stop!" he boomed.

Heads turned his way.

He pointed behind him. "We're going the wrong direction!"

"What?" Jason called back.

"Follow me!"

With no time to explain, Gray turned and waded back toward Lomonosov's study. It was still closer than the distant stairs. Even if the group could've reached the staircase, he suspected it was already a waterfall. The trap's designers would have made sure no one escaped that way.

He also suspected something else about those engineers.

They wouldn't want to be caught in their own snare.

Especially Lomonosov.

The Russian scientist was too smart to risk his own demise if some quake or other mishap disturbed the mammoth tusk and triggered the trap. There had to be another way out, one close to his study.

And I know where it is.

He prayed he was right and not leading everyone to their doom.

As he reached the room, he found the waters inside clogged with floating books from Lomonosov's shelves. He pushed his way through, shoving ancient texts out of his way, forging a path for the others.

"Why are we back here?" Jason gasped, treading water now.

Gray's toes could still touch, allowing him to kick off the bottom the last few yards. As he did, he tried to explain. "If Lomonosov worked endless hours down here, he wouldn't do so without a backup plan. He or the original designers would have engineered a way to escape this trap if it were inadvertently triggered. And that back door would have to be close at hand."

"Where?" Jason asked.

Gray pointed at the answer.

Anna's eyes widened in disbelief. "The fireplace?"

"I thought it was a replica," Gray panted out as he reached its mantel. "But now I wager it served double duty in the past. At one time, it must have been a functioning hearth, one whose chimney to the surface could double as an emergency escape route."

To test his theory, Gray ducked underwater, grabbed the top edge of the hearth, and wiggled himself into the space. With his upper torso inside, his hands blindly pawed above.

He nearly choked in relief as he found a chimney leading up. To be sure, he squirmed the rest of the way inside—until he was able to stand and clear his head out of the water inside the shaft. Under his palms and fingers, he felt handholds carved along the chute's inner wall, forming a stone ladder leading up.

Thank god . . .

Satisfied, he dropped and slid out of the fireplace's hearth.

He popped back to the surface in the study.

"There's a way out," he announced. "But it's not going to be easy."

11:59 A.M.

Jason climbed behind Anna. She shivered—both from cold and terror. Wearing only a bra and underwear, she looked naked. Still, she showed no concern or embarrassment. Like all of them, her focus was on the arduous ascent, on clinging to the hand- and toeholds along one side of the chimney.

The passage was tight. Rock rubbed Jason's back if he leaned out too far to raise a knee or reach an arm. But it was manageable for someone of his small stature. Overhead, Gray struggled a bit more as he led the way.

Luckily, Kowalski wasn't with them.

He'd never have fit through here.

Still, another teammate strained for a different reason.

Below Jason, Yelagin wheezed and coughed. The elderly bishop fought for every yard gained, but so far, he was managing the ascent. Mostly due to the thoughtfulness afforded them by the engineers of this exit. Every thirty feet, a side cubby had been dug out. It allowed for two people to sit, perched above the drop, and catch their breath.

At each spot, the group had allowed Yelagin to relax with Bailey—while everyone else braced their backs against the chimney wall and pinned themselves in place and waited.

"There's another rest stop up ahead," Gray called down.

They had reached this one quicker than expected. The last cubby was only twenty or so feet below them. The gaps between the rest stops must be getting smaller, which was a merciful boon. In the shine of flashlights looped to the men's belts, Yelagin's face had gone deathly white, his eyes pinched from the exertion.

Jason returned his focus above. "Anna, do you need to take a break? Maybe sit for a spell with the bishop?"

"I . . . I'm okay. I can keep going. For now, at least."

Anna stared up the endless chute. Though she didn't ask it, he knew what she was thinking.

How much farther do we have to go?

With no way of knowing, they continued the ascent in silence. Despite her assurance a moment ago, Anna looked longingly toward the cubby, but she climbed past it.

Jason couldn't blame her. By now, his fingers were crabbed, and his shoulders ached. It was actually a relief when Bailey shouted under him.

"I'll help Bishop Yelagin get seated. We may need to rest a bit longer this time."

Sighing, Jason pushed his back against the opposite wall and pinned his legs to a toehold. He felt secure enough to let go with his hands and massage his fingers. Anna did the same. Past her, Gray looked anxious to keep moving, but there was no rush.

The rising waters below had stopped pursuing them for some time, indicative that the library must be fully flooded by now.

Under his legs, lights jostled as Bailey helped Yelagin into the cubby. The bishop thanked him, collapsing heavily in exhaustion. As he did, a loud metallic snap sounded, echoing sharply from the two men's position.

Oh, sh—

It was another boobytrap, likely meant to rid the chute of any trespassers who stumbled upon it, those who failed to note that this cubby was not like the others, positioned differently from the regular run of rest stops.

A wall of heavy water burst from the rear of the cubby, surging out a hidden door. The bishop's body was slammed against the chute's opposite wall, crashing into Bailey, who still clung to the stone ladder. The two men tangled, with limbs thrashing, then Yelagin fell away, vanishing into the torrent.

Bailey managed to keep one handhold. His legs flailed under him, scrabbling for a purchase. But the surge was too fierce. He looked up in a panic, as if recognizing the inevitable.

Jason refused to accept this and headed down. "Hang on!"

Bailey choked on the downpour. "No . . . you'll be pulled with me!"

The priest looked below. "I'll try to reach—"

Then he was gone, ripped off the wall by the current.

Jason cried out, nearly losing his own grip. He searched, but there was no sign of either man. Water continued to flood down the chimney.

Knowing there was nothing he could do, Jason faced back up. Anna stared down at him. He had no words.

Gray did—offering the only option left to them. "We keep going."

12:43 P.M.

Free of the chimney, Gray reached down, grabbed Jason's outstretched arm, and pulled him out of the crack in the rock. The top of the chute had emptied into a cave. The shaft had narrowed precariously at the end, making for a difficult final ascent.

But they had made it.

Just not all of them.

Anna stood to the side. Gray had given her his jacket, which hung over her shoulders. She hadn't even tried to button it. Instead, she had hugged her arms around her body, not in shyness at the state of her undress, but in shock and grief.

Jason remained on his hands and knees. He breathed heavily, plainly as distraught as Anna. "Wh . . . what do we do now?" he gasped out.

"We rejoin the others," Gray answered, doing his best to compartmentalize the loss of the two men.

"Shouldn't we wait here?" Anna mumbled. "In case . . . maybe they'll . . ."

Her shoulders sagged.

Even she couldn't find the strength for hope.

Gray let the two rest for a few minutes. He waited until he got a nod from each, then set off.

Sunlight glared on one side of the cavern, promising an exit nearby. He led Anna and Jason toward the light. As he did, he cast a final glance back. Even this close, the pinched entrance into the chimney was nearly invisible, blending into the surrounding rock.

No wonder it was never discovered.

Gray shook his head and headed off.

The three of them crossed through the boulder-strewn cavern and had to crawl along a low tunnel to reach a grotto on the far side. It opened into a forest. Ahead, between the trees, the towering white walls of the Trinity Lavra glowed in the midday sun. It appeared they had exited a half-mile or so outside the grounds of the monastic compound.

Which is just as well.

Gray saw no reason to return to the Trinity Lavra.

With a long hike ahead of them, they stumbled off into the woods.

Anna looked haunted and forlorn, barely blinking, staring blankly.

Jason turned to Gray, his eyes wide, searching for an answer to explain their loss.

Gray had none.

All he could do was make a promise.

"We're not going to let their sacrifice be in vain." He stared toward the Lavra, but he peered much further, thousands of miles. "We'll find that lost continent."

Still, a warning echoed inside him, one inscribed in wood above a mammoth tusk.

Never go there, never trespass, never wake that which is sleeping.

Gray headed onward without slowing.

Screw that.

FIFTH

Icebreaker

31

Tucker walked Marco across the snow-packed pavement, heading for a sparse patch of yellow grass where a steam grate had melted a swath of the church's yard. He eyed the tunnel below the grate as he stomped over it, shaking a crust of ice from his boots, weighing the vent's usefulness as a means of escape.

His assessment: *No chance in hell.*

Especially now.

A trio of armed guards in white Arctic gear trailed them during this relief break for Tucker's four-legged partner. Elle strode alongside them, bundled in a puffy coat that was too large for her.

Their small group had just finished a meager lunch in their cell. It had consisted of a cold gruel of lentils with a gristly meat of unknown origin. But at least the loaf of bread had only a few scabs of mold on it. Even Marco had turned his nose up at the offering, until Tucker had ordered him to eat. The dog needed to keep his strength up.

They all did.

As Marco sniffed and circled, Tucker gazed out at the spread of the White Sea Naval Base. The sun sat wanly overhead in cloud-scudded skies. It had snowed last night, just a dusting, when they had arrived in Severodvinsk, but a dark line sitting at the horizon suggested a bigger storm would roll in from the sea before nightfall.

Closer at hand, the base looked like the many others that Tucker had
transited through as a Ranger: cement block buildings, yellow dock
cranes, narrow brick stacks churning out smoke. Uniformed men and
women soldiered past, keeping a wary distance, eyes down, huddled in
their jackets. The sound of heavy machinery and the sharper notes of
rivet guns echoed all around the shipyards.

A larger rumbling drew all their eyes to a corner, where an eight-
wheeled armored personnel carrier trundled past, topped by a 30mm
cannon. Tucker recognized the BTR-80A APC. From its larger wheels
and wider treads, this one looked adapted to Arctic conditions, like
much of the base's equipment—not to mention the brigade that trained
out of this base, using the surrounding frozen landscape and seas for
their exercises.

"*Potoraplivat'sya*," a guard barked behind them, hurrying them along
with a wave of his rifle.

"Seems like our leisurely stroll has come to an end," Tucker commented to Elle.

Marco must've understood and finally squatted over the grate and
defecated a wet stream directly into the steam tunnel. Tucker hoped
the smell spread far across the base. That's what they get for the quality
of their food, but Tucker knew that sludgy stool was also likely due to
stress.

Another guard yelled at the dog, raising the butt of his rifle.

Elle stepped in the way before Tucker could. She cursed the soldier
out in Russian, or at least it sounded that way.

The soldier backed down and pointed his weapon toward the church,
ordering them inside. "*Shevelis'.*"

They were herded back toward the sanctuary. The centuries-old
Church of the Holy Sacrament was built of lichen-crusted stone and
hewn pine, gone black with age. But atop its tall steeple shone a golden
orthodox cross, one that looked newly installed.

They were taken to the rear of the church, where steps led down
into the cellar. Last night, Tucker had been surprised at the site of their
imprisonment, then they were herded into the gloomy basement below
the gilded nave of the church. He had quickly identified this level to be

a lingering holdout of the old Soviet era, a site of a former jail, maybe an old black-ops facility.

Clearly, its new owners, the orthodox church—or at least, a certain archpriest—still found such a place useful.

The guards marched them to their cell. Elle had been offered her own accommodation, but she had insisted on joining Tucker instead, clearly not wanting to be alone. Though, he suspected it had less to do with his own presence than Marco's. The dog had slept next to her in her cot. She had kept one arm protectively over him.

Once locked in their cell, Tucker dropped to his bed on the other side of the room, which had a mattress as thick and stiff as a deck of playing cards. They shared a single commode and shower that continually dripped in the open corner. But with their respective backs turned, they managed a degree of privacy.

Elle sank atop her cot.

Without being told, Marco hopped next to her.

Tucker gave him the smallest nod.

Good boy.

Elle stared across at him, leaning back on her arms. She was silent for a spell, then shifted straighter. "Tell me about yourself," she said softly. "How did you end up here, locked up with me?"

"A series of bad choices apparently."

She scowled at him, clearly wanting more than flippancy. He read the pinch of fear that haunted her eyes, along with the thin cast to her lips. She recognized the danger, the likelihood of a fatal outcome, yet she held herself together, maybe from an ingrained Russian stoicism, an acceptance of life's injustices. But he suspected it was just this woman, one who had twice stepped between a rifle and his dog.

Tucker sighed, knowing he owed her an honest response. "I grew up in a country not much warmer than Siberia. Rolla, North Dakota. Near the Canadian border."

"What was it like? Growing up there?"

"Pretty nice. Spent summers at Willow Lake, hiking the North Woods. In winter, it was snowshoeing and ice fishing. But it wasn't as idyllic as that postcard sounds."

"Why's that?"

"My mom and dad died when I was three." He shrugged. "Don't really remember them. They're just pictures in a photo album. It was my grandfather who raised me. Then, when I was thirteen, he had a heart attack from shoveling snow one hard winter. I found his body after coming home from school."

She winced. "How horrible."

He continued, not entirely sure why he was being so forthright. "From there, with no other relatives, I ended up in the foster care system. I petitioned for early emancipation and joined the military at seventeen."

He skipped over the dark years between those two tentpoles of his life.

It's no wonder I like dogs better than people.

"That's how you ended up with Marco and Kane?" she asked, rubbing fingers through Marco's ruff. "Military working dogs."

"Actually, it was Kane and *Abel* first—Kane's littermate brother."

She must have read something in his voice or attitude. She winced again, as if sensing this was a well of pain.

"I lost him during a firefight in Takur Ghar. We were assisting soldiers from the Tenth Mountain Division, securing bunkers in a place called Hell's Halfpipe, when a pair of IEDs exploded. Taliban fighters swarmed from concealed positions."

He shook his head, trying to clear the memory, but it was branded there.

He fell back to that mountaintop.

He and a handful of survivors had been able to reach a defensible position, to hold out long enough for an evac helicopter to land. Once Kane and his teammates were loaded, he had been about to jump off and go for Abel, who was injured, but before he could, a crewman dragged him back aboard and held him down—where he could only watch.

A pair of Taliban fighters chased down Abel, who was limping toward the rising helo, his pained eyes fixed on Tucker, his leg trailing blood. Tucker scrambled for the door, only to be pulled back yet again.

Then the Taliban fighters had reached Abel.

He squeezed those last memories away, but not the haunting voice forever in the back of his mind: *You could've tried harder; you could have reached him.*

If he had, he knew he would have been killed, too, but at least Abel wouldn't have died alone. Alone and wondering why Tucker had abandoned him . . .

"I'm sorry," Elle whispered.

"I've come to peace with it."

Barely . . .

He pictured the arid Arizona desert, and a glimpse of sun dogs chasing across the sky, where he had been able to let go of some of his grief.

But he would never be entirely over that loss.

And he knew why.

I don't want to be.

Abel had earned that pain.

Plus, that grief taught him an important lesson.

He stared over at Marco.

Never again will I allow myself to be held back.

He cleared his throat and nodded at Elle, ready to change the subject. "What about you? How did you end up being a botanist? Especially one who specializes in carnivorous plants."

She looked like she wanted to press him more, but she let it go. "I grew up in Saint Petersburg, raised by a single father. He was an agronomist, specializing in crop production during the Soviet era. I spent summers at the city's botanical gardens, often acting as my father's lab assistant, sometimes traveling across Russia with him. While he leaned toward the practicality of food production, specifically grain crops, I found myself more fascinated by the unusual strategies plants employed to survive, to compete, to thrive."

"And I suspect nothing is more *unusual* than plants that become carnivorous."

She gave him a tired smile. "It's actually an old strategy, going back eighty million years. A way of adapting and surviving in regions of nutrient-poor soils. Even my father was interested in their genes. It was part of his research, to see if some of the thirty-six-thousand genes that are unique to carnivorous plants could be incorporated into food crops to make them hardier."

"So, he wanted to create a field of wheat that would eat locusts, rather than the other way around."

Her smile widened. "Nothing so dramatic. He simply wanted to increase the rate of nutrient acquisition from poor soils."

"Was he successful?"

She looked down. "He had some minor success, then he got cancer, pancreatic, nine years ago, when I was still at the university. Took him down in six months. He died before the advent of gene technology that would have accelerated his research."

"And you're continuing in his footsteps."

"Tangentially. I've been working with those same genes, creating hybrids, studying how certain traits arise from combinations of different chromosomes. It's fascinating how similar so many of those genes—those that produce digestive enzymes or allow for movement—have analogs in animals. It's a stunning example of parallel evolution between flora and fauna. In fact—"

A loud bang made her jump. Even Marco sat up sharply.

Tucker turned toward the door.

A tiny, barred window allowed him to spot the tonsured head of Yerik Raz rush past their cell, heading toward the stairs leading up into the church.

Tucker frowned, sensing the monk's tension.

Did that mean Sychkin had arrived from Sergiyev Posad? And if so, what does that mean for us?

Elle swallowed hard and looked at him. The question was easy to read on her face.

What are we going to do?

As Tucker listened to Yerik's heavy footsteps echo away, he knew only one certainty.

We're running out of time.

5:09 P.M.

Kowalski hopped out of the Siberian bush plane—a single-engine Baikal LMS-901—which sat atop a small lake ten miles south of the town of Severodvinsk. As his boots hit the ice, a loud cracking sounded underfoot. He crouched for a breath, waiting to fall through, but it held—for the moment.

He eyed the parked aircraft with suspicion, expecting it to plummet through the ice.

Off to the side, Yuri crossed with two of his handpicked men, Vinogradov and Sidorov. The trio opened the plane's rear cargo hatch and began tossing out duffels of equipment. The two brothers were twins, but only fraternal. Blond-haired Vin stood a few inches shorter than Kowalski with a quarterback's build, while Sid stood a foot shorter with the stocky bulk of a linebacker. The only feature that was identical were their hard expressions, and even harder eyes.

Both had served with Yuri in the Russian Navy.

Another young man, no older than twenty, named Fadd, had been the Baikal's pilot. The guy spent more time yammering than paying attention to airspeed, altitude, and angles of approach. Still, Fadd landed them squarely on the lake without crashing through the ice.

Not that Kowalski didn't expect that still to happen.

Monk finished making final arrangements with the pilot, then joined Kowalski out on the lake. The last member of their extraction team hopped out. Kane lifted his snout, testing the air, already searching for his missing partners.

The hope was that the Malinois would perform as well as he had in Sergiyev Posad and pick up the scent of their teammates. Clearly failing at the moment, Kane lowered his nose and shook the long trip from his fur.

They had left in the middle of the night, traveling the seven hundred miles in a pair of trucks. It had taken them fourteen hours to reach Arkhangelsk, a portside city on the White Sea. Once there, they had collected the bush plane from a fishing charter, which required Yuri handing over a satchel weighted down with rolls of rubles.

Afterward, they had made the thirty-mile hop to the lake. To continue their ruse as simple fishermen, Fadd would start drilling holes through the ice and set up rods.

But there would be no one to man them.

Monk waved to the western shore, to a snowy forest covering low hills. "Let's head out."

The five men and Kane set off across the ice.

It was a sullen march.

Yesterday afternoon, Gray had returned after nearly drowning in the lost library. He had reported the deaths of Bishop Yelagin and Father Bailey. He had also shared what knowledge that sacrifice had gained them: the possible location of a lost continent, one that came with a dire warning, a danger that could threaten the world if unleashed. Gray and the others, including Sister Anna, were already en route by air to the city of Pevek on the coast of the East Siberian Sea, where they would take a helicopter out to a commercial icebreaker and begin their search of those frozen waters.

But despite the urgency of finding the site, of discovering the nature of that threat before the Russians claimed it, they could not abandon Tucker and Dr. Stutt, or even Marco. Not without attempting a rescue.

To that end, they had recruited additional allies—and resources.

Once off the lake and onto the wooded shoreline, Yuri removed a GPS unit from his pack. He took a moment to get his bearings, then set off into the hills, tracking a red dot on his screen. After fifteen minutes of hiking, they topped a rise.

"We're here," Yuri stated firmly.

It took Kowalski a few breaths to spot the white camouflage netting bulging at the bottom of the hollow ahead of them. It helped that there were some tread tracks leading to the spot, though the overnight snow had partially filled the path.

"Suit up and let's get going," Monk said, searching the skies between the pines. The winds had picked up, blowing snow from branches and dusting over them. "That storm's coming in fast. We want to be in the teeth of it by the time we reach the base."

Yuri and his two men rolled back the netting, revealing a pair of vehicles.

One was a Berkut-2 snowmobile. It had a two-man heated cab built over skids. Atop it was mounted a PKP Pecheneg 6P41 machine gun. In the back was an open-air gunner's seat, positioned over a rear cargo space.

The second vehicle was an A-1 double snowmobile. It looked like a motorcycle with a sidecar, but one sitting on oversize treads.

From the duffels, the team loaded additional rifles and sidearms into the two vehicles, then stripped down and changed into Russian Arctic combat gear, which consisted of camo suits in shades of white and gray. They pulled dark balaclavas over their heads, followed by white helmets with black visors.

As they geared up, Kowalski kept next to Yuri. He asked a question that had bothered him since they left Sergiyev Posad. "Why's your boss so willing to help us?"

"He is paid very well, *da*?" Yuri shrugged.

Kowalski knew that Painter and Kat had arranged the equipment drop-offs with Bogdan, who also coordinated their transportation. The industrialist had plenty of underworld connections to facilitate all of this. Plus, it was well known that a slew of Russian military hardware had the unfortunate habit of falling out of trucks.

Kowalski kept staring at Yuri until the man admitted more.

"I tell him what you do, what you plan to do."

Kowalski remembered catching Yuri on the phone back at the Vatican embassy, speaking to his boss. "You've been reporting in, so what?"

"Bogdan is a happy man. Very rich. Very smart. Sanctions are bad already. War would be much worse. He is not alone in wishing for peace. He sees the wisdom in supporting a cause that will keep his funds flowing smoothly and steadily."

"I thought war was profitable for guys like your boss."

"For a few, *da*. For most others, *nyet*." Yuri stared toward the horizon. "Bogdan also has five children and seven grandchildren. I have two daughters myself."

This last surprised Kowalski.

Yuri tugged on his helmet. "Not all costs of war are measured in profits."

He snapped the visor shut, ending this discourse, and headed toward the Berkut.

Monk crossed to Kowalski, noting him struggling with his coat. "How's your arm?"

"I'll manage." He yanked his limb through the sleeve, a bit too roughly, trying to prove his point. "Barely any seepage through the wrap."

Monk frowned at him. "You should've stayed behind."

As team medic, Monk had tried to sideline Kowalski, but that wasn't about to happen. Tucker got nabbed trying to save Kowalski's ass. So, he wasn't going to sit this out.

Besides, he was needed here—and for more than just his brawn and ability to blow things up. He whistled and signaled to Kane, who crossed over and followed him toward the Berkut. Tucker had taught Kowalski a basic set of verbal commands and hand signals to help him work with Marco. Kane knew those, too, and many more.

Tucker's last instruction had been the most pointed.

Trust the dog, and he'll trust you.

Kowalski hoped that was true.

Once ready, the group split up and set off. Monk climbed aboard the A-1 snowmobile with Sid. Kowalski joined Yuri inside the Berkut, with Kane perched between them. Outside, Vin climbed into the gunner's seat behind the cab.

Two engines choked into roars. The vehicles lurched forward, then gained speed. They flew through the snow-covered woods, riding over hills and across open plains. This rural region was one of the many training areas used by the base's Arctic Brigade. The plan was to pose as late-returning soldiers, hurrying to beat the worst of the evening's storm. They would aim for the back gate onto the base, where they hoped less attention would be paid to them, where their forged papers had a better chance of passing inspection.

From there, their goal was a simple one.

Get in and get out as quickly as possible.

Kowalski stared ahead.

Kane panted beside him, expressing the anxiety they all shared.

Ahead, dark, snow-heavy clouds stacked high, obliterating the sun, casting the world in shadows. Winds blew at them in gusts that rattled their windshield.

The lights of the military town of Severodvinsk glowed in a widening spread before them. It required a special visa to enter the town, but where they were headed was even more restricted.

The White Sea Naval Base hugged the western edge of Dvina River delta, where it emptied into the sea. Its many docks and shipyards serviced and tested the latest submarines and ships in the Arctic fleet. It would undoubtably be highly protected.

But they had to risk it.

Kane whined next to him, a note barely above hearing.

"Quit complaining," he warned the dog. "We'll find them."

Kowalski stared toward the lights, the stormy skies.

Or die trying.

32

Gray crossed through the belly of the eighty-thousand-horsepower beast. The steady rumble spoke to that power, while the nail-on-chalkboard grind of ice along the ship's hardened hull was a near-constant reminder of the harsh seas they traveled through.

He strode alongside Oliver Kelly, the Australian captain of the heavy icebreaker. The *Polar King* was a commercial ship, part of the ESKY shipping conglomerate, whose CEO William Byrd owed Sigma a big favor after events a few months back. Director Crowe had called in that favor, arranging for the use of the icebreaker to conduct the upcoming search.

The *Polar King* had already been in the neighboring Chukchi Sea, repositioned there from the oceans around Antarctica. The busiest seasons for icebreakers in the northern Arctic were spring and fall. A few weeks ago, the *King* had finished a stint with ConocoPhillips, aiding in oil and natural gas exploration near the North Slope of Alaska. The ship had been headed next to the Barents Sea, via the Northern Sea Route, to do the same for a Norwegian firm—until Painter had commandeered the vessel.

From the heavy stride of the former navy officer, Kelly was not pleased with this change of course, especially as it aimed his vessel toward the thicker ice of the polar cap. The current waters were crowded with ice floes, requiring little of the near-bottomless power of the ship's two nuclear reactors. But before long, they would need to strain the upper limits of those powerhouses.

"I don't know what you expect to find out there," Kelly said as he led Gray toward a conference room below deck.

"I'll do my best to fill you in."

Gray intended to explain once everyone was gathered. His team—which included Seichan, Jason, and Sister Anna—had landed on the icebreaker's helipad two hours earlier, just after midnight. They had taken an early morning commercial flight from Moscow to the coastal city of Pevek, which sat at the edge of the East Siberian Sea. There, Painter had arranged for the *Polar King's* helicopter to meet them and ferry them to the ship. It had required stopping on Wrangel Island to refuel before crossing the last four hundred miles out to sea.

It was still going to be a long night, but at least his team had time to rest as they crossed the breadth of Russia. He had napped with Seichan during the flight. She kept hold of his hand, as if ensuring he stayed in his seat. Yesterday, she had looked both relieved and furious when he had walked through the hotel room door. As waterlogged as his gear had been, he hadn't been able to radio the others. The little jubilation of their reunion quickly died away once he told her what had happened to Yelagin and Bailey. It was also a short reunion, just the one night, as afterward their group had split up again.

Voices rose ahead of them, coming from an open door at the end of the passageway.

"Our conference room," Kelly said with a nod. "My navigator will be down shortly with the map you requested. I've also asked another crewman who might be of assistance to join us."

"Thank you, Captain Kelly."

The pair of them passed through the doorway into a wide, shallow room. A large table was bolted in place, running down the room's center. Across the expanse of the back wall, a bank of windows over-looked the bow of the ship.

Gray was momentarily taken aback by the sight. Dark seas spread in an endless stretch to the horizon. Rafts of ice covered the water, reflecting the moonlight. The skies blazed with a sweep of stars, but what truly stole his breath was the shimmering veils of blues, crimsons, and green. They danced and rolled over the starscape, as if a rainbow had been melted across the sky.

Seichan stood limned against that view, looking equally captivated by the lightshow.

"Spectacular, isn't it?" Kelly said. "You're getting a rare display due to a solar storm from a coronal mass ejection, coupled with an X-class flare. It has been raging for the past half day. One of the strongest in a while. We almost didn't get Byrd's satellite call due to the geomagnetic interference."

Kelly looked disappointed that the call *had* come through.

Gray drew his attention from the skies to those seated around the table. Jason stood up from where he had been whispering with Anna. He waved Gray to the side.

Gray excused himself while Kelly poured a cup of coffee from a steel carafe.

"What is it?" he asked Jason.

"I reached Kat in D.C. via the ship's radio. Communication is spotty due to the solar storm. It's probably why we haven't heard from Monk and Kowalski directly. But they were able to phone Sigma Command. Kat relayed their message."

Gray's shoulders tensed. "And?"

"The others are en route to the naval base. Should be arriving in another forty minutes or so. Everything is going smoothly so far."

"But what comes next is the hard part."

Jason nodded, crossing his arms, looking as worried as Gray felt.

"Keep me informed if you hear any further word."

"That's just it. Why I wanted to talk to you. I lost that call with D.C. at the tail end of it. And as we head farther north, the interference will grow worse. The radio tech said to expect a total comms blackout. For several more hours."

Gray sighed.

So much for trying to keep our two operations coordinated.

"We'll have to manage as best we can." Gray waved Jason back to the table. "First, we need to get everyone up to speed aboard the *Polar King*. Decide if what we're attempting is even possible."

As Gray headed to the table, a lanky Black man with a handlebar mustache swept into the room. He wore crisp blue coveralls with the ship's logo on the pocket.

"Our navigator," Kelly introduced to everyone else. "Byron Murphy."

The man lifted a rolled map, a printout from the look of it. He nodded to Gray. "I studied that strange overlay of maps you shared up on the bridge. I was able to chart out a rough approximation of the region that you had blocked off."

"Can you show us?"

Everyone gathered as he rolled out his work across the tabletop. Seichan joined them, stepping next to Gray.

The map showed a cross-section of the East Siberian Sea, along with the northern coast of Russia and several islands. Far out in the water, deep into the Arctic, was a hatched circle.

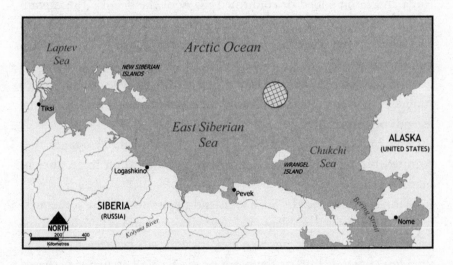

Byron tapped that marked spot. "That's the search zone, as near as I can assess."

Gray pictured that small mountainous island on Mercator's map. It must lay somewhere in that region. There was only one problem. "That's still a big area."

"Around thirty thousand square kilometers," the navigator confirmed.

Jason stared across the map at Gray. "Kat was still working on acquisitioning satellites equipped with magnetometers to pick up micro changes in the Earth's magnetic field. The ideal choice is the European Space Agency's SWARM satellites. They're in low polar orbit and outfitted with both vector field and absolute scalar magnetometers. But the solar storm is wreaking havoc there, too. We may have to wait out this flare."

Gray sensed they did not have that time.

Kelly frowned and tapped a finger on that hatched circle. "What are you looking for here? And what does it have to do with the Earth's magnetic field?"

"You'll have to bear with me." Gray removed his digital tablet. "It's a story going back centuries, if not millennia."

He started at the beginning and laid out all they had learned. Both Anna and Jason added or confirmed many of the details. The captain and the navigator's expressions went from incredulousness to wary curiosity, but never settled on complete acceptance.

Can't blame them.

"And you believe some island is out there," Kelly said. "One with strange magnetic properties. A place that could be the birthplace of the legends of Hyperborea."

"And one that holds a dark secret," Gray added. "A danger that required hiding a lost library and burying its location in an ancient map."

Byron shook his head. "Such an island might not require some mysterious threat to be a problem. The marked search area is in troublesome waters. While it may be *international*, the zone sits between Russia and the United States. In fact, the basin of the East Siberian Sea is shared between those two countries."

"That's why we intend to find it first. Not to plant a U.S. flag, but to try to keep the site *international*, like the waters it sits in."

"Plus, we need to identify the nature of the danger out there," Jason added. "Before it falls into the wrong hands."

Gray turned to Kelly and Byron. "I recognize the risk we're asking you to take. Russia will not sit idly by during all of this. They're already fortifying and arming their northern coast. This is what we could be facing if we're not careful."

Gray brought up a map onto his screen. Two dozen stars marked the locations of the new and refurbished Russian bases. They spread across the breadth of the country's northern coast.

He studied Kelly as the man reviewed the map. Gray wanted the captain to get a better visualization of the stakes at hand before the man fully committed himself and his ship to the task ahead.

"I won't direct you to go along with this," Gray said. "If you wish to countermand the order from your CEO, I'll support it."

Kelly turned to the navigator, seeking his insight, the sign of a good captain. "What do you think?"

"That path leads into deep ice," Byron warned. "Old ice. Centuries old.

I looked into it. The last time those waters thawed was the middle of the 1700s."

Gray shared a look with Anna.

That was the period of Catherine the Great's reign, when it was said she sent out expeditions searching for Hyperborea, based on Lomonosov's research in the Golden Library.

"What difference does it make if the ice is old?" Jason asked, drawing back Gray's attention.

Kelly answered, "Newly formed ice is easier for our ship to cut through. Older ice is more stubborn, compacted, harder to crack. We risk getting trapped."

Yet another danger . . .

"From my charts and satellite maps of ice thickness, the *King* should be able to make that transit," Byron judged, rubbing at his mustache. "Just don't suggest we hang around there long."

Kelly continued to study both the map on the screen and the printout from his navigator. "The East Siberian Sea is one of the least explored regions of the Arctic. Also, one of the most treacherous. With its shallow waters, barely mapped sea ridges, and persistent fogs, sailors despise it, and ships wisely avoid its northernmost reaches."

Byron added to the gloom. "Keep in mind, beyond a few rocky islands near the Russian coast, those seas are *empty* of any land."

From these statements, Gray could guess where the scales on this decision would tilt.

A voice rose behind them, from the doorway. "That's not necessarily true."

Gazes swung to the short form of a leathery-faced man of swarthy complexion and flat black hair. His eyes were squinted by epicanthic folds, as if the man had been staring too long at the midnight sun of the polar north.

"Omryn Akkay," Kelly introduced. "One of the ship's engineers. He hails from this region, so I asked him to join us. We hired him last year for his knowledge of these waters."

"I am of the *Lygoravetlan* people. Or *Chukchi*, as the Russians call us.

Most of my people live inland and are nomadic reindeer herders, but my family has always lived along these coasts. We were the *Ankalit*, the Sea People."

Gray gave a slight bow of his head in greeting. "And why do you disagree with your ship's navigator about there being no islands to the north?"

"Our stories tell of a place, a warm and misty land where undying gods dwell—along with *kelet*, evil spirits that kill any trespassers who approach the gods without proper sacrifices."

Anna spoke up. "That sounds very much like the Greek description of Hyperborea."

"*And* the warnings written about the place," Jason added.

"Have you ever been there?" Gray asked the engineer.

"It is forbidden . . . even to look. But my grandfather, in his youth, was hunting walruses, spent an entire season on the pack ice. He says one morning the low fogs lifted, and far in the distance, he spotted black cliffs rising out of the frozen sea. It so frightened him that he fled home, where he sacrificed many deer to the sea gods to ask forgiveness for his trespass."

Gray remembered the stories of Peary and others spotting distant Arctic lands.

Is this just a similarly wild claim?

To the side, Anna whispered a name to Jason, one inscribed in Latin on Mercator's map, marking a magnetic mountain. "*Rupus Nigra et Altissima.*"

Or in English . . . "Very High Black Cliff."

Like Omryn's father had described.

Maybe it's not so wild a claim after all.

Gray turned to Kelly.

The captain ignored Gray's inquiring look and faced his navigator. "How long would it take to forge a path to the location marked on the map?"

"To its edge?" Byron shrugged. "With a full head of steam, five or six hours. But as I warned, there's a lot of frozen sea to search after that."

"Understood." Kelly faced Gray. He was silent for a long stretch, then came to a decision. "We'll give it a go. But we'll stay no longer than a day."

Gray didn't object to the time limit. He feared they might not even have a day before the Russians intervened. He stared out the windows, at the swirling Borealis, whipped by a gale of solar winds.

He sensed the truth of this moment.

That's not the only storm that lies ahead of us.

33

Elle dozed on her bed, lingering in the shadowlands between slumber and wakefulness. Nightmares haunted any deeper sleep.

A loud *boom* jerked her up onto an elbow.

"What was that?" she asked blearily.

Tucker stood at the back of their cell, on the tips of his toes, peering out the thin barred window. The view opened into a window well, a space excavated to let a little light flow down here, but it offered only a narrow peek at the sky.

"Thunder," he said. "I think."

She shook free of her thin blanket, patted Marco, her stalwart bedmate, and joined Tucker. Snow, mixed with sleet, fell heavily into the window well. The storm had finally struck. Lightning flashed across the strip of sky—followed by another cracking bang.

"Thundersnow," she corrected. "We see it often in the spring in Saint Petersburg. As if Mother Nature can't make up her mind about the season."

Tucker nodded and drifted back to his cot. Elle stared at the storm for a couple more breaths, then did the same. Before either of them could sit, sharp voices echoed down the hallway, accompanied by a hurried tramp of boots.

Elle backed away, fearing they were coming to drag them out.

Tucker stepped in front of her. Marco, his ears tall and tail stiff, jumped off the bed and joined his partner.

A rush of men swept past the door's small window. She spotted the bowed bulk of Yerik Raz. He was followed by Sychkin, who had shed his robes for street clothes. Others crowded with them, easily a dozen.

A stolid-faced stranger strode at the rear. He wore a furred greatcoat over a crisp navy blue uniform. A matching hat crowned his ashy white hair.

He called forward, half order, half exasperation. "This is unacceptable, Sychkin. I've tolerated it once, and I'll not—"

Sychkin answered without turning or slowing, "Captain Turov, time is urgent. We have only this *one* moment. And I have the blessing of our patriarch, along with those who listen to him."

The group continued past, packed together by the urgency expressed.

They vanished out of view, but a loud door slammed shut. Quieter voices continued to reach them from out in the hall, likely guards left by that door.

Tucker turned to her. "What was that all about?"

She told him what she had overheard, knowing he wasn't fluent in Russian. "It seems like the base's commander is being hauled into this mess—and he's not happy."

Tucker looked back at the door. "Join the club."

Elle returned to her cot, to wait out whatever was happening. Tucker did the same across from her. Marco hopped next to Elle. With her heart pounding, she doubted she could even manage a light slumber.

Outside, the storm grew worse. Winds howled over the mouth of the window well. Snow pattered, sticking to the glass through the bars, quickly obliterating the view. It made her feel even more trapped.

She pulled the blanket over her shoulders and leaned against the wall. She stared unblinking at the thickening snow.

Then a scream burst from the hallway, sharp enough to be heard through the distant door. Another followed. Muffled angry voices filled in the silences. Then another cry, full of blood and anguish.

Elle could take it no longer. She burst from her cot, crossed to

Tucker, and dropped beside him. He put his arm around her shoulders and pulled her close. Marco came, too.

Huddled together, all they could do was listen to a chorus of agony. She leaned her face into Tucker, silently pleading.

Make it stop . . .

6:32 P.M.

Parked at the rear gate of the naval base, Kowalski tried to shrink his frame in the passenger seat of the Berkut's cab. He kept his head down and the woolen balaclava pulled over his face.

Yuri stood at the open door, leaning half out toward a stationed guard.

Snow pelted at them. Winds whipped, threatening to tear the door off the cab. Yuri yelled to be heard. One of the guards inspected his papers, then shone his flashlight into Yuri's eyes.

Yuri cursed at him and swatted at the light. He waved at the double snowmobile, which idled behind their vehicle, then chopped an arm toward the gate, clearly pressing their need to get out of the storm.

Kowalski leaned a cheek to his shoulder. A radio earpiece, translating in real time, allowed him to roughly follow the argument.

The second guard strode around the Berkut, bowing against the wind. He circled to Kowalski's side of the cab.

Uh-oh . . .

The guard lifted his rifle. "Papers! Credentials!" he yelled in Russian.

Kowalski took a deep breath, hoping he looked Russian enough because he couldn't speak the language if push came to shove.

Then again, *pushing* and *shoving* might be the only way past this gate.

Kowalski held up a palm and reached for the handle. He had to put his weight into it to fight the wind. As the door popped open, Kowalski lowered his other arm and secretly forked a set of devil fingers toward their third teammate in the cab, then pointed those same horns toward the guard, who leaned in with an arm outstretched for Kowalski's papers.

As ordered, Kane lunged past Kowalski's chest with a deep growl, snapping at the guard's fingers, then barking savagely. Kowalski pretended to try to restrain the muscular dog and make it look like he was losing.

Startled, the guard fell back, tripped, and crashed onto his ass in the snow.

Yuri hollered, motioning to Kowalski's side of the cab. "See, comrade! We *all* want out of this damned storm."

The guard on the ground certainly showed no further interest in inspecting Kowalski's papers.

The other man finally scowled, crossed to his open gatehouse, and struck a button inside. The fence, topped by razor wire, ratcheted open on its tracks.

Yuri hopped back in the cab, slammed his door, and glanced to Kowalski with a roll of his eyes. They set off through the gate, followed by the double snowmobile carrying Sid and Monk. Seated behind the Berkut's cab, Vin gave an exaggerated salute good-bye toward the guards, while keeping one hand on the mounted machine gun.

The two vehicles trundled across the snow-swept streets, which were deserted and wind-whipped. They traveled out of sight of the gate and continued a quarter mile farther, then stopped.

Yuri turned to him. "I got you in here. It's up to you to find the others."

Kowalski stared over at Kane. "It's not me that's gotta do that."

Kane keeps his head down, his nose close to the ice and snow. The order burns bright behind his eyes. SCENT MARCO. SCENT TUCKER. *He needs no command to follow this instruction. The same desire fires his blood.*

His pack is broken, and he intends to close that circle.

Behind him, heavy footfalls follow. Beyond the tall man, two vehicles track them, nearly lost in the storm. His eyes can barely see them, but his ears stay tuned to their rumble, the crunch of snow under treads.

For now, this is his new pack.

But only for now.

As he continues across the grounds, he recognizes familiar scents from camps like this in the past:

—the bitter bite of burnt oil.

—the reek of smoke and ash.

—the ripe melt of decaying trash.

He strips each away, one after the other.

He even dismisses the fear-sweat that mists through the clothes of the man at the end of his leash.

Only one set of scents matters. It is branded into him, meaning home, brotherhood, a warm bed, and a full belly.

He heads into the wind, drawing deep sniffs, carrying each note to the back of his muzzle, under his eyes, over his tongue.

Then he catches the faintest whiff . . . a trail through the air that even snow can't crush. He lifts his nose to it, whines against it, and moves along it. His paws pound faster. His claws dig deeper into the frozen hardpack.

He tugs harder on the lead, refusing to slow.

The other shouts behind him. It is not an order, so it's ignored.

Kane is drawn to the source. The scent rises from a steel grate that steams into the air. He rushes to it and sniffs the wet warmth rising from below, then speeds on—toward home, toward blood shared.

The spoor he follows is tainted. He smells the acid of stress, the looseness of bowel. Still, he picks out the musky note that underlies it all. He has sniffed under that tail often enough.

Marco . . .

He races on—to the next steaming grate, where the scent grows stronger. He barely pauses and hurries on.

To another patch of steel and melting snow.

Then another.

Until he reaches a grate that is so ripe that it fills his senses. He paws at the snow, exposing a frozen dark stain, droplets of that stress. He draws the scent off the steel, too.

He finally stands, stiff-legged with confidence. He stares over at the other, who hulks beside him. He growls, lifting his nose higher.

The other commends him.

Good dog.
It brings no flash of gratitude or contentment.
This other is not Kane's home.

Kowalski radioed Yuri, who trailed in the Berkut, followed by the snowmobile, "Kane's picked up their scent."

Yuri responded. It sounded like a confirmation, but it was hard to tell through the dropouts and static. The heavy snow wasn't the only storm they had to contend with. Higher up, the solar flare continued to pound the magnetosphere.

Still, Kowalski's message was understood.

Yuri pulled up next to him. Vin hopped off the gunner's seat, dropping an assault rifle from his shoulder to his hand. Monk and Sid slid out of the heated seat of their snowmobile. With the two dressed in the Arctic combat gear and of similar builds, it was hard to tell them apart.

Yuri exited the Berkut and joined them. He nodded toward a stone church with a tall steeple. "You think they're in there?"

Monk eyed the place, too. "If they were brought here by Sychkin, it seems likely."

Vin broke out a cigarette and managed to light it despite the wind. He passed it around, pretending they were taking a smoke break. Or maybe the guy simply needed a nicotine fix.

"What's the plan?" Kowalski asked. "Try to find a back door? Sneak in?"

The answer came from none of them.

A scream cut through a lull in the wind, muffled but clear enough.

It rose from the church.

Monk glanced at Kowalski and lifted his rifle, making his point clear.

Kowalski shrugged and did the same.

Looks like we're storming the castle.

7:08 P.M.

At the first blast of gunfire, Captain Turov spun to Sychkin and yanked the man behind him. In his other hand, he drew his sidearm. He barked orders to the two soldiers in the room with them.

A small part of him was relieved for the interruption.

He had little stomach for the agonizing work of Yerik Raz.

Three amputated fingers sat in pools of blood.

An eye hung by a cord from the ruins of a face.

Still, Turov waved to his chief of staff. "Oleg! Get Yerik moving."

One of the soldiers tugged the door open, exposing a firefight in the hallway. He stepped out to join the other men, but a spray of bullets struck him, drove him back into the room. He stumbled and fell, dead before he hit the floor.

The other guardsman knelt to the side and lay down suppressive fire. Shadows down the hall dropped into cells to either side. The only surviving soldier from the hallway used that moment to retreat into the room, taking up a position at the door's other side.

Turov cursed himself for not coming better armed, for his overconfidence in the base's security.

Oleg joined him, gripping a pistol. "Comms are down due to the flare."

He nodded. The radios had been compromised for most of the day. They could expect no rescue. He doubted even the gunshots, muffled by the thick foundations of the church, carried very far through the snowstorm.

"Can't stay holed up in here," Turov noted.

The door into the interrogation room could only be locked on the outside, by dropping a bar across it. Like all the cells.

"Looks like they've got both ends of the hall covered," Oleg said.

"But there are steps that lead up to the nave. Not far away. We'll have more options up top."

The stairs into the church were three meters down the hall to the right.

"On my mark, we unload on the bastards and make for those steps."

He got confirming nods from the two men at the door.

He turned to Sychkin and Yerik. "Stay behind us. Don't stop moving unless we do."

The archpriest's eyes were round with panic.

Good.

Yerik looked angry, not at the threat outside, but at being interrupted, thwarted from his efforts here.

Turov faced the door, waiting for another volley between their forces to end. As the enemy retreated out of sight, he barked at the soldiers. "Now!"

Both rifles sprayed into the hall, ringing off steel cell doors, sparking off stone walls. Turov headed out, pistol raised, flanked by Oleg. Sychkin and Yerik kept behind them.

They set off in a low run, rushing for the steps up to the nave.

One of the soldier's weapon's emptied out. He discharged the spent magazine and struggled to put in a new one. At the lull, one of the combatants leaned out and unloaded a burst of rounds.

Oleg hissed, skipping a step, tagged in the leg.

Turov shifted over and covered his deputy, returning fire, blasting rounds at the door, forcing the shooter back into hiding. With his free arm, he hooked Oleg around the waist and kept him moving.

The soldier finally managed to reload his rifle and lay down a barrage of cover. It was enough for them to reach the steps. They all clambered up. Once at the top, he held their group at the threshold into the church. Frescoes and gold icons glowed in the darkness, lit by a few candles near the altar.

To his left, the main doors had been left open by the intruders. Snow swirled into the church's antechamber. Winds danced the candle flames.

The nave looked deserted.

Directly ahead, the doors to a sacristy lay on the far side. It was where the priest's vestments were stored. Surely it had to have a lock on the inside. If so, it would offer them a place to barricade and wait out this storm.

That's if it wasn't already locked.

He turned to Sychkin, who occasionally held service here. "Do you have keys to the sacristy?"

The priest patted a pocket and nodded with a look of relief.

Turov pointed toward the far door. "We keep going. Don't stop."

They set off, running as a group.

As they passed the church's entrance, a machine gun strafed inside.

Rounds chewed across the floor and tore into the golden altarpieces. Turov caught a glimpse of muzzle flashes through the snow, illuminating the shadowy shape of an Arctic Berkut parked at the curb.

Luckily, their group had been spotted late, and the angle of fire was awkward—or maybe the shooter was merely trying to chase them off.

It worked.

Turov hit the door. Discovering it was already unlocked, he herded everyone into the cramped sacristy. The space was stone-walled with high narrow windows. The door was thick, age-hardened oak.

Oleg threw the deadbolt.

The soldiers shoved a small desk in front of the door, offering further shelter if someone tried to shoot their way inside.

Turov turned to Oleg, whose face was a pale mask of pain. A pant leg was soaked in blood. "Comms?"

"Still down. I'll keep trying. Some message might slip through."

He swung toward Sychkin, who was guarded over by Yerik. He pointed toward the door. "Who the hell are those people?"

7:15 P.M.

Tucker crouched behind a cot. He had overturned it at the outbreak of the gun battle. Elle and Marco sheltered with him. The firefight had died away, but commandos in combat gear barked orders in Russian out in the hallway. White helmets flashed past their cell.

A steel bar scraped, and the door flung open.

A goliath of a soldier barged in. "What're you waiting for? Get moving."

Tucker straightened. "Kowalski?"

Another squattier figure swept up to the threshold. "Got 'em pinned down upstairs. Don't know how long. Can't count on the solar storm keeping everything blanketed. One wrong word gets out, and we're toast."

Monk...

Tucker struggled to understand how they could be here. He helped Elle up and signaled Marco to his side. "How did you find—?"

Kowalski waved and turned. "No time to chitchat. On a tight schedule. Yuri's waiting topside. Kane, too."

Tucker rushed after him with Elle and Marco. In the hallway, another two men in Arctic camo closed behind them, herding them toward the front of the church.

"Wait!" Tucker stopped and barged through the pair behind him.

"Where are you going?" Kowalski huffed but followed him.

Tucker raced down the passageway to an open door. He had to step over bodies, soldiers trapped by the ambush, caught in a crossfire. He pushed into the room. Inside, a steel hearth heated the space. It felt stiflingly hot after the cold cell.

A body was strapped to a chair by leather restraints.

Tucker's ears still rang with the screams of the tortured.

Blood pooled beneath the seat. The air smelled of burned flesh and loosed bowels. Severed fingers lay on the floor. Worst of all, as the man's chin rested against his collarbone, the globe of an eye hung by a cord from its socket.

Tucker rushed up to the stricken man. "Father Bailey."

Elle gasped behind him, having followed him into the room.

Monk, too. "Out of the way," he yelled as he closed the distance. "Kowalski, cut him loose."

Kowalski yanked a dagger from a sheath, while Monk dropped to a knee.

He checked for a neck pulse. "He's alive. In shock."

As Monk quickly bandaged the damaged hands, the priest stirred. He lifted the ruins of his face and stared with his one eye. His features were sunken with despair and agony.

"I . . . I couldn't stop . . ." he moaned through cracked lips, his voice hoarse from screaming. He searched around him, as if seeking absolution. "I told them . . . I told them where Gray and the others went."

34

From the bridge of the icebreaker, Seichan gazed out at the expanse of ice shining in the moonlight and the dazzling curtains of the borealis. She had a panoramic view from this tenth level of the ship's super-structure.

Closer at hand, the bow lamps illuminated the frozen seas imme-diately in front of the ship. The *Polar King*'s red-painted bulk moved steadily across the landscape, curling plates and rafts of ice to either side of its spoon-shaped prow.

"How fast are we going?" Jason asked at the navigation station, watching the radar scan of the region. Sister Anna stayed next to him.

"Three knots," Captain Kelly reported from the helm. "For now, we can maintain a steady pace. But the ice is only two meters thick. It'll get worse before much longer."

"How much ice can the *King* handle?" Gray asked.

"Three times what we're traveling through right now. Up to six meters by ramming the bow and using the ship's weight to crush our way forward."

Seichan tried to picture a wall of ice twenty-feet high. She had a hard time imagining a ship cutting through it, even one as massive as the *King*. Concerned, Seichan turned her back on the sea and crossed to the group.

She challenged the captain as she joined them, "What's the likelihood of us being trapped by that ice?"

Kelly shrugged. "We can travel backward nearly as well as forward. And we're currently only using *one* of our reactors to drive the ship. The second is on standby mode."

Seichan frowned at him, letting him know he hadn't answered her question.

"Low but not zero," he admitted. "Ice is fickle and can shift unexpectedly by currents, closing behind a breaker, trapping it. Happened to a Russian scientific ship in Antarctica a few years back. Everyone had to be ferried off by helicopter."

Gray turned to the ship's navigator. "Mister Murphy, how long until we reach the search zone?"

"We're making good speed," Byron answered. "Another three hours, maybe less. But that ice will grow heavy quick. Once we're in the zone, it'll be slow going."

"What about the radar?" Seichan pressed the man. "Anything showing up yet?"

He shook his head. "Like I said before, there's never been an island found out here." He cast an apologetic look toward the Chukchi native.

Omryn Akkay remained stoic, arms crossed, clearly unswayed by the technology aboard the ship.

Even Bryon expressed similar doubts. "The solar storm continues to muck up our systems. We'll have to hope it clears once we're in the search area."

Jason glanced to the neighboring radio room. For the past hour, he had traveled back and forth between there and the bridge, trying to raise Sigma Command or Monk's team at Severodvinsk. He had no luck reaching either one of them.

"If your radar is compromised by the solar flare," Gray said, "maybe something *could* still be out there?"

Anna nodded and stepped closer. "How well has the Arctic even been mapped?"

"The surface? Fairly well. Satellites are constantly tracking the size of the polar cap. But under all that ice? Little is known. Only a fraction of the world's ocean floors has been mapped to modern standards. Around twenty percent. And the Arctic Ocean is far worse. Less than five percent."

"What about the East Siberian Sea?" Jason asked.

"Even worse," Byron admitted. "We mentioned before how this corner of the Arctic has been the least explored. While the coastal quarter of the East Siberian Sea has been decently mapped, due to the Northern Sea Route passing through there, farther out from the coast almost *nothing* has been charted."

"And these waters are extra shallow, if I recall," Anna said.

"Some of the shallowest of the Arctic—which makes traveling through here so treacherous."

Seichan frowned at him. "Then is it possible that the top of a tall seamount could be buried in thick ice, making it hard for a satellite to detect?"

Gray nodded. "The island is also said to be strongly magnetic. A mountain of lodestone. Maybe that emits enough electromagnetic radiation to blur or mask itself. Especially here in the polar region, in this highly ionized air, with a magnetosphere that's constantly under bombardment by solar energies."

Byron cast him a doubtful look, but he didn't negate this as a possibility.

Kelly interrupted the discussion by clearing his throat and pointing to the windows. "Might want to take a look. You're not likely to see a sight like this again in your lifetime."

Their gazes shifted from the radar screen to the glowing skies and shining ice.

The borealis had grown even more brilliant, shimmering and swirling wildly, no longer a tranquil lightshow. Farther out, near the horizon, it grew more violent. Nimbuses of light raged, radiant and furious, reflecting the severity of the solar storm as it reached its peak.

No wonder we lost communication with the world.

Seichan swore she could hear that storm, a barely audible keening that cut through air and steel, accompanied by cracks and sharper whistles.

And it wasn't just her.

Anna rubbed at an ear, as if trying to erase that noise.

The men seemed unaffected.

Seichan stepped closer to the window, drawn with the others. The skies seethed off in the distance, whipping into a great tempest, forming a shining radiant cyclone across the stars.

Gray bumped her as he dug through his pack and removed his tablet. He flicked it on and scrolled through images, settling on one, a photo from the old Greek book. It showed high cliffs circling a valley. At its bottom, a mountain rose, surrounded by a swirling pattern.

Gray held the picture up to the view outside. "First Nicolas, then Mercator, and whoever drew this in the eighteenth century . . . I don't think they were describing a whirlpool of *water*."

Anna understood, equally dumbstruck. "It was a whirlpool of *light*."

Gray turned to Kelly. "That's where we must go."

35

"Hold tight!" Tucker hollered.

He clutched hard to the wheel of the GAZ Tigr, an all-terrain 4x4 painted in Arctic camo. The team had commandeered the transport vehicle, finding it parked near the church, keys inside, courtesy of the combat force they had ambushed.

Monk and Elle hugged over Bailey, who lay sprawled across one of the two benches that flanked the rear compartment. Marco kept close to them, while Kane commanded the front passenger seat.

Tucker crushed the accelerator under his boot. The eight-ton behemoth shot toward the base's rear gate. Its wipers fought the snow, struggling to keep a view open.

Ahead, a fence, topped by razor-wire, appeared out of the snow. A figure burst from a neighboring gatehouse, rifle at his shoulder, shifting in all directions, momentarily confounded by the wind and white-out conditions, struggling to pinpoint the source of the roaring engine—but it didn't take him long.

The rifle swung toward the truck.

Tucker didn't slow.

Bullets peppered across the Tigr's ballistic windshield and pinged off its armor—then the transport hit the gate. It crashed through with hardly a jolt.

The soldier dove away at the last moment. Still, he rolled to his belly and shot at the back of the retreating truck.

Unfortunately for him, the Tigr wasn't the only threat.

Behind the transport vehicle, the Berkut burst out of the falling snow at full speed. It ran across the crumpled fence, then over the guard on the ground. Braced at the back of the Berkut, Kowalski gripped the handles of the mounted machine gun and strafed the gatehouse as they passed it, shattering glass, pummeling the other guard still inside.

The double snowmobile followed this path of destruction, carrying two of Yuri's associates: Vin and Sid.

It was a savage exit, but after witnessing what had been done to Bailey, mercy wasn't in their current vocabulary.

Tucker continued overland across the snow-covered hills. He aimed for a line of woods, no more than a shadowy smudge through the storm.

The Berkut shot alongside the Tigr and passed it, leading the way from here. According to Monk and Kowalski, they had a plane sitting on a frozen lake some ten miles away. It seemed an impossible distance.

Still, so far, no alarm had been raised at the base, but that wouldn't last.

"How's Bailey doing?" Tucker shouted back.

"Sedated." Monk had his med pack open by his knee and wrapped a bandage around the priest's head, over the gauze-packed wreck of his eye. "But he's far from stable. Needs blood. A hospital ASAP."

Tucker got them moving faster, riding hard over the hills, shattering through icy bushes. They were jostled and rattled, but Monk didn't warn him to slow.

Behind them, a siren blared—first tentatively, then ratcheting into a haunting wail. It spread to other sirens.

The frozen base was waking up.

Their only hope was that the solar storm would slow the enemy, thwart communications, confound radar equipment, and challenge any coordinated response—especially by air. While these northern bases were well-equipped with strategic land-and-sea capabilities, one notable weakness were its air mobility assets.

Tucker knew they had a good lead on land, but—

The thumping roar of a large helicopter rose behind them. Still distant, but closing fast. The bird must have gotten into the air fast, proving the commander of the base was no slouch. From the quick mobilization, Tucker suspected they were being hunted by one of the elite VDV squads, Russia's Airborne Assault Troops, likely their 76th Division, a group assigned to protect the Kola Peninsula.

Whether he was right or wrong, it was bad news.

The trio of ice-hardened vehicles couldn't escape that hawk in the air. Still, they had to try.

7:51 P.M.

Kowalski pounded a fist atop the Berkut's cab, signaling Yuri to slow down. The Berkut swerved wildly, skidding sideways as it braked hard, nearly throwing Kowalski off. He clutched the handle of the PKP machine gun to keep his seat.

He waved his free arm, gesturing for the Tigr to continue past and make for the plane. Tucker didn't need any such encouragement. The armored truck barreled by without slowing. Vin and Sid must have understood Kowalski's intent and swept wide, zipping their twin snow-mobile ahead of the Tigr, taking the lead to guide Tucker and the others to the parked plane.

If it's still there . . .

But one problem at a time.

He searched the sky. The approaching helo roared through the storm, but it remained lost in the snow. Hopefully that was true for their vehicles, too.

Kowalski bent down to the cab's back window, which was cracked open. He yelled his plan to Yuri, who glanced back at him as if he were crazy.

Kowalski answered that look, "Just go!"

The Berkut fishtailed for a breath, then its treads caught traction and it took off. They aimed away from the path of the others, striking for the higher hills and denser pine forest.

Kowalski held tight, staring back over a shoulder.

They had almost reached the forest.

C'mon, you bastard.

Then he spotted a faint glow through the storm, running low.

Beacon lights.

Kowalski leaned tighter to his gun and strafed into the air, trusting the muzzle flashes to draw the eye of the helo's pilot.

If I can see you, then you can see me.

The helicopter's light bobbled, steadied, then swung in his direction, away from the others who remained lost in the snow.

There you go . . .

They hit the woods at full speed. Kowalski ducked as pine branches battered the Berkut and him. It felt like he was flying through the coldest carwash in a convertible. The snowmobile shot up a steep incline, carving a deep trail.

As they reached the top, the little Russian war mobile caught air, flying free for a breath, then crashed back in a jarring thump. Kowalski's forehead cracked into the edge of the cab. His vision narrowed, but he held tight.

He swung around enough to spot the lights above the trees. The helicopter buzzed the tops, swirling snow and frozen needles from branches. From its sweeping pattern, the pilot had momentarily lost them.

As Kowalski had hoped, the aircraft's cameras and FLIR thermal-imaging systems were compromised by the snowstorm and geomagnetic interference.

Still, the pilot had eyes.

"Now!" Kowalski boomed out.

The headlamps flared from the front of the cab. Up until now, they had been running dark, but no longer.

With the Berkut still at high speed, Kowalski jerked to his feet, yanked the long gun from its mount, and rolled off the snowmobile. He hit a snowdrift and toppled several yards, grateful for the cushioning, until he struck a buried log.

The impact nearly tore the machine gun from his grip.

He clamped his hands tighter, earning a complaint from his stabbed forearm. He felt several stitches rip. He ignored the pain.

What's one more scar?

The Berkut, brightly lit, continued onward and dove over the ridge's edge and vanished into the next valley.

Kowalski heaved onto his back and lifted his machine gun, balancing the eight-kilo gun on his shoulder. He waited for the helo to take the shining bait. It didn't take long. Two breaths later, the world filled with roaring. Snow and pine needles whipped into a stinging gale around him.

It blinded him—which was *not* part of his plan.

He winced and squinted against the pounding of the rotorwash.

With no better option, he opened fire and strafed toward the glaring lights.

Hope this still works.

He heard the blast of a rocket launch and spotted the brighter flare of its exhaust.

Guess not.

36

In the rear of the truck, Elle cringed and ducked as a loud blast echoed across the forest. This time, it was not thundersnow.

She stared over at Monk, looking for answers to that explosion. But he simply tucked a blanket more snugly around Father Bailey. There was nothing more they could do. Even sedated, the priest moaned, still lost in a torturous nightmare.

As we all are.

The vehicle braked hard, throwing her forward.

Tucker called back. "Need help! Extra eyes."

Monk motioned for her to go, staying beside his patient.

She pushed up and shambled clumsily to the front, stepping around Marco. As she reached the front, Tucker signaled Kane off the passenger seat. She dropped heavily, taking the dog's place.

Out the window, the woods had dropped away at the shoreline of a frozen lake. With the headlamps off and the sun nearly set, the world had closed down to only a handful of meters past the bumper, all framed by heavy snow.

Tucker edged the Tigr up to the lake's shore.

"Where's the other snowmobile?" Elle asked.

"Lost 'em. I think I caught a glimpse of 'em shooting across the lake."

She turned to him. "Are we supposed to go on foot from here?"

"If so, it seems like the others would've waited for us here."

She continued to stare at him.

"At least, I hope I'm right." He shifted into gear and headed out over the lake. "Can you keep watch on the ice on your side?"

Once they set out, she rolled her window down. The cold bit her cheeks, but it helped calm her feverish terror. Tucker kept a steady pace across the lake, quicker than she would have preferred. Ice popped and groaned under the tires, loud enough to be heard over the low grumble of the engine.

She held her breath and glanced behind the truck. "That explosion . . ."

"I heard it, too. Don't know what it means. But right now, we have to deal with the problem at hand."

Off in the distance, the faint echo of sirens still rang from the base, spurring them to go faster. As they continued, Elle called out a few times, whenever the ice shattered under a tire, spreading outward in a spiderweb of cracks. Stress strained each minute into an agonizing ordeal.

"Up ahead," Tucker said. "Lights."

Wary, he slowed, but there was nowhere else to go.

As they crawled forward, headlamps flared to the right, rushing toward them.

Tucker flinched their truck away.

Out of the snow, the Berkut shot into view. One side was dented and blackened. Kowalski perched on a seat in the back, shouldering an assault rifle. The mounted machine gun was gone.

Kowalski called over to them as the Berkut drew alongside the truck. "Just getting here? This way!"

Yuri guided them forward.

Ahead, shadows emerged, forming the wings of a plane and the bulk of the other snowmobile.

The Tigr closed on their position.

Once there, they unloaded. The plane's single prop was already turning, its engine warming. It explained why the others had abandoned them. They must have shot ahead to alert the pilot and get the aircraft readied. They all knew time was short.

Yuri climbed out of the Berkut. His face was a mask of blood from a deep cut at his hairline.

Tucker looked toward the shore. "What happened back there?"

"Caught the brunt of a rocket blast. Rolled the Berkut." Yuri nodded toward Kowalski. "Could've been worse."

Kowalski shrugged. "My potshots managed to bobble the trajectory of the first rocket. But its launch-flash offered a perfect target, even for someone snow-blind. Then it was just flames, smoke, and an explosion."

He mimicked the blast, fanning out his fingers.

Elle failed to entirely follow this; even Tucker frowned.

But Monk interrupted any further inquiry, calling from the back of the truck as he popped the rear gate. "Need help moving Father Bailey."

They all headed over.

Tucker climbed inside and lifted the priest by his shoulders. Kowalski took his legs. Monk winced as Bailey groaned, thrashing slightly. Blood sprayed through the bandages over his hands. Even in the gloom, the stricken man's face was ashen, his lips blue-tinged.

"Hold on." Monk set about tightening the wraps, looking grim as he did so.

"How is he even alive?" Kowalski asked, but he wasn't referring to the aftermath of the torture. "I thought he drowned back at the buried library."

Monk shook his head. "Before I sedated him, he explained. When he was flushed down the chimney, the water column below broke his fall. Luckily, it seems the designers of the trap only meant the library to remain flooded for an hour or so. Long enough to drown any trespassers, but limit the risk to the books."

Elle struggled to follow this story, recognizing there was much she had missed after being captured.

Monk continued, "The water was already draining by the time Bailey fell. He was sucked out of the fireplace by the undertow and managed to find air while it emptied. But he broke his ankle. Took a hard hit to his head. No way he could try to scale that chimney again. Then soldiers burst inside and grabbed him, hauled him to Sychkin."

Kowalski winced. "Seichan spotted a Russian squad hightailing it toward the Ringing Tower. Nearly caught her, too. But what about Yelagin?"

Monk shook his head. "Didn't make it."

Elle breathed hard, despairing, picturing the elderly bishop.

"And Bailey won't, either," Monk warned. "Not unless we can get him to a hospital, to a trauma team."

Yuri hopped into the truck and waved for Bailey to be lowered back to the cot. Sid jumped in, too. "We can take him. Once you all get airborne, you'll need to strike immediately for international waters. You'll have time for nothing else."

Monk winced. Clearly, he knew Bailey's care could not wait.

"I can get him to a rural hospital," Yuri offered. "I still have enough rubles to keep everything quiet. Plus, my boss's ties with the Russian *mafiya* will reinforce that."

Monk took this all in and came to a fast decision, knowing the priest's life depended on it. "Do it."

Still, Monk looked at the plane, then back at Bailey, clearly pulled in two different directions.

Yuri grabbed Monk by the arm, staring hard into his eyes. "I will keep him safe, comrade. Trust me in this. The others will need you. If that bastard Sychkin knows where your friends are . . ."

Monk took a deep breath, nodded, and drew the Russian into a brief one-armed hug. "Thank you, Yuri."

With the matter settled, the two parties quickly separated.

Tucker drew alongside Elle. "Go with Yuri. Bogdan can keep you hidden."

"I'm done hiding," Elle snapped at him. "If there's anything I can do to help, I'm doing it."

She broke away and strode toward the plane.

Tucker followed, drawing Kane and Marco with him. "Elle . . ."

"If you're going with," she called back to him, "then I'm going, too."

8:18 P.M.

Inside the cabin of the Baikal LMS-901, Tucker leaned behind the two seats at the front. A young Russian named Fadd commanded the pilot's seat. Monk sat next to him at the auxiliary controls. The engine revved into a high-pitched whine as the propellers spun up and started dragging the aircraft across the ice.

As they taxied up to speed, Tucker studied the sky, watching for another helicopter, but the dense snow and lack of sunlight kept the world pressed tight atop them.

Monk focused to the starboard side, where the Tigr and the lone snowmobile had vanished. From the pinch of his eyes, it looked like he might be regretting his decision to leave Father Bailey's side.

Unfortunately, they were both searching the wrong way.

Fadd cursed and stiffened.

The Baikal sped across the ice. The shoreline rapidly approached, limiting their runway. But that wasn't the problem.

Out of the gloom, a huge bulky shape crashed through the tree line and careened out onto the ice, trundling toward them.

Tucker recognized it. He had spotted it earlier at the base, during Marco's short walk. It was a Russian BTR-80A armored personnel carrier. Atop it was mounted a 30mm cannon. Luckily, at the moment, the Russians seemed just as surprised to see them.

He knew these APCs could go sixty miles per hour, especially over open roads. The base commander must have dispatched it out the main gates, sending it to search for them. Then the fiery crash of the helicopter had been spotted and drew the APC—right into the Baikal's path.

Fadd reached to the throttle. As he started to pull back on it, Monk leaned forward and shoved it back forward.

"No," he warned. "Keep going."

Tucker knew he was right. They were committed. The plane and the APC raced toward each other in a terrifying game of chicken. The massive cannon swung toward them.

Tucker cringed.

They needed to catch air fast, but their speed was still too slow for liftoff.

The cannon fired, ripping 30mm rounds across the ice. The first rounds struck the windshield, driving everyone low—then the lake shattered under the APC's fifteen-ton bulk. Its nose dipped, sending the remainder of the barrage tearing into the ice in front of the Baikal.

Their speed increased.

The plane's tires lifted, then settled again.

Still not enough . . .

By now, Kowalski had come up front. He spotted the APC. "For once, I'm not the one falling through the ice."

Unfortunately, such vehicles were amphibious. The APC settled into the water, but it failed to sink. As it buoyed up, it tires paddled. Its front end rammed through the frozen water, becoming an ice-breaker, forging toward them.

Still, the mishap had bought their team a few extra breaths as the soldiers inside struggled to compensate.

The Baikal finally caught air—and kept it.

Fadd brought their nose up into a steep climb, angling to the side.

Below, the cannon pivoted toward them.

They weren't going to get clear in time.

Then a small shape raced into view below, flying across the ice. It was the double snowmobile, driven by Vin. The Russian thrust out an assault rifle, holding it one-handed, and strafed across the side of the APC. He could do no real damage. He was like a gnat attacking an armored elephant. Still, Tucker had ridden in such vehicles. He knew what such a barrage sounded like inside that steel drum.

Caught by surprise, the soldiers were clearly rattled, bewildered at which target posed the most danger. The cannon's direction bobbled, reflecting that confusion.

It was enough.

The Baikal swept over the foundering APC and shot away, angling toward the White Sea.

Below, Tucker spotted the snowmobile vanishing into the storm, its mission accomplished.

Kowalski followed its passage. "Really need to get me a snowmobile."

They had made it.

Just not all of them.

Fadd leaned forward into his controls. He coughed, spraying blood. As he fell back into his seat, a small hole in his chest poured a crimson stain through his clothes. He must have been hit during the opening volley but said nothing.

The plane's nose dipped precariously.

Monk hollered, hitting a series of switches, transferring control of the Baikal to his seat. "Get him on his back! Put pressure on the wound."

Tucker and Kowalski obeyed, manhandling the pilot out of the seat and to the floor. Monk pulled on the wheel, drawing their nose up. He was the only one who knew how to fly the aircraft.

He called back, doing his best to instruct them, but it was no use. Tucker shared a look with Kowalski. Both had seen enough death to recognize the inevitable. The young man stared up at them, gasping, choking out blood. Mercifully, after another few breaths, his body slumped, but his eyes stayed wide, as if he were surprised to find himself dead.

Tucker fell back onto his heels, his palms bloodied.

Elle covered her face.

Kowalski simply swore.

They had come so close to a clean break, but Tucker had learned a hard lesson years before.

Everything comes with a cost.

And too often it's in blood.

A hush fell over the cabin as Monk sped them onward, flying low over the White Sea, trying to stay under any radar that was still operating during the geomagnetic storm. Hard winds buffeted the small aircraft. Snow kept the visibility tight around them.

They continued their race for international waters, not that such seas were necessarily a safe harbor.

And not just for them.

They had all heard Bailey's warning, learned what information had been tortured out of him. With the ongoing blackout, only one path was left open to them.

To find Gray and the others—before the Russians did.

37

Standing over his office desk, Turov slammed his receiver down, hard enough to send the encrypted phone skittering across his desk. The base's landlines still functioned, but little else.

He had already learned that the enemy made a successful escape, fleeing aboard a small aircraft. The plane remained lost. With the solar flare continuing to pound the region, the base's over-the-horizon radar systems—which bounced signals off the ionosphere—were plagued by ghosts and static. It made picking out a small craft nearly impossible.

That alone had infuriated and humiliated him enough.

But worst of all, men under his watch had died.

After everything, Turov had been forced to reach out to Vice Admiral Glazkov in Severomorsk, the commander of the Northern Fleet. Turov related all that had happened, all the way back to when Sychkin had tortured and killed two Moscow students.

The admiral's fury had been palpable, burning Turov's ears. Glazkov's anger was not solely directed at Turov's failure in securing the prisoners, but for what that threat posed. The Americans now had an opportunity to make landfall and establish a foothold out in the East Siberian Sea. Both Turov and Glaskov knew such a geostrategic site, deep in the Arctic, could be vital for Russian security and its hopes for expanding the country's territorial reach. Not to mention, the Americans now had a chance to secure whatever unknown danger might be hidden on that island—to possibly weaponize it.

Upon learning all this, Glazkov had screamed at Turov, ordering him to mobilize a strike team—and to lead it. His final words tolerated no argument: *Get your ass out there, or I'll strip you of your command.*

The admiral would also be repositioning the *Ivan Lyakhov*, the military's newest icebreaking patrol boat, a vessel full of Arctic-hardened soldiers and weaponry. Turov was to meet them, along with a *spetsnaz* team of twenty-four men, a group that he had handpicked after his first meeting with Sychkin. His team would depart the base within the hour aboard an An-74 transport plane fitted with wheel-ski landing gear.

The only problem was that the intel gained from the priest had only given them a rough approximation of the site's location. To pinpoint it further would require a coordinated search across a vast swath of ice.

In the meantime, Glazkov would be dispatching one additional vessel.

Turov frowned at this last inclusion, knowing it was a bad decision. Still, he was in no position to countermand this order.

Again, Turov felt trapped, like he had in the past, during the war games that had marred his record. Similar to back then, Turov knew, if this decision led to a disaster, any repercussions would fall on his head—not that bastard Glazkov's.

His anger was interrupted by a knock on the door.

"Enter!" he shouted.

Oleg pushed inside, limping on a bandaged leg. He led in a trio of others, while waving for a pair of guardsmen to maintain a post outside.

Sychkin entered with a triumphant air that infuriated Turov. Yerik Raz shadowed his master, looming behind the archpriest's shoulders.

Turov suspected Sychkin had already made his own calls, possibly alerting Glazkov of what had transpired through back channels. During the call, the vice admiral's reaction and swift mobilization of forces suggested Glazkov had some foreknowledge.

"When do we leave?" Sychkin pressed him.

Turov ignored the question and focused on the third member of this group: a snowy-haired woman with pale skin stained by a tattoo. Yesterday, Valya Mikhailov had arrived with Sychkin's group, along with the prisoners. Turov had forbidden the mercenary from entering his base, keeping her at arm's length over in the town of Severodvinsk—which, in retrospect, may have been a mistake.

Her ice-blue eyes drilled into him, her anger matching his own.

Turov refused to back from that fury. "You know these Americans. Those who escaped. And their allies. You've dealt with them in the past."

These were statements, not questions.

She turned her anger toward Sychkin, sneering at the archpriest. "I warned him not to underestimate them."

Turov pointed at her. "Then you're coming with us."

She faced him. "Where?"

"To the East Siberian Sea. Where the others are headed."

Some of the anger bled from her expression, revealing a dark satisfaction in its place. She clearly had her own grudge against this enemy.

She shrugged her acceptance.

With the matter settled and some final details arranged, Oleg led the others away.

Alone in his office, Turov turned to the windows that overlooked the storm-swept White Sea. Snow continued to fall heavily as winter refused to bend to spring. Dark clouds lay low over the water.

The view matched his mood.

He lifted a hand, where a gold ring circled a finger. He stared at the wings and sword, the emblem of the Arkangel Society. Over the next day, the hopes and dreams of the group could be fulfilled.

To find Hyperborea.

He felt no stirring at this possibility.

Only trepidation.

He remembered what Sychkin had told him, what was found in a letter from Catherine the Great's son, concerning what lay hidden on that lost continent.

Wonders and horrors.

He didn't know how much of this was true. All he knew was that a true *horror* was sailing toward that region—upon the last order of Glazkov. In addition to the massive patrol boat and Turov's forces, the admiral had dispatched another vessel, the latest in Russia's fleet of submarines. It had been on a shakedown cruise near the Bering Strait, not far from where everyone was headed.

The boat was code named *Project 09852 Belgorod*.

But to all, it was known by a more fitting name.

The Doomsday Sub.

SIXTH

Hostile Shores

38

Aboard the *Polar King*, East Siberian Sea

Huddled in a bright-red coat and woolen sweater, Gray stood at the bow of the icebreaker. A heavy fog smothered the ship, slowing their speed to a crawl. It was so thick that wisps hung in the air like cloudy veils. He waved his fingers through one.

"Never seen anything like it," Jason said next to him.

Gray lowered his arm. "Wish we weren't seeing it now. This fog will make our search nearly impossible." He stared at the wan glow of the morning sun through the mist. "And now that it's daylight, we don't have the borealis guiding us any longer."

Gray pictured the swirling, brilliant cauldron of light that had led them to these waters. That had been more than seven hours ago. It had been their beacon through most of the night. Anna had posited that if the lightshow was indeed the whirlpool described in the old texts, that perhaps the *four rivers* said to lead into it might represent the cardinal points of a compass—east, west, north, and south—all merging into one at the North Pole.

Still, by morning, they had pushed into this fogbank sitting atop the ice, and the mystery vanished away. Though they had lost sight of the whirlpool in the sky, Byron had gotten a relative fix on its location during the night.

The ship continued to ply painstakingly toward those coordinates. But it wasn't just the lack of visibility that confounded them.

Gray braced himself as the bow lifted, ramming high over the ice below, driven by the force of its twin nuclear-powered engines. A thunderous cracking erupted as the ballasted weight of the *Polar King* crushed two stories of ice under it. The entire ship quaked as it fell. Air-bubbling bow thrusters to either side pushed the displaced ice away from the hull, allowing the ship to slide forward.

They had entered this heavy ice three hours ago, riding through it like a thirty-thousand-ton porpoise across frozen seas. Captain Kelly had expressed his doubts about how much farther they could travel if the ice grew any thicker, especially when it was this stubborn, compacted over a span of two centuries.

"We must be close," Gray muttered.

The radio in his hand crackled with static. He lifted it to his ear. Even this close, transmissions remained garbled. Still, he made out Seichan's voice. "Get back . . . the bridge. You're . . . to want to see this."

He pressed the transmitter. "What is it?"

"Just get your asses . . . here."

Gray frowned and lowered the radio. "They want us back at the bridge," he told Jason.

"Good. I can barely feel my toes and fingers any longer."

The two of them crossed into the towering superstructure and took an elevator to its tenth level. Men and a few women bustled along the hallways, part of the hundred-and-twenty-person crew aboard the *King*.

Gray and Jason reached the bridge. Seichan noted their arrival and waved them to the navigation station. They had to push through a group gathered around it, including Sister Anna, who had changed into a borrowed set of crew coveralls.

"What's got everyone stirred up?" Gray asked.

Anna pointed. "What do you make of that?"

Gray stared down at the face of the ship's compass. Its needle jittered right and left, then swung full around several times before returning to its dancing pattern, as if confused where to point.

"Definitely picking up some strong magnetic interference," Byron reported as he leaned on his fists atop his station.

Gray pictured the churning lights in the sky. "Could the compass be reacting to the solar storm? Like the borealis had?"

Byron shook his head. "Not likely. Something more localized is fouling the reading."

With his words, the needle spun once more, shivered a moment, then settled into a fixed position. No one spoke for a few breaths, waiting to confirm that the strangeness had passed.

Jason turned to Byron. "Did we sail out of range of whatever was causing the aberration?"

The navigator shifted and checked a glowing chart. "That magnetic compass is mostly decorative, a nod to our sailing past. We now rely on gyrocompasses, which fix our position by the rotation of the Earth." He tapped at his colored screen. "This ECDIS system calibrates the gyro, along with speed logs, NAVTEX, GPS, and other nav-equipment, to plot our nautical position."

"What does all that show?" Gray asked.

"While the storm is wreaking havoc with some systems, we're still getting decent data. Enough to display both the geographical North Pole and the last charting of the Earth's magnetic pole."

Gray stared back at the old compass. "Let me guess. That's not where the needle is pointing."

"Not even close." Byron looked at him. "Commander Pierce, I owe you an apology."

"What for?"

"For not believing you. Something bloody strange is out here."

"*Do not be deceived by its false pull,*" Anna whispered, quoting from Nicolas of Lynn's *Inventio Fortunata.*

"Can we follow that needle's course?" Gray asked Byron, glancing over to Captain Kelly, who still manned the helm, consulting with a pair of crewmen.

"We're roughly doing that already," the navigator answered. "It lies in the same direction as the coordinates I determined from the borealis's spinning."

Kelly broke away and crossed toward them, his lips thin and drawn with worry. He had clearly heard enough of the conversation to offer his own opinion. "The crew reported on the depth soundings and ice thickness ahead. The waters grow very shallow, less than twenty meters deep, and the *King* drafts eleven of those. We'll be scraping our keel before long. Even worse, the ice is steadily thickening."

"How much farther can we go?" Gray asked.

"Maybe another two miles. But I'd prefer to err on the side of caution and go no more than half that." The captain responded to the dismay on Gray's face. "You can always take the helicopter and search ahead. That's if there's anything to see through the fog. Or go overland, using our snowmobiles."

A firm voice called from across the bridge. "That won't be necessary."

They all turned and watched Omryn Akkay back away from the bank of windows. His manner looked dismayed, almost fearful. Past the Chukchi native, the view outside had partially cleared, the fog shredding in front of the bow.

Through the haze, the midday sun reflected brightly off open ice. Scraps of dense mists still hung in places, mostly near spires of black rock rising out of the ice, as if snagged by those sharp points. The bluffs rose four or five stories high, climbing in sheer faces. The outcroppings formed a rough circle, like a jagged crown poking out of the ice.

In the center, though, a lone peak climbed higher, easily ten to fifteen stories high. Fog draped its rocky heights, which fell away in steep cliffs. Lower down, a massive sheet of ice rode up its eastern flank, as if a wave had struck long ago and frozen in place.

Gray noted that the compass needle pointed straight toward that spire.

"We found it," he said, his voice hushed with awe.

Anna spoke its name, one lost in time and myth. "Hyperborea."

1:08 P.M.

As the exploratory team set off over the ice, Jason glanced back at the mountainous crimson bulwark of the *Polar King*. The icebreaker had come to a stop a mile from the peaks. The ship had dared come no closer. The waters were too shallow, and likely frozen solid nearer the buried shoreline.

Jason rode at the back of a four-person Arctic Snowcat. It trundled on double tracks across the ice. Another Cat followed, exiting a hold near the *King's* stern and driving across a ramp that extended to the frozen sea.

It carried Omryn, whom Gray had convinced to join them, as the Chukchi crewman might have some insight concerning this home of his peoples' sea gods. The burly red-haired driver, Ryan Marr, was from Boston, a former Coast Guard officer who had served on cutters in the Arctic. He was accompanied by his Aussie wife, Harper, the *King's* medical doctor, a blonde spitfire with a no-nonsense attitude.

Jason hoped no one would need her services today.

He turned his attention forward. Anna sat up front with the ice-breaker's captain, who aimed them toward the black peaks. It seemed Kelly hadn't wanted to miss out on this opportunity. Jason couldn't blame the guy. After traveling thousands of miles across featureless ice, to make landfall and explore such a strange site had to be irresistible.

Ahead of them, the final two members of the team sped across the ice on Polaris snowmobiles. Gray and Seichan switched back and forth across each other's path, clearly enjoying the freedom after the cramped days of travel. Still, they kept their speed tame enough for the others to follow.

Not that anyone could be easily lost.

All the vehicles were painted in red and black, to match the *Polar King*, and for another important reason. The bright colors made them easy to spot on the ice in case of emergency.

Let's hope we don't run into any of those.

Especially because they were all on their own.

The solar storm continued to wreak havoc on long-range communications. The short reach of their radios had some degree of reception, but even that was spotty. The only positive news was that Byron believed the geomagnetic interference should start to wane in the next four or five hours. The navigator had stayed behind to try to shorten that time frame.

Jason hoped he was successful. He was anxious to reach Kat, to reconnect to the world. They needed to share this discovery, start spreading the word before the Russians learned of this place. And if there was a threat to the world hidden here, it needed to be identified and secured.

Anna spoke up front, glancing back at him, perhaps sensing his anxiety. "Do you think that central peak could truly be a mountain of pure lodestone, as Nicolas of Lynn claimed in his book?"

From his lap, Jason lifted a small compass given to him. The needle pointed at the spire of black rock. "I doubt it's solid magnetite. More likely the outcropping has rich veins of the magnetic stone running through it." He waved to encompass all the peaks. "This whole grouping might be the same. All part of a huge massif, a sea ridge with only these topmost tips cresting through the ice."

Anna looked forward. "I wonder . . ."

Jason scooted closer. "What?"

"You could be right. According to the annotations that Mercator included with his map, the *Rupus Nigra et Altissima*—this magnetic mountain—was thirty-three miles around. A measurement he likely gleaned from Nicolas's *Inventio Fortunata*."

Support came from an unusual source. "Byron performed some preliminary measurements," Kelly stated as they approached the outer ring of cliffs. "The circumference of the exposed outcroppings is roughly fifty kilometers—thirty-one miles."

Anna sat straighter, looking back at Jason, her eyes shining as blue as the skies. She was clearly thrilled, but there was an edge of melancholy in her expression, the way her gaze seemed to stretch far beyond their vehicle's confines.

She deflated with a sigh. "How I wish Igor were here to see this, to see history—what was inscribed in the ancient texts we both studied— come alive."

Her words sobered Jason, reminding him that this discovery had come with a steep price. Not just her brother, but all the others who had fallen.

And more might, too, before this is over.

He took a deep breath as the Snowcat swept between two of the mist-shrouded peaks of the outer ring. As they entered the heart of this mysterious landscape, he swore he could feel the powerful energies buried here, the magnetic pull of this place.

Kelly cursed and jerked the vehicle hard, throwing Jason to the side. The Snowcat lifted off one tread before crashing back down.

As it did, Jason caught a glimpse of the obstacle that Kelly had sideswiped. It stuck out of the ice, but it wasn't a rocky outcropping—it was a tall spar of wood, tangled by frosted ropes. Other oaken slabs, peppered with nails of black iron, lay embedded or buried around the pole.

"What was that?" Anna asked.

Jason answered. "I . . . I think it was the top of an old ship's mast. Maybe the remains of a weathered crow's nest."

"There are others," Kelly said, nodding ahead.

Across the ice, other poles of wood poked crookedly. Some had shattered. One still had an intact crossbar, as if it had been turned into a grave marker—which was surely the case.

Jason pictured the old sailing ships locked in ice under them.

"They must mark the remains of Catherine's ships," Anna said.

Jason stared across the frozen graveyard. "Clearly not all of them made it back."

He swallowed hard, wondering if they'd suffer the same fate.

He looked toward the bulk of the *Polar King*, a crimson rampart in the distance. A chill of misgiving swept through him, as if he had stepped on his own grave.

Maybe Omryn was right.

No one should come looking for this place.

39

Gray raced his Polaris snowmobile up to the towering spire of black rock. It climbed four hundred feet in sheer, unscalable cliffs. Mists shrouded its summit, while the frozen sea framed its base. The eastern side was covered by a shoulder of ice that climbed a quarter of the way up. At this northern latitude, the winds mostly blew from that direction, known as the polar easterlies.

Must've taken centuries of thawing and freezing to build that mass of ice.

He waved to Seichan and the two trailing Snowcats. The group intended to circle the peak and search for a way inside. If this site had been habitable at one time, it was likely not on the surface. Still, he didn't hold out much hope of finding an entrance.

He glanced back to the old masts sticking out of the ice. According to Byron, the last time this ice had melted down to the open sea had been nearly three centuries ago, when Catherine's expeditions had sought out Hyperborea. Any entrances were likely buried under the ice.

Still, they had to look.

Gray sped away, leading the others around the flank of the peak. Seichan drew alongside him, leaning tight to her machine's handlebars. The two Snowcats followed. Gray kept a slow pace, eyeing the black rock.

Seichan noted the oddity first and radioed. This close to each other, the interference was just a staticky background. "I think there's a rim of open water where the ice meets the rock."

Gray squinted and spotted the gap, less than a foot wide, along the bottom edge of the cliff face. He slowed his Polaris and braked to a stop. He hopped off to investigate, while the Snowcats closed in on his position.

His boots crunched across the ice as he crossed to that frozen lip. He stared down into the gap and spotted dark-blue waters far below. To investigate closer, he leaned out, bracing an arm against the rock. His gloves disturbed a slippery layer of moss over the rock. It was millimeters thick, little more than furrier lichen. His disturbance stirred up a cloud of gnats, no larger than grains of pepper. Up higher, the dark stone was scribed with more of the same, thinning to regular lichenous fungi in hues of yellows, reds, and oranges, forming some cryptic petroglyph across the rock.

Returning his attention below, he identified a misty haze that had nothing to do with the fog. It matched his own exhalations, the misty condensate of his warm breath in the cold.

He pulled off his glove and placed his palm against the stone. The surface was cold, but far from icy. The moss under his fingers was damp, moistened by the rising condensation.

"It's warmer than it should be," he mumbled.

He stared up the length of the peak, at the surrounding ring of cliffs. He wondered if these outcroppings created their own microclimate, holding back the ice fog that covered this region.

"What are you doing?" Seichan called from her snowmobile, not bothering with the radio.

He turned and headed back to his own vehicle. He hooked a leg over his seat. "You were right. The rock is warm enough to hold the ice at bay. Something must be heating it down deep."

As he got moving again, he remembered how Sister Anna had told them that much of northern Russia was geothermally active. He stared up at the peak as he rode alongside its flank.

Is the same true here?

Their group continued around the spire, which was roughly a mile in circumference. He slowed a few times to inspect deeper shadows, hoping they might mark the mouths of a tunnel, but he found only more rock.

Finally, they reached the shoulder of ice on the eastern side. He felt defeated. If there was any opening here, it would be covered under meters of ice. He searched the expanse. The frozen surface had been polished to a bluish hue by winds and periodic melts. The midday sun blazed off it, turning the ice a fiery cobalt.

Gray squinted against the glare. He shaded his eyes with a hand as he edged along it, going even slower. Sections of the ice wall had calved away over the centuries and had left shattered cliffs littered over the ice.

He searched through them, peering into the bluer gaps of the exposed ice.

Still nothing . . .

Then he reached a region that was misted over, just a haze. It reminded him of what he had noted rising from the gap between the ice and rock. He drew his snowmobile closer. It rose from one of the broken sections. He flicked on the snowmobile's single headlamp, a customized add-on for a vehicle that had to operate during the sunless months of winter. A toggle let him swivel the beam around.

The haze seeped from a crack near the bottom, maybe a foot tall and four times as wide. He stopped his machine and cut the engine. He slid off the seat and continued on foot. The mist-dampened ice grew slippery near the opening, but his Arctic boots had studded grips.

Seichan followed as the Snowcats drove into view behind them.

He freed a flashlight and dropped to his belly. He shined a bright beam down the crack. Blue ice glowed in the brightness. He followed a trickling flow of meltwater. It ran steeply away, toward a wall of black rock three meters away—then vanished through an arched opening in the stone.

Gray pushed farther in, tilting his head to the side to do so. He stretched his arm and light. Past the archway, he spotted a chute of ice that continued downward. The meltwater flowed along it, vanishing into the darkness.

Frustrated, he pushed back and rolled to his side. As he did, he noted the nearby broken tips of masts sticking out of the ice. "I think there's an opening," he said. "Maybe an old port entrance to this place before it froze over."

By now, the others had exited their Snowcats and gathered closer.

Jason dropped to a knee to peer through the crack. "No way we're fitting through there."

Kelly offered his own insight. "Luckily, you have an icebreaking crew with you."

Gray stood. "What do you mean? Do you think we can use axes and chop a way inside?"

"Too risky." Kelly straightened and headed toward one of the Snow-cats, drawing Gray and Jason with him. "There's an easier method."

The captain waved to Ryan Marr, the former Coast Guard officer, to accompany them to the rear of the Snowcat. Kelly opened the vehicle's cargo hold, which doubled as a weapon locker. To one side rested a wide case. He undid the latches and cracked it open.

Jason whistled appreciatively at the cellophane-wrapped blocks of white clay, stenciled with PE4-MC. It was the Australian military's version of C4 or Semtex. Plastic explosives. Inside the crate were blasting caps and remote detonators.

"I mentioned that icebreakers could get trapped." Kelly nodded to the explosives. "This is how we get out."

Ryan reached inside and grabbed an electric drill and screwed a fat bit in place. He then faced the cliff of ice and scratched the scruff of his red beard. He studied the frozen surface, as if trying to read a map.

"You intend to blast a way through?" Gray asked the captain. "And that's *less* risky than using ice-axes?"

"With the right expert, yes." Kelly eyed Ryan. "It takes a real artist."

Jason grinned up at the shoulder of ice. "Kowalski is going to be sorry he missed this."

Kelly glanced to Jason.

Gray explained. "He's our team's demolition expert. And Jason is right. He will be sorely disappointed."

Gray searched to the west.

Wherever he might be.

40

Airborne over the East Siberian Sea

"They've got to be down there somewhere, right?" Tucker asked.

He crouched in the copilot seat of the Baikal, serving as an extra pair of eyes as Monk glided them over a featureless fogbank. It stretched to the horizon in all directions.

Behind them, Elle and Kowalski searched from the windows back there. The only two who remained unconcerned were Kane and Marco, who slept in tight curls on two chairs.

Monk leaned forward. "Keep an eye out for any sign of them."

Despite the tension, Monk stifled a jaw-cracking yawn with a fist. The man had had little sleep during the eight hours of flight. Tucker had briefly relieved him after catching Monk's chin resting on his collarbone, drowsing off. With the plane on autopilot, Tucker had kept vigil during Monk's nap, nervously watching the instrument panel, while the night skies had swirled with shimmering veils of the borealis.

They had to stop at daybreak to refuel at the northernmost tip of the Novaya Zemlya archipelago. They landed at a small gravel airstrip next to a Russian Arctic park. Elle spoke with the lone keeper of that remote spot. Luckily, the park allowed dogs, so Tucker was able to let Kane and Marco run free over the rocky landscape, stretching their legs and releasing some of the tension from the past days. He kept them close, though, as distant white specks marked the presence of polar bears.

But there was another reason they had stopped, too.

Out of sight of the airstrip's lone caretaker, he and Kowalski had carried Fadd's body to a remote barren gully. They built a cairn of rocks over the young man, promising to come back and give him a proper burial.

When the two had returned to the plane, Tucker found Elle sobbing inside. She did her best to hide it, rubbing a fist over her eyes. A bloody rag lay next to her, where she must have tried to clean the floor of the plane.

Tucker had pulled her close and held her as Monk got the Baikal back in the air. At that moment, Tucker had needed her warmth as much as she did his. During his years with the Rangers, he had buried too many, too young. One never grew numb to it.

"Check to the right!" Elle called out, drawing Tucker back to the present. "Is that a break in the fog?"

Tucker leaned over to search in that direction. Off in the distance, thirty or forty miles away, a patch of glaring light shone from the featureless expanse of the gray fogbank. It looked like the sun reflecting off open ice.

"You're right," Tucker confirmed.

"I thought I saw a brief flash of fire from that direction a moment ago," Elle said. "It caught my eye. But it's gone."

"There's smoke, too," Monk said. "Just a thin trail."

Tucker squinted and saw he was right. "Could that be coming from Gray and the others?"

"Let's hope so." Monk swung the aircraft in that direction. "We're running low on fuel . . . and they're running out of time."

Tucker nodded.

Two hours ago, from the air, they had spotted a shattered dark trail through the white ice, heading north. The route had led straight into the fogbank and vanished. They had turned and followed it, recognizing the path of an icebreaker. They prayed it was the ship that Gray and the others had boarded.

But Tucker's group wasn't the only one following that well-marked trail.

Just before reaching the fogbank, they spotted another ship. They swept low, then quickly angled away once they saw it was a Russian vessel, an icebreaking patrol boat. Tucker had used binoculars to study the gray-blue ship. He made out the massive AK-176MA naval gun mounted at its bow. A Kamov Ka-27 anti-submarine helicopter sat on the boat's stern pad.

They all knew what that Russian vessel, alone in these waters, must have been dispatched to do.

The same as us—to find the others.

Like Tucker's group, the patrol boat must have come across the broken path through the ice and now steamed hard along it, making good time with the route already shattered for them.

It was what made Tucker's current search so desperate.

Gray and the others needed to be warned, to know what was coming.

Still, Tucker knew such foreknowledge would do little good, especially out here, locked in ice. He scanned across the unbroken landscape.

Where could any of us go? Where could we hide?

41

Seichan sheltered with the others behind one of the Snowcats as shards
of ice rained around them. Larger boulders crashed in front. Even with
her face turned and her eyes closed, the flash of fire still dazzled her
vision. Smoke had briefly blasted over their position, then the easterly
winds had battered it back, blowing it past the tall black peak.

"All clear!" Kelly shouted.

The team rose from behind their parked vehicles. They staggered
out, rubbing at ears and shaking heads. The group had retreated three
hundred yards from the detonation site. They all stared toward the ice
wall—or what was left of it.

A stubborn haze of smoke persisted.

Gray crossed and mounted his snowmobile. "Let's check it out."

Seichan rushed and hopped onto her Polaris.

The others prepared to follow in the Snowcats.

Gray didn't wait, clearly anxious to discover if Ryan's mastery of
reading ice was as accomplished as Kelly had claimed. Earlier, they had
all watched the former Coast Guard officer drill holes into the frozen
wall, shape a set of charges, and place blasting caps. After making some
final adjustments, Ryan had given a thumbs-up, and they had retreated.

But did it do any good?

Seichan followed Gray, racing across the ice, skirting larger blue sledges that had slammed to the ground. It took them less than a minute to reach the site. A quarter of the shoulder of ice had been blasted off the peak's side. They were forced to slow, to pick their way through the debris field.

Once close enough, Gray edged his Polaris to where the misty crack had been. He flicked on his headlamp and pointed its beam toward the center of the blast zone. Seichan drew alongside him, adding her light.

"Kelly was not lying," Gray concluded. "Ryan is a true master of icebreaking."

"Ice-blasting," Seichan corrected him.

Gray cut his engine and hopped off. Seichan did the same. They stepped together through the last of the debris field toward the ice-free wall of rock. The archway that Gray had spotted earlier now lay exposed. Past it, a rubble-strewn slope of ice descended into the peak. A blue boulder broke loose and rolled and bounced along the ice chute, vanishing beyond the reach of their light.

Gray crossed to the arched opening, running his hand over its edge. "This must be the top of a larger cavernous opening into the mountain's heart." He pointed to the end of a mast sticking out of the ice. "Not far from where those ships must have once docked when the waters were still open."

Seichan crouched and peered past the archway. "Hopefully that ice ramp leads all the way to the bottom. It looks wide enough for our snowmobiles to traverse. Maybe even a Snowcat." She stared up. "Still, we'll have to be careful."

Hanging high above them, a stubborn mass of ice clung to rock. It looked like a frozen ax waiting to fall.

"Even the vibrations from our engines could bring that crashing down," she warned.

"We can consult with Ryan. Get his assessment."

The growl of the two Snowcats drew their attention around, announcing the arrival of the others. Gray and Seichan crossed from under that hanging lip of ice and hiked out to meet them.

The lead Snowcat braked hard. A door popped opened, and Kelly exited. He strode quickly toward them. He carried a handheld radio in his hand, his expression darkly worried.

Seichan's heart pounded harder, sensing something was wrong.

"What is it?" Gray asked.

Kelly lifted his radio. "Byron just called in. There's a plane on approach, casting out a nonstop SOS."

Seichan craned her neck and searched the skies. A slight haze persisted as fine ice crystals hung in the air, reflecting the sunlight. But she spotted no aircraft.

Gray joined her, shading his eyes. "Who is it?"

"Pilot says his name is Monk Kokkalis. Claims he knows you."

Seichan's breath clamped in her throat. Gray reached out and grasped her arm, squeezing all his hope into that grip.

To the west, a small prop plane flew into view, entering the well of blue skies framed by the fogbank. It began a slow circle.

"He's requesting permission to land," Kelly said.

"Tell him to do so." Gray's voice was raw with relief. "To touch down out here."

But Kelly was not done. "Your friend says we've got trouble coming our way. Big trouble."

2:55 P.M.

Kowalski gathered with everyone out on the ice. There was much hugging and claps on backs. Even Marco had recognized his sometime-partner and had come bounding over, leaping at him in a canine greeting, one paw landing squarely in his crotch.

Stories were quickly exchanged in thumbnails of victories and losses. The latter dampened the initial joy.

"We still don't know if Bailey survived," Monk said. "We can only hope."

Kelly shoved forward, concentrating on the immediate threat. "Describe the patrol boat that's following the *King*'s trail."

"Definitely Russian," Tucker said. "Looks new. Especially the weaponry it's carrying. My guess is that it holds a crew of at least a hundred."

Monk nodded at this assessment. "By my estimate, clocking their speed, they'll be here in two hours, maybe less."

Gray faced Kelly. "Any further word from your navigator and radio crew? We need the world reopened. To get eyes looking this way."

Kowalski scowled. "Why? So everyone can get first row seats at our slaughter?"

"These are still international waters," Gray reminded everyone. "An unprovoked attack here, one witnessed by the world, would risk triggering a global war. Such a threat might make the Russians pause."

"*Might* does not instill a lot of confidence," Tucker said.

Kelly had a worse response. "Doesn't matter. Byron says the solar storm will keep us blacked out for at least another three hours. Until then, we're on our own. Which means we have only *one* option."

"Does it involve surrendering?" Kowalski asked.

Kelly ignored him. "We need to delay that patrol boat."

"How?" Gray asked.

The captain surveyed the newcomers. "Which one of you is Kowalski?"

Eyes turned his way.

Oh, crap.

Kowalski stepped back with a groan, suspecting why he had been called out, what it probably meant. He didn't want to raise his hand, but those stares forced his arm up.

As he did, he made a firm promise to himself.

This is the last time I travel to the Arctic.

But first he had to survive this outing.

"You're coming with me," Kelly told Kowalski in a voice that brooked no argument. He pointed to one of his crew. "Ryan, you're with us, too. Grab the demo kit."

The man nodded and strode toward one of the Snowcats.

Kelly turned to Monk. "Can you taxi us back to the *Polar King*? We'll need your plane after that, too, if you're willing to fly again?"

Monk nodded. "Whatever is needed."

Kelly passed him with a pat on the shoulder. "Good man."

Kowalski sighed heavily and prepared to follow, but first he called over to Gray. "What're you all going to be doing while we're gone?"

Gray turned to the blasted wall of ice and a steep tunnel descending into darkness. "We're going to see if this patch of rock is worth dying over."

42

Captain Turov strode through the stark cabin of the An-74 transport plane. He nodded to his strike team, patting shoulders along the way. Several of the *spetsnaz* soldiers lounged or slept, conserving their energy for the threat ahead.

The team, including Turov, wore the latest in tactical gear designed by the Russian arms manufacturer Kalashnikov. It included multilayered, vented outerwear for cold-weather maneuverability, along with camo helmets and body armor. The team carried upgraded AK-12s, fitted with underbarrel GP-34 grenade launchers. Their kit also included bayonets that could be quickly attached for close-in fighting.

He had offered the same weaponry to the final two members of the group: Valya Mikhailov and her lieutenant Nadira Ali Saeed. The two women had refused the weapons, preferring their own rifles, side-arms, and daggers. The pair also wore body armor that was clearly customized to their form, hugging snugly, patterned in grays and blacks.

The two were seated behind the five-man cockpit. Across from them, Sychkin dozed next to his hulking aide-de-camp, Yerik. The two wore the same body armor as Turov's team, except the archpriest had declined any weapons, not even a side-arm. Sychkin trusted Yerik to keep him safe. The monk had a steel ax hanging from his belt and an MP443 Grach strapped to his thigh.

Turov reached the cockpit and leaned inside. "Have you been able to make contact with the *Ivan Lyakhov*?"

"Only sporadically," the radioman answered. "They're still following the trail left by the other icebreaker. From the condition of the water and ice, the *Lyakhov's* captain estimates he's running two hours behind the enemy."

"And no radar contact?"

The shake of a head answered this. "But the ship's hydrophones picked up what sounded like an explosion a short time ago. The *Lyakhov* also noted that the steady rumble of breaking ice in the distance went silent."

Turov rubbed his chin. "The target ship must have stopped."

"The *Lyakhov's* captain made the same assessment, but with radar systems still compromised and the dense fog shutting down visibility, confirmation can't be made. Unfortunately, the geomagnetic interference grows steadily worse the farther north the vessel travels. For us, too. I keep losing contact with the *Lyakhov*."

"Has there been any revised estimate when this solar storm will abate?"

"Still showing another three hours, sir."

Turov frowned. The enemy needed to be subdued before then. He pointed to the radio operator. "Keep trying to reach the *Lyakhov*. If successful, order them to push their engines to flank speed. To hold nothing back."

"Yes, sir."

Turov stared at the spread of ice and the approaching fogbank.

The third component of this assault remained unreachable. The last word from the Belgorod-class submarine was when it vanished under the polar ice cap, sailing its thirty-thousand-ton bulk toward the search zone. Its code name was *Siniykit*, chosen for the largest oceangoing creature—the blue whale—which was fitting as the submarine was nearly two hundred meters in length.

The boat needed to be that large to hold its arsenal of six massive Poseidon 2M39 torpedoes. The stealth weapons were the latest in

Russia's underwater arsenal, tested for the first time in 2023. The bus-size weapons were more drones than torpedoes, capable of remote operation, with a range of ten thousand kilometers. Powered by a nuclear reactor, the torpedoes were capable of carrying up to a 100-megaton payload. Such beasts were designed as a second-strike nuclear option, to devastate a coastline and trigger a radioactive tsunami.

It was the reason the boat had earned its nickname the "Doomsday Sub."

The *Siniykit* had been out in this polar region to test its weaponry, using unarmed Poseidons. But it also carried one that was loaded with a nuclear warhead. Its payload was only a hundred kilotons, but that was still five times stronger than what had been dropped on Nagasaki. He also knew that some in the military were anxious to do a live test of that bomb.

It was what made Turov balk when Vice Admiral Glazkov had included the boat on this mission. It was a disaster in the making.

I can't let matters get that far out of hand.

Turov turned his attention to the plane's navigator. "How far are we from the *Lyakhov*?"

The man lifted his nose from his station. "We should reach their position in eighty-seven minutes, sir."

Turov pointed to the pilot. "Shorten that timetable. I want us there in under an hour."

The man nodded and edged his throttle forward.

Turov surveyed the fogbank ahead as it swept toward them. The enemy had to be subdued as quickly as possible. If he failed to do that, the consequences could be dire, possibly even triggering a nuclear war.

That must not happen.

Even if it meant annihilating the enemy, with no quarter given or mercy offered, it would have to be done.

He turned to the ice-hardened soldiers behind him, resolute on this point.

So be it.

43

Gray sat atop his Polaris at the mouth of the misty tunnel. He pointed his headlamp across its threshold. Beyond, meltwater traced down a sloped ramp, tracing away into the darkness.

Seichan climbed onto her snowmobile. "The others are all set in the two Snowcats. I warned them to maintain a distance, to let us forge a path ahead of them."

Gray glanced back, hearing engines throttle up.

Omryn sat behind the wheel of one Cat. The Chukchi crewman had the most experience with the vehicle. He carried Jason and Sister Anna, along with the ship's doctor, Harper Marr. Tucker drove the second Cat, with the botanist Elle Stutt and his two dogs.

Gray felt this exploratory team of eight was too small for the challenge ahead—or possibly too large, considering the civilians in tow. But with the constrained timetable, he needed all their expertise, especially not knowing what awaited them.

If anything.

He had to accept that possibility, too.

Before leaving, his group had also armed themselves from the vehicles' weapon lockers. All of them now carried sidearms. Though, Seichan undoubtedly also had knives hidden under her winterwear at strategic locations. Sister Anna refused a pistol, but with some pressure, she settled on a flare-gun.

Omryn brought his own firearm, a Remington 870 DM Magpul. The 12-gauge shotgun was fitted with lead slugs in a detachable six-round magazine. He carried two more mags in a sling over his shoulder. He explained his choice of Arctic weaponry with an economy of words: *polar bears*. While no one expected to encounter such a creature here, such stopping power would be welcome if there was trouble.

Tucker still had an AK-12 that he had secured from the assault on the naval base in Severodvinsk. He gave a spare rifle to Gray, which was slung over his back.

Gray radioed the group. "Single file. We proceed with care."

He twisted the throttle and edged his Polaris over the lip of the slope, then began a slow descent down the icy chute. The treads of his tracks dug deep, keeping him from a deadly slide.

Seichan followed.

Gray studied the ramp under him. He pictured water trickling down here for centuries, building up into this natural slide into the heart of the mountain. He swiveled his light, inspecting the chute, watching for any worrisome cracks, wending his way around jagged boulders that had gotten blasted down here.

He also studied the rock walls to either side. As he descended, the walls slowly climbed higher and spread wider, forming a huge opening into the peak, easily forty feet high. The icy chute broadened under him, like a glacier spilling down a valley.

With the extra room, Seichan drew alongside him. The two Snowcats followed, keeping single file.

Gray glanced back. He pictured the tall archway and imagined a three-masted ship docked outside, maybe moored in the deeper waters.

He made the mistake of staring back for a breath too long.

Seichan shouted a warning. "Stop!"

She reinforced this by nudging her snowmobile into his, sending him in a sideways skid.

He braked hard, spinning a bit more on the ice, then came to a stop.

He quickly identified what had panicked her.

Twenty yards ahead, the rock walls vanished, opening into a gargantuan cavern. The ramp that they had been following spilled over an edge, forming a frozen waterfall that tumbled into the abyss.

Seichan stopped next to him and scolded, "Quit sightseeing. Eyes on the road."

The two Cats trundled up to them, then cut their engines.

Doors popped, and the team exited, wary of the meltwater-slick slope. Flashlights clicked on.

Gray waved everyone together. "Keep close. Watch your footing."

They carefully edged down the last of the ramp, aiming toward the drop-off.

Jason stared at the trickling water underfoot. "Definitely warmer down here."

Anna whispered as she kept close to the young man. "It's like the stories the Greeks told of Hyperborea, how its lands were said to be sultry and hot."

"A land we now know was heated by geothermal energy," Jason noted.

Elle supported this. "I smell sulfur in the air. Pretty strong."

Gray had noted it, too. It was the rotten-egg smell found around hot springs and geysers.

Tucker offered his own explanation. "It might just be Marco. His bowels still haven't fully settled after all that Russian prison food."

His attempt to lighten the mood failed.

The weight of the place—the history, the rock overhead—hushed the group into a wary silence. Sunlight still reached this deep, reflecting down the ramp behind them in a silvery-blue sheen. But ahead, where the chute dropped away, the world vanished into a Stygian darkness.

As they drew closer, Harper called to the group. "Oy! There are stairs over here!"

Gray turned. To the left of the waterfall, stone steps descended in a swooping arc, falling away into the shadows below.

"Same over there," Jason called out, pointing to the far side of the icy fall.

Gray guided everyone toward the doctor's side, wanting them off the ice as soon as possible. "Keep together."

They reached the stairs without mishap and gathered along the steps, which appeared to have been chiseled out of the rock. Gray stared past the frozen waterfall. On its opposite side, a matching staircase arched along the wall on that side. The two sets of steps formed a grand U-shaped promenade.

"How deep does this go?" Tucker asked, leaning over the edge of the steps with his flashlight in hand.

"Stay back," Gray warned. He turned to Anna. "Sister, you brought your flare gun, yes?"

Her eyes widened with understanding. "Of course."

She withdrew the yellow gun from a belt holster and handed it over.

Gray checked it was loaded, then pointed its muzzle high, aiming for the cavern's ceiling. He squeezed the trigger. A short bang launched a flare across the chamber. When it reached its apex, it burst into a blinding red sun. It hung in the air and slowly descended.

Despite Gray's warning, they all moved closer to the edge of the stairs.

"My god . . ." Jason exclaimed.

"I don't think *your* god has anything to do with this," Tucker said.

Gray gaped at the wonders revealed in the firelight. Stone pyramids, much like those of Egypt, climbed high. Below them, a contiguous spread of homes and structures formed a multilevel jigsaw puzzle. Several spires poked higher, topped by a sculpted mix of Nordic animals—whales, mammoths, walruses, seals, reindeer, caribou, and muskoxen—as if each were a totem to a clan of these ancient people.

As he stared, Gray remembered what had been carved in ivory on the mammoth tusk hidden at the Golden Library.

This is what that ancient artisan was trying to depict.

Before the flare expired, Gray turned to Jason. "Start recording *all* of this. We must bring this to the world. Show that this archaeological wonder belongs to all nations. Not just one."

"Like on the other side of the world," Tucker noted. "With Antarctica. A continent that by treaty belongs to no one."

Gray nodded. "We must preserve this *continent*, this lost Hyperborea, in the same manner. Before the Russians get here."

"You mean before all hell breaks loose," Tucker added.

3:39 P.M.

Recognizing the danger and the closing window of time, Gray got them moving quicker down the steps. They needed to record as much as possible, to be ready to share it with the world if given the opportunity.

As they continued, Gray dispatched another flare, both to light their descent and to assist Jason in capturing the wonders below. This second flare also allowed them to get a better sense of the place's breadth. They had been too overwhelmed the first time by the beauty and spectacle. They had failed to appreciate that this cavern, easily a half-mile across, was only one of many, all interconnected like the homes themselves.

It reminded Gray of the layout of the Golden Library, how it extended outward under the Ringing Tower across a series of rooms, forming a labyrinth. But the discoveries hidden here were far more ancient than any book found in a gold-plated chest.

Anna offered her own theory. "I think this place spreads out to those surrounding peaks, forming one great metropolis. These sea-faring people must have overwintered here, then ventured outward during warmer months."

"Which would make this the Rome of the Arctic," Jason added.

Anna smiled. "The old texts—of Greece and Rome—mention travelers, emissaries of Hyperborea who visited them. Such accounts were likely draped in mythological terms, by societies that could not comprehend the Far North or the sophistication of the people who had learned to survive here."

Gray could not argue against this—all he could do was keep them moving.

As they neared the bottom, finer details emerged. Across the spread of homes, and more dramatically across the pyramids, their surfaces had been carved with scenes of home life, of battle, of great hunts, and a bestiary of mythological creatures.

Gray remembered Bishop Yelagin's account of vast swaths of petro-glyphs found across the lands of northern Russia, some so beautiful and advanced that they had to be preserved under a glass dome. Then there were those stone pyramids and tombs found on outlying islands of the White Sea.

Were they all the handiwork of these Hyperboreans?

With no way of knowing, Gray drew the others to the bottom of the steps. The group slowed, as if fearing to trespass any farther. Or maybe it was because they faced a larger obstacle.

"Where do we go from here?" Anna whispered. "It would take teams of archaeologists and anthropologists decades to study and understand this place and its people."

Gray heard the longing in her voice. She clearly wanted to be part of any such exploration.

Let's hope she gets that chance.

The group abandoned the stairs and spread out, examining the closest structures. The shoulder of a pyramid rose to the left. A match-ing one climbed on the chamber's far side. The structures looked to be made out of sandstone, either quarried or maybe manufactured in some geothermically-heated kiln. Elsewhere, roofs looked buttressed by ribs of whalebone.

Clearly *wood* would've been a rare commodity this far north. But apparently these ancients found ways to compensate with bone and stone—and not just with those materials.

"Look," Jason called over as he examined a home. He rubbed a finger along the green patinaed edge of a doorway. "I think this is copper."

Gray joined him and looked closer.

Definitely copper.

He straightened and pictured mines somewhere out there. Maybe these ancients had discovered more than veins of lodestone in this giant massif of rock.

Omryn offered additional anthropological insight. "Some Inuit were skilled in such metalcraft, going back three thousand years. They called themselves the Copper Inuit." He glanced significantly at the others. "It is said many of them had blond hair."

Gray frowned and stared across the expanse, again wondering how far these Hyperboreans had spread. Could they be the ancestors or teachers of the Copper Inuit?

Tucker waved an arm, drawing attention. "Kane and Marco are picking up something over here. Plus, you might want to see this—or maybe not. Not if you have a weak stomach."

The Ranger had wandered toward the towering waterfall, which glowed with their reflected light. Gray led the rest of the group over to him.

He stood near a cluster of old tents. They had been set up in a small square off to the side. The fabric, the wooden spars, all were remarkably preserved by the cold. Pots and pans lay scattered. Leather clothing dried on racks, stiffened to boards by age.

"It's the remains of an old camp," Jason said. "Likely left behind by Catherine's team or someone who came earlier."

"It's not just the camp's remains," Tucker said and crouched by one of the tents. He shined his light through its open flap. "But the campers, too."

Gary joined him, dropping to a knee.

Two bodies lay inside, mummified by the cold, preserved by the same. There was clearly something wrong with them. Their features, while withered and shrunken, also sprouted with strange growths, as if their bodies had become the beds for some malignant fungus or plant. Fibrous structures vined over them, entwining the two together. But whatever afflicted the pair had died long ago, turning brown and dried.

"What happened to them?" Anna asked, backing away and turning to Harper, the team's medical expert.

The doctor shook her head, keeping a distance herself. "I have no bloody clue."

Gray turned to the only person who might have any further insight. "Dr. Stutt?"

The botanist drew closer, showing no fear, only fascination. "It appears to be some form of infestation. Whether antemortem or postmortem, I can't say."

Gray was reminded of the other reason his group had sought out this place. It wasn't just to record the wonders found here, but to identify the danger hinted at by so many others.

He stared at the bodies.

Is this it?

Tucker reminded them again. "Something over here has Marco and Kane spooked."

Gray turned, noting the two dogs standing stiffly to the side, facing the icy waterfall, noses low, hackles high. Both growled in low warning tones.

"They're scenting something they don't like," Tucker said. "And I've learned to trust their noses more than my eyes."

Gray crossed closer to investigate. Framing either side of the waterfall, half buried in the ice, rose two tall stone thrones, all carved with symbols. The closest was inscribed with a riotous garden of twisted leaves and thorns, like a macabre version of Eden. On the far side, the tall seat appeared carved with sea life in all its myriad forms, as if waiting for Poseidon to rest his weary bones.

He remembered Yelagin mentioning the discovery of an oversize throne on one of the White Sea islands. The bishop had also shared a Greek account of a towering trio of Hyperborean brothers. Gray tried to picture someone three cubits in height sitting there, but even these chairs appeared too large, which suggested they were meant to be symbolic, rather than practical.

"There's a space *behind* this carved throne," Tucker said. "It extends behind the fall of ice, too."

Gray shifted over, stepping between Marco and Kane to get a peek into the gap. He pointed his flashlight into the narrow space.

"Anything?" Jason asked.

Gray nodded and faced the others. "Appears to be a tunnel in the wall between the thrones. It's reachable if we go single file."

Tucker frowned. "I think my partners would argue against trespassing there."

Despite the risk, Gray knew they had to investigate.

"Something must be down there," he said. "That tunnel is positioned grandly near the entrance, framed by those thrones, also by the pyramids to either side." He swung an arm toward the tents. "Even this lost group set up camp here."

"And look what happened to them," Tucker reminded the group. "You all can go inside, but I'm keeping my dogs out. That's if I could even get them to go in there."

"Just as well. It's best if we leave someone behind." Gray searched up the wall of ice. "In case we get stuck."

Tucker shrugged, looking more than happy to stand guard. "Keep in mind, our radios won't work once you're in there. Not through all that rock and ice. If you get in trouble, I'm not going to know. And vice versa."

"Understood. We'll have to make do." Gray faced the others. "If anyone else wants to stay here, I would understand. Just don't wander far."

He searched their faces. No one took up his offer, though Omryn looked doleful and worried.

Gray nodded and shifted behind the throne. "Then let's head out."

44

Standing on the ice, buried in dense fog, Kowalski cursed his life. He tugged at the crotch of his dry suit. The scuba gear was courtesy of the *Polar King*, but apparently none of the dive squad was taller than six feet. It made for a snug, ball-pinching fit.

Still, the gear was not the worst of his complaints.

He stared over an icy cliff. Twenty feet below, black water washed and sloshed. Two of the *King*'s dive team flanked him. All three wore their tanks, waiting for the word to go. Another crewmate pounded a motorized winch into the ice. Its line would lower them into the polar sea—and hopefully raise them later.

Everyone moved about swiftly, as if they had done this before, and maybe they had. For a crew of an icebreaker, tackling problems in deep ice was likely a regular necessity. But he doubted any of them had ever tried to ambush an eight-thousand-ton Russian patrol boat, one armed to the teeth with cruise missiles and naval guns.

Captain Kelly stood a few yards away, radio at his ear, yelling into it, as if that would help with the spotty reception. But at least the other half of this assault team—the dry half—was only a quarter mile away, led by Ryan Marr.

Monk strode from the captain's side and joined Kowalski. "The others will be ready in five. They've finished their drill holes and are placing charges now."

Kowalski pictured that five-man team out on the ice. Twenty minutes ago, they had leaped from the plane as it came to a stop, trudging off with huge drills over their shoulders, each with bits three feet long. They had quickly disappeared into the fog.

Afterward, Monk had flown the rest of the party here, a quarter mile farther up the channel created by the *Polar King*'s passage. The flight to this area had been harrowing enough. Monk had kept the Baikal skimming the ice the entire time, all but flying blind through the fog, not that there were any trees or hills to worry about.

From the hydrophones aboard the *King*, they had been able to determine a rough position of the approaching patrol boat. The sound of its diesel engines and spinning props had been easy to track. It was how they knew it was traveling under full steam, faster than when it had last been spotted from the air, which necessitated a quick change in plans.

The ambush site was only five miles from where the *Polar King* was parked. They had hoped for a greater distance, but the Russian ship was sweeping in fast, which also shortened their timetable.

Kelly crossed to them. "Let's get you in the water," the captain called over. "You'll not have much leeway once Ryan's charges go off."

His fellow divers—Mitchell and Renny—nodded and stepped toward the winch. Across their chests were strapped underwater ordnance packages, already primed with blasting caps. Kowalski carried another. All were his own design, after cannibalizing the resources aboard the *Polar King*.

The captain held Kowalski back. "Ryan's efforts should force the patrol boat to slow, to cut its engines temporarily. That's the window you'll have to complete this mission."

Kowalski stared off into the fog, picturing the other team planting charges across an arc of drill holes. They were all counting on Ryan's ability to read the ice. The plan was to break free a massive ice floe from one side of the channel and send it careening across the path of the patrol boat. It would create a temporary dam, one that would challenge the smaller boat.

"Will a floe like that truly intimidate the Russians?" Monk asked. "Their vessel is an icebreaker, too."

Kelly scoffed. "The *King* is a nuclear-powered *icebreaker*. The patrol boat is an *icebreaking* vessel. There's a difference. It runs on diesel engines. It can only break ice six feet thick. That floe we'll be sending their way will be fifteen to twenty feet thick."

"Then won't that be enough to stop them?" Kowalski asked, hoping to avoid a dip into the freezing waters.

"It'll no doubt slow them. But that floe will be loose. They can push it, and failing that, they have guns that can chew the blockage into slush." Kelly pointed to the first diver riding the winch down. "The only way to stop the boat is to take out its propellers after it slows to address the ice floe."

"What about the patrol boat's helicopter?" Monk asked. "We spotted it from the air. Even if the vessel is stranded, they could send it aloft."

"Better that than the ship's entire arsenal," Kelly reminded them. "And the Russians certainly can mobilize ground forces, too, and send them overland across the ice."

Monk looked grim.

"Remember our goal is a *delaying* tactic. To buy us time until this infernal solar storm ends. There's little more we can do. The *King* has a small armory, but it's meant to ward off polar bears, or in a worst-case scenario, a small pirate attack. Not the full force of the Russian Navy."

Kowalski sighed heavily. "So, it looks like I'm going for a swim."

Kelly nodded as the second diver vanished over the edge. "Remember, the patrol boat has *two* stern propellers. You'll need to destroy both. Even if *one* is left functioning, they could still keep moving."

Kowalski nodded and pointed to the ordnance package strapped to his chest. "I know. That's why I'm bringing a spare charge. Just in case."

The radio, still in the captain's hand, squawked. Ryan's voice reached them. "Blowing in thirty, Cap. Counting down now."

Kelly pointed to Kowalski. "Move it, soldier."

"Seaman," Kowalski corrected him as he turned away. "I'm former navy, like I told you."

"Then why are you whining about a swim?" Kelly asked, following him to the winch. "I thought seawater was in a sailor's blood."

"Not when it's colder than a polar bear's nutsack." He yanked on his snug dive suit. "And speaking of nutsacks, your ship's tailor really sucks."

Kelly looked back at Monk, as if wondering how he put up with his teammate.

Monk merely shrugged.

Kowalski crossed to the edge. He secured his mask and dry hood, then hooked his foot into the line's loop. With a huge breath, he dropped over the edge. The winch operator swiftly lowered him.

The captain called down. "Good hunting!"

Kowalski saluted back with a raised middle finger.

Then he hit the icy water.

4:24 P.M.

Valya Mikhailov had no tolerance for fools—especially those who put their faith in anything more than bone and steel. She ran a thumb over her holstered Glock 21 as she stared out the window of the transport plane.

The featureless expanse of the fogbank failed to hold her attention.

She listened as the archpriest whispered to Yerik Raz, their two heads bent in prayer. She cast Sychkin a sidelong glance. She knew the man had no true faith in anything but himself and the power he could wield. The monk, on the other hand, seemed devoted, both to the priest and to his faith. She noted Sychkin placing his palm on Yerik's fire-ravaged cheek, not shying from the scarring.

Still, the monk turned his face away. There was clearly a well of pain attached to that disfigurement that had nothing to do with the touch of flames. She knew the man had been burned in a fire that had killed his mother, and that Sychkin had taken him in afterward, as ward and mentor.

Valya scowled.

Better you had died in that fire.

For now, she had no choice but to remain with these others. They were taking her where she needed to go. She pictured the dark figure rushing through smoke in the apartment building opposite the Vatican

embassy. The firefight had been short, and Valya had not escaped unscathed. Her shoulder was no longer in a sling, only wrapped against
the fight to come. The pain remained, but it helped focus her.

She would not be caught off guard again.

Next to her, Nadira slept, her arms crossed over her chest. Valya had
wanted to bring along a larger contingent of her own people, but she
had been refused. Still, she had already taken measure of the team that
Captain Turov had handpicked. She could not fault him. His *spetsnaz*
crew kept silent, reserving their strength. None of them bothered to
double-check their weapons. True professionals had them ready at all
times.

She caught one staring toward her, his eyes cold and hard, likely
sizing her up as well. She turned away, feeling no need to impress
anyone.

She returned her attention to the landscape passing under the plane.
They were due to rendezvous with the other prong of this assault, an
icebreaking patrol boat that was following the path left by the enemy's
ship. The *Lyakhov* came with guns, missiles, and a complement of a
hundred Arctic-hardened soldiers.

Turov clearly thought such a force was overkill.

Valya did not.

As she stared below, a fiery glow flickered through the gray-white
fog. But in a blink, it was gone. She squinted toward it, but it never
repeated. She cocked an ear to listen for any indication that the flight
crew had spotted it, too, but the low murmur up front remained steady.
Still, she trusted her eyes and continued to watch that section.

Concentrating there, she noted another brightness in the same region,
just north of where she had spotted the flicker. It appeared to be a patch
of open ice, reflecting the afternoon sun.

She clenched a fist and shoved up, stirring Nadira, who looked inquiringly at her.

Valya shook her head and stepped over her lieutenant to reach the
cockpit.

Turov was bent next to his navigator, both studying a plotting map.
The captain tapped at it. "This is where the *Lyakhov* should be?"

"By my best estimate, from speed and last known position, yes sir. We should rendezvous in the next fifteen minutes."

Valya interrupted. "Captain Turov."

He turned to her, clearly noting the urgency in her voice. "What is it?"

She answered tersely. "An open area of ice. Free of fog. At least for now. If you're looking to land, this might be our opportunity."

He straightened. "Show me."

She scooted into the cramped cockpit, searched through the front windshield, oriented herself, then pointed. "There."

Turov leaned forward and stared for a breath. "You're right."

The navigator also looked. "I don't think that's far from where we plotted the *Lyakhov*'s location."

Turov confronted the pilot, sounding peeved that the man had depended more on his instruments than his eyes. "Can you land us there? Is there enough clearance?"

"I'll have to make a sweep to be certain, but yes, it looks good."

"Then do it."

Turov turned to her and nodded his thanks, but she was already recalibrating, taking this new factor into account, as she returned to her seat.

Still, she pictured that brief flash in the gloom.

What the hell was that?

4:25 P.M.

Still on the water's surface, Kowalski gaped as a blue mountain of ice slammed into the channel. A moment ago, a series of muffled detonations had gone off, accompanied by spats of fire—then the world had closed in front of them, blocked by that bulldozing wall of ice.

Ahead of him, the iceberg thundered as its bulk splintered and crashed into the opposite side. A wave of water welled toward him, pushed by that frozen behemoth.

That was their signal.

And a big one at that.

All three dove, letting that wave crest over them. They were pulled by small sleds with electric motors.

Kowalski followed behind the other two men. Both were experienced polar divers. Renny led the way, driving deep toward the newly birthed iceberg.

With the sun shrouded by fog, the visibility sucked, but still the little light that did reach these depths cast the world in shades of aquamarine. Blue walls rose on both sides. Their undersides formed inverted mountains, scalloped and scribed with algae. Fronds waved in the current created by the explosive calving of the ice floe. Small fish darted in flashes of silver. Roils of shrimplike crustaceans sped in panicked schools.

But Kowalski had no time for sightseeing as he sped after the others.

The trio reached the berg as it churned heavily, spun leadenly. It appeared to be half the size of a football field. They dove under it, and the world darkened, occluded by that mass of ice. Once beneath it, Kowalski was rocked by its motion, like a cork in rough seas. His ears filled with its creaking, popping, and cracking.

Renny swept onward, aiming for its far side. He clicked on the small dive torch at the tip of his sled. Kowalski pursued that tiny star through the darkness. Finally, the waters brightened ahead. Mitchell slowed his board and lifted an arm, spinning slightly, like an astronaut in space. They were to pause here, wait for their target.

Kowalski drew to a stop with the others. His insulated dry suit covered him from crown to toe. But now, hanging in place, Kowalski shivered in the cold. He pictured his girlfriend, Maria, who was in the Congo at a gorilla reserve on a special project. He wished he was there with her. He tried to draw that African warmth to him. But all he kept picturing was a cold beer, sweating in the savannah heat.

That would be nice, too, right now.

Renny and Mitchell swam closer to him. Both had backgrounds in the Aussie Navy. They checked on his status, offering okay symbols with their free hands. He returned it, but without enthusiasm.

And for good reason.

He was far from okay.

They all heard the growing rumble of the approaching patrol boat. It steadily rose in volume. Kowalski felt it in his gut, thrumming across his chest. He stared past their dark shelter to the brighter water.

Time ticked away, marked by the pounding of his heart.

Finally, a massive shadow swept toward them, a thundercloud across blue skies. The engine's timbre changed, slowing, dropping to a low roar, then subsiding further.

Kowalski pictured the boat's captain studying this dam across his boat's bow. The hope was that through the fog, with the charges buried deep into drill holes, no one on board would have noted the brief explosive flashes. Additionally, the blasts could easily be mistaken for the natural cracking and thunderous pops of unsettled ice left in the wake of the *Polar King*'s passage.

But at the moment, *hope* felt like a feeble shield against the immensity of the task ahead. Still, Kowalski clung to it.

The boat's diesel engines continued to rumble, gliding the vessel's four-hundred-foot length the last of the way. Bow thrusters engaged, sounding like fire hoses at full blast, which helped steady the craft in the channel.

Renny chopped an arm toward the boat.

Time to go.

Kowalski secured his sled under him and twisted its throttle. They didn't know how long the Russian captain would ponder this obstacle, to judge if his boat could nose this massive floe out of its way or not.

The answer came fast, with the thudding chatter of heavy guns.

Kowalski flinched as rounds pounded into the berg overhead, churned out by the turreted AK-176MA naval gun mounted at the boat's bow. The Russians weren't holding back, firing on full auto, more than a hundred rounds per minute, clearly planning on bandsawing the berg into pieces.

Still, twenty feet of ice was as tough as ballistic armor.

For now, it kept Kowalski and the others shielded.

They fled from the deafening barrage and set out from under the floe. Keeping together, they sped toward the deep shadow of the boat's keel. Once there, Renny led them along the hull's centerline. The bulk of the massive boat hung overhead, a great steel whale. As they continued, the bow thrusters finally subsided to either side.

Nearing the stern, the trio slowed to a crawl. Through the murk, lit by their dive torches, they made out the two propellers, positioned to the port and starboard sides. The pair still turned, but only slowly as the engines idled. The props' blades were three meters long, curved like bronze scimitars.

Knowing they dared not wait, Renny and Mitchell split off. Each glided toward one of the props. Kowalski stayed put, maintaining his role as back-up. He lifted a hand to the ordnance strapped at his chest. The bombs were equipped with Mag-Lok hooks for securing them in place, and timers set for five minutes.

Renny reached his side first. He looked like a sparrow hovering before a huge fan. The diver's neck craned as he studied his target.

Earlier, Captain Kelly had explained that it was not uncommon for an icebreaker to damage or break a propeller. It required divers to repair them regularly, like these two. The weakest spot was where the shaft met those blades.

Renny planted his ordnance package where it would do the most damage, magnetically locking it in place. He stared over at Mitchell, waiting for his partner to do the same. Finally, the other succeeded and gave a thumbs-up. Both engaged their bombs' timers, yanked their sleds up from where they hung on straps, and sped back toward Kowalski.

Again, Renny was faster, clearly the more experienced.

Mitchell lagged behind, struggling with his sled.

Something was wrong.

And then got immediately worse.

The propellers spun up, churning through the water, first slowly, then faster. Mitchell jerked a glance behind him, then back again, fighting his sled.

Renny failed to note his partner's distress, concentrating on his flight away from the stern. The tidal pull of the turning screw caught Mitchell. He got his sled sputtering, but its small, foundering motor was no match against the giant diesel overhead.

Mitchell thrashed, momentarily holding his place, but it was a losing battle.

Kowalski swore, already working quickly, blindly. Then he ducked his head, twisted his sled's throttle, and sped past Renny—who finally recognized something was wrong and fumbled into a turn.

Kowalski rushed to Mitchell, who had begun to draft back toward the starboard propeller. Once there, Kowalski spun, somersaulting to reverse his position. He kept hold of his sled with one hand and yanked Mitchell over to him. The panicked man abandoned his dying sled and snatched on to Kowalski's belt.

Better hold tight.

Kowalski reached to his shoulder and flung his ordnance package behind him, toward the propeller. He had already flipped the timer from five minutes to five *seconds*.

This is going to hurt.

With two men on one sled, they could not fight the suction.

Then the world exploded behind them.

The concussion crushed his lungs, popped both ears, spurted blood from his nostrils. He got tossed forward by the blast, momentarily spinning. He managed to keep hold of his sled. Mitchell got thrown off.

Tens meters farther on, Renny was less affected by the explosion. He rushed in and recaptured his dazed partner. Kowalski got his sled under him, and they fled back toward the ship's bow. Behind them, the starboard propeller still spun, crookedly, and with only one blade.

Luckily, the charges that Kowalski had crafted were not that powerful. They were meant as sabotage, to break joints, not sink a ship.

Still, his head would be ringing for days.

They raced along the hull of the patrol boat. The muffled barrage of the bow gun continued nonstop. Hopefully with all that noise, no one aboard had noted the smaller blast at the stern—or at least, not yet.

Kowalski and the others needed to be gone before that happened.

As they reached the front of the boat, the reason for the engagement of the propellers became evident. The massive naval guns had already chewed a deep gully through the massive floe. The boat had been moving forward to continue that trenching.

Kowalski stared ahead.

Above him, the huge gun chugged away. Its heavy rounds shattered both into the ice and through the water. White cavitating streaks shot across the dark blue, creating a deadly gauntlet.

Renny cast him a worried look, but they had no choice but to risk it.

Kowalski returned a nod, and they sped away. Burdened by Mitchell hanging on his belt, Renny fell behind. Kowalski tried to aim away from where the gun ate at the berg, but as the weapon strafed, rounds still sped around him, marked by collapsing pops of their passage. Still, he made it safely under the iceberg.

He raced another few meters, then twisted around.

Renny reached the floe, too—but not unscathed. A dark trail of blood flowed in his sled's wake. The men sped up to Kowalski. Mitchell's face was a mask of pain and fear. His left leg hung crookedly, nearly torn in half by a strike to his calf.

There was no time for aid.

They all continued at top speed under the berg. When they reached the far side, a distant blast echoed through the water, marking the explosion of the other ordnance packs.

Kowalski could not savor this success, not with the blood trailing them.

Two minutes later, they reached the winch line and abandoned their tanks. Kowalski sent Renny up first, with Mitchell hugging around his partner's neck. As Kowalski waited, staring up, blood spattered down. He expected Mitchell to lose his weakening grip, but the man kept hold. The two vanished over the edge.

Kowalski followed next. Once topside, he found Monk securing a tourniquet on Mitchell's leg. Any additional care would have to wait. Most of the team had already boarded the plane. The Baikal's engine was idling.

Once Monk was finished, the last of the group hurried to board.

Renny and Kowalski carried Mitchell between them.

Captain Kelly greeted them inside, his face dark and grim. "Well done. You've bought us some breathing room back there."

Kowalski glanced over a shoulder, hoping that was true. He turned back around as Monk taxied for a liftoff. As Kowalski stared dully, he wondered what awaited them ahead.

He had no way of knowing, but he was certain of one thing. Despite Kelly's words, they had better keep holding their breaths.

Because this isn't over.

45

Elle followed the rest of the group down the tunnel behind the frozen waterfall. She was the last in line. She glanced back at the exit, where the two giant thrones flanked the ice wall—one carved with sea life, the other with a riotous garden.

But her thoughts were on another.

She had hated to abandon Tucker. Marco, too. Earlier, as she was leaving, the young shepherd had taken a few steps toward her, as if preparing to follow despite whatever spooked him. He only stopped when Tucker had whistled Marco back to his side.

Still, Elle knew she had to continue on. She pictured the state of the bodies in the tent. Whatever lay hidden here would most likely need her expertise.

Knowing that, she hurried forward and followed the bobbing lights of the others. After the chill of the icy waterfall, the warmth of the passageway was welcome—if not the smell.

The sulfurous taint to the air grew heavier.

She pushed through it, tasting it on her tongue.

Ahead, the tunnel delved steeply, heading deeper underground.

"Everybody stick together," Gray called out. "Close up our ranks."

Elle joined the two from the *Polar King*, Omryn and Harper.

Ahead, Anna and Jason followed Gray and Seichan.

Lights swept along the walls, illuminating carvings etched full around. It was quickly evident that the same motif found on the giant thrones continued along this passageway. To the left, the surface swam with images of sea creatures. To the right, a dense garden climbed with thorny vines and drooping flowers.

"What does this all mean?" Anna whispered, searching around.

Jason drew to a sudden stop, turning to one side. "Don't know. But look at this totem." He bent closer. "It's set off in its own niche. As if significant."

They all gathered to him. Inside the cubby, a sculpture depicted a beautifully rendered whale. Its eyes looked ancient, almost mournful.

"*Balaena mysticetus*," Omryn intoned, naming the specimen. "In English, 'the mystic whale.'"

"Or as they're more commonly known, the bowhead whale," Harper added. "These beasties are unique to these waters. They can live for up to two centuries, making them the longest-lived mammal."

Gray ran a finger along the totem's back. "From this level of artistry, the species must have been highly regarded by these Hyperboreans."

"By *all* the Arctic people," Omryn corrected. "Many groups, including the Chukchi, have myths and legends tied to such grand creatures."

Elle drifted to the far side of the tunnel, drawn by another piece of sculpted artwork. Directly opposite the whale totem, the wall had been deeply carved, showing a collection of strange flowering plants with spiky thorns. They looked very much like what had been engraved on the throne. Only these examples looked as finely rendered as a botanist's anatomical drawing, so perfect that they appeared to have sprouted from the wall, then calcified in place.

As Elle studied them, she knew she had spotted this specimen before, depicted in another manner.

She drew the others' attention from the whale totem. She pointed her flashlight. "I believe these are the same plants we found drawn in the Greek book. The page marked with the word *sarkophágos*. Or 'eater of flesh.'"

Gray drew out his tablet and pulled up that sketch again. He held it before the carving.

"You're right," he said. "They're the same. Even down to the vine snaking out from one of them."

He glanced back the way they had come.

Elle could guess what he was picturing.

The bodies in the tent.

A frightful thought intruded, likely shared by Gray.

She voiced it aloud. "Maybe these specimens fed on *more* than just insects. Maybe the Greek word written on that page was not a name, but a *warning*."

"Eater of flesh," Gray said.

By now, Jason had drifted farther down the passageway, video-recording the stretch of wall on that side. "There are more carvings over here, framed in niches. Two of them. Related to whales."

The group crossed and inspected the artwork, while Jason recorded everything.

The first niche showed small boats and tiny figures, likely the Hyperboreans themselves. Above, a flotilla of whales swam across the stone. There was a sense of majesty and pride in the depicted scene.

"It's a whale hunt," Anna noted. "And the two most prominent specimens appear to be bowheads again."

Jason drew them two steps farther down. "And shows what happens *after* those hunts."

Elle frowned as she shifted over.

The next niche was more gruesome, depicting the slaughter and butchering of another bowhead. It appeared the laborers were harvesting something vital from the cetacean. The rendering was cruder, almost as if the artist was ashamed of what he had been forced to illustrate.

"What are they trying to show with all of this?" Anna asked.

No one had an answer.

To seek more meaning, Elle turned to the opposite wall. Another niche sat across from the whale hunt. Again, this diorama showed workers laboring intensely. Only strewn across the floor and hanging on racks at the back were dried plants.

Elle waved the others closer. "This diorama illustrates another *extraction* process—only from plants this time. Most likely the same carnivorous specimen from before."

"But to what end?" Gray asked.

"Maybe *this* end," Seichan called out. She stood several meters farther down the tunnel, having drifted off on her own.

They continued toward her, sensing the press of time. She stood where the passageway ended at a domed chamber.

As Elle approached, the sulfur in the air grew intense, increasing with each step. It burned her eyes and nostrils. She coughed harshly, as her body struggled to clear her lungs.

The Aussie doctor held everyone back, shrugging a med pack from a shoulder. "We can't stay down here long, folks," Harper warned.

The doctor soaked a pile of 4x4 gauze sponges, then passed two or three to each person. "Keep your mouth and nose covered. Wipe your eyes down regularly."

Elle followed her instructions, grateful for the relief.

The source of the burning stench was readily evident. It rose from the middle of the next chamber, where a deep pit bubbled with noxious black mud. It cast up belches of sulfurous gas, staining the air a foul yellow. The same, in powder form, was caked on the floor, walls, and ceiling.

"It's a mudpot," Jason said. "A blister of that geothermal energy that warms this place."

"Only this will suffocate us if we don't keep moving." To hurry them on, Seichan pointed to what had caught her attention. "What do you make of these?"

Framing the entrance to the domed chamber, two tall pots— amphora-like jars—rested to either side of the tunnel.

"Whales and plants again," Elle said. "Like on the walls."

Jason held a wad of gauze over his lips and nose, while recording the pot on the left. "It's not just whales carved into this pot, but all sorts of sea creatures."

Gray moved to the pot on the right side, examining its carved images. Elle followed and dropped to a knee, sweeping her light over its sculpted surface. "It's the same carnivorous plant again."

Gray stepped back to allow Jason to continue filming. "Both pots are empty," he noted, "as if waiting to be filled."

Gray pointed his flashlight back the way they had come. He cast his beam down one side of the tunnel, then the other. His expression was pinched with concentration.

Elle joined him. Despite the danger, curiosity throbbed through her. She noticed Gray's expression softening, as if he were coming to some understanding.

"What are you thinking?" she asked him.

He turned, not rudely, just still ruminating. He faced the chamber with the bubbling cauldron. Three passageways extended outward from it: to the right and left and directly across the pit.

"We need to see more," he simply stated and strode along the lip of rock surrounding the boiling mudpot.

The others followed. He cast his light into the two side tunnels as he passed them. The one to the left was covered in images of whales and sea life. The other was inscribed with a tangle of malignant-looking plants.

Same motif again.

Gray aimed for the far tunnel, where niches framed its entry. He was plainly drawn by the two amphorae inside, each three feet tall and sealed with lids. They were identical in appearance. One half of each pot had been carved with whales. The other half of each pot was inscribed all over with plants.

Gray brushed the caked sulfur off a pot. "Two sides of the same coin," he muttered.

"But what's up there?" Anna asked, pointing higher.

Above the passageway, another niche had been carved. Only this one was huge, half the size of the tunnel's mouth. It showed figures gathered in a cave. Some looked as if they were beseeching their gods, raising their arms high. Others were down on their knees. Strange totems lined the back wall. The roof of the niche was inscribed with strange symbols and shapes.

"It looks like a ceremony or ritual," Anna whispered.

Omryn nodded. "The Chukchi people do something like this. A prayer for the well-being of a family."

Gray nodded, as if this made sense to him, then he passed into the tunnel under the niche. Elle kept up with him, no longer wishing to lag behind. The rest followed. The tunnel was short and featureless— but the chamber it dumped into was not.

Anna entered behind them, gawking all around. "This looks exactly like the carving outside."

Elle nodded.

The ceiling bore the same arcane symbols. Totems stood stacked along the walls. In the room's center, an elongated shallow depression stretched three meters, lined by rune-like markings. More of those two-faced pots rested along the walls.

Elle wandered deeper inside, forgetting for the moment the burning stench outside. She swore she could hear ancient chanting, the beat of drums, but it had to be her imagination.

Jason, though, noted another oddity. He lifted his camera and examined the device from all angles. "It stopped filming. The visuals were clear, then started waving, before going dark."

Gray crossed to a wall. He pressed a palm against it, then removed a spoon from his pocket. It was tarnished nearly black. Elle recognized the same patina from the pots and pans at the campsite. He must have pilfered the utensil before the team left.

He placed the spoon against the wall and pulled his hand away. It remained in place. "Lodestone," he said, turning to face the group. "This entire cavern has been carved out of a magnetite vein."

Jason stared down at his camera. "Those energies must've knocked out the electronics."

"It's likely affecting us, too," Harper warned.

Elle searched the chamber. "But why build this room out of lodestone?"

Gray crossed to the divot in the floor. "To be a place of healing. People have long believed that magnetism can cure disease, relieve pain."

Harper joined him. "Don't be so dismissive, commander. There are many proven therapeutic benefits from magnetism. Treating headaches, depression, high blood pressure, insomnia, even multiple sclerosis."

As Gray took this in, his face returned to that pinched, thoughtful look. He stared toward the exit, likely picturing the dioramas that led them here.

Elle kept her attention in the room, on the collection of two-faced pots, showing the strange plants on one side, and whales on the other.

As she did, she was suddenly thunderstruck.

Gray turned toward her, maybe hearing her gasp.

"All those carvings in the tunnel," she said. "I think they're ancient flow charts. Showing how these people manufactured a product that they harvested from *whales*."

"And *plants*," Gray added. "Considering where this all led, to a place of healing, I believe they were recording recipes for the production of a medicine."

Elle turned to one of the room's pots. "Which once done, required combining the two medicines to create a final elixir."

Gray stared over at the trough in the floor. "The final treatments must have been performed here, in this magnetic chamber, leaning on the energies of the room to enhance the elixir's effects."

Seichan joined him. "Even if you're right, what *disease* were these ancients treating?"

Gray turned to her, as if the answer were obvious. "Old age."

Anna covered her mouth, then lowered it, as she clearly made the connection, too. "All those stories about the amazing *longevity* of the Hyperboreans. While not immortal, it's said they lived to extraordinary lengths." She stared around the room. "Could it be true?"

"Are you asking if the medicine worked?" Gray shrugged. "I don't know. I'm not sure how the harvested essence of a whale and a plant, combined with magnetism, could achieve such a result."

The ship's medical doctor raised a hand. "I may know."

All eyes turned to her.

"I've always been fascinated by ancient remedies, especially among the northern people. The Inuit, the Dorset, the Sámi, even Omryn's people. But I'm still a Western scientist. Last year, I came across a research paper from the University of Rochester in New York regarding the longevity of whales, specifically *Balaena mysticetus*."

"The bowhead whale," Elle said.

Harper nodded. "It's why the paper caught my attention, especially considering the oceans I travel through."

"What did the study show?" Gray asked.

"As I mentioned, the bowheads can live for up to two hundred years. The Rochester study discovered the *source* of this astounding longevity. It was because bowheads possess a unique set of genes that suppress cancer. The genes miraculously repair damaged DNA, the leading cause for most cancers. The reparative agent is a strange protein—CIRBP— that's produced by those genes. After this discovery, those same scientists have been trying to find a way of engineering those genes into us. Trials with mice have already been partially successful."

"And you think these ancients stumbled into a successful way of doing that?" Gray asked.

Harper shrugged. "The tribes out here, living a hard life, cut off and isolated, had to develop innovative strategies to survive. Many of their native remedies required complicated formulations—producing pharmaceuticals that baffle modern medicine, yet have shown to be effective."

Omryn nodded at this.

Anna waved behind them. "And keep in mind, these people were clearly advanced. Look at the city they built."

Elle offered her support, too, leaning on her background. "I told you before how carnivorous plants carry many analogs to mammalian genes."

"Parallel evolution," Gray said.

She nodded. "Such species also produce an astounding number of enzymes, some whose function we don't fully understand. They're unique to these carnivores. Maybe these ancient people learned to utilize those enzymes to take advantage of the bowheads' cancer-fighting genes. Maybe to extract that CIRBP protein. Or maybe even to achieve gene transfer into the patient." She lifted her palms. "I don't know, but someone should research this, to see if it's possible."

Harper nodded her head, as if ready to do just that.

Jason added a few final words, approaching from a different angle. "Remember the Hyperboreans were said be *huge*, too, toweringly tall. Maybe, beside the whale's longevity, the treatment also instilled a level of gigantism."

Seichan sighed heavily, clearly done with this matter. She offered a more cynical outlook. "Or maybe the Hyperborean shamans were just very good at spreading their own hype, spinning a tall tale about their snake oil—or whale oil, in this case—which grew more outlandish as the story was passed from ear to ear."

Gray straightened, still looking undecided on the matter, but not on another. "Okay, we've gained all the information we can at this point. We should head out. Maybe that solar storm has subsided enough for us to reach the outside world, to share what we discovered."

"If not," Jason said as they departed, "let's hope Captain Kelly and the others managed to strand that Russian patrol boat. Or all of this will have been for nothing."

The group quickly returned to the room with the mudpot, greeted by its noxious belches.

Anna clutched her wad of gauze tighter over her mouth. "This stench certainly can't be healthy. No wonder Marco and Kane were so bothered."

"In the past, this chamber must have once been better ventilated." Gray stared down the side tunnel inscribed with sea life. "I wager that passageway once led to the open sea, where the Hyperboreans set off on their sacred whale hunts."

Elle turned the other way. "And that tunnel must lead to where they grew their specimens."

She drifted in that direction, wanting to get a view of that long-dead garden.

Support to do so came from Seichan. "I see light shining back there."

Gray joined her, stared for a breath, then nodded with a frown. "Maybe it's another way out."

"A back door," Seichan said. "If we need it."

A look passed between the two. Their worried expressions were easy to read.

Elle understood.

Those two expect to need it.

SEVENTH

Fire and Ice

46

As the transport plane rushed low over the break in the fogbank, Captain Turov gazed down at the massive bulk of an icebreaker. A triumphant surge rushed through him, but it was equally quelled by relief.

"They're here," he gasped out, then called to the pilot. "Circle us over."

Behind him, others crowded at windows, either in the cockpit or the main cabin. Excited murmurs echoed throughout the plane.

Sychkin shoved up front, abandoning his lapdog, Yerik.

"We found them," Turov announced.

"Not just them!" Sychkin exclaimed, his voice booming as if from a pulpit. He shifted Turov's attention to the collection of black rocks sticking out of the ice. "That must be Hyperborea. Or at least, the mountainous tip of a greater plateau buried beneath it."

Turov frowned back at him, "Why do you think that?"

Sychkin scowled. "Look closer." He pointed at the tall peak in the center of the grouping. "Someone blasted ice off its flank."

Turov squinted and saw the man was correct. "There's a tunnel opening, too."

"And the ice is chewed up at the entrance," Sychkin added.

"By tread marks."

Sychkin grabbed Turov's arm. "A party must have already gone below. If so, they could ruin all our hopes. All of Russia's future."

The archpriest's eyes shone with a rabid fervency.

"We must stop them," Sychkin insisted.

Turov drove the man back into the cabin with the others. "Then let us do our job."

As the archpriest retreated to a window, Turov addressed the entire cabin, taking the pulpit himself this time.

"We land in three minutes. As soon as we touch down, we'll drop the rear door and split into two teams. The eleven under Lieutenant Osin will secure the landing site, using the snowmobiles to establish a cordon. Your priority will be to lock down that icebreaker, to keep those aboard at bay."

He turned to the second team. "The eleven with Lieutenant Bragin will be with me. We're going to strike for a tunnel into the mountain."

"I must go with you," Sychkin demanded, his eyes still fire-bright.

Turov frowned, ready to refuse.

"You don't know what's down there," Sychkin pressed. "You may need my knowledge of Hyperborea. And Yerik can keep me well protected. I won't burden your men."

Turov still wanted to balk, but ultimately he didn't care if the bastard got himself killed. *As long as he stays out of my way.* Plus, he knew the archpriest could become problematic later if Turov refused. There were many in positions of power who still bent an ear to this fool. And Turov had a future career to consider.

He pointed to both Sychkin and Yerik. "You will obey our every word. Do not step out of line. Is that understood?"

Sychkin bowed his head, but there was nothing submissive in his manner.

Another raised an arm. "I know this enemy," Valya Mikhailov asserted. "You saw what they did back at your base. Don't make the mistake of sidelining me again."

In truth, he welcomed her input, but her abrasive attitude rankled him.

Before he would commit, he swung into the cockpit. Before landing, there was another force that needed instructions. He spoke to his radioman. "Any further word from the *Lyakhov*?"

"Yes, sir. Just now. Message came garbled, but clear enough. They've run into a mishap with their propellers. Maybe engines. They're working on repairs now."

Turov frowned. "How long?"

"I lost them before they could clarify. I'll keep trying to reach them. But we'll be clear of the solar storm in another hour."

"Reach them *before* that. Get the *Lyakhov* to send whatever forces they can by helicopter to this spot."

Turov turned around and found Valya standing there. She had moved silently, as ghostly as her pale visage.

"That was no accident at the patrol boat," she stated firmly. "That was the enemy again."

He frowned. "How can you—"

"I noted a flash of fire just before I spotted this icefield. It could've been anything, but with the *Lyakhov* being stranded, I wager the enemy is trying to delay the vessel's arrival. To gain enough time to outlast the solar storm."

Turov took a deep breath.

It made frightening sense.

He pointed at her. "Then you're coming with me."

47

Jason covered his mouth, trying not to gag. "What's that smell?"

He hurried after the others, who had continued farther down the side tunnel by now. Jason had stopped to check his camera. After leaving the lodestone chamber, the device had started working again. Best of all, the exposure hadn't damaged the videos he had already recorded.

Can't lose any of this.

Chasing after the others, Jason started filming the tunnel's walls. Their surfaces were inscribed with a gnarled entanglement of thorny vines, pendulant leaves, and crested flowerheads. It was like traveling through a petrified garden, one grown by Medusa herself. While recording, he had to be careful not to brush against the walls. Those thorny barbs snatched at his clothing. Some of the spikes extended a foot out, as if warding against trespassers.

As Jason finally caught up with the others, the stench grew worse. It made his eyes water, more than the sulfur of the boiling pit. He wasn't the only one suffering.

"It smells like rotting meat down this way," Anna said. "Like something died under a hot sun."

Elle called from the front of the group, where she strode alongside Gray and Seichan. "Maybe it's *this* scent that spooked Marco and Tucker. It's definitely making me want to turn back."

Jason knew that wasn't true. After entering this tunnel, the botanist had set a fast pace, one that had nothing to do with their short time-table, and all to do with her curiosity about the Hyperborean garden.

Ahead, the brightness that Seichan had first noted continued to grow. It was far from blinding, but it was enough for them to continue without their flashlights.

As they reached the tunnel's end, gasps rose from those up front. Jason tried to get a look, but the others blocked his view. Finally, Omryn retreated back, stumbling clear so Jason could push forward.

The Chukchi crewman muttered a single word in his native tongue. *"Kelet . . ."*

Jason remembered what that meant. It was a name for what shared this island with his people's sea gods.

Kelet.

Evil spirits.

Jason drew alongside everyone else. They were lined across an apron of rock at the edge of a cavernous chamber, easily the size of a football stadium, only the domed ceiling was suffocatingly low, draped with stalactites of limestone. The roof was also riddled with cracks, as if a god's hammer had struck it. The hundreds of gaps shone with sun-light, but there would be no escape that way, not even if they had a ladder that could reach that high. The top was sealed over by the surface ice, but a translucent glow still seeped through, illuminating the garden below. A few of the higher cracks, though, appeared open to the air, showing azure skies.

"Careful," Gray warned him.

Jason looked down and backed a step.

The apron of rock was more like a beach, sloping a few meters and disappearing into a silty, bubbling bog. Pockets burst with beachball-size belches of gas. Hot mud simmered and churned everywhere. A few islands of rock rose higher, but they were unreachable without asbestos waders.

Still, all this paled to what lay out there. Across the steaming floor, waist-high growths rustled gently, as if stirred by unseen winds. The plants were clustered in stands or spread across muddy fields. Leafy fronds shivered, curling at their edges, as if urging them closer.

"The garden," Elle gasped. "It's still here?"

Jason gaped at the palm-size lobes, frilled by long cilia that waved seductively. Spiked stalks lifted those fleshy appendages high, making a mockery of true flowers.

"How could they have survived?" Gray asked.

Elle tried to answer. "I think they're coming out of a dormancy period. With the spring. Some of the plants out there, those getting less light, look yellowed and drooped, likely still dormant."

"What do you mean by dormant?" Anna asked.

Elle explained, "In the Arctic, mosses and other plants, even insects—bees, ants, spiders, some caterpillars—will freeze solid, only to revive in the springtime. Whereas this species, while kept warm down here, they likely go dormant during the winter when there is no light for months."

Anna searched higher. "So the returning sunlight stirs them back to life?"

"Or the freshening of their food source." Elle waved to a swirling cloud of gnats and buzzing flies. "The Arctic, even here on the ice cap, is not a lifeless void. In fact, it's notoriously buggy. Just try walking through the Alaskan tundra. The mosquitoes alone will suck you dry. Out on the ice cap, decaying algae, rotted fish, and the bodies of dead seals, walruses, birds, even polar bears, all attract hordes of ravenous insects."

"Is that what we're smelling?" Harper asked. "Dead animals?"

"Yes and no," Elle answered. "It's the *sarkophágos* themselves that are giving off that scent, wafting it through the cracks up there, using the reek of decaying carcasses to attract their insect prey."

"But how can they survive in all that scalding mud?" Jason asked. "I'm sweating even standing this close."

"Their stalks must have some crystalline protection. Incorporating silicates or carbonates. I wager the *sarkophágos* get additional sustenance from that mud, too, as it constantly refreshes this cavern, rising up from down deep. Maybe the species even incorporates photosynthesis during the summer months."

"Still, that's not all that feeds them," Seichan interjected, as she pointed to one of the hillocks of rock.

Jason shifted a step to get a better look. He wished he hadn't. And it wasn't just that one spot. As if washed up onto distant shores, bones accumulated along the edges of those islands like driftwood, all covered in a sulfurous silt blending with the rock. He recognized the horned skulls of caribou and muskox. The tusked remains of a walrus. There were also human skulls, many dozens if not hundreds. Along with cages of ribs, long femurs, chains of vertebrae.

"Clearly those big animals didn't venture down here on their own," Seichan said.

Even Elle looked stricken. "The caretakers must have been *feeding* their garden, too."

"What about the bodies back at the camp?" Harper asked. "The dried growths sprouting from those mummies looked a lot like what's planted here."

"Maybe that's the danger everyone warned about," Elle said, looking worried now. "Maybe their spores can be contaminating, spreading seeds into fertile soil."

"Into us?" Anna asked.

"Possibly any warm flesh. But I don't see any germinating bodies at the moment. Maybe only at certain times of the year does the species become dangerous. Such an action might serve to spread the species, utilizing a host to carry those germinating spores to other lands."

"If so, no wonder it was deemed hazardous," Gray said. "If this escaped and spread . . ."

"It would be the very definition of *invasive* in *invasive species*."

"And the men back in that camp?" Harper pressed.

"While their flesh might have fed that early growth, without sunlight, without access to insects and other nutrients, the rest eventually withered away."

Seichan turned from the sight. "We should get back up. We've wasted enough time. There is no way out this way."

Elle hung back. "We're still missing something."

She motioned to a pair of copper boats to the left that Jason had not even noticed. There were also a bunch of corked water jugs and sets of thick leather clothing draped over a copper rack, including little caps.

Jason realized the outfits matched what the tiny figures had worn in the plant-extraction diorama.

Elle waved over at the collection of gear. "Clearly the Hyperboreans harvested this field to concoct their medicinals. They must've found a way to live in harmony with this species."

"It's something we can explore later." Gray waved for her to follow. "First, the world needs to know about this place. About the wonders and dangers hidden down here."

She nodded and turned away with clear reluctance.

Jason remembered the duty assigned to him. He lifted his camcorder and edged down the bank, dropping to a knee. He studied the digital viewfinder as he scanned over the fetid field. He zoomed in on the closest plant, a yard or so away. He filmed its shivering movement, its lolling fleshy lobe.

Gray scolded him, "That's enough. Let's—"

The catch in the commander's voice was the only warning.

Through the viewfinder, he captured a snap of movement. A vine shot out, like a striking snake. It hit Jason under the angle of his jaw as he jerked back. Something stabbed deep—it felt like the sting of the largest murder hornet.

He fell back as the vine dropped to the stone. It writhed for a moment, then slowly retracted toward the plant. It left a crimson oily trail across the stone, dribbling from its thorny tip.

Jason scooted back on his butt. "What the hell?"

Gray helped him stand.

"Thanks. I can manage on—"

Pain lanced through him, so agonizing he couldn't find the breath to scream. He opened his mouth. Then the fire spread throughout his body. He collapsed into Gray's arms. His limbs tremored uncontrollably. His breathing gasped in convulsive gulps, then he lost all strength.

He waited to black out, prayed to do so.

But the fire remained, just no control.

He felt his body being lifted. Through unblinking eyes, he watched Gray rush him down the corridor. He heard Harper, but her words were a panicked jumble of medical jargon.

"... *hemotoxin ... neurotoxin ... paralytic ...*"

Elle added her own assessment, one even worse. "*Infected ...*"

Then they were back in the chamber with the mudpot. Before Gray could head toward the main tunnel, loud blasts echoed.

Jason recognized that unique concussion.

Seichan confirmed it. "Grenades."

"We're under attack." Gray shoved Jason into another's arm. "Omryn, guard over everyone. Keep them here. Harper, Elle, Anna. See what you can do to stabilize Jason."

With his head lolled crookedly, Jason watched Gray and Seichan race away.

Through the agony, he screamed, if only in his skull.

I'm still here ...

48

Tucker lay on his stomach on the second floor of a stone home. He had the butt of his AK-12 rifle at his shoulder, his cheek on its stock, and one eye peering through his weapon's holographic sight with magnifier.

From his sniper's perch, he watched a long line of lights bobbling down the arc of steps. He counted eighteen to twenty in that company. The exact number was hard to determine as shadows danced, but one thing was certain.

Way too many.

He needed to cull that herd.

Earlier, shortly after he heard the scream of a jet engine echoing down from above, a firefight had broken out topside, too. Grenades had exploded. Automatic weapons had rattled. Fearing the worst, Tucker had retreated with Kane and Marco into the labyrinth of homes. As he did, a new noise intruded. The rumbling roar of small engines, echoing hollowly, traveling along the ice chute. This was confirmed by a cascading fall of loose ice over the edge above, then lights had bloomed up there.

With that, he had quickly sought this higher roost among the homes.

Through his scope, he noted the familiar Arctic camo and body armor worn by most of the strike team heading down here.

Russians for sure.

Not that he had any doubt.

He scowled, knowing he could not let that group look too closely at the frozen waterfall—and what lay hidden behind it. To that end, he picked a target, zoomed his scope, and squeezed his rifle's trigger.

The sharp bang stung his ear, but he remained focused. A figure crumpled from the headshot. He shifted to the next in line, but lights blinked out, nearly in unison. A few lingered, then snapped off. In the last afterglow, he caught the barest glimpse of shapes leaping off steps or rushing headlong and heedless down them.

He winced at the swiftness of their reaction. He imagined they must be Russian special forces, the elite of the elite. He waited two breaths, but the lights never flicked back on. They must have come with night-vision gear.

Two could play at that game.

He pulled goggles over his eyes and tapped a button. The world revealed itself in shades of gray and green. He turned his gaze away and blind-fired a burst of three rounds. The slight muzzle flares stung, amplified through the night-vision gear. The flashes, confined inside the small room, were like camera bulbs exploding.

As he had meant them to be.

He needed to lure as many of the soldiers as he could into this maze, to get them to ignore the waterfall. He rolled into a crouch, dropped through a hole in the floor, and exited the home. He rushed away from where he had been roosted.

He had no way of knowing the number who would enter this laby-rinth, but he had to be prepared.

And not just me.

He tapped another button on his goggles. The view through his lenses changed. In the outside corner of each eye, two video feeds played. One from Marco's vest-mounted camera. The other from Kane's. Kowalski had hauled in all of Tucker's customized gear when he had arrived with Kane and the rescue team in Severodvinsk.

Tucker touched his throat mike. His comm gear operated on dual band and was currently switched to UHF, which worked decently underground, as long as the trio kept close. With the channel open between his dogs, he let them know the plan.

"Boys, let's go hunting."

5:30 P.M.

Turov crouched next to Lieutenant Bragin. After losing one of his men, the *spetsnaz* leader's bloodlust was up. The man coordinated with his second-in-command. The other nine soldiers had quickly vanished into shelters along the edges of the stone city. They had moved swiftly. Even outfitted with night-vision gear, Turov had lost sight of them almost immediately.

Bragin had forced Turov into a small low-roofed abode, along with Sychkin and Yerik. Outside, Valya and Nadira had posted themselves to the left of the doorway. Another *spetsnaz* soldier was down on a knee to the right.

Turov stared up.

On the ice cap, the initial barrage to secure the landing site had quieted into occasional short bursts. As expected, the commercial ice-breaker was ill-equipped to withstand a well-armed force. Lieutenant Osin's orders were to keep the crew cowed and on board the ship until the *Lyakhov* could finish repairs and sail here.

To the side, Bragin snapped quick orders, preparing to dispatch six of his teammates in parties of two to hunt down the enemy, reserving five to secure this immediate area.

Valya pivoted into the space. "Don't," she warned, sweeping her gaze across the men. "Keep your main force here. That was a lone shooter. Someone intent to pull your strength into that dark maze."

"One man or not," Bragin said, "I can't leave a sniper at our backs."

"Then send no more than a pair to harass him. Keep the rest in place." She stared outside. "If that shooter is trying to lure us in that direction, then we should be looking the *other* way."

Bragin turned to Turov.

Turov nodded, trusting Valya's judgment. "She may be right. For now, let's keep your men closer at hand until we gain a firmer grasp of the situation."

"Then let me send *three* after the sniper," Bragin argued. "One to draw out, two to kill."

Turov considered this. Bragin had decades of experience in urban warfare. In Syria. In Mali. Across the Crimean Peninsula. There was no reason to second-guess the lieutenant.

"Do it," Turov ordered.

Bragin revised his instructions to his second-in-command.

As the man ran off to pass on the orders, Nadira hissed outside. She waved without looking inside, drawing Valya and Turov to the doorway. The woman pointed toward a massive frozen spillway. At the top, sunlight flowed through the distant tunnel mouth and blazed off the ice, amplified to a blinding glare through their night-vision goggles.

Nadira wasn't pointing up there, but at the fall's base. The ice darkened as it dropped away from the sunlight—then brightened again near the bottom. "Something is lighting the far side," she whispered.

"And growing brighter." Valya turned to Turov. Satisfaction shone on her face. "Someone's coming."

5:35 P.M.

Gray rushed down the last of the tunnel. The beam of his flashlight reflected off the wall of ice at the end.

His heart pounded in his throat. He pictured Jason collapsing into his arms, poisoned by the harpoon strike of that plant. But he knew there would be no hope for the young man—for any of them—if the Russians got the upper hand.

As he neared the exit, he strained for the grenade blasts that had drawn him away with Seichan. Occasional gunfire reached him, but little else.

Was it already over?

He slowed as he reached the ice wall and edged toward the narrow gap behind the throne—and paused. An instinct warned him something was amiss.

"What're you doing?" Seichan asked, crowding at his back.

He lifted a palm as he realized what had raised his hackles. He took a single breath, firming his conclusion. Then took the only action he could. He lobbed his flashlight through the gap and out into the open, sending it spinning wildly—then swung around, cupped his palm over Seichan's light, and shouldered her toward the far side.

Behind him, he heard gasps, confirming the worst.

A spatter of gunfire sparked off the ice.

Now Seichan understood and flicked off her light.

A moment ago, the part of his brain honed during his years in the military, sharpened further by his decade with Sigma, had noted that it was too dark beyond that throne. His ears had also failed to pick up any murmur from Tucker, any shuffle from his two dogs. That paranoid section of his mind that was always on high alert put those pieces together in a heartbeat and had screamed *ambush*.

Additionally, as it was dark, it suggested the lurkers were using night-vision. Under those sensitive scopes, his spinning flashlight would burn as brightly as a flare, momentarily blinding anyone out there. And if he had been wrong, the only outcome would be a shattered flashlight and a couple startled dogs.

But he was not wrong.

He drove Seichan out the gap on the far side, scooting behind the throne carved with sea life. They dared not retreat toward Jason and the others or risk putting them in a direct line of fire.

Taking advantage of the momentary shock, Gray barreled out from behind the throne and into the open. He ran low, in case anyone was posted on this side and hadn't been looking when he tossed his makeshift flash-bomb. Behind him, his flashlight continued to twirl on the floor, strobing enough illumination for him and Seichan to reach the edge of the stone labyrinth.

Within steps, though, sweeping between two buildings, the world fell into deep shadows. The distant glow from the reflected sunlight offered little help. Gray rushed with one hand on the wall next to him, the other extended in front.

The only teammate with night-vision gear was Tucker and his two dogs. He cursed his group's lack of equipment and ducked into a doorway and tried his radio, but all he got back was low static. He ran a palm over the stone wall.

Still, too much rock.

Seichan leaned next to him, her voice a breathless whisper. "What now?"

5:37 P.M.

Valya cursed under her breath, her retinas still flared.

How had they known . . . ?

Her goggles sat atop her forehead. One of the soldiers had already smothered the flashlight and extinguished it. To rest everyone's eyes, a few red lamps had been set up and glowed on the ground. The *spetsnaz* team sheltered at the edge of the city, out of the line of fire of any sniper.

Bragin had already dispatched three men in the direction of the fleeing pair, but it would be hard to flush them out of that labyrinth. Recognizing this, the lieutenant's instructions had been to canvass that side, to hold the line until a strategy could be worked out.

Valya had little patience, especially as she had caught a brief glimpse of one of the two who had fled. The slim shape, even the gait of her flight, was branded into Valya's memory. She was prepared to begin this hunt on her own, taking only Nadira. But she had acted rashly in the past and had paid a steep price for it.

Another hadn't learned that lesson yet.

Sychkin confronted Turov. "Those two came from somewhere well hidden, a location clearly meaningful with those two thrones flanking it. It must be important."

"It can wait," the captain said.

"It can't," the archpriest insisted. "We must know what they learned. Before communications fully reopen following this solar storm. When they do, we must be the first to announce it, to claim it for Russia. Nothing else matters."

Turov groaned, clearly perturbed and done with the archpriest. "Then go. Take Yerik. I'll give you three men, but no more. Not until we secure this area."

Sychkin smiled, showing too many teeth. He opened his mouth to say more, possibly to gloat, but the look on Turov's face dissuaded any further discussion. Taking advantage of this boon while he could, Sychkin hurried to Yerik and Bragin.

The lieutenant listened, then glanced askance at Turov.

The captain waved. "Let him go. He's best out of the way as it is."

Bragin nodded, agreeing with this judgment, and waved three of his men to follow the archpriest and his hulking aide.

Valya watched them leave. The five men pushed past the throne and vanished behind the ice curtain. After a few seconds, lights flared back there. Valya understood. As deep as that group would likely travel, it would be pitch dark—and night-vision required some ambient light to function, unless one employed special IR illuminators. But she knew Sychkin would only be satisfied with what he could see with his own eyes.

The glow slowly faded as the small group departed.

Turov returned. "We're ready. We'll be deploying a bombardment of grenades, to squeeze them into a narrowing net. Then we'll hunt them down with thermal scopes."

She nodded at this plan.

"I assume you'll want to accompany us," Turov said.

She smiled, showing too many teeth. "Try and stop me."

She followed Turov toward the gathered team. Two men freed rocket launchers and fitted them with warheads.

As she waited, she stared over at the ice wall, momentarily curious. *What the hell is down there?*

49

Elle paced around Jason's body. She had to keep moving, if only to hold her panic at bay.

This can't be happening again . . .

She flashed to the young Russian pilot, Fadd. His body had lain for hours inside the plane while they had flown here. Jason's face had Fadd's same bloodless complexion and blue lips, but at least his chest still moved. So, there had to be hope.

Anna knelt beside Jason and held his hand. "There must be something else you can try," she pleaded with Harper.

The ship's doctor knelt next to Jason on the floor. Omryn had carried his limp form into the lodestone chamber, draping him across the rune-lined trench in the floor. The Chukchi crewman now guarded the tunnel entrance.

"I've tried everything I could," Harper explained, waving a hand over her open med pack. "This is little better than a first-aid kit when it comes to severe reactions like this. If this was an anaphylactic reaction, the EpiPen should have helped. Same with the corticosteroids. He needs fluids, a hospital, labs, a tox screen."

Elle summarized her answer. "He needs to get out of here."

Harper sighed and lifted her stethoscope, ending with her own terse conclusion. "He doesn't have much time."

Anna searched for another answer, her gaze falling on Elle. "Those plants. The Hyperboreans made that elixir out of them. The same species that poisoned Jason. Maybe the medicine could help him."

Elle knew the nun was grasping at straws. Still, she stared over at the tall pots inside the room. "Even if there's anything in those containers, they're long past their expiration date by now."

"What does it hurt to try?" Anna said. "He's already dying."

Elle conceded this point. She crossed to one of the jars and attempted to pry off its lid. It wouldn't budge. The sealant had turned to cement over the passing centuries.

Omryn noted her effort and stepped over. He tried, too, but with no better luck. Rather than give up, he picked up a loose rock. It was twice the size of his fist. He lifted his arm, swung hard, and cracked the lip of the pot. Two more strikes, and Elle was able to pick the shattered pieces of the lid away.

Omryn pointed his flashlight into the jar's depths.

A dark sludgy liquid filled the pot to three-quarters. It smelled far from medicinal, more like rancid fish oil that had been fermenting—in this case, over centuries.

Anna hurried to them, carrying Harper's canteen. The nun had already emptied the water out. Without hesitation, she dunked the bottle into the black slurry and filled it to the brim. Once done, she rushed back to Jason.

Elle followed, while Omryn returned to guarding the door.

Anna handed the canteen back to the doctor, who looked dismayed.

"Do we bathe his wound with this?" Harper asked. "Force him to swallow it?"

Elle lifted her palms. "We've come this far. Do both."

Harper nodded. She grabbed some gauze sponges and soaked them thoroughly, keeping her nose turned away from the stench. She then placed the dripping compresses over the puncture wound under Jason's jaw. She left them there and shifted over to fill a measuring spoon from her med kit. Grimacing, she dribbled the sludge past Jason's lips, across his tongue. He failed to swallow, so there was no telling if anything reached his stomach. It appeared most of it drooled back out.

Anna knelt next to him, one hand clutching her throat with worry.
Elle resumed her pacing.

Harper checked Jason's pulse and blood pressure.

"His vitals are getting worse," the doctor concluded.

Anna covered her face. "Then it's been a waste of time after all."

Elle didn't have the strength to console her. Anna sought solace elsewhere and shifted her hands to lips, whispering a prayer.

Still, Elle knew their effort hadn't been a total waste. The exertion,
the movement, even the flicker of hope, had stirred her enough to think
more clearly, to push her panic further back.

She took a deep breath and pictured that steamy garden. She remembered her earlier quandary, wondering how such a garden could
be so deadly, so invasive, yet the ancient gardeners here had harvested
those fields on a regular basis. And from the old Greek legends, Hyperborean emissaries had visited foreign lands. Yet, none of those stories
told of a sporulating affliction that spread wider.

"Maybe the Hyperboreans were naturally resistant to the toxic
spores."

Harper heard her. "What are you getting at?"

"I don't know. Somehow the Hyperboreans were able to live with
the *sarkophágos* species and not fall ill. Back at the garden, I saw copper
boats that the harvesters must have poled across those hot mudflats.
And there were those hanging leather outfits, likely meant to cover
skin. Still, the gardeners must have occasionally gotten stung by those
poisonous tendrils."

"I would think so," Harper admitted. "If the Hyperboreans were
smart, they'd have had an antidote handy. Back on the beaches of
Australia, during the summer months, we're plagued by box jellyfish,
which deliver a burning, deadly sting. Kills people. So the beaches
installed these metal stanchions full of vinegar bags to counteract the
venom. Saves many lives."

Elle nodded, then more vigorously. "Of course . . ."

"What?" Harper asked.

"Remember, the Hyperboreans *were* smart." Elle turned to Anna.
"I need your help. I'm not sure how much I can carry on my own."

Anna looked confused, but she stood up. "From where?"

"We're going back to that infernal garden."

Elle rushed for the exit, drawing Anna with her.

Harper called after them. "Hurry. His body's starting to tremor."

Elle glanced back. Jason's arms and limbs were quaking against the stone. She turned to Omryn. "Help hold him down. Keep him safe until we return."

She didn't wait for confirmation and set off at a fast walk, then a run.

Anna chased after her.

Elle didn't slow when she reached the chamber with the mudpot. She angled to the side and over into the vine-encrusted corridor. She continued along it, breathing hard, driven by fear, but also by hope.

The distance to the garden was easy to gauge. The reek of decaying flesh grew richer with each passing meter. When it finally watered her eyes and churned her stomach, the end of the tunnel appeared.

Elle slowed as she neared it, not wanting to run headlong into the bubbling mud and the dangers growing there. As she crossed the threshold, she ducked to the left, to where a pair of copper boats were beached on the stone apron. Next to them, a rack held an entire outfit of leather, made to cover a gardener. She ignored it all and dropped to a knee before a row of stone-corked jars, each a foot tall. Earlier, she had thought they were primitive canteens, clay water jugs.

But they're not—*hopefully* they're not.

She slid one closer, struggled with its stone cork, but she had no better luck than she had with the amphora pot. She grumbled and resorted to Omryn's technique. She grabbed a rock and smashed the neck off the jug in one swing. The cork and the top of the jug bounced and rattled into the mud. Some of the container's contents—a blue-green oil—splashed out.

She sniffed at it, appreciating the wintergreen scent. "This sure as hell isn't water."

Anna joined her. "Will this help Jason?"

"Only one way to find out."

Elle grabbed a fresh jug, shook it to make sure it was full, and passed it to Anna. She considered giving the nun a second jar, but her thin limbs struggled with just the one.

Frustrated and scared, Elle hauled a new one for herself, while cradling the open jar under her other arm.

I can carry two.

She didn't want to be frugal. Jason was deep into his affliction. She didn't know how much antidote he might require at this point. Unfortunately, the ancients had never carved a formulary of dosages into a wall.

They should have.

"Let's go." Elle stood up, hefting her two jugs.

They set off again, moving slower with their burden. Each laden pot weighed more than thirty pounds. Elle's heart pounded with urgency. She pictured Jason's limbs quaking, while blurring his features with young Fadd's.

We can't lose him, too.

She considered abandoning the jar she had broken into, to lighten her load, so they could move faster. But she hugged it tighter, knowing Jason would not likely last another lap back to the garden if she needed more. She planned on bathing his entire body in this elixir and forcing as much down his throat as she could without drowning him.

I need every drop.

They half-trotted, half-plodded their way up the tunnel.

As they rounded a curve toward the exit, hushed voices echoed back to them. She flinched, fearing she was already too late and that Harper and Omryn had come to tell them as much. Then shouting erupted, followed by rifle fire, and heavy blasts of a shotgun.

Someone found the others.

Elle paused, but Anna continued ahead, plainly intent on delivering the antidote even if it meant getting caught. Already committed at this point, Elle followed. She couldn't let Anna go alone.

They passed around the curve, and lights shone brightly at the end, illuminating two men in body armor. The newcomers stared toward the magnetite chamber. Elle had no trouble identifying the two, especially the giant.

Anna recognized them, too. "Sychkin . . ."

The vehemence she poured into each syllable of the archpriest's name was palpable. This was the man who had killed her brother, Igor. Maybe not directly, but he was definitely as much to blame as the one who had pulled the trigger.

Unfortunately, that anger was not just tangible to Elle.

Yerik turned toward the tunnel. He either heard Anna or spotted their arrival. His scarred features hardened, and he swung a huge pistol toward them.

Elle dropped a jug. Before it crashed to the floor, she grabbed for her holstered sidearm with her free hand. Still, her reaction was too slow.

Another was not.

Anna held forth her yellow flare gun and fired at the pair. In her fury, the nun's aim was poor. The flare struck the floor, ricocheted off a wall, and bounced into the next chamber with a flare of crimson fire.

Still, it proved enough.

Yerik bellowed, covering his face, already gnarled by an old burn. Panicked, unnerved by the flare's fire, he tumbled backward. He snatched at Sychkin for help, but it was no use. Gravity had hold of his massive frame.

Yerik twisted and fell, one arm still reaching for Sychkin. A single word burst from this throat, breaking his vow of silence for the first time. "Papa . . ."

Then he crashed headlong into the boiling quagmire.

Sychkin got dragged to his knees by that last desperate grab of the terrified man. He fell at the pit's edge as Yerik's bulk struck the mud. A heavy, steaming wave splashed up, striking his upturned face. He screamed and rolled away. His fingers dug at his cheeks and eyes. He bellowed through the scorching mud, while writhing on the floor.

Anna lowered her flare gun, showing no remorse, only satisfaction.

Before they could move, another armored figure ran into view from the magnetite chamber. It was a lone Russian soldier. He had lost his helmet. Blood covered one side of his head. Though panicked, he grabbed Sychkin by the wrist and dragged his screeching body toward the main tunnel. With his other arm, he pointed his rifle. The soldier fired toward the lodestone chamber, failing to note the two silent women in the side tunnel.

Then the soldier and his burden were gone, trailed by Sychkin's screams.

"C'mon," Elle urged and crossed the last of the way.

Reaching the mudpot room, she shied from the body sprawled facedown in the molten clay and sulfuric water. A scuffle of boots drew her attention. Omryn stumbled out, clutching an arm around his stomach. Blood soaked around his limb.

"They caught us off guard," the man explained, waving them toward the chamber. "When I was holding Jason down."

He led them back inside, then remained posted at the exit, leaning on the wall.

"Omryn . . ." Elle mumbled.

"Go." He nodded to the jug in her arms. "Try your medicine."

Inside, two men lay dead from huge wounds. Omryn's shotgun was designed to drop polar bears in their tracks—and apparently, Russian soldiers, too.

Harper rose as they entered. She had thrown her body over Jason, protecting her patient with her life. The doctor snatched up a six-inch roll of gauze and stepped toward Omryn.

She glanced back at Jason. "Gave him a shot of valium to calm his seizures. Nothing more I can do. Time for you two to play doctor, while I see to a patient I can help."

Elle didn't argue. Omryn needed his belly wound wrapped. And from here, Jason's survival was mostly out of their hands. It was up to the Hyperboreans.

She and Anna rushed to Jason's side. Elle still held the jug she'd broken open. She dropped to a knee and poured its contents over his face, across his neck wound, and down his body, baptizing him with the blue-green oil.

Without being told, Anna snapped the neck off her jug. "What now?"

Elle took her jar. "Hold his head up."

The nun dropped and pulled Jason's shoulders across her knees. As Anna cradled his neck back, Elle tipped the jug and washed the oil across his lips, dribbling it down his throat with as much care as she could manage, trying to time it with his exhalations. Again, there was no swallowing. She might be drowning him, but she poured until the last drops fell away.

She then tossed the empty jug. "Better pray this works."

Anna took her words literally, lifting her fingertips to her lips, bowing her head over Jason.

They waited for some sign.

Elle studied his body. At first, there was no reaction. Then a slight flutter of his eyelids and fingers. She feared he was starting to seize again. Then the movements became more purposeful. His eyelids blinked. His palms pressed against the stone. His knees bent. It was like he was trying to push himself out of the toxic storm within. Finally, his body relaxed. His legs extended, dropping flat.

But not in defeat.

Jason mumbled, and the roll of his eyes focused, staring up at Anna's bowed face.

"You're awake," Anna whispered.

"I . . . I was never asleep." He groaned. "Heard everything. Saw most."

Elle cringed, realizing the toxin must have been a powerful paralytic, trapping him in his body—but not numbing him.

"Hurt so bad. The burning." He tilted his face. "But worst of all. That black sludge. It was horrible. Tasted like sh—"

He was cut off by a huge blast, then another, and another.

Elle turned toward the exit as the salvo built into a deafening barrage. She recognized the source.

Grenades . . .

50

Tucker ignored the explosions. He was again on his stomach, hidden high in a second-story roost. His rifle was at his shoulder, his cheek at the weapon's stock. Through his night-vision goggles, he stared down his sights.

Below and directly ahead of him, a narrow street ran between two homes.

C'mon, Kane, you can do it.

For the past half hour, the trio had led a game of cat and mouse across the city's maze. With the dog's cameras, Tucker's vision expanded for blocks. It had allowed him to identify three hunters, whom he had led deep into this labyrinth, away from the others. More soldiers were probably heading into the city, using the cover of those grenades and rockets.

With those forces moving in, Tucker knew he had little time left. Still, the soldiers on his tail had proved challenging. He couldn't shake them. Plus, there had been a few close calls. His side burned from where he had failed to roll out of the way fast enough.

The game was taking its toll.

And not just on me.

Finally, movement drew his eye. A dark shape rushed into view on the street, running low, but limping badly on one limb. It was the foreleg Kane had injured last year.

There's my good boy. Knew you wouldn't let me down.

Tucker flinched as a soldier appeared behind Kane. The Russian stayed hidden around a corner, surveying the street.

Move it, Kane.

Tucker reinforced this, subvocalizing a command. "KANE, SHELTER RIGHT."

The dog hobbled into that turn, nearly losing his balance. But he rushed through the home's door on that side. The soldier ran to follow, sticking close to a wall, intent to eliminate one of the stubborn targets.

Tucker swallowed and checked Kane's video feed. The home was a single room, a blind alley, trapping the dog.

The soldier swept to the doorway, still cautious, sheltering to one side.

It was right where Tucker wanted him.

"MARCO, TAKEDOWN BRAVO ONE."

From the door across the street, a huge sleek shadow burst forth. Marco leaped through the air and slammed into the man's back.

"KANE, TAKEDOWN SAVAGE."

The older Malinois lunged low out of the doorway. Kane hit the soldier in the legs, sending the Russian flipping through the air. When he landed, both dogs savaged him, ripping the soft flesh between armor. The man screamed, garbled, then gurgled.

Another two soldiers rushed in, coming from both flanks.

Clearly, as Tucker had used a dog with a fake limp to lure the first soldier into a trap, these two had sent their man as a forward decoy to flush the enemy.

Like I wasn't expecting that.

All this time, Tucker had never moved his rifle's sights, even when Kane had limped past and the first soldier closed in. He squeezed a three-round burst at the closest man. Before the soldier fell, Tucker shifted on his elbow and fired a second burst at the other target.

The shots had been clean, raising not even a cry.

Tucker gathered his gun and leaped to the ground. "TO ME," he ordered his two partners.

Marco and Kane broke free of the soldier, though Marco gave the man a final shake, like a dog with a snake.

Once together, Tucker dropped to a knee, offering pats and reassurance. "Good boys."

He stared off toward the city ahead of him, where the barrage of grenades had waned into occasional blasts, suggestive that the enemy was closing in on it.

Got to get back there.

Tucker had lured this trio far into the labyrinth, but now he had to return. Earlier, he had caught the lightshow by the waterfall. Even from a distance, the twirling light had blazed through his enhanced vision like a solar flare.

Someone had made a break for it.

Gray? Seichan? Maybe both?

He knew the commander must have heard the earlier firefight up top. The man would've come to investigate—running himself full tilt into trouble. And now someone had to get him out of it.

Tucker straightened and pointed in the direction of a rocket blast. "MARCO, KANE, TRACK FRIENDLIES."

They set off together. By now, the two dogs had spent enough time with this crew to hopefully register the others' scents, to know who was friendly and who was not, odors distinct from the borscht-swilling Russians.

The trio rushed swiftly, moving in unison.

But Tucker knew the battle ahead would be tougher than the one played out here. There were many more soldiers, likely hunting with night-vision and thermal gear.

Knowing this, Tucker needed a wider scope of view.

"MARCO, FLANK CLOSE RIGHT. KANE, FLANK CLOSE LEFT."

The two dogs split off, forging their own paths across the dense urban jungle. Through his goggles, their eyes became his. He followed their camera feeds, while whispering orders, coordinating their paths.

He found an easy rhythm with the pair.

While this might be new for Marco, for Kane and Tucker, this was

as familiar as an old dance, one they knew well, a cadence forged in the
sands of Afghanistan. As Tucker ran, he sensed a fourth flowing with
him, the one who had once danced with them, but no longer.

You were a good boy, too, Abel.

Tucker ran onward.

Some called him a lone wolf, but he knew the truth.

I'm never alone.

Especially now.

*Kane races over raw rock and across carved stone. He lifts his nose as he
fords a bridge over a chasm. The air rising from below burns his nose. Not
from heat, but acid. His ears prick to the deep-throated belches calling from
down there. He feels the heat buffeting through his fur, even with his body
covered in a hard vest.*

*He spans onward. His pads find rough rock, and he is off, nose dropping
low or riding high, sifting through each note.*

—the melt of ice that releases old musk.

—the mold off rock that is fungal and ancient.

—a nest of desiccated bones that still have the iron scent of marrow.

None of it is what he seeks.

*Marco leaps from one rooftop to another, riding high across the stone
forest. He hunches as he skirts a tall spire, topped by the shadow of some
huge horned beast. He sniffs, but it gives off no scent. It is as much rock
as the bricks under his paws. He moves on, gaining speed. In his ears, he
hears notes of warning in a brief command to* SLOW, *to keep with the pack.
He obeys, less out of obedience as the draw of home and a full belly and a
scratch behind the ear and a tussle under the sun. He listens sharply, not for
commands, but to the other's breath in his ear. It warms through him as
much as any hot sun. As he strains, other sounds ping through him.*

—the trickle of sand off a roof's edge.

—the pop of distant ice.

—the blast of another explosion.

The last is closer now.

As Kane runs, the tang of hot smoke rolls high overhead. His ears ring with each boom. He tastes the bitter drifts of older blasts, marked in age by their pungency as their smoke settles denser between walls. He leads a path toward where those notes are less potent, where the smoke still drifts, where the blasted stone is still hot.

His path leads toward the heart of the bombardment.

He knows this path.

He has run it countless times, toward the sting of steel, the burn of flames, the cries of the wounded. He does not balk. Not ever. Not now.

But not forever.

He races with this one hard truth locked in his bones, a hard lesson taught by his brother. Still, this only makes him run harder, ignoring the ache in his limb, the breaths that come less easily.

He runs onward, heart pounding with both lust and joy.

The other's breath fills his senses.

He wills his own command to his packmate.

One more time, one more time, one more time . . .

Before it ends forever.

51

Sensing death was near, Gray rushed low. The left side of his face burned. A grenade had struck too close, shattering stone, pelting him with shards, several still embedded to bone. He fisted blood from his left eye, clearing his vision—the little that there was.

Seichan kept her flashlight muffled with a palm, only periodically letting a bright sliver shine through to illuminate their path. And it wasn't only the darkness that stymied them, but also the thickening smoke.

The initial salvo of grenades and rockets had chased them deeper into the city, then back again as a fusillade of blasts exploded in front of their path. Both knew what was happening. The Russians were driving them into a kill zone. Gray and Seichan had tried hiding, believing they had found a deep enough rabbit hole, but a rocket had struck, nearly collapsing the structure atop them.

So, they ran on, trying to keep one jump ahead of the enemy.

But the soldiers were closing that noose, coming from multiple directions.

"On the left," Seichan hissed.

Gray dropped, his rifle at his shoulder. He caught the merest shift of shadows. He fired at it, raging on full auto for three seconds. He heard rounds ricocheting off stone—then a sharper cry.

They both turned and dashed through a doorway, across a room, and out a far door into a small yard, walled by stone. A flash of Seichan's light revealed steps up to the next home. They rushed over and climbed quickly, leaping steps. At this point, it felt like they were fleeing through an M.C. Escher painting—one that was slowly burning around them, leaving them little room to maneuver.

Shots rang out, sparking around their feet in the darkness.

A sniper.

Still a ways off.

By now, Gray was certain the soldiers were not only aided by night-vision, but also with thermal scopes. He and Seichan jumped off the roof into the next street. Gray gasped as he hit his ankle wrong, the one already badly sprained. He fell to a knee.

Seichan crouched next to him. "Can you keep going?"

"Don't have much choice."

He shoved up and hobbled on, more hopscotching than running. They passed a recent rocket impact. The area still smoked. The site's heat was an open oven.

Seichan grabbed his arm and pointed to where a wall had fallen crookedly, balancing on the stump of one of the city's many pillars. "Under there," she said. "It's warm enough it should mask our body heat."

He nodded, limping after her. "We're not far from the icefall. There's a little reflected light reaching here, which should help us."

As they reached the shelter, a savage barking erupted, picked up by another.

Gun blasts followed.

"Tucker," Gray whispered.

He and Seichan had heard spats of automatic fire from deeper in the city, indicating the former Ranger was still on the run, putting up a determined fight. But this barking was far closer.

A soldier ran past their position, weaponless and panicked.

The Russian moved too fast for Gray to pick him off. Then a shape burst low and sped after the fleeing man. A body thudded heavily, followed by a scream and savage growling. Another armored shape pushed into view, his face hidden by a helmet and night-vision goggles.

Seichan twitched her SIG Sauer in the soldier's direction, but Gray pulled her arm down. A dog hugged this newcomer's side.

Kane.

The Malinois whined and pointed his nose toward their hiding spot. Gray pushed up. "Tucker."

The Ranger lifted an arm, clearly unsurprised. He stared in the direction that Marco had gone.

Distracted, Tucker failed to notice a shadow running across the rooftops toward them, rifle at his shoulder, heavy with a grenade launcher. It was likely the sniper who had taken potshots at them earlier and was now rushing in for the kill.

Gray lifted his AK-12, took a breath, then let it out slowly as he pulled the trigger. The weapon rattled out a short burst. Startled, Tucker ducked low. Kane spun in a circle. But no one was more surprised than the sniper. The impact of rounds lifted him off his feet. The Russian fell backward. As he crashed, his weapon fired. A grenade flew—but not at them.

A trail of smoke through the darkness led to the ice wall.

The grenade blasted into a ball of fire that reflected tenfold off the ice.

Gray grimaced at the unlucky shot.

If that all came crashing down . . .

Marco raced back, joining Tucker and Kane. "Time to move," Tucker warned. "Don't want to stay in one place too long."

Gray and Seichan headed over, both eyeing Tucker's combat armor.

"Borrowed it. The guy wearing it no longer needed it."

"How did you find us?" Seichan asked.

Tucker patted Kane, then Marco. "A dog's nose is better than any thermal scope."

They set off.

With each step, Gray's ankle shot electric fire up his limb. After a minute, a howl of raw agony echoed to them, coming from the direction of the waterfall.

Gray stopped and stared that way. As he did, a large sleeve of ice calved away and fell like a dagger. It shattered to the ground with a crystalline ring.

Tucker tried to lead them deeper, but Gray grabbed his arm. "Everyone else is still down that tunnel, behind that icefall."

Tucker understood and looked at Gray's leg. "We need eyes on the situation. Can you manage?"

He nodded. "Let's go."

Tucker set a hard pace, which Gray appreciated. Tucker cast his dogs to either side, to extend their range of sight. The guy's lips were set in a grim line. Gray knew who the man must be especially worried about. The Ranger had grown close to the botanist over this long ordeal.

After a few minutes, Tucker led them to a three-story structure. It stood thirty yards from the frozen waterfall. They climbed to the second story, which offered a decent view. Tucker left his dogs to guard below. They wanted no surprise visitors.

A wide doorway out to a balcony offered the best vantage.

To the right of the icefall, red lamps glowed, illuminating a cluster of men, all dressed in camo. The angle made it hard to estimate their number.

A wounded man moaned loudly, whimpering in turns. His face was a ruin, bleeding heavily. His eye sockets looked empty, giving him a sepulchral appearance. A soldier injected him with something, likely a sedative or pain reliever.

Another soldier looked to be cursing, pointing toward the waterfall.

Gray struggled to understand.

Tucker made sense of it, clearly zooming in with his goggles. "The angry one is Captain Turov. I remember him from the naval base. The one next to him looks like he's got the stars and bars of a senior lieutenant, likely the strike team's leader."

"What about the wounded man?" Seichan said. "One of the soldiers?"

Tucker turned with a lean grin. "Oh, that's Archpriest Sychkin. Seems he's having a bad day."

"What happened to him?" Gray asked.

Tucker turned back to the scene. "As far as I can tell, I think he came from that tunnel of yours. Evacuated by one of the Russian soldiers."

Gray cursed under his breath. "Our friends?"

"No clue. No sign of them out there."

"Then they must still be in there."

"Or dead," Seichan offered coldly.

Gray recognized this possibility, too, but . . . "Considering Sychkin's condition, *someone* put up a fight." He turned to the others. "If it was our group, then they could still be alive. We need to find out before we run out of time."

This was reinforced by another resounding pop of ice. A huge section of the icewall broke away and crashed to a scintillating ruin in front of the thrones.

"It's coming apart for sure," Tucker said. "I can make a dash with my dogs, try to get through. For now, with all that ice raining down, the soldiers are keeping their distance."

"No," Seichan said. "I know what's back there. You don't. You and your dogs will be more useful here. Someone needs to lock down that exit before I bring the others out."

Gray heard the unspoken caveat to her statement.

If we get out . . .

Tucker nodded. "We'll cover you from here."

"Only shoot if you must. Don't give your location away."

She turned to leave, but not before leaning over and kissing Gray, hard and desperate—then she shoved away, rolled to her feet, and set off.

Gray and Tucker maintained a vigil. A full minute ticked by, which felt like forever. Then a shadow darted out of the cityscape. Using the coverage of the tumbled blocks of ice, Seichan made it behind the throne carved with sea life—and vanished away.

Gray's finger rose to touch his lips, feeling the lingering bruise of her kiss. It was as if Seichan were pouring all that was unspoken between them, expressing her fears and hopes.

He lowered his hand.

It had also felt like good-bye.

52

Kowalski crouched by the side door of the aircraft. "It's now or never," he hollered up to Monk, who continued to pilot the Baikal. "If we keep circling, I'm going to hurl all over my fine work."

"Then get ready," his teammate called through the crowded cabin.

Captain Kelly leaned over Kowalski's shoulder. "Do you know what you're doing?"

Before he could reply—which was going to be a firm *eff-you*—another interceded. "Looks good to me," Ryan said.

Kowalski rolled his eyes, which made his stomach churn worse. "Let's get this over with. If we're going to be shot down, I'd like to do it on a full stomach."

Earlier, on the flight back to the *Polar King*, after the sabotage of the Russian patrol boat, a midsize jet had swept through the fog overhead. Its passage was noted by the hot swirl of the plane's contrail through the icy mists. Luckily, Monk had been sticking to his previous route, skimming the ice cap. The maneuver kept their small craft from being spotted.

Afterward, Monk had sped them deeper into the fog. A short time later, they all heard the concussive blasts of grenade fire. It reached them through the preternatural acoustics of the polar region. It was easy to conclude what was happening.

The *King* was under siege—but it was a tall castle to breech.

Or so they hoped.

Kowalski and the others had compared notes, trying to judge how many Russians could have been aboard the midsize jet. The conclusion was that there were not enough to commandeer the icebreaker. Likely, the arriving force had been ordered to keep the vessel locked down—until that heavily armed patrol boat or its mobile forces arrived and finished the mission.

The dive team's earlier sabotage had bought their group a small window of opportunity. They had used it to come up with a plan—and to build their only weapon.

Kowalski stared down at the jury-rigged bomb. He had used spare parts from their prior mission. Unfortunately, the amount of leftover plastic explosives had been meager.

About the size of a goose egg.

Better be enough.

"Inbound now!" Monk called back.

Kowalski grabbed the door handle. Monk tipped the Baikal on its wing and aimed them out of the fog. They had been skirting the bank's edge for the past forty-five minutes.

The waiting was over.

The Baikal burst free of the mists. The sunlight glared after so long in the fog. Still, Monk kept the plane on its attack path. He dove for the jet. It sat on the ice, about three hundred yards from the crimson bulk of the *Polar King*.

The Baikal managed a full thirty-three seconds of free flight—then gunfire strafed at them. The air-threat was finally noted by the ground forces.

Rounds pinged and ricocheted. Several tore through their wings. A few zinged through the fuselage, luckily missing everyone inside. Mitchell curled tighter. He had lost enough blood as it was. The man didn't have any more to spare.

A rocket sped past one wingtip and arced back to the ice, where it burst into a fireball that spun into the sky.

"Now!" Monk hollered.

Kowalski shoved the side door open. The world sped under him.

He lifted his makeshift device by a strap. The bulk of the jet appeared below. As the Baikal swept from its nose to its tail fin, Kowalski tossed his ordnance. The device spun, flapping its strap.

"Is that bomb big enough?" Kelly asked, still second-guessing Kowalski.

"That's *not* the bomb."

Kowalski pulled the door shut as a muffled blast echoed up to them, near the back of the jet, by its fuel tank. A moment later, a massive fireball lit the world behind them as the tank exploded.

"That's the bomb!" Kowalski clarified.

The blast wave caught the small aircraft. Flames and smoke burst around them. The Baikal got tossed like a paper airplane in a hurricane. Kowalski regretted his wisecrack toward the captain—because he had failed to fully latch his door.

It flung open as the plane cartwheeled.

With his hand gripping the handle, Kowalski got yanked out. For a death-defying moment, he hung in midair. Then the plane's wing strut struck him in the gut. He wrapped around it.

A strobing view of the world opened below him.

The jet's fireball had blasted across the ice in all directions, all the way to the hull of the icebreaker. In its blackened wake, bright fiery torches ran across the ice or rolled in agony. A snowmobile exploded, flipping through the air.

Then hands grabbed Kowalski and hauled him inside. Monk stabilized their flight into a swaying wobble.

Once inside, Kowalski slid his ass to the floor.

He tried to thank his rescuers—but all that came out was his lunch. It splattered between his knees and washed across the floor.

He wiped his mouth and shook his head.

Fuck the Arctic.

6:22 P.M.

Turov stared up as the thunderous blast echoed away. The flash had been so bright it had wiped out the sun. Flames had shot inside the upper cavern, blasting through the distant archway and lapping across the roof before dying out.

"The transport plane," Lieutenant Bragin concluded.

Turov slowly nodded.

Somehow the crew of the icebreaker had blown it up. The enemy's shipboard munitions must have been more formidable than he had expected.

"What now, sir?" Bragin asked, clutching a fist to his chest.

Turov searched the dark city. Smoke fogged rooftops and billowed higher in spots. He returned his attention to closer at hand, to the four other soldiers guarding this small encampment.

"We don't have enough manpower. We need to regroup. Topside. Wait for the *Lyakhov* to reach us." He stared at the bloody, blistered ruins of Sychkin's face. The archpriest moaned and rocked, still in agony despite the heavy morphine injection. Turov shook his head. "There's nothing more for us down here. Sound a retreat."

Bragin fished in his armor and pulled free a whistle.

From the city, a pair of stragglers stumbled into view, haggard with smoke-stained armor. One had to carry the other with an arm under his shoulders. The injured one could barely use his leg. He was dropped leadenly to the ground.

Turov squinted at the ancient city.

How many more soldiers are still out there?

The answer came in a flurry of gunfire. The two arrivals lifted their rifles and fired into the remaining soldiers. The attacker on the ground strafed low. The other remained standing and picked off any who escaped.

Bragin yanked out his pistol, but the one on his knees fired, shattering the lieutenant's hand with a burst. Bragin never screamed, just fell back a step, and turned. The lieutenant eyed a rifle abandoned on the ground. Before he could move, a huge dog unfolded from the shadows. It stalked with head low, teeth bared.

Off to the side, another appeared, same posture, same threat.

Bragin backed away, lifting his free arm in plain surrender.

The attacker on his feet closed in on Turov and centered his rifle at his chest. As the man lifted his face, Turov was surprised to recognize his former prisoner.

"Seems our roles are reversed," the man said coldly.

Turov simply lifted his palms. As he stared into the hard eyes of these two men, he recognized how badly he had underestimated his enemy—even when forewarned by Valya Mikhailov.

He stiffened with this thought and searched around, realizing who was still missing.

Where is that woman?

53

Valya hunted along a tunnel carved with a snarl of vines on one side and a swirling seascape on the other. She had paused briefly with Nadira when a deafening boom had blasted, briefly turning ice to fire behind them. But the world fell back into darkness, and they continued onward.

A firefight had followed, too, so brief that Valya had never slowed.

Her focus remained ahead.

Earlier, she and Nadira had hidden at the city's edge after Sychkin came howling out of this passageway, without Yerik, hauled by a wounded soldier. Something lay hidden back here, but that was not Valya's goal. After the archpriest had returned, Valya had counted on her true target to show herself, to come searching for answers to the man's screams.

This proved true when Valya spotted a lithe figure dart out of hiding, dance through the icy shadows, and duck in here.

Valya and Nadira had quickly followed. Once into the dark tunnels, they had donned their night-vision gear and trailed the flare of light that marked Seichan's passage. They kept their distance, wary of any allies.

For now.

6:25 P.M.

Seichan fled along the carved tunnel, her heart in her throat. She had heard the gunfire behind her. It had to mark the assault by Gray and Tucker, but had they been successful?

She took a deep breath and shoved her fear down. It served nothing. If the Guild had taught her any useful skill beyond murder and terror, it was to remain focused upon the task at hand, to look forward and not back.

But that did not mean to put on blinders.

Her ears remained attuned to her surroundings. She heard the cracking of ice behind her, loud and more regular now. The huge explosion must have weakened the waterfall. This was confirmed by a resounding crash behind her, crystalline and bright. The waterfall was coming apart even faster than she'd thought.

If it should collapse, her only exit would be blocked by thousands of tons of ice. She and the others would suffocate before any rescue could be mounted, poisoned by the sulfurous air.

Recognizing this, she ran faster, her light bouncing across the walls.

As she did, she heard a scuff of sandy rock behind her. She might have missed it—except she had been holding her breath at the thought of suffocation. Plus, the acoustics of this tunnel amplified even a whisper.

She kept her pace steady, so as not to alert those behind her. She knew who must be sharing this tunnel. Though she had never spotted Valya among the Russians, it had to be her. No plodding Russian soldier moved so silently. No doubt Nadira was with her, too.

Seichan took the only action available to her.

While still running, she bent and gently touched her flashlight to the floor, abandoning it there. She then fled onward into the dark. She needed time, more than she needed light. She ran her fingertips across the carvings, feeling the thorns of the plants, letting the tortuous garden lead her forward.

Behind her, the abandoned flashlight should slow Valya. It would force the woman to proceed more cautiously, thinking Seichan had stopped or had reached the end of the tunnel. Plus, the dazzle of the brightness would make Valya pause. Those two hunters would need time to abandon their gear and let their eyes readjust to the dimness.

Taking advantage of this, Seichan ran onward until starlight glowed ahead of her. She blinked, trying to understand it—then did. It was the lights of the others, flowing from wherever they had holed up.

As she rushed forward, strategies flashed behind her eyes. Panicked, she momentarily forgot her training.

Her left leg struck a low boulder and sent her into a wild roll. Behind her, the crash of pottery revealed the true nature of the obstacle.

One of those damned sculpted jars.

She halted herself before tumbling into the mudpot that boiled and belched ahead of her. She pushed ahead on her hands and knees.

Lights flared on the far side. The glare stung her eyes. She raised a hand against it. A figure stepped into view, decked in Arctic camo. One of the soldiers. She snatched at her holstered SIG, but a voice called over, high-pitched and confused.

"Seichan?"

She recognized the voice. Still, she freed her pistol, arming herself until she understood the situation. The botanist came running around the steaming pit. Only then did Seichan notice the body floating atop the quaking mud.

Yerik.

Elle helped her to her feet. Omryn came around the far side. Like Tucker, he had donned a dead man's armor.

"The others?" Seichan asked, quickly assessing the situation.

"Anna is inside with the doctor and Jason. He's recovered. But weak."

"How?"

"Long story. I found—"

Seichan cut her off. "Don't care. Everyone back into the chamber. All lights out. No sound." She glanced back. "Trouble is coming. Valya and Nadira."

Elle looked sickened at this news, but resolute. "We can make a stand here."

"No time. We can't get pinned down."

Elle looked confused.

"That waterfall is one bad shake from crashing down, of turning this place into a tomb. That's why I came here. To get you all moving. But—"

She glanced back to the main tunnel as the lighting shifted. Far down the passageway, the steady glow now bobbled.

Valya found my light. Knows it was a ruse.

Seichan swung back to the others. "Hide. I'm going to lead them off." She pointed at the side tunnel that headed to the toxic garden. "Once they follow me, you all need to run for the exit. As fast as you can sprint. Carry Jason if you must."

"I will do my best," Omryn promised, lifting a palm to his stomach.

Seichan finally noted the belly wrap under his armor. She grimaced. This group needed to get moving ASAP. Burdened by the injured and afflicted, they would be moving slower than she had hoped.

She started to turn for the garden passageway, then swung back around. She held out her pistol toward Omryn. "Trade me."

He looked down at his Remington 12-gauge, clearly reluctant to part with it. But he passed over the shotgun.

She hefted it, testing its weight.

I'll need a weapon like this to deal with Valya.

Omryn took her SIG, but he added a warning, nodding to the Remington. "That's my last magazine in there. Only six slugs left."

Seichan nodded.

It will have to do.

That and one other item.

She held her hand out to Elle. "Your flashlight."

The botanist handed it over.

"Now go," Seichan ordered.

Trusting them to obey, she fled around the mudpot and dashed down the garden path. As she ran, she made a promise to herself, one she had made earlier, one she intended to keep. She pictured Valya.

Only one of us will walk out of here—or neither of us will.

6:32 P.M.

Valya approached the end of the dark tunnel, hugging one side, where stony thorns tugged at her body armor. Nadira flanked the other side. They both kept low and ran dark. Small lights—IR illuminators—were fixed to their rifles and cast an invisible spectrum that their night-vision gear could detect.

The two scanned the next room, careful of the broken pottery underfoot. A pit bubbled and popped with molten mud, spitting and hissing in the dark. A body floated atop the quagmire.

The archpriest's lapdog.

As Valya had suspected, there must be others besides Seichan down here. Unfortunately, her target knew she was being hunted, evident from the trick with the abandoned flashlight.

A search of this chamber revealed three tunnels leading away. Her sensitive goggles picked up a flare of light rising from the passageway to the right. Nadira spotted it, too, motioning with her hand in that direction.

Valya sidled into the chamber with her rifle raised. She edged toward the tunnel's mouth, while signaling Nadira to sweep around the mud-pit and approach from the other side. Her lieutenant moved swiftly, a dark, silent shadow. Valya waited until they were both in position. She kept high, while Nadira dropped low.

Valya counted off on three fingers. As she curled her last digit, they both leaned out, rifles tucked to cheeks. The light rose from around a curve of the tunnel, retreating away. The glare was blinding, but clearly no one was in sight.

Satisfied, Valya nodded to Nadira and tugged off her goggles. She would not let herself be blinded again. Nadira followed her example. They set off in pursuit, still running dark, using the meager light ahead to guide them. Then she heard a faint echoing whisper: Seichan warning those who were with her to stay quiet.

Valya tightened the grip on her rifle.

The light continued to retreat ahead of them.

Where are you going?

A loud blast and a flash of muzzle fire dropped Valya low. A dark shadow rolled from the floor ahead. Seichan must have lain in wait in the shadows, sending the others ahead with her light.

On her belly, Valya opened fire with a deafening barrage on auto. Her rounds sparked brightly off the sculpted walls. Nadira used the cover to run forward, to get a bead on Seichan as the woman retreated around a curve of the tunnel. As Nadira opened fire, Valya burst to her feet and followed, closing the distance.

Two more thunderous blasts—clearly from a shotgun—pounded Valya's ears. One slug shattered stone. The second caught Nadira in the shoulder, hard enough to slam the woman back. She struck the wall hard but continued firing, strafing wildly, clearing the tunnel ahead.

Valya reached her, keeping low.

Nadira groaned, but she remained standing. Her combat armor had protected her from a worse outcome.

Valya focused forward. "On my mar—"

Nadira's rifle slumped, falling slack, then her weapon clattered to the stone.

Confused, Valya retreated a step. Nadira still stood, but the woman's knees bent under her. Only then did Valya note the black blood running down her lieutenant's neck—and the spear of rock, one of the sculpted thorns, poking through her throat. While the shotgun strike hadn't killed her, the impact into that wall had.

Nadira gurgled, then went slack, hanging on that sharp spike.

In the silence that followed, a rapid pounding of boots sounded behind her, echoing from the mud chamber. As Valya listened, she heard frantic whispers. Then the noises receded, fading off into the distance, marking a panicked flight out of here.

Valya sneered as she understood. Seichan's allies hadn't been running with her. They had been left hidden behind. Valya stared ahead, calculating. She couldn't know for sure if one or two allies were still with Seichan, offering support, but her gut told her otherwise.

Valya knew her target.

She's alone.

A moment ago, Seichan must have rolled her flashlight down the tunnel, making it look as if others were retreating with it—while setting up the ambush that killed Nadira.

Valya growled in annoyance, but she had to respect the tactic.

She weighed whether to leave or not, to abandon this hunt. She shook her head and crouched lower. It wasn't pride that kept her fixed. If she ran, Seichan would follow. And Valya had no knowledge of how many of the woman's allies had taken flight down the other tunnel, or how they might be armed. She pictured Sychkin. Plus, two *spetsnaz* soldiers had never returned with the wounded priest. That was enough reason to be cautious of those others. She dared not get pinned down, between Seichan behind her and an unknown enemy ahead.

Valya grimaced, having another reason to continue her hunt.

She pictured her brother, cold in an Arctic grave in Greenland, and tightened her grip on her rifle.

It was time to end this.

She set off, moving silently toward the light. It had stopped retreating. Her ears strained for any telltale warning. She breathed softly through her nose. She edged around the corner and spotted a flashlight, again abandoned on the floor. But it was not a delaying tactic. Seichan had no more need of a light. The end of the tunnel lay ahead, opening into a cavernous chamber that shone with a wan glow.

Valya increased her pace, fearing she would lose her target inside there.

Still, she kept her rifle pointed, her eyes searching for any movement. Then a small metallic ringing reached her. She tried to imagine its source but failed. Its distance was also hard to discern, like a faint bell chiming over hills.

This mystery slowed her again.

As she reached the abandoned flashlight, she flicked it off. She did not want her shadow to be cast ahead of her, giving away her approach. Paused there, she heard a strange rustling. It was not the brush of cloth. It sounded expansive and stretched far across the next cavern.

Frowning, suspicious, she slunk lower and hugged the wall, cautious of those stony spikes. Finally, she could see into the cavern.

The sight froze her.

Under a cracked roof, shining with sunlit ice, a vast garden spread across a steaming mudflat, which burbled and spat in accompaniment to that rustling. The landscape stirred and waved, as if swept by winds—but there was no breeze down here. She remembered how Sychkin had wanted a botanist to aid in the search, one with experience in carnivorous plants.

Valya now knew why.

Movement drew her eye to the left.

A tarnished skiff drifted rudderless across a skim of acidic water and mud. It looked made of copper. She recalled the metallic ringing.

Copper over rock, she realized now.

From the distance and angle, she could not tell if anyone was aboard, sprawled flat and out of sight. She leaned farther into the cavern, trying to get a better view. Another boat lay overturned on the shore, as if inviting Valya to tip it over and follow.

Then she spotted the trap.

A glint of light revealed the muzzle of a weapon hidden under that overturned boat, which rested crookedly on a rock. The shotgun pointed directly at her from that copper bunker.

She had a fraction of a moment to react, less than a single clench of her heart.

She dove headlong to the side, crashing across a pile of pottery jugs. She hit her wounded shoulder. Agony burst through her, narrowing her vision to a pinpoint. Sliding on that bad shoulder, she strafed under the lip of the overturned boat. Rounds pinged and sparked fire off the copper. The boat shifted and rattled under the barrage.

She did not wait, ready to leap for another angle of attack. She shoved to a leg, extending the other for balance. She never stopped firing.

Then a snake bit, just above the back of her boot. The pain was sharp. Her foot wobbled, suddenly unable to support her weight. She sprawled forward, striking her forehead against the rock.

Then a weight landed on her back, pounding her flat.

She twisted enough to spot Seichan straddling her.

How . . . ?

Behind Seichan, a drape of leather waved and answered Valya's question.

Seichan hadn't been hiding out on that drifting boat, or under the one on shore, but behind a rack of old clothing. The muzzle of the shotgun had been a decoy to hold Valya's attention.

Valya struggled, but one arm was deadened after the crash onto her wounded shoulder. She had no purchase with the opposite leg. She knew why. The pain by her boot hadn't been a snake strike, but the slice of a knife—across her Achilles tendon—hobbling her.

Still, Valya kicked with her good leg, trying to roll from under Seichan. With her rifle pinned beneath her, Valya grabbed for her pistol. She managed to free it, but before she could bend an elbow and fire behind her, a blade slammed into her forearm and drove her limb down. The steel twisted, severing tendons. Her pistol clattered free.

Seichan snatched the gun, leaving the blade embedded.

Valya gasped—not in pain, but in shock. She recognized the black handle sticking out of her arm, the cast of its steel. It was her *athamé* dagger, her grandmother's ceremonial blade.

"You left this behind," Seichan hissed at her ear. "Thought I'd return it."

6:42 P.M.

Seichan felt Valya go slack under her, but she didn't trust it. She kept the pistol at the back of the woman's head, another blade at Valya's throat. Her heart pounded, demanded that she plunge the knife deep, to end not just this life, but to sever Seichan's past from her present.

Valya was the last vestige of her former life, a pale ghost that had been haunting her, a reminder of who she had once been. The monster inside Seichan wailed to be released, to be let loose, if only this one last time, to end the long, bloody journey that had led here.

"Do it," Valya said coldly.

There was no defeat, no fury, not even resignation.

Just acceptance.

Seichan knew this woman was her pale doppelganger, brutalized into who she was as readily as Seichan had been. If it hadn't been for

Gray, this might still be her. In this moment, she wondered if Valya's long pursuit of her had not been solely fueled by revenge, but driven more by an underlying envy.

I escaped.

Still, Seichan knew that wasn't entirely true.

A monster remained inside her, one that still wailed for blood. She recognized it would never be sated. There was one way to kill such a ravenous beast.

To starve it to death.

She climbed off of Valya, sheathed her dagger, and yanked the rifle from under the woman. Seichan flung her arm, sending the weapon out into the steaming mud. All the time, she kept her pistol pointed, never wavering, never trusting.

She stared down at Valya. The woman's blood flowed down the stone.

The beast wailed inside her, wanting more.

"I won't be that monster," she whispered, knowing she had made this pledge before. She intended to keep it this time.

For Gray, for Jack, for my future.

Still . . .

She reached down, tugged free the *athamé* dagger, and severed Valya's other Achilles. She flung the blade far, then fled the poisonous cavern, casting back a final promise.

"But I won't be a fool either."

Not ever.

54

Gray stood his ground as another section of the icewall cleaved away. It fell like a spear and shattered against the stone. A blast of shards stung him, peppering any exposed skin.

Still, he remained fixed, never taking his eyes away from the nearest throne. Behind him, Jason and the others gathered with Tucker and his dogs. They had safely escaped long minutes ago. The returned group kept themselves armed, guarding over their three Russian prisoners: Turov, his lieutenant, and Sychkin.

The latter continued to moan, half delirious, half sedated, but still in pain.

The noise scratched like nails along Gray's stretched nerves.

He wanted to put a bullet in the man, a mercy killing—not that the bastard deserved any mercy. Still, at least it would shut him the hell up.

A thunderous popping drew his eye up. Cracks spiderwebbed across the waterfall. More sections fell away, crashing with massive explosions. It finally drove him back. It would do no good if he was crushed to death.

"It's all coming down," Tucker warned. "We should get on the stairs."

Gray waved to him. "Go. Get everyone moving up."

Tucker stared at him, recognizing that Gray intended to stay here. But the Ranger finally nodded, turned, and started shouting orders.

Gray took a deep breath. The others had told him how Seichan had lured Valya and her cohort down the side tunnel that led to the steaming garden. He took solace in the fact that those two mercenaries had also not returned.

He took a step toward the nearest throne, eyeing the gap behind it. Tucker had stopped him from entering earlier. Gray could barely walk, let alone offer any true back up. Tucker summarized it best: *You'll only make matters worse. Trust your woman.*

Tucker even offered to go in with his dogs, but Gray knew he could not endanger more lives. Seichan had risked her life to save those behind him. He wasn't about to send any back in.

He took a deep breath, a mantra repeating in his head.

Trust your woman.

Still, as more massive sections broke from above and crashed hard, spilling ice across the neighboring city, he found it harder and harder. The floor had filled with slush and mountains of shattered ice. The far throne was already buried. The gap behind the closer one was only open because a fat plate of ice had fallen over it, forming a roof, sheltering the opening.

He shifted to peer along it when a shout rose behind him.

"Gray!" Tucker bellowed. "Above you!"

He craned his neck. A gargantuan slab of ice tilted away from the waterfall. He fled backward, hobbling on his bad ankle. Then Tucker joined him, hooked an arm under Gray's shoulder, and dragged him away.

The thunderous boom sounded like a cannon blast behind them. Cold air and shattered ice threw them both forward. They hit hard and slid. By the time they stopped, their bodies were coated in a layer of powdery ice.

Gray shoved up, shaking his coat free. He turned and searched through the frosted air. When some of it settled, the view opened, and his heart sank. The nearest throne was gone, crushed and buried.

Tucker joined him. "I . . . I'm sorry."

Gray shook his head, refusing to accept this.

Trust your woman.

He did.

He stumbled forward. The cold numbed his ankle—or maybe it was due to the adrenaline. He forded through a crush of knee-deep ice and around jagged boulders until he could reach the wall. The latest collapse had deeply scraped the base of the waterfall, leaving a crystal-blue surface.

His reflection mirrored off it as he stumbled closer.

Then, through the translucency, a shadow appeared on the far side, rushing forward, merging with his reflection. He recognized that silhouette. His hands had explored its every curve.

"Seichan . . ."

He rushed up and put his palms against the ice.

A meter away, she did the same.

"No," he gasped out.

This wasn't an utterance of defeat, but defiance.

I won't lose her.

He waved to her, yelling. "Get back!"

She clearly could not hear him, but he pulled the AK-12 rifle from his shoulder. He had stripped the fully equipped weapon from one of the dead soldiers. He lifted and pressed it against the ice, then waved an arm, pantomiming for her to retreat.

He waited, still not sure she understood.

But her shadow fell back, fading into blue ice.

He backpedaled in turn, retreating a safe distance. Then he lowered the weapon, aimed it at that azure mirror, and fired.

A grenade shot from the rifle's undermounted barrel. The round sped and struck with a fiery explosion. Smoke blasted, and ice cracked. Before it could clear, Gray rushed forward through the ice and fire.

Blinded, he still ran headlong.

Then something struck him, wreathed in crystals, smelling of sulfur.

Arms wrapped around him.

He pulled Seichan tightly to him.

She gasped in his arms, breathing heavily. "I . . . I didn't think I'd get out of there."

Gray hugged her hard. "You need to learn to trust your man."

7:10 P.M.

Tucker followed the last of the group up the steps. They had traversed three-quarters of the way toward the top. To the side, the waterfall continued to fragment into massive sheets that crashed into the city. The thunder was nearly nonstop now, becoming a storm underground.

Ahead, everyone stumbled along, exhausted, most having to support another. Anna helped Jason. Seichan gripped Gray as if she would never let him go. Turov and Bragin hauled the archpriest between them. Harper kept a steadying hand on Omryn, who hugged an arm over his wrapped belly.

Directly ahead, Elle climbed with Kane and Marco.

A change in timbre of that thundering storm drew Tucker's gaze. He watched the entire top section of the waterfall give way. It tilted far, a glacier about to give birth. Then the section toppled away, falling into the darkness. When it struck, the ground shook. A huge cloud of frost and ice blasted to the roof, casting rainbows in the last shine of the day's sun.

Tucker gaped at the sight.

Elle spotted the danger. "Look!"

With the top of the fall gone, the ramp that led down to it cracked into pieces and slid over the edge. One of the Russian snowmobiles was carried along atop one slab, then tumbled away with the ice.

Tucker's heart clenched.

If more of the ramp broke free, they'd be trapped. Or at least, it would be a long, treacherous climb to reach the small arched opening in the peak.

Tucker bellowed to the group. "Go! As fast as you can!" He waved an arm toward the falling ice. "It's all collapsing!"

The group paused, staring in that direction, then set off again.

At first slowly, then gaining speed.

Tucker herded everyone in front of him. They reached the top and set off for the collection of snow machines. The ice quaked underfoot, shaking each time another section broke away. Cracks skittered around and ahead of them.

Jason fell and slid down the slope on his stomach, but Omryn caught him and hauled him up. The two forged ahead together.

They reached the machines and split their group up—including the trio of Russians. Tucker took Turov into a Snowcat with his dogs and Elle. Gray and Seichan guarded Bragin and Sychkin, not that the blind priest needed much oversight. Jason and Anna doubled up with Omryn and Harper on the Polaris snowmobiles. The *Polar King's* crew had more experience with ice and snow, so they drove the machines.

Engines started, and the group fled up the ice chute. Massive floes cracked and slid away. The destruction chased the retreating group. Behind them, the crashing ice filled the cavern with more crystals and frost. The rainbows grew more brilliant back there, while sunlight beckoned ahead.

The two Polaris shot through the exit first, vanishing into the glare. Then the two Snowcats followed.

As Tucker trundled free, he saw the world had vastly changed since they had departed. Past the ring of outer peaks, a crater had been blasted into the ice, framed by twisted metal. A pall of smoke hung low and heavy, competing with the surrounding fogbanks. Fires burned everywhere.

In the rearview mirror, Turov's expression was dismayed, mournful, as he looked at the wreckage.

"Your plane, I'm guessing?" Tucker said.

The captain simply stared.

The team raced toward the blast site, drawn by the vehicles painted in red and black. The colors of the *Polar King*. The icebreaker looked intact, with a smoky stain across its hull on this side.

As they drew nearer, bodies in combat armor lay across the ice, burned, some still smoking. Tucker took little solace in the sight. These were someone's sons or fathers.

He shook his head at the waste.

Tucker spotted a familiar grouping and aimed for it. They stood near the small Russian plane, the Baikal. The aircraft looked hard-driven, resting crookedly on the ice. A group of the crew carried another in a stretcher, rushing hurriedly toward the ship. The plane must have just landed.

Tucker led the other vehicles toward them. Once there, they all staggered out, or climbed off their machines. Captain Kelly spotted the ship's doctor and hurried to her, pointing at the retreating crew. She was clearly needed aboard. She nodded, turned, and hopped on the snowmobile behind Omryn. The Chukchi crewmate also required more than a med kit to deal with his injuries.

As Tucker climbed out of the Snowcat, with Turov held at gunpoint, Kowalski met them. The big man covered his privates as Marco raced up and leaped, knocking Kowalski back a step.

Tucker looked across the chaos, the fires, the confusion. "Let me guess. Your handiwork?"

"With help from some friends." Kowalski nodded to the bedraggled group by the plane. He then eyeballed Turov. "Looks like you've been making friends, too."

Before Tucker could answer, a loud roaring rose to the south. Everyone froze, still shellshocked, fearful. Gazes lifted and searched the skies.

From the fogbank, a large helicopter burst into view, tearing through the mists and diving low. It was the Russian gunship—the Ka-27— from the patrol boat. It was designed to fight submarines and came with a battery of weapons, including depth charges and torpedoes. Enough to sink the *Polar King*.

The helicopter made a low pass, likely assessing the ground situation—then arced into a turn.

Gray rushed up to Tucker and Turov.

Seichan followed with Lieutenant Bragin, who dragged Sychkin along with him and dropped the man to the ice. The skin on the archpriest's face was blackened, swollen, and bloated. His nose showed raw cartilage. His eye sockets were knots of raw tissue.

Kowalski cringed at the state of the man on the ground. "What the hell . . ."

Gray confronted Turov, pointing an arm toward the circling aircraft. "Call them off."

"Why?" Turov asked calmly. "Despite conditions here, we still have the upper hand. Our patrol boat will arrive before much longer."

Gray raised his other hand. He held one of Sigma's encrypted satphones. "The solar storm has passed. Comms are wide open. I've been in touch with D.C. since we exited the mountain."

Tucker stared up.

Gray lifted his phone to his lips. "Putting you on speaker, Director."

As Gray held out his arm, the familiar voice of Painter Crowe addressed the Russian captain. Even coming out of that small device, Crowe's voice was authoritative and assured.

"Fifty minutes ago, we acquired NOAA polar satellites with high-rez cameras. We have live feed of the area. Wave to the audience, if you'd like. It's being broadcast to all intelligence agencies, and to a global audience if need be."

Gray stared hard at Turov. "These are still international waters. The next action is your call. Halt hostilities now or risk a global war."

Turov searched the skies, then looked back to the commander. His shoulders sagged, but he kept his spine straight. He held out a hand. "I'll need a radio."

Tucker felt a surge of relief.

Another did not.

Sychkin cried out, more moan than words, but one demand was clear and easy to translate. "*Nyet.*"

Gray ignored the priest, clearly not interested in his input.

Sychkin tossed something from a pocket. A small transmitter with a blinking red light. It was meaningless to all of them—but not to Turov.

The captain backed away as if the archpriest had thrown a cobra at his feet.

"What's wrong?" Gray asked.

Turov stared at Gray, at all of them, his expression grim, his words worse.

"It's doomsday."

7:32 P.M.

Turov closed his eyes, balanced between fury and remorse. "This is not the outcome I had wished for."

That statement had layers of meaning beyond regret. He had feared this very scenario. It was why he had fought so hard—not so much to secure this little plot of land, as to keep this nuclear option from being deployed. Still, he knew that wasn't entirely true. It was his own ambition that led him here as much as it had Sychkin.

"I thought I possessed the only failsafe device, a way of reaching the *Siniykit*," he said. "Or so I was told."

He stared at the blinking transmitter, a match to the one couriered to him, arriving locked in a secure case from the Northern Fleet Joint Strategic Command. Clearly someone had doubted that Turov would resort to this option, even in defeat. Turov could guess who that was, the only one with authority enough to dare do this, someone whose desires were in lockstep with Sychkin.

Vice Admiral Glazkov.

Still, Turov knew there were many others up and down the chain of command, the vocal minority who had wanted to perform a live-fire test of the Poseidon torpedo, who also played a role in this subterfuge.

And now we must pay the price.

Not just those gathered on the ice, but the hundred crew aboard the *Lyakhov*.

"We're all trapped," he said.

The American with the phone—Gray—approached him, challenged him. "What do you mean it's *doomsday*?"

Turov saw no reason to prevaricate. "There is a Belgorod-class submarine, the *Siniykit*, the third prong of this mission. It was ordered to surface fifty miles away, to offer support if needed, but also as a failsafe, to make sure no one but Russia had territorial control of this location."

"And what does that mean for us?"

"Are you familiar with our Poseidon torpedoes?"

Gray nodded. "Unmanned stealth weapons. Eighty feet long. Nuclear capable."

"Not just *capable*. On the *Siniykit*, the boat has one loaded with a hundred-kiloton warhead."

"That's your failsafe?"

"It's already been dispatched. Underway." Turov waved to the transmitter on the ground. "With satellite comms open, the *Siniykit* would've received the command to launch."

"Can you countermand it?" Gray asked.

Turov shook his head. "After firing the Poseidon, the boat was under orders to dive beneath the ice cap and go into hiding." He stared across the group. "There is no way of reaching them."

Tucker looked at his dogs, no longer bothering to point his pistol at Turov. "How much time do we have?"

"At a range of fifty miles, accounting for the Poseidon's rate of travel . . ." Turov shrugged. "Thirty minutes, maybe less."

Gray searched to the south, speaking rapidly. "A hundred kilotons. Meaning a fireball of four hundred yards. Blast radius of two miles. To escape the worst of it—radiation, thermal damage—we'd need to be nine or ten miles away." He turned to another man in the colors of the icebreaker. "Captain Kelly?"

Turov looked at the two men.

"With both engines going, the *King* can push twenty-two knots. But that's over open water. Even if we reverse along the path we took, we'll manage no more than fifteen to eighteen. And that's pushing it."

Gray paused for a breath, clearly doing calculations in his head—then he sagged. "We can't get clear in time."

Turov understood what they were contemplating and offered some hope. "Those numbers you stated, Mister Gray. Those are air-blast numbers. For a nuclear bomb that explodes *above* a target. This will blow underwater."

Gray straightened. "And *under* ice."

Kelly nodded. "It should offer some insulation."

"It'll still be close." Gray pointed to the icebreaker. "We need every-one back aboard."

Kelly turned and passed instructions. Radios were lifted, spreading word. Seconds later, a siren wailed. The captain turned to them. "Reached Murphy. He's getting engines started. Thank God, they were still warm."

They all set off for the ship.

Turov hesitated, not sure if this applied to him.

Tucker grabbed his elbow. "What are you waiting for?" He stared up. "Let's give the world a show they won't forget."

As they set off, a huge man called after them. "Wait!"

Tucker looked back. "Kowalski, what's wrong?"

"You're all forgetting something!"

55

Valya crawled across the rough stone. Blood flowed from her forearm, from both ankles. It filled her boots, soaked through her armor. Where it pooled under her, it ran in streams to the bubbling mud behind her. The blood and her wounds drew flies and gnats, buzzing and divebombing, clouding the air around her.

I will not die like this.

She used her elbows and knees to propel her. She scraped and dragged herself toward the copper boat still overturned on the shore. Seichan had left her shotgun hidden under the false blind.

Valya struggled toward it. In the past—abandoned, brutalized, and blood-oathed—she had lost so much control of her life.

No longer.

She reached the boat and shouldered it aside. She clutched the stock of the 12-gauge and pulled it to her. Better to end this now, by her own hand, rather than succumb to the injuries inflicted upon her by another.

She intended to take back this much control.

She rolled to her shoulders.

As she did, she stared past her toes to the mudflats and the rustling growths.

She squinted. She did not remember the plants being this close to shore, gathered where her blood seeped into the mud.

As if noting her attention, the nearest plant curled its leaves, in a nearly hypnotic rhythm. Two fronds parted, revealing a coiled vine. She instinctively pulled back her legs, but she was too slow, too weak. The vine snapped out like a whip, striking at her ankles where her grandmother's blade had cut deep.

She yanked the leg back, her foot flopping in her boot.

A breath later, fire shot up to her knee, then higher. She scooted on her elbows, trying to escape the agony, but it followed her.

And that was not all.

The plants shivered closer, propelled by roots that swam and pushed through the hot mud. One, then another, and another. A second vine lanced out at her, missing by inches, stabbing into rock. Crimson oil spattered where it struck.

She swung her shotgun around, struggled with her aim, and fired.

The slug tore through the closest plant, shredding leaves, decapitating those fleshy flowerheads. Panicked, she fired again. But there was no lasting damage. A plant on her left crawled onto the stony bank, casting out roots, gripping the rock with thorns. It pulled itself closer, following the blood trail toward its source.

Its movements were slow, relentless, determined.

She twisted and fired, shattering through the plant's anchor of roots. It rolled back into the hot mud. As she lowered her gun, a sharp sting bit her wrist, near where the *athamé* blade had impaled her forearm. She jerked her limb away, breaking free of the vine that had stabbed her.

Still, the damage was done.

Acid burned through her veins, up her arms. The fire reached her heart and exploded, pumping everywhere with each panicked beat. She fled away, dragging the shotgun.

More of the plants clustered along the shore.

Roots snagged and pulled.

She tried to reverse the shotgun, to bring the muzzle to her chin, but her hands, then her limbs, refused. The weapon fumbled free and clattered on the stone.

No . . .

She let her body fall toward it, to retrieve its promise of release.

Only she ended up slumped across the rock, unable to move—yet, still burning inside.

She blinked away tears—even this control was stolen from her.

As she stared, unable to look away, the plants continued their slow, inexorable march through her blood, coming for her.

The first one scrabbled close enough to bow its many heads. A frill of dancing cilia probed the air, leading those malignant flowers to kiss her bare wrist. At first, it felt like the whiskers of a cat, tickling her hot skin—then those hairlike tendrils burned with acid into her, drawing the head closer. Petals opened, curling back, revealing a tangle of waving tendrils, far larger than the cilia.

With their touch, acid melted flesh, leaving only raw nerves that screamed.

Then the others joined the feast.

56

From the bridge of the *Polar King*, Gray watched as Captain Kelly transformed his massive nuclear-powered icebreaker into a thirty-thousand-ton bulldozer—only one running in reverse.

"Ten minutes!" Byron Murphy shouted from his nav-station, counting down the time left to them. "We're crossing the five-mile mark."

Halfway to safety.

Gray stared past the bow, toward the spires of rock that marked Hyperborea. As the icebreaker reversed down the channel, the legend receded into the mists. He pictured the massive Poseidon torpedo and its warhead speeding toward there.

He was not the only one.

Tension was evident across the bridge. Sweat pebbled brows, small crucifixes were kissed, lips whispered in silent prayers. Only *one* of them seemed unperturbed, as if he had done this countless times.

"Hold steady," Kelly called out calmly, guiding his ship via exterior cameras.

Gray kept vigil on the starboard bridge wing. Its windows, front and back, allowed him to view the ship's bow and stern. He shared this spot with Kowalski and Seichan. Across the bridge, Tucker and Monk manned the portside wing, along with Marco and Kane, who had earned their place.

Everyone else was below deck, at the orders of the captain. Though, many of them were in the small med ward, where Harper was playing triage with the wounded.

Maybe I should be there, too.

He gripped a hanging strap to keep himself upright, his ankle throbbing and swollen in his boot. But he did not want to miss this.

"Maybe we shouldn't have scuttled that vessel after all," Kowalski said, staring past the stern to the *Ivan Lyakhov*, the Russian patrol boat.

Kowalski had warned them of this problem. Sabotaging the *Lyakhov* had served them earlier, but now it was an obstacle in their path.

The Russian boat sat in the channel carved by the *Polar King*. Its bow thrusters churned to either side, holding the craft in the center of the waterway. The massive icebreaker bore down on it, still running in reverse. There had been no time to try to turn the massive ship in the thick ice. Even now, every minute counted, which meant this union was going to be a rough one.

While the *King* had slowed as it neared the Russian ship, the icebreaker dared not lose too much speed. The huge ship swept through a thick crush of broken ice and small bergs. It was the debris left behind by the massive floe that had been blasted into the channel.

"Brace for impact!" Kelly yelled, broadcasting his message ship-wide. But this announcement was less for the *King* and more for the *Lyakhov*, which also heard his warning through the radio.

The bow of the *Lyakhov* swelled behind the icebreaker—then the *King*'s stern slammed into the front of the boat. Due to the icebreaker's momentum and its massive weight, the crash felt no worse than a speedbump. The *King* jolted, then shrugged off the impact.

The same was not true for the smaller patrol boat. Its bow crumpled and lifted, riding for a moment atop the breaker's stern. The two continued down the channel this way for a hundred yards, before the *Lyakhov* finally slid into the water.

"Engage second engine!" Kelly ordered. "There's no slowing from here, mates."

The *Polar King* picked up speed as the engine crew added the horsepower of the breaker's second nuclear powerplant. Past the *King's* stern, the *Lyakhov* struggled to hold the center of the channel, having to rely solely on its bow thrusters on either side. The boat shimmied and swayed like a salsa dancer in the frigid water. The Russian boat dared not lose its line. If it slipped sideways, it would jam across the channel, trapping everyone.

To pull off this Russian ballet between the two huge ships, it required timing and trust across the two bridges. All their lives depended on mutual cooperation.

As a sign of good faith—a truce formed by necessity—Captain Turov had already been shuttled via helicopter to the *Lyakhov*, taking along his lieutenant and the archpriest. At this point, recriminations and punishments could wait.

Especially considering what they all faced.

Byron bellowed out the time and distance. "Five minutes to go. Seven miles out."

Gray searched Kelly's features to see if there was any information to be found there. But the captain remained stoic. Still, a single bead of sweat shone on his forehead. It was easy to read.

It'll be tight.

Making matters more nerve-racking was that no one knew for sure *when* the torpedo would hit. Their timetable was all guesswork. It could hit at any moment.

The *Polar King* sped along, no longer gaining speed.

This was all the engines had.

"Three minutes," Byron called out. "Eight miles."

No one acknowledged this, as the bridge crew grew breathless, smothered by the tension.

After another minute, Kelly waved an arm high. "That's it. Lock us down. No more sightseeing."

Storm shutters lowered over the windows. Then its louvres closed tight, cutting off the view. Before that happened, Gray noted the same was true over at the *Lyakhov*. When that warhead struck, its flash could blind instantly, even at this distance.

Kelly was taking no chances, considering the unknown variables.

"One minute," Byon announced, though his words were barely above a whisper. "Nine miles out."

Kelly nodded to the navigator. "That'll—"

The world brightened beyond the shutters. Every louvre stood out starkly, limned against a brilliance that shocked. It was still blinding, as if a sun had crashed before their bow.

It was also eerily quiet—then the world fell dark again.

In the silence, no one breathed. Then a sharp bang shook the ship, but it was no louder than a thunderclap. It was not the concussive world-shattering explosion shown in movies. A loud rumbling followed, rapidly growing in volume, sounding like a freight train running across the top of the icebreaker.

Winds buffeted and rattled the ship.

With the flash over, Kelly found his voice. "Open us up."

A button was hit.

The shutters remained down, but the louvres ratcheted wider.

Through the panoramic spread of the bow windows, a shocking sight revealed itself, dreadful in its power, stunning in its scope. Off in the distance, a fiery plume rolled into the sky. The fog banks fled to all sides, opening an ever-widening view, exposing that hellish heart.

Around that mushrooming cloud, ice shoved up into a huge wave, sweeping toward them and outward in all directions. At the top, its frozen crest shattered into massive, jagged pieces, becoming an icy gristmill, grinding across the top of the world.

"Maintain speed," Kelly said, gulping out his words as that monster pursued them.

The *King* and *Lyakhov* raced down the waterway.

But no one was fooled.

They would not escape the inevitable.

"Look!" Tucker called out, pointing directly across the bow.

The churning wave slowly lost some of its power, weakened by distance and the deepening water. Yet, not enough to keep it from reaching them.

Still, the channel that the *Polar King* had forged through the ice was full of open water. Past the bow, the dark blue trough cut like a knife through the ever-expanding circumference of the blast-driven wave. As the swell approached, it ripped the channel wider ahead of them, piling and pulling ice away.

"Hang tight!" Kelly warned.

The wave struck. The water lifted the bow high, tilting the boat, then dropping it down the far slope. Walls of ice swept to either side, spinning and grinding past them. The noise of its passage was worse than the nuclear blast. It ate at Gray's ears, accompanied by a mournful, deep-toned dissonance, like the death rattle of the world.

Then the surge was gone, rolling off into the distance, before eventually subsiding and sinking into the sea.

In its wake, the waters continued to rock. Ice bumped and scraped the hull.

Kelly radioed the other ship, checking on the state of the *Lyakhov*, but it wasn't necessary. A muffled cheering rose and echoed from the Russian ship. They had made it, too.

As the celebrations spread, Gray crossed to the bow windows with Seichan. She hooked an arm around his waist. They stared at the dark column that glowed at the heart of the fog-cleared skies. He pulled her closer, needing her warmth.

Together, they gazed at the fiery death of Hyperborea.

It was a reminder of a hard lesson.

Nothing lasts forever.

Not even legends.

57

Tucker crossed the veranda of the colonial-era mansion. The three-story, sprawling home sat in a remote corner of the Spitskop Game Preserve, far from the tourist area of the park.

This was his home—as much as any place truly was.

Past the porch's white-washed railing, wide swaths of lawn—composed of indigenous buffalo grass—rolled out for half an acre. Farther out, the larger twenty-acre parcel was dotted with barns and outbuildings. A neat gravel drive led to a packed-dirt road. There, a pristine sign stood, carved of native ironwood and painted in brilliant shades of orange, white, and black. The letters spelled out LUXURY SAFARI TOURS.

He shared this business with the Nkomo brothers, old friends who ran the photo safari. Tucker came often to visit, to rest up. It was here he had recuperated with Kane last year, where he had first met Marco as a pup.

Presently, the Nkomo brothers were out of the country, rehabbing a spot in the Congo for their next venture. For the moment, Tucker had this place to himself—well, *mostly* to himself.

He carried two tall bottles of cold beer, which already sweated in the morning swelter of the savannah. The sun glared off the grasslands, shadowed by stands of acacia trees. He stepped over to a pair of rattan rocking chairs, which stirred under the breeze of a large ceiling fan.

Kane rested in the shade. The dog lifted his head inquiringly, staring intently, but not at the beers in Tucker's hands. A large red Kong football sat atop a table.

"In a sec, bud." Tucker called to where Marco ran in circles on the lawn, barking and panting with puppyish delight, "C'mon in!"

It wasn't a command. It wasn't even directed at the young Malinois.

Elle Stutt lifted an arm, about to whip a Frisbee for the dog, then lowered her hand. She waved acknowledgment and headed over. She climbed the porch steps, drawing Marco with her, who went straight to the water bowl.

"Think you can use a drink, too," Tucker said, proffering a beer. "Best to stay hydrated, I always say."

She accepted the bottle, raising it a touch. "*Spasibo.*" She stared over at Marco. "Nothing tires that dog out."

He grinned. "You said the same thing about me last night."

She settled to the chair and cast him a sidelong glance. "Ah, but we did find your limit, did we not?"

"That's the scientist in you, always testing boundaries." He dropped into the chair. "But I believe further research is still needed."

"We shall see."

After the events in Russia two months before, the pair had been visiting each other often.

He also kept in touch with Yuri. Tucker owed the man a large debt. Not only for saving his own life, but for getting Father Bailey to a hospital in time. The priest had survived his ordeal, but his recuperation would be a long one. Yuri had also arranged for the body of the young pilot, Fadd, to be recovered from its stone cairn in the Arctic park and given a proper burial.

As a small recompense for Yuri's efforts, Tucker had finally relented about the dogs that his boss, Bogdan Fedoseev, had wanted. Tucker had refused to give up Marco or Kane, but he had agreed to train a new pair—although he had never promised which breed.

Maybe a pair of French bulldogs.

Still, any training would have to be performed here, not in Russia. He was certainly not welcome back, not after all that had happened.

And it wasn't just him.

Elle had resigned her position at the botanical gardens in Saint Petersburg. Life in the Russian city had become untenable. Though the dust had settled, there were many, especially under the current regime in Moscow, who had failed to appreciate her efforts in the Far North.

The same was true for Sister Anna, who experienced an unspoken animosity among the hierarchy of the Patriarchate's Holy Synod. Painter Crowe had arranged a spot for Anna in a diocese in Chicago, where she was settling well. Jason made sure of that, following her like a smitten puppy under the guise of helping her.

Tucker recognized a lost cause.

Keep hoping, kid.

He stared over at Elle—not sure himself where this would lead, especially as she had taken a position at the University of Cape Town. Elle clearly still missed her home in Saint Petersburg, but Africa was a hothouse of plant life, many species still yet to be discovered. She was clearly excited for this next step in her career.

And she hadn't totally abandoned her former life.

A loud hiss announced the arrival of a large orange tabby, who must have finished his round of mousing and ratting in the outlying barns. The male cat bounded onto the porch rail and growled at the domain before him. It had taken Elle a week to trap the feral stray near her apartment in Saint Petersburg and bring him here, but he was adjusting well to his new surroundings.

Marco lowered his head and backed away cautiously. A few claw smacks across his nose had taught him respect.

"Hush, Nikolai," Elle scolded. "We're guests here."

The cat swiped his tail twice, spat his disagreement, and leaped away.

Marco retreated to Elle's side. She patted his flank, reassuring him. "He's not as mean as he looks."

Marco wasn't buying it and slunk lower.

"Keep him company," Tucker said. He took a final swig of his beer and stood. "I need some quality time with someone who is feeling sorely neglected."

Tucker picked up the red Kong football.

Kane leaped up, his front leg giving out slightly for a moment.

"Who's up for some catch?" Tucker asked, while signaling Marco to stay.

Kane ran across the veranda, vaulted over the steps, and raced across the sunlit grass. There was no limping, no favoring of a limb, simply joy.

"That's my boy."

Kane spies the spin of the rubber ball through the brightness. He tracks it with one eye as he races under its flight. It arcs high, then falls earthward.

He rushes to meet it.

As it comes down, he jumps high, twisting his length, muscles stretching. His teeth catch and clamp. He savors this victory, landing in the warm grass. He spins a circle, showing his triumph.

He then rushes back, flipping the ball high.

His packmate catches it just as deftly.

They are one.

Always.

Kane prances away, dancing his jubilance, knowing down deep it can't be forever. It won't be always.

But for now . . .

He faces his man.

One more time, one more time, one more time . . .

11:44 a.m. EDT
Takoma Park, Maryland

"Sixteen minutes until D-day," Monk sounded off.

Gray paced the small room off the main chapel. The ceremony was set to begin at noon. He checked his watch, then shook down the sleeve of his black Armani suit. He straightened his tie, clipped with a silver Σ symbol. He ran a hand over his slicked hair, but a stubborn cowlick defied his efforts.

"Quit fussin'," Kowalski said. "You're not gonna get any prettier."

The two men were his groomsmen, as stiffly dressed as he was. None of them looked comfortable in their suits. They were built for tactical gear and boots. He scowled down at his polished dress shoes. He rubbed at the toe of one with the heel of the other.

"If you scuff that," Monk warned, "Kat will murder you in your sleep. She's already read the riot act to the wedding photographer."

"Because she's taking her maid-of-honor duties seriously."

Monk feigned offense. "Are you slighting my efforts as best man?"

Kowalski grunted. "That bachelor party sucked. You ran out of alcohol."

"A problem very much due to you," Monk reminded the large man. "I ordered enough for a small platoon."

Kowalski rubbed his forearm where he had been stabbed. "It was for medicinal purposes. For the pain. Doctor's orders."

Monk scowled. "It's been two months and—"

They were thankfully interrupted by Painter as he knocked and entered. "The bridal party is all set," he reported.

"So, Seichan didn't make a run for it," Kowalski noted.

Gray knew the man was joking, but that worry did lurk at the back of his mind. Still, even with the pressure of the wedding, Seichan had seemed more settled over the past months. There was a new calmness to her. It was not necessarily a sense of peace—that was not Seichan—but more the impression of an inner resolve, a centering that had escaped her until now.

He knew a large part of that had to do with Sigma regaining its footing. The group had identified and eliminated the bomber of the Smithsonian Castle. The remainder of Valya's organization was systematically being picked apart and snuffed out. Likewise, the events in Russia, especially on the polar ice cap, had been acknowledged by those in the upper echelons in D.C. Through Sigma's efforts, a global war had been avoided. Since then, all talk of dissolving the group had faded.

Still, Gray knew Seichan's calmness was not solely due to the firming of Sigma's standing in D.C. With the fall of Valya and her organization, Seichan was less shadowed and haunted. Gray and Seichan had talks about this, usually in bed, in the dark, where it was easier to bare one's heart. Her past with the Guild had scarred her deeply. It was never going away, but by finally burning away the last vestiges of the

Guild, those lingering shadows left behind, represented by Valya and her group, Seichan now felt freer, able to heal that old wound.

Maybe not fully, but enough.

Painter crossed to Gray, resting a hand on his shoulder. "Don't know if you want to hear this now. I got news from Russia about an hour ago."

Gray frowned, worried, but happy for any distraction. "What is it?"

"Archpriest Sychkin hung himself in his gulag cell. His body was found this morning."

Gray nodded, not surprised, only disappointed. The bastard deserved to suffer longer, but the world was better off without him drawing air. Gray suspected that Sychkin's activation of the failsafe device, calling hellfire upon Hyperborea, had nothing to do with preserving Russia's position in the Arctic, and was all about ending his own suffering—and taking down as many people with him as possible.

Dying alone in his cell?

Gray could live with that, especially knowing the lingering effects of that selfish act. He had seen photos of the blast's aftermath. The residual heat of the explosion and the radioactive glow continued to keep the ice melted for miles around the site. The peaks had been shattered or damaged, marking the grave of those ancient people.

Still, Jason's recordings of what had been found below were being studied by academics around the globe. Likewise, there was renewed interest in the unusual genetics of bowhead whales, and their ties to longevity. As to the *sarkophágos* species, it was not likely any plants survived, but for now, no one would get any closer to look, not until it all cooled down.

Gray inquired when that might be. "Any further word about the radiation levels up there?"

Painter sighed. "It'll remain hot for years. And the environmental effects will last even longer. Still, the act has forced the Russians to throttle back their ambitions in the north. After the NOAA satellite recorded and broadcast what had happened, the Russians have been more cooperative, maybe begrudgingly so. Still, that accommodating attitude has extended to another site."

Gray looked at Painter. "Where?"

"The Golden Library—or at least what remains of it. Russia has opened its doors to researchers around the globe, including those from the Vatican. Likely it's their attempt at regaining a measure of goodwill."

"Has Father Bailey had a chance to revisit the site?"

Painter lowered his eyes. "Not yet. And I'm not sure he'll ever want to. Lots of ghosts there. Plus, his rehab continues. He's having a hard time of it."

"Understood." Gray tried to change the subject. "I heard that Captain Turov has been named as the new admiral of Russia's Northern Fleet."

"He has. Nothing like being cheered as a national hero after he saved all those lives aboard the *Ivan Lyakhov*. The world all watched that daring rescue. While a few of his superiors might have resented some of his choices and actions, none dared challenge the surge of public opinion. Especially for a country that needs to make amends to the world."

"What happened to his boss, the former commander of the Northern Fleet?"

"Glazkov?" Painter shrugged, showing a slight smile. "He's vanished, but I don't believe it was of his own volition."

Gray nodded.

Good riddance.

"On better news," Painter said, "the *Polar King* is again plying the seas. As I understand it, they are being greeted at every port with raucous celebrations for their efforts. And not a single member of the old crew chose to abandon the icebreaker."

Gray was happy to hear it.

"Two minutes," Monk warned them all, tapping at his wrist.

Painter headed for the door. "Which means I'm needed elsewhere."

Once the director was gone, Gray took a deep breath. Monk's countdown reminded him of Byron ticking down the time left to them on the *Polar King*. Only this time hopefully it wouldn't end in a nuclear explosion.

He pictured his last sight of Hyperborea, burning under the polar sun. He recalled a discussion he'd had with Sister Anna back in the Golden Library. It concerned Catherine the Great's decision to keep the lost archive hidden, along with the secret it held: the location of Hyperborea. According to Anna, the Russian empress must have believed that her world wasn't ready for the wonders and horrors of Hyperborea. All of Catherine's puzzles and hoops were aimed toward one goal—as a test to prove some future generation was *wise* enough and *cautious* enough to receive such knowledge.

Gray shook his head.

After all that had happened, the answer was grimly clear, as plain as a fiery plume mushrooming into the Arctic sky.

We were not.

"Time's up," Monk announced.

Gray stirred back to the present. He gathered with the other men. There were some final congratulations and jokes as they departed the room and crossed the short hall to the front of the chapel.

Once there, Gray took a breath and stepped before the altar, where a priest clutched a book to his chest. The man nodded to him, as if checking to make sure he didn't have cold feet.

Gray turned away. He had leaped through fire, been shot at countless times, stabbed even more, and faced down ferocious beasts, and now—he had survived a nuclear blast.

I can do this.

He faced the small gathering, forty or so of their closest friends and family. Monk and Kowalski stayed at his side. As the music started, his gaze fell upon his son, Jack. The boy fidgeted next to Jason, whose sole wedding duty was to keep the young boy out of trouble, likely one of the hardest chores.

Jason nodded back to Gray. Sigma's tech expert had recovered after everything and had even put in a request with Painter for future field assignments.

The kid must be gunning for my position.

Gray returned Jason's nod.

Fat chance.

Motion drew his eyes as the rear doors opened. The first through were two flower girls, the daughters of Monk and Kat. They cast petals from baskets and crossed with all the solemnity of priests at a high mass. But halfway down, the pair started throwing petals at each other, and much giggling ensued. Still, they made it to the front and were scooped up by an aunt and uncle.

The bridal party came next, floating in billows of crimson chiffon, with Kat trailing the last of the bridesmaids.

Monk whispered next to Gray. "I'm the luckiest man."

"I might argue with you about that," Gray said as Seichan stepped into the chapel.

Painter presented her, holding out an elbow.

Seichan rested a hand delicately on his forearm. She was dressed in dark crimson, her veil and train snow-white lace. Her bodice was snug, sculpted of oil-black leather that accentuated her every curve.

Gray gaped at her approach down the aisle, at her leonine grace. When they had first met, she had been dressed in motorcycle leathers. He appreciated this small nod to that moment, marking the anniversary of their first encounter, a meeting that ended in a fierce firefight.

He silently promised to never let that passion wane.

Upon reaching the end of the aisle, Painter stepped aside to let Seichan cross the last steps to the altar on her own. She turned and squeezed the director's arm, not to hold him there, but to express her thanks.

Kowalski used this moment to lean and whisper to Gray, "Last chance, buddy. Getting married? Sure that's wise?"

In the big man's words, Gray heard an echo of his earlier ruminations.

As Seichan climbed toward him, he reached down and took her hand.

Wise or not . . .

Gray didn't care and smiled with all his heart.

And to hell with being cautious.

He stared into her eyes, challenging her.

Let's throw caution to the wind.

Epilogue

Early autumn

In an apartment overlooking the Pontifical University of the Holy Cross, Bailey sat in the comfort of a deeply cushioned chair. A small hearth glowed with a few embers, holding back the evening's chill, a kiss of the winter to come.

The warmth soothed the aches that had settled into his bones. Dusty shelves surrounded him. A book lay open on his lap. He reached to turn a page, but there was no finger to do so. He cringed at his body's betrayal, at its stubborn refusal to accept what he had lost.

He clenched a fist of three fingers. His left hand was also missing a digit, its middle finger. But that was not the worst damage. He lifted a palm to his right eye, or where it had been. A patch covered it. He was still adjusting to how it had changed his depth perception. He had trouble even climbing the stairs up here.

The cane hadn't helped much. But he continued to need it as his left ankle had mended poorly and would require a second surgery.

But that could wait.

It had taken him a long time until he was fit enough to reach this apartment on his own. A doorknob rattled in the next room. He sat straighter. The apartment door creaked open, a light clicked on, followed by footsteps. A soft whistling of breath approached this room. Then those footfalls stumbled near the threshold, expressing worry, concern.

The door into the study swung open.

A tall, gray-haired man stood framed against the light, his body stiff with fear, but then he relaxed with recognition.

"*Prefetto* Bailey," Cardinal Samarin gasped out. "What are you doing in my apartment? Do you need some help?"

The cardinal eyed the cane resting next to the chair, which remained comfortable and warm. Bailey settled deeper.

"I've been waiting for you," Bailey said. "I'm glad you were late returning home from your evening classes at Holy Cross. It gave me a chance to search your apartment more thoroughly."

"But why?"

"It's taken me months, far too long, to finish this investigation, even with Monsignor Borrelli only keeping a small circle of confidantes. Those whom he might trust with information concerning a discovery in Moscow."

"I don't understand."

"Back in Moscow, Monsignor Borrelli must have been suspicious after being ambushed in Red Square. He must have feared someone had betrayed him, someone he spoke to in Rome, someone he thought he could trust."

"You can't think that I had—"

Bailey pointed at the cardinal's desk, where a drawer showed a broken lock. Bailey lifted what was hidden under the book in his lap, what he had found in that locked drawer. As he raised it, the gold shone in the glow of the hearth. The ring carried an embossed emblem of wings and a sword.

Bailey read what was inscribed on its inside, translating the Russian Cyrillic. "Arkangel Society." He tossed the ring at the cardinal's toes. "Apparently, the Vatican isn't the only Church with its own *intelligenza*. It seems the Moscow Patriarchate has their own, too."

Cardinal Samarin took a step back, raising a hand. "Let me explain."

Bailey sighed, knowing there could be no explanation. After all that had happened, the injuries and agonies that he had sustained, he had no patience. He pictured Bishop Yelagin, Monsignor Borrelli, Igor Koskov, and so many others.

Bailey reached to his lap, to what else was hidden under his book.

He pulled out the Glock 19 fitted with a silencer. He squeezed off two shots, which sounded like sharp gasps. Samarin stumbled two steps away, then crashed to the floor.

Bailey shoved out of the comfortable chair with a small grunt of complaint. He pocketed his weapon, collected his cane, and headed for the door, which required stepping over Samarin's body.

As he did, he did not look back.

He knew this act was a mortal sin.

He would seek absolution with a confessor from his intelligence group. Even with such an ally, he would undoubtedly have to recite hundreds of rosaries to wash away this sin—which he would do.

For a simple reason, one that had nothing to do with forgiveness. Those rosaries would serve as a reminder of the justice served here this evening.

So I'll savor every one of them.

Author's Note to Readers:
Truth or Fiction

At its core, *Arkangel* has been a puzzle-box of a story—one with a nuclear blast of an ending. It's been a tale of maps and legends and how they can blur the line between fact and fiction. But now, here at the book's conclusion, I thought I'd share how much of *my* story is fact and how much is fiction. I also thought I'd dig a little bit deeper and tell how this story came about: the inspirations and strange tangents that became this novel.

Let's start at the beginning.

For decades, I've collected all manner of esoterica in my "idea box." Typically, it's pieces of history that end in a question mark, something I can try to answer within the pages of a book. Or it's scientific articles that make me go "what if" and allow me to speculate where they might lead.

In this case, I had notes and articles regarding all the Hyperborean legends, which seemed to blend historical mysteries with scientific speculations—but I had no idea *how* to build a story around it.

Then I learned about Aleksandr Dugin, a Russian philosopher who believed the roots of the Russian race stretched back to a lost continent, what the Greeks called Hyperborea. As mentioned in the opening notes to this novel, Dugin's ultranationalist viewpoint led to the man's work being required reading by the Russian military and at the country's top political science academies. It is said this theological view of Russia's destiny was used to justify the invasion of Crimea and Ukraine. So much so that Dugin is often referred to as "Putin's Brain."

Likewise, there is indeed an offshoot of Dugin's philosophies—the New Scythians—who seek the origins of the Russian people elsewhere: among the nomadic tribesmen of Eurasia.

To me, this supported what Anna Koskov espouses in this novel: *Myths can move mountains.* And thus, it gave me the jumping off point for this story.

But before we move on, and further separate truth from fiction, I thought I'd share another small inspiration, one not birthed from that "idea box." Instead, it sits behind me as I write this afterword.

In the prologue, explorers discover a mammoth tusk that had been inscribed with a hidden message, turning that artifact into a large piece of scrimshaw. Years ago, I had obtained a mammoth tusk at an auction for the estate of an archaeologist. It, too, had been inscribed, becoming a piece of art. I thought I'd share it here, too.

This artifact inspired that moment in the prologue. And while that tusk is more than two hundred thousand years old, I don't think we need to go that far into the past to dig deeper into this novel's historical subject matters.

VASILY CHICHAGOV & CATHERINE THE GREAT

As the beginning of this novel, we find Vasily Chichagov leading a trio of survey ships into the Arctic during the spring of 1764. This is a true account of an excursion by the commandant of Arkhangelsk. And according to a memoir written by his son years later, Vasily did indeed receive a letter after leaving port: a secret decree from Empress Catherine the Great, penned by Mikhail Lomonosov, who ordered Vasily to travel north, toward the pole, to search for the lost continent of Hyperborea.

Catherine remains a fascinating figure of history, a queen who usurped her husband to take the throne, and who was an advocate of the sciences and a new progressive view of Russia's future. Toward those ends, she not only sought out the Golden Library, but she also researched the historical origins of the Russian people—first, looking toward the Scythians, then later at the Hyperboreans. I found this parallel to what's happening today in Russia to be fascinating.

THE GOLDEN LIBRARY OF THE TSARS

In the fifteenth century, Ivan III (Ivan the Great) did indeed acquire a vast library as a dowry from his new wife, Sophia Palaiologina, a Byzantine princess. It was said to be a collection that rivaled the world's greatest archives, containing books and texts thought to be lost forever. But after the emperor's death, his grandson—Ivan IV (Ivan the Terrible)—took possession of it. He grew convinced it held the secret to Russia's future, believing it contained secrets to black arts, and he did indeed task scholars to begin translating the books, many of whom fled in fear of that black magic. Later, he became so paranoid that he hid this library so well that after his death, the vast archive vanished into history. In 1724, a Russian officer reported discovering a room full of trunks in a secret passageway beneath the Kremlin. After that, it was forbidden to trespass down there. This detail inspired the opening chapter to this novel.

And the search for this lost library continues to this day. Many believe it may still lie undiscovered in some walled-off chamber beneath Moscow, while others have ventured farther out, searching outlying areas with a historical tie to Ivan the Terrible—including the Trinity Lavra and the town of Sergiyev Posad. So, who knows what might be uncovered one day? Fair warning, though: be careful not to disturb any mammoth tusks.

A LOST CONTINENT TO THE NORTH

The Greeks truly believed that there were a long-lived people who populated a verdant continent "beyond the north wind." This myth persisted over the passing millennia, becoming deeply entrenched—all the way into the twentieth century. Early Arctic explorers claimed to have seen it. In 1905, Robert Peary reported in his book *Nearest the Pole* that he had spotted a distant landmass far to the north, which he called Crocker Land. Another explorer, Frederick Cook, said he found a lost land even farther north during an expedition in 1908. Searches persisted for decades after that. In fact, in 1923, US Navy Lieutenant-Commander Fitzhugh Green declared in *Popular Science* that *"experts are in nearly unanimous agreement that a new arctic land will be found."*

So, I decided to go find it—and I'm not the only one.

I learned that there are indeed groups searching for evidence of this lost continent today: across the Kola Peninsula, at the island of Vaigach, in the Ural Mountains, and in other regions. Those teams have uncovered vast swaths of petroglyphs, with one site so astounding that it is indeed being sealed under a glass dome to protect it. The most intriguing find, though, is the discovery of pyramids, stone labyrinths, and a giant throne on islands in the White Sea. Could this be evidence of the descendants of a lost civilization?

If you'd like to read more about expeditions to the north and the Arctic's unending allure for explorers and adventurers, I highly recommend two books:

Arctic Dreams, by Barry H. Lopez

Beyond the North Wind: The Fall and Rise of the Mystic North, by Christopher McIntosh

OLD MAPS AND LOST BOOKS

As mentioned above, the legend of Hyperborea persisted in written accounts all the way to present day. Yet, this same blurring of myth and truth also found its way into maps. Gerardus Mercator drew the chart featured in this book (*Septentrionalium Terrarum*) in 1595. It's considered the oldest map of the Arctic. Mercator was also well regarded—both in the past and present—for his meticulous accuracy. Yet, in his Arctic map, he shows a mysterious landmass, one divided by four rivers that form a whirlpool around a magnetic mountain. This strange continent found its way into future maps for two more centuries.

Yet even Mercator admitted he didn't believe the location of the magnetic North Pole was where he had drawn that large mountain in the center of his map. He claimed that it lay elsewhere, marking a little island on his map. I found this small detail intriguing.

Likewise, the accounts upon which Mercator based his Arctic map came from a long-lost source, the legendary *Inventio Fortunata*, written by Nicolas of Lynn in the fourteenth century. As related in the novel, the English friar traveled to Norway, then continued farther north, sailing deep into the Arctic. He wrote a travelogue of his account, which he presented to King Edward III upon his return—along with a silver astrolabe.

Unfortunately, this book vanished into history. The record of its existence could only be found today in references by Mercator, and in another book, *Itinerarium*, written by Jacobus Cnoyen—a text that also disappeared. I found this gap in the written record to be highly suspicious. But who knows? Maybe copies do still exist in the lost Golden Library.

Before moving on to the modern section of the novel, I thought I'd address a subject that bridges past and present . . .

TRINITY LAVRA OF ST. SERGIUS

The details of the history of the monastic compound are accurate, from its founding to its present day. The presence of sacred springs—holy waters summoned by St. Sergius—is a true legend of the sacred site. Likewise, it was Ivan the Terrible who tore down the old wooden palisades that once protected the Lavra and constructed the massive walls and its twelve watchtowers.

I chose to hide the Golden Library under the Ringing Tower (*Zvonkovaya Bashnya*) because this site is somewhat neglected by the public. It's hidden behind a theological school, away from the splendor of the main collection of churches and cathedrals. It's so ignored that I could find only a few pictures of the place. The photo that is featured in the book is actually of the Drying Tower (*Sushil'naya Bashnya*) near the Lavra's main gates—of which there were abundant dramatic shots. Luckily, the two look very similar, so I used the Drying Tower as a stand-in. But I thought you should see a true picture of the Ringing Tower. Here it is:

As related in the novel, Russia's second-largest budget expenditure—after the military—is devoted to restoring the Russian Orthodox Church. It's seen as a means to a spiritual renewal for the country, a way of instilling national pride. But there remain darker shades to this funding, one tied to the Tikhvin Icon, one of Russia's most sacred treasures.

The story of the icon's history—vanishing from Constantinople and reappearing to Russian fishermen—is held as holy proof that Russia is destined to be the Third Rome, the future spiritual center of the world, with the Trinity Lavra as its new Vatican City. This belief is one of the main reasons that a vocal number of the Russian Orthodox Church, including its patriarch, sanction Russia's military conquest of other countries.

But that is not Russia's only ambition.

THE NORTHERN SEA ROUTE AND THE NEXT COLD WAR

The Arctic is heating up—and not just in temperature and thawing ice. The construction of new bases and the restoration of old Soviet installations along Russia's northern coasts is as described in the book. The stated explanation for this build-up is that Russia intends to better guard its coasts as the Arctic ice melts, to help protect the Northern Sea Route—that shortcut from the Pacific to the Atlantic.

But Russia is also seeking to push its territorial boundary farther into the Arctic, staking flags, doing geological tests—and for good reason. The Arctic is a vast storehouse of rare minerals, oil, and natural gas, not to mention being strategically important. Even with the war in Ukraine straining resources, Russia has not slowed its expansion in the north. That alone highlights the importance that Russia places upon its ambitions in the Arctic.

The entire region is an icy powder keg waiting for a match.

For a more comprehensive look at this subject, I recommend these two articles:

"The Ice Curtain: Russia's Arctic Military Presence" by Heather A. Conley, Matthew Melino, and Jon B. Alterman (from Center for Strategic & International Studies)

"Russia's Military Posture in the Arctic" by Mathieu Boulègue (Chatham House, The Royal Institute of International Affairs)

LOCATION, LOCATION, LOCATION

I thought I'd quickly bullet-point my way through a few key locations that appear in the book.

Tucker has a little chase across Apothecary Island in Saint Petersburg. The history of the place is as described, as is its botanical park—from the Japanese garden that confounds Kane's nose to the huge glass-walled arboretum with a lily-pad-filled pond.

The ruins of the Simonov Monastery are a real location in Moscow, located next to a children's park and overlooking the Moskva River.

The Dulo Tower and the history of its name are accurate. Likewise, there is a newly restored church on the property: Theotokos of Tikhvin Church. And the monastery's old dyehouse is indeed the oldest surviving industrial building. Sorry for making such a mess of the place.

The Apostolic Nunciature—the Vatican's embassy in Moscow—is roughly as described. There is even a seventeen-story apartment building that overlooks the site. Some of the interior details of the embassy were adjusted to fit the story. On a side note, the Vatican does indeed have its own *intelligenza*, its own spy network. For decades—if not centuries—it has dispatched operatives to infiltrate hate groups, secret societies, hostile countries, wherever the concerns of the Vatican were threatened. For example, during the Cold War, Walter Ciszek—a Polish-American priest—played a cat-and-mouse game with the KGB for years, before being captured and spending two decades in a Soviet prison. As Father Bailey would attest, Ciszek was lucky not to have run into Archpriest Sychkin back then.

On very minor notes: ADX Florence—the Alcatraz of the Rockies—is indeed a real place, and considering it does have a Bomber's Row, it seemed fitting that Valya would seek out intel from such a facility. Likewise, the Smithsonian Castle is currently undergoing a multiyear restoration, so again it seemed an opportune time for Valya to strike. Hopefully, some of the Castle's restoration budget will be devoted to improving Sigma's rehab facilities. After this adventure, the team is going to need it.

EAST SIBERIAN SEA

Those icy waters are indeed the least explored corner of the Arctic—and treacherous, especially its northernmost extremes. With its thick ice, dense fogs, shallow waters, and poorly mapped seabed, it's a sailor's nightmare. So maybe something does lie hidden out there, undiscovered, partially masked by electromagnetic radiation and the strange vagaries of polar energies.

COLD TECH

This novel featured some of Russia's latest Arctic weaponry, vehicles, and boats. All are as accurate as I could make them. Most are in use today (or soon will be). That includes the Berkut-2 snowmobile mounted with a PKP Pecheneg 6P41 machine gun, the A-1 double snowmobile, even the new Kalashnikov tactical gear. Most worrisome of all is the Belgorod submarine, what has been dubbed "Russia's Doomsday Sub." It's one of the few boats that can carry the bus-size Poseidon 2M39 torpedoes, a stealth shark capable of delivering a warhead of 100 megatons, of unleashing a radioactive tsunami along a coastline. The current consensus is that this weapon is "very real" and already in production.

BOWHEAD WHALES

Please consider this book as further proof that we need to save the whales. Bowhead whales (*Balaena mysticetus*) clock in at a mighty eighty thousand kilos and can live for two centuries. According to a recent article in *New Scientist*, this longevity is due to the whales' unique sequences of genes that suppress cancer development. This is accomplished via a group of genes that produce a protein called CIRBP that repairs damaged DNA, a condition that leads to most cancers. Scientists at the University of Rochester are researching how to engineer this same genetic advantage into humans, both as a means of preventing cancer and of extending lives. But maybe *someone* has already learned this trick, a people who have been subsisting on whales for millennia.

CARNIVOROUS PLANTS

Okay, I may be as equally intrigued by carnivorous plants as Dr. Stutt. The biology and evolution of such unusual flora showcased in this book are accurate, even the ability of some plants to switch between being carnivorous or not depending on conditions and availability of nutrients or energy. Considering the pattern of sunlight in the far north and the overwhelming abundance of flies and other insects, the Arctic seemed the perfect place to create a new species of carnivorous plant.

MAGNETIC CURES

Our bodies are electric. Each cell is a little powerhouse, whose main engines are mitochondria. As we age, those engines become less efficient and are a major cause for our bodily decline. The use of ultrasound, bioelectricity, even magnetism, has shown an amazing ability to repower those engines: to heal, to strengthen immune systems, even to slow aging. In fact, the U.S. Department of Defense has started clinical trials to showcase how bioelectricity can cut the healing time of severe injuries in half, possibly even regrow nerves. Now all I have to do is figure out how to get on their waitlist.

MILITARY WORKING DOGS AND THEIR HANDLERS

I love Tucker and Kane (and now Marco). I first encountered this heroic pairing of soldier and war dog while on a USO tour to Iraq and Kuwait in the winter of 2010. Seeing these pairs' capabilities and recognizing their unique bonds, I wanted to try to capture and honor those relationships. To accomplish that, I spoke to veterinarians in the U.S. Veterinary Corps, interviewed handlers, met their dogs, and saw how these duos grow together to become a single fighting unit. I also vetted their stories with former and current handlers to be as accurate as possible. If you'd like to know more about war dogs and their handlers, I highly recommend two books by the author Maria Goodavage:

Soldier Dogs: The Untold Story of America's Canine Heroes

Top Dog: The Story of Marine Hero Lucca

In this novel, I introduced Marco, whom Tucker first acquired as a pup in the novel *Kingdom of Bones*. At the end of that novel, I requested suggestions to help me name this pup—and I received thousands (thanks!). I picked Marco at the recommendation of Jeffrey Adamec, who is a retired Green Beret and Ranger. He was also a handler and K9 Trainer for the Third Special Forces Group. His military working dog was named Marco. The brave four-legged soldier located some thirty

IEDs and saved countless lives—so how could I not honor such service by naming Tucker's newest companion after such a stalwart warrior?

By the way, if you'd like to read more about Tucker and Kane, the dynamic duo first appeared in the Sigma novel *Bloodline* and continued in solo adventures: *Kill Switch* (where you meet Yuri and Bogdan) and *War Hawk*. You can also check out how Tucker comes to terms with the loss of Kane's brother, Abel, in the novella "Sun Dogs," which is included in the anthology collection *Unrestricted Access*.

So, thus ends another Sigma outing. I hope you enjoyed the adventure. As you might suspect, there is much more to come. But for now, we'll let Gray and Seichan enjoy their honeymoon—where they'd better get good rest. Because what comes next is a major turning point for Sigma. As one chapter closes, another opens. And what unfolds will be a challenge unlike any that Sigma has faced in the past, one that will shake the organization to its core—and where no one will be safe.

You have been warned.

Rights and Attributions for the Artwork in This Novel

p. 9—Pindar Hyperborea
The Odes of Pindar including the Principal Fragments with an Introduction and an English Translation by Sir John Sandys, Litt.D., FBA. Cambridge, MA., Harvard University Press; London, William Heinemann Ltd., 1937.
(image created by author)

p. 13—The Golden Library
Secured with an Enhanced License
ID 118570552 © Jjustas | Shutterstock.com
(image edited by author)

p. 24—Encrypted Page
Golden book image secured with an Enhanced License
ID 445653853 © Brothers Art | Shutterstock.com
Composited with separate art developed with Midjourney
(images edited by author)

p. 89—Hunting Party
Secured with an Enhanced License
ID 1675994395 © Anna Kostenko | Shutterstock.com
(image edited by author)

p. 106—Cropped Encrypted Page
Golden book image secured with an Enhanced License
ID 445653853 © Brothers Art | Shutterstock.com
Composited with separate art developed with Midjourney
(images edited by author)

p. 108—Trinity Lavra Photo
Secured with an Enhanced License
ID 2017874282 © Maykova Galina | Shutterstock.com
(image edited by author)

p. 136—Sketch of Landscape
Writing from *The Odes of Pindar including the Principal Fragments with an Introduction and an English Translation by Sir John Sandys*, Litt.D., FBA. Cambridge, MA., Harvard University Press; London, William Heinemann Ltd., 1937.
Composited with separate art developed with Midjourney
(images edited by author)

p. 147—Carnivorous Plant A
Graphic created by author with Midjourney and edited by author

p. 147—Carnivorous Plant B
Graphic created by author with Midjourney and edited by author

p. 148—Sarcophagos
Image created by author

p. 151—Faded Frontispiece
Golden book image secured with an Enhanced License
ID 445653853 © Brothers Art | Shutterstock.com
Composited with separate art developed with Midjourney by author
(images edited by author)

p . 177—The Unholy Trinity
From Pexels.com (photo by Danil) under free Pexel License
(image edited by author)

p. 186—Faded Frontispiece
Golden book image secured with an Enhanced License
ID 445653853 © Brothers Art | Shutterstock.com
Composited with separate art developed with Midjourney
(images edited by author)

p. 188—Row of Astrolabes
Graphic created by author with Midjourney and edited by author

p. 189—Single Astrolabe
Graphic created by author with Midjourney and edited by author

p. 189—Photo of Spherical Astrolabe
History of Science Museum, CC BY-SA 4.0 <https://creativecommons
.org/licenses/by-sa/4.0>, via Wikimedia Commons

p. 190—Highlighted Glyphs on Sketched Astrolabe
Graphic created with Midjourney and edited by author

p. 192—Numbers on Astrolabe
Graphic created with Midjourney and edited by author

p. 192—Glyphs and Deciphered Numbers
Graphic created by author

p. 194—Photo of Ringing Tower
Secured with an Enhanced License
ID 1721521297 © Yurii Sabelnikov | Shutterstock.com
(image edited by author)

p. 195—Tower and Monk
Graphic created with Midjourney and edited by author

p. 227—Tile and Letter
Graphic created with Midjourney and edited by author

p. 229—Glagolitic Row
Graphic created by author

p. 229—Glagolitic Row Deciphered
Graphic created by author

p. 230—Ivan in Glagolitic
Graphic created by author

p. 235—Burying the Truth
From Pexels.com (photo by Ylanite Koppens) under free Pexel License
(image edited by author)

p. 240—Incomplete Cyrillic Letters
Graphic created by author

p. 241—Completed Cyrillic Letters
Graphic created by author

p. 250—Lomonosov's Name
Graphic created by author

p. 252—Hyperborean Carving 2
Secured with an Enhanced License
ID 2266005189 © Creative rabbit hole | Shutterstock.com
(image edited by author)

p. 254—Mercator Map A
Public Domain (edited by author)

p. 255—Mercator Map B
Public Domain (edited by author)

p. 305—Russian Bases
Secured with an Enhanced License
ID 1956422059 © Peter Hermes Furian | Shutterstock.com
(image edited by author)

p. 322—Sketch of Landscape
Writing from *The Odes of Pindar including the Principal Fragments
with an Introduction and an English Translation by Sir John Sandys,*
Litt.D., FBA. Cambridge, MA., Harvard University Press; London,
William Heinemann Ltd., 1937.
Composited with separate art developed with Midjourney
(images edited by author)

p. 339—Hostile Shores
From Pexels.com (photo by Tobias Bjørkli) under free Pexel License
(image edited by author)

p. 385—Whale Totem
Graphic created with Midjourney and edited by author

p. 386—Stone Plants
Graphic created with Midjourney and edited by author

p. 387—Carnivorous Sketch
Graphic created with Midjourney and edited by author

p. 388—Whale Hunt
Graphic created with Midjourney and edited by author

p. 389—Whale Harvest
Graphic created with Midjourney and edited by author

p. 389—Plant Harvest
Graphic created with Midjourney and edited by author

p. 391—Whale Pot
Graphic created with Midjourney and edited by author

p. 391—Plant Pot
Graphic created with Midjourney and edited by author

p. 393—Ceremony Chamber
Graphic created with Midjourney and edited by author

p. 399—Fire and Ice
Secured with an Enhanced License
ID 2223090883 © Apisit Suwannaka | Shutterstock.com
(image edited by author)

p. 482—Mammoth Tusk
Photo by author

p. 486—Ringing Tower
Secured with an Enhanced License
File# 108044469 © icemos | Adobe Stock
(image edited by author)

About the Author

James Rollins is the #1 *New York Times* bestselling author of international thrillers that have been translated into more than forty languages. His Sigma series has been lauded as one of the "top crowd-pleasers" (*New York Times*) and one of the "hottest summer reads" (*People*). In each novel, acclaimed for its originality, Rollins unveils unseen worlds, scientific breakthroughs, and historical secrets—and he does it all at breakneck speed and with stunning insight. He lives in the Sierra Nevada mountains.